BAKER STREET IRREGULARS

THIRTEEN AUTHORS WITH NEW TAKES ON SHERLOCK HOLMES

EDITED BY
MICHAEL A. VENTRELLA
& JONATHAN MABERRY

DIVERSIONBOOKS

Diversion Books
A Division of Diversion Publishing Corp.
443 Park Avenue South, Suite 1008
New York, New York 10016
www.DiversionBooks.com

For more information, email info@diversionbooks.com

First Diversion Books edition March 2017.
Print ISBN: 978-1-62681-840-8
eBook ISBN: 978-1-62681-838-5

TABLE OF CONTENTS

INTRODUCTION

Who is the most popular fictional character ever? Given the number of books, movies, plays, stories, comics, and games about the amazing Sherlock Holmes, the answer is elementary.

We can't get enough of the great detective, the most unlikable and unlikely hero. His superpower is his intellect. We could never be Superman, but when Sherlock examines the evidence and provides the solution, we all realize that with proper observation and deduction, we too could be heroes.

The character of Sherlock is so iconic that he can be rearranged in many different formats and still be recognizable. So when Jonathan and I started discussing the possibility of a collection of "Alternate Sherlock" stories, excitement grew. Sherlock as an alien! Sherlock as a computer program! Sherlock as a monk!

We invited some great writers to give us their interpretations with the only limitation being that we needed a mystery solved by a personality that was clearly Sherlock's. Some of the writers kept the names and others created new ones but our favorite detective is still recognizable in each story.

The game is afoot!

—Michael A. Ventrella

'LOCKED

BY MIKE STRAUSS

"You've been 'locked!"

Sherlock posed with an 88 percent audience-approved smug smile and outstretched pointer finger until he was certain the camera had gotten enough footage. Cognizant that there was also a camera on me, I maintained my façade of awe, even while fuming internally.

I've hated that line and that pose for years now. I've hated the man who utters that phrase and the exuberant manner in which he does so. I've hated his undeserved ego and his constantly increasing monetary demands for the placation of that ego. I've hated the way that this insipid twit and his ridiculous slogan have seeped into the public conscious.

In short, I, John Watson, hate Sherlock Holmes.

"*Cut!*"

The moment the director called the scene, Sherlock's camera-friendly grin dropped and he immediately stomped toward Mary Morstan, an assistant producer. "Yesterday, when I got back to my trailer, my coffee was cold. If it is cold again today, I want you to fire the entire catering company," he fumed.

"Immediately, Mr. Holmes."

Mary's response was precisely the right degree of respectful and groveling to keep Sherlock from lashing out further. It was a practiced response and Sherlock wasn't discerning enough to realize that he was being handled. The irony of that was not lost on Mary or on me.

I've seen him act like that dozens of times in the past and I still

7

have trouble comprehending how he gets away with it. Admittedly, he is the star of the highest-rated reality show on cable television, but even Charlie Sheen got fired from *Two and a Half Men*. About the only guess I've managed to muster is that he has never abused anyone except for the producers, who pretty much accept his diva attitude as part of the price of success.

Mary was brought in as an assistant producer literally to be the main target for his bile. Sherlock doesn't know, but she was a child psychiatrist who specialized in children with high-risk behavior before joining the show. That experience has helped her control and mollify his regular outbursts—though even she occasionally needs to vent a little after one of his tirades. Today looked like it was going to be one of those days.

The moment Sherlock disappeared from view, she marched over to me, slipped her hand behind my head, and pulled me close for a long, deep kiss.

"Indian food, a walk by the fish pond, and then a long, hot soak with you rubbing my shoulders."

The actions might have appeared abrupt and almost callous to a casual observer, but her fingers were gently massaging my neck and her whisper was passionate. Mary wasn't demanding of me. She was requesting, just in a way that hid the seriousness of our relationship from any observers.

• • •

"I wanted to give you a heads-up, Jack," she said as I placed a second blueberry pancake on her plate. "The network is looking to boost ratings."

"That's insane. We are already getting three times the audience of the next-highest-rated reality series."

"Yeah, but we are about 10 percent down from last year. That is enough to get advertisers worrying." She played with her eggs for almost a minute before continuing. "Sex and violence get ratings, Jack, and the executives know it."

There was something in her voice that made me realize she wasn't talking about just a robbery at a strip club.

"What are talking about? Aggravated assault? Date rape?" I asked, frowning.

"Murder."

Shockingly, she was standing next to me with a firm grip on my arm before I could leap to my feet. "I know, Jack. I argued against it, too. But I was outvoted."

Mary wrapped her arms around me to comfort me even before I started crying. Her tight embrace warmed my suddenly chill body and dispelled my shivers almost as quickly as they came. She waited until my storm had passed before speaking again.

"Honey, you knew from the start that murder was a possibility. If it helps any, I got the executives to agree that this would be billed as 'A Very Special Episode' and we'd wait at least three years before doing it again."

I took a very deep breath and reached for my tablet.

"Okay. Have you sent me the scenario yet?"

"No, and you won't be getting an electronic copy this time. Verbal scenario only. Absolutely no paper trail on this one."

The precautions made sense, but it was a first for me. There were a couple of episodes where the scenario was on a thumb drive and I had to read it on a computer that was completely cut off from the internet. There was even one episode, the one that involved child pornography, where the scenario was handwritten and the only copy was shredded and burned after the episode was complete. But I never expected to have to hear the details of a scenario verbally.

I poured myself and Mary another cup of coffee. "Best get started."

• • •

"Perfect," Mary said happily, and gave me a sisterly kiss on the cheek.

I had just described all the details of the scenario to her, two times in a row, without making any mistakes. All things being equal, the scenario wasn't too complicated. There were plenty of misdirection points, but the basic scenario was that Jenna Moriarty killed her late husband's mistress because she had stolen most of the money that Jenna was supposed to inherit and frittered it away.

Technically, the facts were true, but only because the mistress, Danielle Carter, was previously supposed to be the criminal on a different episode. She stole the money, but by the time we were ready to start shooting, she realized she was pregnant. The producers were not keen on the idea of an episode of *Locked* where a pregnant woman was the villain, so the episode was scrapped and the evidence of the theft was quashed.

But now everything had changed. Danielle had given birth to a baby boy and couldn't afford to raise him. At the same time, Jenna was having trouble making ends meet. Despite the fact that both women had received sizable payments for agreeing to participate in the first episode, they were now at the end of their rope and the promise of two million dollars to their children, after taxes, was enough to get one woman to agree to commit murder and the other woman to agree to be murdered.

Despite the fact that I had been watching people get paid to commit crimes or have crimes committed against them for years, I still couldn't believe that two people had agreed to this, for any price. But, somehow, they had agreed, and according to Mary, the murder had already been committed. At this point, my job was the same as always: make sure that idiot Sherlock discovered the various clues that would eventually lead him to solve the crime.

Honestly, the hardest part wasn't convincing the public that a man who had just barely managed to get an associate's degree in criminal justice from a community college was an investigative genius. Most of that was accomplished by the editing team. The real challenge was keeping Sherlock from realizing that I knew all the details of the crime and was essentially leading him around by his nose.

"You okay, Jack? You've been really quiet for the last few minutes."

"Sorry about that. I was just musing."

"Need to talk about it?"

"Nah. I'd just be venting about Sherlock and that's the last thing you need to hear." I smiled at her and then noticed that all the breakfast dishes were still on the table. Cursing, I quickly started clearing the table.

Mary calmly walked over and slipped an arm about my waist. "No need to rush at this point. A few more hours won't hurt anything and tomorrow is going to be a long day. Why don't you put down the dishes, cuddle up with me on the couch, and watch some black-and-white movies with me?"

There's a reason I love this woman.

• • •

"*Action!*"

It was time for my opening monologue. Every episode started with one and while I always prepared a little for it, most of it was ad-libbed. Testing panels showed an unprecedented 93 percent approval rating for the monologues that I ad-lib.

"London, Ohio, is a small town with a population just under ten thousand. It has roughly the same level of crime per capita as most other towns this size. But London is different from other small towns in one major way. It has the lowest number of unsolved felonies of any town in America, roughly half as many as the next best. What makes London so special? That is simple. London is home to the greatest investigative mind in the country, dare I say the world—Mr. Sherlock Holmes."

I said that last sentence with a perfectly straight face. Give me my fucking Emmy.

The camera panned to Sherlock, as is always the case when I first mention his name. The man was really hamming it up for the camera today, casually sitting in a lounging chair and vaping an e-cigarette. The camera always stayed focused on him for thirty seconds at this point, using him as the backdrop for a title sequence that would be added in postproduction. Today, Sherlock pulled out a key guitar and played a few notes of "Every Breath You Take" by the Police. I knew Mary would be fuming at having to pay for the rights to use the song.

When the camera panned back to me, I continued. "While solving crimes is old hat for Sherlock, today he received a very special case. Instead of getting a text or phone call from the victim of a crime, today Sherlock received a call from Sheriff George Lestrade, requesting assistance with a new case: the murder of Miss Danielle Carter.

"We are currently standing in the living room of the deceased, inches away from where her body was first discovered."

"Thank you," Sherlock said, putting his e-cigarette away. "Now tell me, Watson, do you see anything suspicious about this scene?"

The question was patently ridiculous. There were half a dozen suspicious things about the scene. The contracts that the perpetrator and victim both agreed to required them to perform a particular set of actions that were consistent with the narrative of the scenario. One of those required acts was to set up the scene of the crime in a particular way.

As I looked carefully at the scene, I saw roughly half a dozen books strewn about the floor, obviously having fallen off the nearby bookshelf. Between that and the fact that an easy chair was clearly out of place, it was undeniable that a struggle had taken place here.

As much as I wanted to point out these things, it was my job to make Sherlock look good, which meant I had to point out something trivial or simply wrong. This was an important episode, so I opted for the latter, because it made Sherlock look smarter.

"On a cursory inspection, I think it is odd that there is no bullet hole in the wall or floor."

Sherlock chortled. "Ah, my dear Watson, as usual you find mystery in the commonplace. The lack of a bullet hole is easily explained by the open window."

Actually, according to the autopsy report, the bullet had lodged in the victim's skull, but postproduction could easily make sure that little bit of information never showed on the air.

"The important clue is these three open books on the floor. My keen eye for detail has noticed that the word 'car' is visible on the pages of all three of them. It is quite clear to me that in her dying moments, Miss Carter intentionally left this clue that would help us identify her assailant."

I will admit that part of me was impressed by the insane leaps of logic that Sherlock could make on the spur of the moment. But mostly I was just disgusted by the nonsense he spewed and the fact that the American public fell for it so easily.

But I enjoyed my paycheck, so I didn't say that. Instead, I said, "So you think we should look in the car?"

"So simpleminded, my dear Watson. What would you ever do without me?"

I was tempted to find out.

"No, Watson. You have forgotten one very important detail. Miss Carter is a woman who has recently given birth to a child. Her child is the most important thing in her life. The word 'car' doesn't refer to her automobile. It is short for 'carriage,' as in the baby carriage we passed when we first entered the foyer of this house. That is where you will find the hidden clue."

I took off like a jackrabbit, while Sherlock followed at a measured, gentlemanly pace. This was characterization for both of us. At first Sherlock had wanted to be first on the scene for everything, but the producers insisted that he be the sedate one and that I be the aggressive one. It cost an extra thirty thousand dollars an episode to get him to agree.

This characterization wasn't just the result of audience polling or the whim of some producer. It was necessary to allow me to hide evidence at whatever location Sherlock had just proclaimed was important, without the cameras seeing me do it.

This time, as soon as I reached the baby carriage, I hid a small cell phone under one of the pillows nestled inside of it. The cameras were currently following Sherlock, so I knew I hadn't been caught on film. When Sherlock finally arrived in the foyer, I was diligently searching the exterior of the carriage.

"Excellent, Watson. Have you found anything?"

"No, but I haven't searched the interior yet."

I delayed my search a few moments until I was certain the camera was pointed directly at the interior and then began to run my hand along the inside walls of the carriage. Feigning excitement, I triumphantly drew the phone from its hiding place.

Sherlock immediately grabbed the phone from my hand. "Now let us see what clues this phone offers."

A few hours ago I had deleted all of the outgoing calls made on the phone during the last two weeks except for the ones made to a specific phone number. This made it remarkably easy for Sherlock to find the relevant information. Of course, he still spent a good two minutes babbling about investigative techniques and the mindset of the victim.

"Quickly, Watson, to the car. There is no time to lose. You drive while I research this phone number on my iPad."

Our corporate sponsors at Apple would be thrilled that he name-checked their product.

• • •

"Counsel, I need to speak with you about Danielle Carter immediately."

If anyone in the world other than Sherlock had walked into Mrs. Vallejo's office without an appointment and interrupted this attorney's work, she probably would have had that person thrown out of the building. But because *Locked* brought in so much revenue to the town, Sherlock could get away with just about anything.

"I know who you are," the woman at the desk said, "but I am simply unable to help you. Attorney/client privilege extends beyond death."

"Certainly, my fair lady. I apologize for the interruption."

Sherlock made a dignified exit from the office. For once, even

I was mystified. I knew he believed he had figured something out, but for the life of me I couldn't figure out what. The simple solution was to ask him.

"Are we abandoning this lead?"

"Quite the contrary, my dear Watson. We are following it to the very end."

"I don't understand. She didn't tell you anything."

"Actually, she told me everything. That is why we are headed back to the victim's house."

I was quite tempted to strangle the man for his vague response, but I was certain he would explain if I feigned a look of complete confusion.

"I can see from the look on your face that you don't follow. It is actually quite elementary. Despite the fact that I didn't make an appointment and simply walked into her office, Mrs. Vallejo was not surprised to see me. Thus I was able to deduce that she saw me on camera before I entered the building. And since the only cameras in the area belong to the London Savings & Loans across the street, she must have an agreement with the bank to monitor their cameras."

I steeled my features carefully to avoid laughing in his face. Somehow he managed to ignore the fact that Mrs. Vallejo could have easily heard the ruckus of a small production team walking into the waiting area of her office suite.

Sherlock had paused in his explanation. I took the obvious cue. "How does that help us?"

"Simple. Mrs. Vallejo would only have such an agreement if she also uses the bank to store important evidence for her clients. Therefore, we must simply search Danielle's residence for the key to a safe deposit box."

"That could be hiding anywhere in her home," I objected.

"Ah, my dear Watson, you forget that Miss Carter is a woman. I am quite certain that the key will be found hiding in her makeup case."

Amazingly, his mild misogyny actually polled at an 88 percent approval rating among female viewers. The primary reason that fans gave for the positive response was that he was too perfect otherwise.

I couldn't stand it, but I was actually a bit grateful for it at that moment. A makeup box was a very easy place to hide a key. In fact, his explanation would have been perfect except for one small problem. Danielle Carter had a safe deposit box at Suncrest Bank, not at London Savings & Loans.

Fortunately, we had long ago worked out a solution to problems like this. The show had rented a number of safe deposit boxes at banks throughout the town. All I needed to do was send a text to Mary to tell her which bank Sherlock had stated and where he claimed the key was hidden. By the time we arrived back at the house, there would be a key waiting for us.

• • •

Using slightly exaggerated movements, specifically for the sake of the camera, I carried the box from the wall to the table. Both the cameraman and Sherlock stood on the opposite side of the table from me. This was planned. I had instructed them that I intended to use a surprise reveal for this evidence.

Ostensibly, the surprise reveal was to increase suspense and to offer an opportunity for a commercial break. The truth was that I needed to palm a key into the box and I couldn't do that with two sets of eyes and a camera staring at me.

The sleight of hand went off without a hitch. After a moment of stunned silence, I turned the box around toward the camera and Sherlock.

"I don't understand, Holmes. What does it mean?"

Holmes reached into the box and pulled out the Suncrest Bank safe deposit box.

"It means, my old friend, that the late Miss Carter was a very cautious woman. The villain responsible for this foul deed is even more dangerous than I first thought."

Twenty minutes later, I unlocked another safe deposit box at a bank halfway across town, this time in full view of the camera. The box was half-full with financial documents. Mentally crossing my fingers, I stepped aside so Sherlock could examine them.

A few minutes passed before he spoke. "Watson, I have solved the case. Call Sheriff Lestrade and have him pick up Mrs. Joan Vallejo, Mr. Theodore Ramsey, and Mrs. Jenna Moriarty. I'll meet them all at the Carter residence and reveal the identity of the killer."

• • •

"George," I said, as gave the sheriff a strong handshake.

He responded with a broad grin. "Jack. Always a pleasure to see you. The suspects are waiting in the kitchen with one of my deputies. I hope that is acceptable," he said, giving a meaningful look to the cameras.

George's words were directed at me, but Sherlock responded anyway. "Quite fine, Sheriff. Let's not keep them waiting."

I followed Sherlock as he walked into the kitchen. Curiously, the sliding door that opened to the back yard had been left open, but that wasn't likely to affect the scenario, so I didn't worry about it.

Sherlock was in his element. He pulled out his e-cigarette and vaped for a few moments in order to heighten the tension. By the time he spoke, all eyes were upon him.

"You are probably wondering why I have assembled you here. The answer is quite simple. The three of you are the main suspects in the case," he said, gesturing to Vallejo, Ramsey, and Moriarty. All three attempted to protest, but Sherlock cut them off.

"Enough with that. I said you were all suspects, but only one of you is guilty."

The sheriff had been involved with enough episodes to know that Sherlock wanted someone to ask who at this point in his speech. Usually I asked the question, but George spoke up today.

"Excellent question, Sheriff. Let's consider all three suspects.

"First, there is Mr. Theodore Ramsey. He is the brother-in-law of the deceased. Public records show that he also owns a .22 caliber pistol, which is the exact caliber of the bullet that killed the victim. Finally, financial records show that Miss Carter recently purchased an expensive luxury minivan for her brother-in-law.

"Second, there is Mrs. Jenna Moriarty. She is the recently widowed wife of James Moriarty, the man that Miss Carter stole nearly a hundred thousand dollars from. Her late husband also has a .22 caliber pistol registered in his name.

"Finally, there is Mrs. Joan Vallejo. She is a lawyer who specializes in paternity law. Financial records indicate that she received a retainer for five thousand dollars from Miss Carter before the death of Mr. Moriarty. Then, a day later, Suncrest Bank stopped payment on the check. In the past week, Miss Carter's cell phone shows that she and Mrs. Vallejo called each other at least eight times. And finally, Eric Scott, the personal secretary of Mrs. Vallejo, has a .22 caliber pistol registered in his name."

The three suspects objected forcefully. Mrs. Vallejo was the loudest and most ardent in her objections. But there was something about the way that all three objected that made it obvious to me they were playing up to the camera. After years of filming this show, most of London's residents considered it a point of pride to be named a suspect and then exonerated. Luckily, none of them were badly overacting, so the scene wouldn't require much editing.

Sherlock allowed the objections to peter out and then once again took control of the scene. "Please bear with me. Shortly I will exonerate two of you."

He took another long drag of his e-cigarette.

"First, Mrs. Vallejo. You were rightfully angry that Miss Carter reneged on her agreed-upon retainer. But you have a thriving law practice and the money wasn't that important. Furthermore, public records also show that you had already negotiated a deal to avoid a civil suit. I am quite certain the phone calls were simply further negotiations regarding payment of that deal."

Mrs. Vallejo looked quite satisfied.

"Next, Mr. Ramsey. While you would have been legitimately concerned about losing your new minivan if Miss Carter's crime came to light, you also took custody of her child after her death. Since she had no inheritance to speak of, money obviously wasn't a motivating factor in that decision."

Jenna Moriarty didn't even wait for Sherlock to begin his accusation. She sprinted out of the kitchen, just as she had been instructed to do by one of the producers. Making sure to block the path of George, I ran after her.

This chase was supposed to end in the master bedroom, where I would corner her, but she apparently forgot her instructions and raced through the front door. Cursing lightly under my breath, I continued the chase. Once she was outside, she seemed to realize she was in the wrong place. Looking panicked, she ran toward the back yard. I followed, hoping I could salvage this situation.

The yard was completely fenced in. Jenna looked around in confusion and then appeared to notice the open door to the kitchen. I could only assume she planned to run back into the house and follow the original instructions.

It was actually a rather astute plan, except for one flaw. Sherlock stepped out of the house just as she was about to run through the kitchen door. She quite literally fell into his arms.

The situation was a disaster. I was supposed to catch her, search her, and find the murder weapon on her. In actuality I was going to plant the murder weapon on her, but with camera behind me that would be easy enough to do.

Instead, Sherlock searched her while I ran up to them. There was absolutely no way I could slip the murder weapon on her after he searched her. Besides the fact that either he would notice or the camera would catch the subterfuge, it would make him look bad on camera.

It was the most important episode of the season, possibly ever, and it was about to end anticlimactically.

"My dear Watson, I believe our Mrs. Moriarty here threw something into the bushes as she ran past. Would you be a good fellow and see what it was?"

For a few moments I simply stood frozen. There was no way

Sherlock could have seen such an action and I was reasonably certain that he knew no such thing had happened. But, with that one statement, he had saved the climactic scene of the show.

Shaking off my stupor before it ruined the scene, I walked over to the bush. Making a big deal of searching diligently, I triumphantly revealed a .22 caliber pistol.

Sherlock gave me a knowing wink. A wink that changed our entire relationship forever. A wink that he carefully hid from the camera.

Turning back to look at both the cameras, he donned his 88-percent audience-approved smug smile and pointed at Mrs. Moriarty.

"You've been 'locked."

IDENTITY:
AN ADVENTURE OF SHIRLEY HOLMES AND JACK WATSON

BY KEITH R. A. DECANDIDO

I *hated* oncology rotation. I never told anybody this, because nobody gave a damn. I was a fourth-year med student. It was December. Everybody who mattered at the hospital—basically, a mess of people, none of whom were me—got the first shot at vacation, including all the oncologists at New York Presbyterian, which meant I pinch-hit for whoever they told me to. This week it was Dr. Antropov.

Mostly, it just meant seeing people who had regular treatments who were on a strict schedule. Anything that needed more than your basic babysitting wasn't gonna happen until Antropov got back, which meant I was gonna spend my week supervising ongoing chemotherapy and radiation treatments.

Monday morning, my first appointment was Martha Hudson, in for her weekly chemo. She was a white lady in her forties, looking haggard, like most chemo patients. Her chart told me that she was most of the way through month number two of chemo for endometrial cancer, and that four months ago she had a hysterectomy. Her appearance told me she was well off, since she wore elegant name-brand clothes, fancy jewelry, and a nicely styled butch haircut—she had the money to pay someone to style what little hair she had left.

"Ms. Hudson, I'm Jack Watson—I'm filling in for Dr. Antropov this week."

"I know, Dmitri told me he was flying home to visit his family for the holidays."

That was more than he'd told me. Then again, he didn't let me call him Dmitri, either. "How you feeling, Ms. Hudson?"

"Please, call me Martha. And I feel like hammered shit."

I smiled. "Hammered shit?"

"Yes. It's where you take regular shit and pound it repeatedly with a hammer, wham-wham-wham!" She used her right fist as a hammer and pounded it into her left palm.

"So pretty shitty, then?"

"Yes. I'm taking naps all the time, and the techs are finding it harder and harder to find a good vein."

Looking down at her right arm, I noticed bruising around the bandage from where the IV was inserted. "Yeah, that's gonna happen sometimes. They may need to switch arms before this is over."

"Really? Dmitri told me not to worry and that it was all in my head."

"No, it's all in your arm, and it's gonna hurt like a son of a bitch." I didn't usually use foul language with patients, but Martha started it with "hammered shit."

"Oh, it does, believe me. But I'd rather stay with the right arm in any case. I'm left-handed, you see, and if my left arm becomes as useless as my right, I won't be able to draw."

"You're an artist?" The chart didn't list her occupation.

She chuckled. "Hardly. I simply enjoy drawing. It relaxes me, and I need all the relaxing I can get right now."

"Thought you said you were taking a lot of naps. Sounds like you're already pretty relaxed." I grinned to let her know I was just teasing.

Sure enough, she chuckled again. "You're very droll, Dr. Watson."

"It's Jack, and I don't get to be called that until May."

"Ah, that explains it. If you're still a med student, then you're allowed to have a bedside manner. I understand they have that removed when they give you the doctorate."

"Actually, that's elective surgery."

"In any case, Jack, my need for relaxation is mental rather than physical. My home situation has become more…challenging since the cancer diagnosis."

She didn't go any further, and I didn't ask. Her home life wasn't my problem, especially since she wasn't even really my patient. I checked the chart over, but nothing leaped out. "Is there anything else you want to ask or talk about?"

"No, I'm fine. I mean, I'm not *fine*, I'm undergoing chemo, but the alternative is far worse. I just wish—" She cut herself off. "Never mind. Are you attending Columbia's med school?"

I nodded. "Yeah, I did two and a half years at Hopkins, then I joined the Army. Once I got back from Afghanistan, I enrolled in Columbia to finish off."

"So you're from Baltimore?"

"Originally. After I got home I needed a fresh start. And I heard this was a helluva town."

She smiled. "Oh, it very much is, Jack. In fact, the Bronx is up *and* the Battery is down."

"Yeah, and I get to ride in a hole in the ground every day."

I'd left my smartphone on the desk, and it buzzed, vibrating an inch to the left.

"Excuse me," I said as I grabbed it. I'd learned the hard way to make sure I checked my text messages soon as I got them, otherwise the docs who needed me to run some errand or other *right now this second* would get all pissed.

But it turned out not to be a doctor. "Dammit."

"What's wrong?" Martha asked.

I shook my head and put the phone back down. "Sorry, just found out I didn't get the apartment I was shooting for." She looked at me funny, and I added, "I'm rooming with a guy who has a place on 84th. It's rent-controlled, two-bedroom, and we're both grad students, so we're never home to get in each other's way.

Unfortunately, it's going co-op in the new year, and my roomie decided to just take campus housing at Columbia."

"You're not doing that?"

"Hate dorms. Too much like the barracks."

"That makes sense." She put a finger to her chin, and then let out a long breath. "I'm sorry, Jack, I'm starting to fade. Is there anything else?"

I looked at the chart again, but that was just to make it look good. "No, we're done for now. Next week is your week off, and Dr. Antropov'll be back in the new year, so he'll take care of you then."

She nodded and slowly got to her feet. "Ooooh. Not good."

"You okay to get home?"

"I have a car service. It's not far, in any case. I'm right over on Riverside Drive." She looked at me. "You're a very good listener, Jack. Might I be so forward as to make you an offer? One that will solve your housing problem?"

I frowned. "I guess?"

"I have a niece. She's—well, difficult, and she needs a companion, someone who listens well, and can engage her without asking what she deems to be stupid questions. That was me until a few months ago, but—you know."

With a nod, I said, "Right."

"She is also a student at Columbia, and she has rejected every person she's interviewed. She might reject you as well, of course, but it's gotten to the point where I just took down the Craigslist ad. I'm rather desperate."

I hesitated. This was totally out of left field, and I'd only just met the woman.

She then said, "You would have an entire floor of a Riverside Drive townhouse to yourself, rent free."

That got my attention. "Okay. What do I have to do?"

"Talk to my niece. Are you free this evening?"

• • •

Since it was late December, we were between semesters, so I had shit-all to do on a Monday night anyhow. I'd been thinking of going to see a movie—Mondays and Tuesdays are the best nights to see a movie in the theater; the place is almost totally empty—but a free crib in exchange for listening to some kid? I'll take that interview.

When Martha said townhouse on Riverside, she wasn't kidding. It was a beautiful five-story place on the corner of 107th that had to go back to the early twentieth century. It was all red brick and white stone, with fancy wrought-iron patterns on the front door.

I rang the bell. About a second later, a voice said, "Who is it?" over the speaker.

Now that was impressive all by itself because intercoms like that in New York usually just gave you a burst of static. This one, though, was crystal clear. "It's Jack Watson."

There was a pause, and then: "I don't know anyone by that name, though it's a very common name, and I suppose I might have met one at some point. Obviously if I did, they were spectacularly boring."

Okay, maybe listening to this kid was going to be more of a challenge. "Uhm, I'm here about the, ah, companion job."

"Oh, you're the person my aunt met at the hospital?"

"Yes."

The door made a light buzzing noise, and I pulled it open.

To call this place huge undersold it. High ceilings, fancy furniture, and the foyer I walked into had a massive staircase on the right, and led to an even bigger room. And there was wood *everywhere*—hardwood floor, wooden banisters on the wooden staircase, wood paneling on the walls, a wooden coat rack near the front door.

The young woman who walked in from the far room was small and slight, with just enough curves to make you realize she was female. She was well fed, though—three years in Afghanistan taught me the difference between people who were skinny because that was how they were built and people who were skinny because they didn't eat. She had brown hair that she kept short, and I thought she had brown eyes—she wasn't looking at me. Her skin was the coffee color you see on some mixed-race folks. But even with that mocha flesh tone, she was pretty much the dictionary definition of *nondescript*. I also couldn't tell how old she was at all—if you'd told me she was twelve or twenty-eight or anything in between, I'd believe you.

"Please place your coat on the coat rack and then come with me," she said.

After I did that, she asked, "How long did you serve as a medic in Afghanistan?" as she led me into the next room.

"Your aunt tell you that?"

"No, she just said that she met you at the hospital, but that means you're obviously a medical professional of some sort, and you carry yourself in the manner of someone who served in the military, specifically in combat situations, to wit, the way you continually check your surroundings. When you shrugged out of your coat, it was as if you were expecting there to be a backpack and your hands moved toward your head as if to remove a helmet. Plus, there is a particular cast to your eyes that I have observed only in those who have been involved in armed conflict—some would call it haunted, if they preferred to be vulgar. So, therefore, your service was recent and involved combat—but your fingers have none of the calluses associated with use of firearms and since you are involved in medicine, it stood to reason that you served as a me—"

"Okay, I'm impressed." By this time we'd gone through what I figured was a sitting room and then a dining room. "But how'd you know it was Afghanistan? I could've served in Iraq."

She turned around and stared at me, and I stopped dead in my tracks. I got my first good look at her brown eyes, and her stare was *intense*.

"Your fingers have none of the calluses associated with use of firearms and since you are involved in medicine, it stood to reason that you served as a medic. Now then, enough of my stating the blindingly obvious. Please answer the question: how long did you serve as a medic in Afghanistan?" She took a seat at the head of the table.

I just stared at her for a second, but she was back to looking away, which, I got to tell you, was a huge relief. After another second I sat at the seat perpendicular to her and said, "Three years."

"My aunt seems to think that you could replace her as my companion. What Aunt Martha fails to understand is that I do not require a companion. I am, of course, grateful to her for assisting me all these years while my parents have traveled, but I am no longer of an age where I require a guardian or someone to speak to. In fact, I would much rather not have someone." She frowned. "Under what circumstances did you meet my aunt?"

"I was filling in for Dr. Antropov to supervise her chemo."

"Which means you're a fourth-year medical student, since Aunt Martha would have identified you as a doctor, and you would likely have introduced yourself as 'Dr. Jack Watson,' and supervising a standard procedure is typical of the duties given to internists such as yourself. This means that you are working long hours at the hospital in addition to your studies, which means that you will not have the time to irritate me." She nodded. "Excellent. I accept your application, Mr. Watson."

"You just said I wouldn't have time to—to irritate you." Honestly, that had been my biggest worry about this whole thing from jump: I didn't have all that much spare time.

"Which suits us both. You do not need to be encumbered by the additional duties my aunt thinks are required, but the act of having you here will placate her and create the illusion that I am being taken care of. Do you accept?"

I just kind of sat there with my mouth hanging open. Pretty much from the minute this kid opened her mouth, I figured the job was a lost cause. I didn't think I *could* listen to her for more than five minutes without wanting to strangle her.

But getting a free room in *this* house and not having to put up with her bullshit? "I'll gladly accept, Ms. Hudson."

She frowned again. "Don't be stupid, my name isn't Ms. Hudson. Aunt Martha is my mother's sister, and she committed the barbaric act of changing her name to that of her husband when she married, and kept it following his death. That practice derives from an era when women were considered to be the property of their spouses and so subsumed their birth names for that of the husband. That is no longer the case, so I do not comprehend why women continue to engage in the idiotic practice. In any event, I would properly be identified as 'Ms. Holmes,' which is my father's last name—and my mother's, actually, as she also underwent the barbaric practice. However, you may address me by my first name of Shirley."

"And you can call me Jack."

"Is that how you are referred to by friends and colleagues?"

I started to say that my Army buddies all called me Doc, because that's what you usually call the medic, but I really didn't want little Shirley Holmes calling me that, and she was literal enough that she might. So I just said, "Yeah."

"That was a lie. You hesitated before answering. Nonetheless, I will abide by the terms you set out and refer to you as Jack. You may bring your belongings whenever you wish. Aunt Martha lives on the second floor, I am on the third, and my parents—on those rare occasions when they darken this townhouse's doorstep—are on the fourth. You will have the top level where my brother once lived before he moved out. I am afraid it will require a considerable amount of stair climbing, but you seem to be a fit specimen."

I chuckled. "The place I'm about to move out of is a fifth-floor walkup, so I'm good. I'll move in tomorrow."

• • •

The first few weeks living at the Holmes townhouse were interesting. I had my own bathroom, with a claw-foot tub, and even a kitchenette, plus a bedroom that was bigger than any apartment I'd ever lived in, never mind the shitholes where I hung my helmet in the desert.

I didn't see that much of Shirley. She spent all her time researching. I checked in on her a few times after I moved in, just to keep appearances up, for Martha's sake. In her room on the second floor, she had four computers on her desk: a purple iMac from the turn of the century, a Dell laptop from about 2004, a MacBook Air, and an Acer laptop that looked more recent. Plus, I saw a big pile of smartphones on the desk, starting with a Treo, a BlackBerry, and the first-ever iPhone model and going all the way up to the latest models, and Apple, Droid, and Windows phones. One of the desktops was playing music (sounded like something classical), another had some kind of graphics program, another had an Excel spreadsheet, and the Air was running a word-processing program.

First thing she said was, "What is it you want, Jack?"

"Just checking in to make sure you're okay."

"Of course I am okay. In addition to the placation of my aunt, your presence serves as a useful and immediate aid should I not be okay, as you are a semester away from being a fully trained physician and are located only two flights above me. However, I have not summoned you, which is an indication that I am, in fact, okay. You may rest assured that you will be informed if that situation changes."

All righty, then.

When she wasn't home, she was going off to some library or other.

Once the semester started, we didn't see each other hardly at all. Which was fine. I saw more of Martha, honestly, and we spent a lot of time making fun of "Dmitri." She told me she wished I was her regular doctor.

One Friday night I came back from the hospital to see a tall Indian woman standing outside the front door. She was staring at the wrought-iron pattern.

"Can I help you?" I walked up to the door next to her.

"Do you live here?" She spoke with an accent that sounded a little British.

"I do, yeah."

"Oh. Is this Shirley Holmes's place?"

"Uh, yeah, it is. I, ah, rent out the top floor. You here to see her?"

"I *think* so."

That was a weird answer. "You a friend of hers?"

"Oh, no! That is to say, we've taken a class together, and she's *brilliant*, but…"

After she trailed off, the uncomfortable silence went on way too long, so I said, "You wanna come in?"

"I suppose so, yes." She gave me a big smile. "Thank you, I'm so *sorry* for being ridiculous."

"It's fine." I pulled my keys out of my slacks and opened the door. "By the way, I'm Jack."

"My name is Kirti. Thank you *so* much for your help."

Martha was coming downstairs as we came in. Before I could say anything, Kirti said, "Shirley, is that you?"

Chuckling, Martha said, "Afraid not, but thanks for the compliment." Turning, she yelled up the stairs. "Shirley! You've got a client!"

I frowned. "Client?"

"Didn't I tell you about Shirley's hobby? She helps people with things."

The kid herself came down. "Hello?"

"Is that you, Shirley?" Kirti asked.

"Of course. And you're Kirti Prakash. You and I both took the 'Ecology: A Human Approach' class two semesters ago."

"Oh, good, you do remember me."

"I remember everything—well, everything important, and many things that aren't, including every excruciating moment of that class. I should have realized from the name that it was a waste of time. It isn't as if there's such a thing as a robotic approach to ecology."

Shirley took Kirti into the sitting room, and I was about to go upstairs. Martha, though, stopped me. "Stay. You should watch this."

"Watch what?"

"My niece in action. Trust me."

I was about to say no, but I was curious, and besides, I was supposed to be Shirley's "companion." Maybe I could help with whatever Kirti's problem was.

This time Shirley took her meeting in the sitting room. In the weeks I'd been in the townhouse, I hadn't been in this room except to walk through it. There was a back staircase to the kitchen that I used occasionally if I needed something that wasn't in my own kitchenette, but otherwise I didn't hardly use the first floor except to walk in and walk out.

Shirley sat in a nice easy chair that was pretty well worn, but looked real comfy. Kirti sat on the couch, and I took a smaller chair that was near the big fireplace.

First thing Shirley said was, "I take it your shift at Starbucks just ended?"

"Yes, I—" Kirti's eyes got all wide. "*How* did you know I work at Starbucks?"

"It's obvious. The coffee that is sold at Starbucks has a particular odor—not, I might add, a particularly pleasant one—and enough of it lingers to indicate that Kirti was in the store for many hours. In addition, there are coffee grounds under her fingernails, indicating that her lengthy stay in the establishment was due to her working behind the counter rather than as a customer. Every time I saw her on campus, she had her hair down, even in warm weather, much less the just-above-freezing temperatures of today, but it's tied up in the style of baristas at Starbucks to wear under their regulation caps."

Kirti shook her head. "I *knew* I was right to come to you, you're *so* brilliant! And yes, I *do* work at the Starbucks on Broadway. I don't really *need* to—my college bills are paid by my trust, and I live with my parents—but the extra money is useful sometimes, and I like interacting with people." She let out a breath. "But *none* of that matters. Shirley, you're the *only* one who can help me. My fiancé has gone missing!"

"And you haven't reported him to the police since they would then talk to your parents, and they disapprove of the union?"

Kirti opened her mouth and closed it. "How did you know that?"

"It doesn't matter." She let out a long sigh. "But if you insist, you aren't wearing an engagement ring, but since you entered, you have fiddled with your left ring finger several times, and stared down longingly at it several more times. You're devoted enough to your fiancé to seek out my help, yet you're not wearing the ring, which means you've been pressured into not wearing it, and such pressure would likely come from your parents."

"It's primarily my father. Well, actually, he's my stepfather—he married my mother two years ago. My biological father died when I was a girl, but he left me with a trust."

Shirley nodded. "You already mentioned that. Do you have access to this trust?"

Shaking her head, Kirti said, "Not until I get married. My stepfather has been *very* strict about who I might date, which is his right, of course."

I snorted and then turned it into a cough so I didn't piss Kirti off.

"He doesn't even like me to go to parties. The last six months or so, he's been *particularly* adamant. I still go, but usually only when he's away on business—he travels a great deal for his job."

"You met your fiancé at one of these parties?"

Kirti nodded. "His name is José Hernandez. We met at a party at a friend's apartment on 117th Street. He was off in the corner, not talking to anyone, and wearing dark glasses even though we were inside and at night. I was attracted to him right away—he's completely bald, but with a thick beard, and I've *always* found that look to be rather sexy." She got a shy smile when she said that. "In any case, I struck up a conversation. Turns out he's been *very* sensitive to light his whole life, which is why he wears the tinted lenses. I had a difficult time speaking to him at first, because his voice is *very* quiet, so I could hardly understand him, but we went up onto the roof of the building and then I could hear him properly. He used to be in the Army, and he was wounded in the throat when he served in Iraq and it damaged his vocal cords. *That's* why he grew the beard, to cover the scarring."

"You began dating after that party?" Shirley asked.

"Yes. We went out twice, but once my stepfather returned from his business trip we didn't see each other. I told him I met someone, and he was *furious* that I went out with a man he didn't know or approve of. The fact that he's a Latino didn't help matters, unfortunately—my parents are *very* old-fashioned."

I swallowed another snort. That much was kind of obvious.

"Unfortunately, José became *very* skittish after that. We texted each other constantly, and he said the most *wonderful* things, but he was afraid to see me for fear of what my stepfather would do. But we did get together a few times when my stepfather was away on business, and on one of those dates, he proposed! It was *so* romantic—we were at the Metropolitan Museum of Art, and he suddenly got down on one knee and gave me the ring! He not only asked me to marry him, but to swear eternal devotion to him, which of course I did! We promised each other, right there at the Temple of Dendur, to always be true to each other. We agreed to marry the next week!"

"Since you keep referring to José as your fiancé, I take it that he disappeared before the wedding?"

Kirti let out a huge sigh. "Yes. We were to meet at the courthouse a week and a half ago. He met my mother and I at our apartment—"

I couldn't help blurting out, "Wait, your mother? You said your parents didn't approve."

"My mother changed her mind after he proposed. She said that all that mattered was that I was happy. But he forgot the wedding rings, so he had to go back to his apartment. He put my mother and I in a cab and said he'd meet us at the courthouse." Her lips started trembling. "I never saw him again. We waited at the courthouse for *hours*, and I texted him, but *nothing*! I've *been* texting him, and I even sent him an email and left him a note on Facebook, even though he doesn't check either of them all that often. *Nothing*."

"Did you try going to his place?" I asked.

"I'm not sure where it is," Kirti said ruefully. "He said he lives in Harlem, but I never went to his apartment. He shares it with two other men, and he says they've agreed never to bring anyone home."

Shirley stared at the floor for a couple seconds, and then looked up. "Do you have pictures of José and of your parents?"

"Of course, I've got them on my phone." Kirti frowned. "Why my parents?"

"It will help me with the investigation," Shirley said, and then gave Kirti her number so she could text the pictures.

Kirti played with her smartphone for a bit, and then Shirley's own phone made a clanging noise.

Then Kirti stood up. "May I please use your bathroom?"

Shirley nodded, but didn't look up from her phone, which she was running her fingers over like a kid with a game console.

I pointed to the dining room. "Go through there to the kitchen, then hang a left. There's a little bathroom there you can use."

"Thank you so much." She headed the way I pointed.

I shook my head. "You do this a lot?"

Shirley was still staring at her phone. "Hm?"

"Help stupid people. I mean, she wants to marry a guy and she doesn't know where he lives. Plus, she didn't even know what you look like."

Now Shirley looked up. "What do you mean by that?"

"When Martha came downstairs after we walked inside, Kirti asked if she was you, and then she asked if it was you when you came down. I mean, she *came* to see you, and you were in that ecology class together, so why didn't she recognize you?"

"Jack, you may well have put your finger on the solution to what happened to José Hernandez."

I blinked. "What?"

But Shirley didn't answer me, just went back to playing with her phone. I was gonna get up and leave, but then Kirti came back in.

"Ah, Kirti," Shirley said, "now that you've provided me with this information, I must ask you some questions. Who is the executor of your trust?"

"My parents, until I marry, at which point I control it."

"As I suspected. What are your parents' full names?"

"My mother is Nipa Kapoor, and my stepfather is Ganesh Kapoor."

"What do they do for a living?"

"Well, my mother keeps house, of course, and my stepfather is a vice-president for Chase Bank—I'm not sure which actual office he's in, but it's somewhere in midtown. Anyhow, they have him travel a great deal, and I believe he goes from branch to branch for his work as well."

Shirley started typing furiously with her thumbs on her smartphone, probably noting down all that info. "Next, would you please describe me?"

Kirti blinked. "I'm sorry?"

"Tell me what I look like."

"Uhm…" Kirti's mouth kind of just opened and shut. "I mean, you have medium-sized hair, and—I'm sorry, I don't understand what this has to do with finding José."

"I'm just confirming something Jack noticed. Are you familiar with a condition known as prosopagnosia?"

"No," Kirti said.

But I was nodding my head. "Face blindness. Basically, it means you have trouble recognizing people, even if you've met them before." It was more complicated than that, but unlike Shirley, I was just as happy not to bury people in jargon and long-winded explanations.

"Oh." Kirti sounded confused. "I *do* have difficulty with that—but I'm *still* not clear as to what any of this has to do with José."

Shirley stood up and held her smartphone display out toward me. "Jack, this is a picture of Ganesh Kapoor."

I looked at it. It showed a dark-skinned man with hair that had enough product in it to count as a deadly weapon. He had a sharp nose, wide brown eyes, and small ears, and was clean-shaven. Also, he was wearing a gray suit. "Okay," I said with a shrug.

Then she swiped a finger across the display and showed it to me again. "This is José Hernandez."

I looked at a bald guy with a thick beard. He was wearing shades, and just a sweatshirt and jeans.

And then I saw it: he had the same nose and the same ears. I shook my head.

Shirley then turned to Kirti. "Is it reasonable for me to assume that your intention is to wait until José is found and marry him?"

"Of *course*! Why do you think I want you to find him?"

"And until that time, your mother and stepfather are in control of your trust?"

"Yes."

Shirley nodded. "Excellent. I will take on your case, and I promise that I will have José's location by this time tomorrow."

I shot Shirley a look.

Kirti's eyes went all wide again. "You can find him *that* fast?"

I was more wondering why it was going to take that long, but I didn't say anything.

"Absolutely."

"Oh, *thank* you!" Kirti got up and moved toward Shirley, but she flinched.

"Please!" Shirley cried out, and it was the loudest I'd heard her say *anything* in the month or so I'd been living here. "Do not touch me!"

Kirti backed off. She looked like she'd accidentally stepped on a puppy. "I'm *so* sorry! But thank you *ever* so much!"

A few seconds later, Kirti left, and I just stared at Shirley. "Why didn't you just tell her that her stepfather was posing as this José guy?"

"Were you not even paying attention, Jack? Every time I state the obvious, the person to whom I provide the statement asks for proof. You can't just accept that I know that you served as a medic in Afghanistan or that Kirti works at Starbucks, I must explain it. For that reason, I prefer to provide Kirti with documentation to supplement my declaration that the man who wooed her is her own stepfather in disguise."

"Wasn't a bad disguise," I said, "especially with her being face blind, but the Army part of the story doesn't hold up."

Shirley tilted her head. "How so?"

"If he's that sensitive to light, the Army wouldn't have sent him to the desert. Hell, they probably wouldn't have taken him at all."

"Yes, well, your assessment of Kirti's intelligence was not altogether unfair, Jack, and I'm sure that Kapoor was counting on her not knowing such minutiae. Now then, let us commence with the verification."

• • •

The next day, Kirti came back to the townhouse. Shirley and I had been up half the night digging stuff up online, and then I took a trip out to talk to people while she stayed home and sent emails and made some phone calls.

I gotta admit, I was enjoying this, mostly because I was really looking forward to Kapoor's comeuppance. This asshole manipulated his own stepdaughter, and my plan was to offer to walk Kirti to the 24th Precinct myself to file charges.

When I opened the door to let Kirti in, she didn't even say hi or anything. "Did you find him?"

"C'mon in, Kirti. Shirley's waiting in the sitting room."

I took her coat and hung it up on the coat rack, shaking my head at the fact that I'd just talked about a sitting room. Never in a million years did I see myself ever even *being* in a sitting room, much less living in a house with one.

Anyhow, we sat in the same spots we were in the previous day, except Kirti was actually on the edge of her seat.

"So where is José?"

"Before I answer that, I must ask you a question," Shirley said. "Where is your stepfather right now?"

"He took my mother out to dinner tonight to Rosa Mexicano near Lincoln Center."

"In that case, the answer to your question is the same: the person who asked you to marry him, who identified himself to you as José Hernandez, is currently taking your mother out to dinner at Rosa Mexicano near Lincoln Center."

There was a quick pause, and then Kirti shook her head. "Is this some sort of *joke*?"

"I believe our interactions to date should have made you realize, Kirti, that I do not joke. I find humor to be confusing and imprecise and frustratingly subjective. Nonetheless, even if I were the kind of person who would joke, I'm not doing so now. The fictitious José Hernandez is, in fact, your stepfather, Ganesh Kapoor, in disguise."

Now Kirti stood up. "That is the most ridiculous thing I have *ever* heard. You've hardly done *any* investigating or searching—it's only *been* one day!"

"I actually made this particular determination yesterday before we finished talking. With Jack's help, I've spent the last twenty-four hours acquiring evidence, since I assumed that—despite the fact that you specifically came to me because of my brilliance—you would not simply accept my word."

"This is the most *absurd* thing—"

I got up out of the chair and put a hand on her shoulder. "Look, Kirti, I know it's hard to accept, but hear her out, okay? Trust me, you need to listen to her."

Kirti stared at me for a few seconds, then let out a noise like a burst pipe and sat back down, folding her arms. "Very well. *Tell* me your ridiculous story."

As I also sat, Shirley shot me a look that I couldn't figure out—maybe it was her way of saying thank you?—and then she turned her intense stare right at Kirti. "Ganesh Kapoor is a liar. He does *not* work for Chase, though he used to, albeit not in a position that would afford him many travel opportunities, as he was a teller at a branch located in Rockefeller Center. He was fired for cause ten months ago due to multiple—"

"You're lying!" Kirti screamed.

Shirley stared more intently. "He was fired for cause ten months ago due to multiple sexual harassment complaints from both coworkers and customers. And I am not lying, I never lie. I find it even more irritating than humor."

"Kirti, I talked to the bank manager," I said, leaning forward, "and she told me all of this." I didn't mention the part about how I told the woman that I was Kapoor's doctor and that I was worried about his mental health. She was reluctant to say anything until I said that part, and then she couldn't shut up about what an awful guy he was and what he did.

"He allowed himself to be fired so he could collect unemployment while he searched for another job, but was unsuccessful. However, not wishing to be viewed as unable to support his new family, he pretended to work, having already talked up his job as something far greater than what it truly was. At that point he realized that he had control over your trust, and would continue to do so as long as you remained single. So he became stricter regarding your dating practices, and at the same time created a simple disguise. A false beard covered his nonexistent wound that was his excuse for altering his voice, he contrived a reason to wear tinted lenses, and he removed his toupee. That would combine with your prosopagnosia to make the disguise effective. Living with you for so long made him aware of your habits and your preferences, and he played to them while pretending to be José. He kept other details vague, and also chose a very common pseudonym that would discourage attempts at an online search."

I just nodded. Shirley had checked whitepages.com and found more than one hundred men named José Hernandez in Manhattan alone.

"His proposal was sufficiently romantic that you could not possibly have said no—and then extracted a promise from you to always be true only to him, thus decreasing the likelihood of you even finding another relationship, much less someone to marry, after his 'disappearance,' which was, in fact, him simply removing the disguise and becoming Ganesh Kapoor full time again. Thus he has guaranteed indefinite control of your trust, allowing him to maintain the fiction of his being a bank vice-president to the general public."

Kirti was just shaking her head and looking away. "No, no, I don't believe you—"

Shirley, though, was relentless. "I also was able to obtain the financial records of Ganesh Kapoor." She pulled a first-generation iPad up off the floor and handed it to Kirti. "As you can see, he has been making weekly transfers from the bank that houses your trust to his own account."

I shuddered again. This civilian kid had no business getting her hands on financial records. I had asked her that morning where she got it, and she had just said, "A friend of the family." Since she didn't lie, that was actually true, but she wouldn't tell me anything else past that.

Kirti stood up, tears running down her cheeks. "I can't *believe* you would say this about my *father*! Maybe I just *will* go to the police—it's obvious you don't understand a *thing* about what I'm going through! José loves me and I *will* find him!"

And then she just walked out. She probably would've slammed the door, but the wrought iron was too heavy for that.

Shirley was staring at the doorway to the foyer through which Kirti had just stomped out. Her mouth was hanging open, and she had a look on her face that I'd never seen before: confusion. "I don't understand. I provided her with incontrovertible proof. The bank records alone should have done it. This makes no sense to me."

"Actually, it's pretty simple."

"I doubt it." She shook her head derisively. "If I can't figure it out, I'm not clear as to how you might."

I ignored the dig. "She's in love."

"What?" More confusion. "How can she possibly love someone who doesn't exist?"

I sighed. "Look, Kapoor did his job way too well. Kirti's in love with 'José Hernandez,' and nothing we say's gonna change that. She won't believe anything bad said about him."

She looked at me like I was nuts. "And this makes sense to you?"

Chuckling, I said, "I don't know if I'd go that far, but at the very least I can understand it." I looked over at the doorway. "Hell, I wish I loved someone enough to be that stupid about."

"There is nothing in this world that justifies stupidity—which you'd think would mean there'd be less of it." She sighed. "Ah, well, it was an interesting problem at the very least. Very engaging. And you were quite helpful, Jack—I would not have known of her prosopagnosia without you, and that was the key to the problem.

She would surely have recognized her own stepfather even with the false beard and dark glasses and false voice but for that. Also, your verification of his employment history was quite valuable. That required prevarication, which is not something at which I excel."

"Wow, you're actually admitting to sucking at something."

She almost sneered. "I would never admit such a thing, particularly not in such vulgar terms. My lack of facility with lying is by choice, not ability. Lies are the source of much of what is wrong with the world—though it is hardly the only culprit in society's failings."

I didn't have anything to say to that, so we just stood there in an awkward silence for a couple of seconds before I said, "I better get back upstairs. Got the overnight shift tonight, and I wanna grab a nap before I go."

"Before you retire, Jack, I just wish to say that I may have been mistaken in my initial assessment of you. Perhaps, if you are amenable to the notion, you might aid me with other clients that ask for my assistance?"

"Depends." I grinned. "Do all of them stomp out like four-year-olds?"

"Hardly. In fact, just yesterday I received a prototype for a new smartphone that isn't actually on the market yet, which was sent in gratitude by one of my previous clients. I was going to spend the evening testing its capabilities."

I smiled. "You do that. I'm gonna take a nap."

"Wait," she said testily.

"What?"

She sighed. "You haven't answered my question, Jack. Please do so before departing."

I remembered her comments on humor, which probably extended to sarcasm. "Yes, I'd be happy to help you out if I can."

"Good."

Then she turned and headed toward the kitchen without another word.

Definitely not what I was expecting. Maybe hanging out with this kid was going to be more interesting than I thought.

THE SCENT OF TRUTH

BY JODY LYNN NYE

I braced myself as the Great Investigator launched himself at me. His flapping jowls smelled of slightly old meat as he reared up and ran his broad, black nose up and down my body. I almost regretted that I had taken off my air-conditioned environment suit—Baskur left traces of saliva all over my under-robe and billowing trousers, face, arms, and even my mustache.

"You have been in Alpha Ganston recently, I perceive," he said, through the translation charm on the collar about his neck. "Mmm! I love the smell of Alpha Ganston!" He sniffed ardently, circling around and around my shoes on all fours.

"Yes, I know," I said. I had been advised to immerse myself in complex odors in preparation for the meeting with Baskur. Call it a currency, if you will. I needed his assistance. No one else, I had been reliably informed, would be able to disentangle the bizarre circumstances that had been transmitted to me while I returned from my last assignment. I was lucky that I had not yet laundered the last outfit I wore on my previous visit to the well-forested tropical outpost on the second planet that circled our star. Panettiere, the fourth planet, upon which I now stood, was cooler, with a humid atmosphere that had evolved the Norridings. They communicated largely by scent, but Baskur had gained a reputation for uncovering hidden truths that was known far beyond our system.

After a time, Baskur retreated a pace or so away from me and sat down upon the broad oval floor cushion. A long, narrow, purple tongue like a snake darted out of his mouth and laved his face, so as not to lose even a particle of the scents he had just vacuumed off me. That visage, covered as it was with short, golden-brown fur, made me think irresistibly of a basset hound, but with even more intelligent eyes.

"And to what do I owe this delectable treat, middle-aged male visitor of human extraction?" he asked, as three smaller Norridings, similar in build and coloration to Baskur, brought bowls of clean water to both of us.

"My name's Shoqan al-Hamish ibn Malik," I said, bowing deeply over the broad krater. "There's been a difficult situation, and I have been directed to ask you for help."

He scratched his right ear vigorously with a rear claw. "Why not call it what it is?" he asked. "You call it murder."

I admit that I goggled, nearly dropping the water. "How would you know that?"

"In the same way I know you to be a journalist," he said, fixing me with those warm brown eyes. "You have never visited me before. Most of those who seek me are upset. Not only are you not upset, you had the presence of mind to bring me a form of payment in advance, odors of an interesting place. I sense that you live on Thumberlia, our chilly fifth planet, and have recently come all the way from the Oort cloud surrounding our system, yet your news concerns yet a third world in our system. Therefore you are not personally involved in the matter. You are curious, but not on your own behalf. I am intrigued. Nay, fascinated. More fascinated than I have been in some time."

I felt hope rise in my heart. "Then you will come with me to Al-Boeme?"

"No," Baskur said, settling down with his paws crossed before him like a sphinx. "Have they not told you I'm retired? I don't go out on cases any longer. I prefer to remain among my own kind."

"But a man was murdered!" I exclaimed, dropping to my knees on the guest cushion and setting the bowl aside. "Prunli of Cinque Narangova, the ambassador from a planet of five large continents that circles an orange sun eight light years from here, was found dead in his chambers in the capital city on Al-Boeme." I named our third planet from the sun, the chief of the satellites circling Dayel and the center of government for the system.

"Humans die all the time." Baskur lifted a paw. "It is an ordinary occurrence."

"But there are no clues to this murder," I said. "None at all."

At last I saw a hint of interest on his mobile face.

"No clues? I am sure there are surveillance cameras, communication records, trace evidence, and eyewitnesses who can help the authorities to determine the perpetrator."

"None at all," I said. "Captain Boycott, my source on Al-Boeme, said that the electronic surveillance was turned off and all records from the hour involved were wiped irretrievably. The room was swept clean and sanitized before anyone realized that there was a body concealed within. Prunli was alone when he died, and the door locked with his own code. Captain Boycott immediately put the room into stasis. Knowing I was coming to Panettiere, she asked me to request your help. Please come. I have a ship waiting." I gestured toward the exit. "Sir, the circumstances are mysterious, and the matter is a vital one. Cinque Narangova has become a valuable trading partner with Dayel in recent years. Prunli's murder could jeopardize that."

"Most interesting," Baskur said. He shook his great head, and his jowls flapped. "It is not the victim who interests you. No, Boycott is someone you're very fond of. An old romance, one that ended amicably. No!" He got up and circled me again. "Ah, those Ganston aromas! Yes, I sense Al-Boeme, but from long, long ago. The odor of violets is pervasive. Thank you for letting me absorb the scents."

"The worker is worthy of the fee," I said, with another polite nod.

"A parlor trick." Baskur laughed, a snorting, snuffling noise. He studied me for a long while with a curious look on his long face, then held up a paw. "Come closer. I have not yet taken my fee."

Curious, I moved nearer to the Great Investigator. Baskur turned his broad muzzle up to my hand. I held it out for him to sniff. *SNAP!* He clamped his jaws upon my hand.

"Ow!" I felt his teeth pierce my skin. Baskur opened his jaws and drew back. I clasped my hand to my chest. It throbbed and dripped blood onto the carpeted floor. Another of the Norridings darted forward with a roll of white bandage. Reluctantly, I allowed her to stanch the bleeding.

"I perceive that you've been the recipient of many a worthwhile fee yourself," Baskur said, his tongue darting out to clear all my blood from his face. "Your system is rich with particles from many a distant world, ones you have absorbed as well as those that you have consumed. In time I will identify all of them. You are married or attached to a female of your species. I sense that you also have offspring. Three, I believe. Two of the same gender as yourself, and one indeterminate."

"But how would you know that?" I asked, astounded by his accuracy. "None of them have been with me since before I landed on Alpha Ganston."

"With your physical relationships, there is an exchange of microbes and cells," Baskur said. He shook his head vigorously and his jowls flapped noisily. "You retain traces of everyone with whom you have had contact. Even airborne particles become part of your physical self. The female has not had frequent contact with you of late. I perceive this by the weak concentration of her cells in your body. Yet there are three distinct clusters of cells that share traits with her and also with you. Hence, three children. You may of course have others with whom you are not in contact."

He had precisely pinpointed the relationship between me and my current mate. We were in the last months of our second ten-year contract. The marriage had broken down irretrievably years before and was due to end, but I shared custody of my beloved children.

"Remarkable! You can tell that people are related by the combination of cells in their bodies? Are you able to distinguish generations? You can perceive my brother, or my father, and how often we have come into contact with one another?"

"Oh, yes," Baskur said.

"Astounding," I said. "My assignments never brought me to Panettiere before. What an amazing species you Norridings are. But humans frequently change partners and have offspring with more than one. We come into casual contact with many others of our kind, and with other species. Don't they blur after a while?"

The Great Investigator flapped his jowls once again. "That is one of the reasons that I have retired. Everyone is becoming too homogenous, including my people with yours. Now that I have consumed some of your cells, you're part of me, too. And I of you. But it means I am less of myself and more of everyone whom I have ever touched or smelled. To maintain my individuality, I need to remain apart from contact with other beings and not gather further artifacts within my person. But you have intrigued me with your tale, middle-aged human journalist. For your sake, I will break my self-imposed exile. A true locked room mystery! It will be my last and greatest case. Let us go to the scene of the crime."

The transit within the system took a matter of hours, half of it accelerating to a near-light speed and the other half decelerating. Most of that time the Great Investigator spent rolling around on a mat of irregular, long-pile carpeting that his three assistants installed in the cabin. He was, they confided, a bit addicted to shag. Although the rubbery backing of the mat sent horrible odors circulating through the ventilation system of my fleet craft, I felt it was a small price to pay for obtaining Baskur's services.

As a reporter for the popular news media, I was eager to observe him in action, though my chief motivation was to protect my contact. As Baskur had deduced, Ariana Boycott was a dear friend, one with whom I had once been very close. We had nearly joined our lives together.

After our affair ended, Ariana had become involved with Prunli. At the time, he had been an attaché to the previous envoy. Their relationship had been stormy. I worried how deeply she was involved. Could she be responsible for his death? The clues had been destroyed. Calling in an outside authority made it seem as though all she sought was the truth, when the action might be a cynical blind.

I caught Baskur's eyes upon me. He flipped upright.

"It would be daring if she asked you to bring me if she was in fact guilty," he said.

I flicked my fingers. "I see too many vids to think that isn't possible, but I hope—I pray—that it isn't so." Then I blinked. "How did you know what I was thinking?"

"Because it was all over your face," Baskur said, with a growl that sounded like a chuckle. "I hope the case is not as easy to solve. Otherwise, I would rather have stayed at home."

When we arrived at Security Headquarters in Al-Boeme's capital city of Prak, Captain Ariana Boycott was waiting upon the landing strip, clad in the narrow, floor-length blue coat and hat of her rank. She looked as cool and beautiful as she had the last time we had been together, five years before. Her thick auburn hair was all but hidden beneath the tall hat, but the warm, honey-colored complexion and deep green eyes like tourmalines gladdened the eye. My heart pounded in my chest, something that I fancied was not lost upon my companion. An entourage of fifteen officers, both human and android, surrounded her. Its size indicated that she had grown considerably in importance since the last time we had seen one another. Our eyes met. She smiled, and my heart pounded more strongly. She still had the power to move my soul.

As he had with me, Baskur snuffled her all over. She spread her arms out and waited patiently for him to complete his examination.

"I'm grateful that you came, sir," Ariana said. She gestured to the waiting throng. "This is my staff. Each of them has either examined the hotel room or been instrumental in preserving evidence. Besides these, there's the hotel staff, the ambassador's own aides, and fourteen members of other diplomatic services who had several meetings with Prunli during the three days before his death."

"So many?" the Great Investigator asked, regarding them with dismay. "Ah, well." He leaped up onto every one of the police escort in turn, giving them the thorough going-over that he had me, though I noticed that he was getting more nervous all the time. His long, whiplike tail switched back and forth.

"We must proceed to the location," he said. "Quickly! I do not want to make contact with more particles than is absolutely necessary."

Boycott nodded. We exchanged no more than the briefest glance before escorting Baskur into a waiting hovervan marked with police livery. The Great Investigator and I, along with his minions, occupied a spotlessly clean compartment alone.

The city of Prak had changed little since my last assignment there, except to grow in size. The buildings all seemed to be part of a grand design, ornate and beautiful as well as functional. Small details struck the eye as we passed them. I turned often to mention them to my traveling companion, but found him deep in thought.

The rooftop of the pink stucco Grand Hotel Al-Boeme was empty when we set down. I fancy that Captain Boycott had seen to it that we made contact with no one else, as per the Great Investigator's wishes. From there, she led us into a mirror-walled turbovator encrusted with gold scrolls and cherub's heads. We descended only one floor. It made sense that the ambassador had occupied a penthouse suite.

"Nothing has been disturbed since we found him," Ariana said, leading us through an opulent and quiet corridor. "Once our evidence drones found there were no traces, we sealed the room."

"In hopes of attracting my attention," Baskur said, with an amused glance. "You must have been very confident that I would come."

"Hopeful, that is all," Ariana said. "You must understand that we want to avoid an interstellar incident."

A featureless, all-gray android waited outside the door of the suite. Boycott presented her credentials. A slot popped open in the android's chest cavity to accept the card. The mechanical placed one manipulative extremity against the wall beside the door. The double portals parted. A rush of air gusted out into our faces. Baskur inhaled deeply.

He turned to the rest of us, then his gaze lighted upon me.

"I know that you are not involved in this matter, and I have your scent stowed," he said. "Pray accompany me. You persuaded me to come. You may as well see it out."

"It would be an honor." I bowed deeply.

The door shut upon the police contingent, leaving us alone in the crime scene. I set my data drone on full record mode and let it float up toward the ceiling of the room. Baskur's inspection of the chamber would be a treasure for my broadcast channel, providing he allowed me to use any of it.

"What do you see here, human?" Baskur asked.

I scanned the chamber. The body lay as it had been left, on the floor beside a yellow upholstered divan. Now that the stasis lock had been removed, the corpse would begin to decay. I sensed no putrefaction, only bodily functions that normally accompanied the final moment of mortality.

Ambassador Prunli had been a handsome human, although he had begun to gain weight around the belly. He had a square jaw, broad cheekbones, noble forehead—growing more noble by the year, I was pleased to say, as time had plucked more and more of his rich chestnut hair from it—and a sweeping mustache that put my facial adornment to shame. I admit to some satisfaction in seeing that deterioration of a rival, although the rivalry was long in the past. His face bore the expression of surprise. The brutal attack had been swift as well as bloody. As the stasis had kept all things fresh, the bodily fluids remained liquid. Even his eyes still glistened, as though death had occurred only moments before. Cringing at the notion that he might at any moment sit up and speak, I stayed at a distance. The Great Investigator, though, dived onto the corpse and began to sniff from top to toe and back again.

"Most interesting," he said, gathering in great gulps of air. He tasted the body, the carpet, the surface of the furniture, and even the artwork displayed upon the walls. A bronze statue of a feather in a paneled recess particularly attracted his attention. Now and again he emitted little cries of encouragement to himself. I found it repellent that he could lick a corpse so happily.

"You look as though you enjoy that," I said.

"I do! Now, please be quiet. I must concentrate."

He circled around and around the body, gathering up particles of scent and matter with his nose and tongue.

"The scene is not so devoid of clues as we were told," Baskur said. "If anything, we might thank the cleaner, because it removed a lot of the extraneous material with which we would otherwise have to deal. Instead, I can almost *become* Ambassador Prunli." He gave one final sniff to the terrible wounds in the neck and chest, then bit the man's hand. I cried out.

"Did you have to do that?"

Baskur didn't answer, engaged as he was in licking the congealing blood from his face, absorbing, as I knew, the essence of the dead man before us.

At that moment, the door to the suite slid open, and Captain Boycott entered with two of her officers at her back.

Baskur looked up at her, his warm brown eyes fixed on her face.

"I love you," he said.

"What?" she asked, bewildered. "Have you found anything that can help me solve this murder?"

The Great Investigator shook his head vigorously as if to clear it. He let out a deep sigh.

"Yes, Captain, I have. There's nothing more I can do. I must see all of those who have been with or near the suite before too much time has passed. Quickly!"

"That's impossible," she said. "Many of those who passed through here are honored diplomats, all engaged in important trade and peace discussions. I can't compel them to come and be interrogated."

"Of course you can! Tell them that there is a scandal brewing that will affect all of Al-Boeme! I can only hold it back if I learn the truth, and swiftly!"

Ariana's green eyes flicked to me. I nodded. Her mouth twisted in a wry grimace.

"All right, then. I'll do my best to get them together. Shall we say two hours?"

"Arrange it. Ah, but wait," he said, as she began to leave. Let your assistants make the calls. Will you remain here for a moment?"

"Certainly," Ariana said, though she looked puzzled. She signed to her associates, then let the door close. "What is this about?"

"What was your relationship with the victim?"

She shot an uncomfortable glance at me.

"Why, nothing. I hadn't seen him for several years."

Baskur let out his grunting laugh.

"Come, come, Captain Boycott. You called me in. You must know what I can do and what I have learned."

She looked shamefaced at being caught in a lie.

"We were lovers. When he asked to see me, I came out of curiosity. I stayed…out of curiosity."

"It's none of my business," he said, but the expression on his long face said otherwise. For myself, I was trying to control a feeling of unreasonable jealousy. We were no longer together. I had no right. "I'm going back to the ship to wait."

Once reensconced upon the unspeakable shag carpet, the Great Investigator threw himself back and forth, pondering the evidence. His minions brought him food and water, each of which he spurned impatiently.

"Is there really a scandal?" I asked, watching him toss and turn like a restless sleeper.

"Oh, yes," he said. "And your friend knows it. That's why she called me in, instead of relying upon local investigators to uncover it. As for what it is, I won't know until I examine the witnesses." He glanced at me. "And you need not worry. She's as attached to you as you are to her. I don't need to have sampled her cells to determine that. Pure observation proves it to me. When does your current marriage contract expire? Soon?"

"That's rather tactless of you, as well as none of your business," I said, offended and surprised at the same time.

"You've made it my business, both of you," he said, sounding weary. His eyes drooped. "And because you are so attached to her, and I have sampled your cells, so am I. I love her, even though she's not of my species. But she is of yours. Now, go. I need to think."

I departed, sputtering in confusion.

• • •

The gathering we joined was a truly distinguished one. I recognized diplomats and envoys from several planets within the Dayel system and from many worlds outside. As Baskur's temporary chronicler, I was admitted, but not strictly welcomed. While they reclined on cushions and chaises longues, I and several members of the hotel staff were relegated to straight-backed chairs in the corner. At least my drone could rove unrestricted.

Their curiosity about Baskur overwhelmed their indignation and discomfort at being summoned, even more so when he began to examine them.

"Is this really necessary?" demanded Honored Otso of Caledon, a human of indeterminate gender like my youngest child, as Baskur snuffled his way down xir long blue silk dress and paid special attention to the jeweled chains hanging around xir neck and wrists.

"Not only necessary, but vital," Baskur insisted. He returned to xir face and sniffed it again. He withdrew and allowed his long tongue to cleanse his facial fur of all traces. He moved on to Tik-tik, a tall, narrow-waisted being with a striped coat from Susk. From here, the envoy smelled like honey. I wondered what other traces Baskur discovered among the black and gold fluff.

"Captain, I have to protest," said Ambassador Eugin of the exoplanet Ni Hao Xiao Mao, a stocky being with smooth white fur that covered his entire body. "None of us is responsible for this foul crime. Of course we are sorry for the death of our colleague, but why are we gathered here?"

Baskur reclined upon the square of smelly carpet that had been removed to here from my ship for his comfort.

"I am reliably informed that Prunli was here to negotiate trade with all of you. His is a minor system with few resources that are unavailable in other places. So, why have so many of you gone to such trouble to visit him not once, but many times over the last few days? Shall we say, perhaps to obtain…personal emoluments that would make you consider him and his system with greater favor?"

"Bribery?" Honored Otso protested. "How dare you! What do you know about the intricacies of interstellar cooperation?" But xe clutched the jeweled chain at xir neck. Baskur followed xir movements with an amused look on his jowly face.

"Yes. I don't need to know very much about the ins and outs of your practice to know that there were several ancient artifacts on the walls of the ambassador's suite, artifacts that smelled enough like him for me to determine that they originated on the same world. Many of those are missing now. Many of you," he said, glancing at those around him, "retain the odor of those empty wall niches, hooks, and drawers in his suite."

"Well, what of it?" Eugin asked, waving a hand. "He gave us valuable gifts! It's a common practice in diplomatic circles."

"More than physical gifts, in many cases," Baskur said, with significant glances at Honored Otso and Tik-tik. Both of them squirmed, as did Ariana Boycott, standing near the door. "He made love to several of you. But it wasn't so much what he gave as what he *took*. Each of you smells of desperation. He commanded your presence again and again, but how? There is no odor or particle, therefore it had to be compulsion. Information. He was blackmailing each of you, wasn't he? Threatening to publicize each of the illicit gifts and negotiations among you? To reveal that bribery, smuggling, and blackmail are everyday parts of the diplomatic lifestyle?"

"Yes!" Eugin burst out. "He seemed to know everything about us, all of our passwords, our secret trades. Our internet searches.

Everything! Our data was supposed to be secured with the latest in microft protocols. He could *never* have worked out those numbers. How could he have obtained them?"

Baskur smiled. "Only if he had access to the gatekeeper. Most programs have a back door, in case of emergency. It would be easy for a diplomat to convince an ordinary person that such an emergency requiring access existed. His powers of persuasion would not have been lost upon this one." He leaped from his mat and fixed his teeth into the arm of a young human and dragged xir forward. Xir name, if I recalled it correctly, was Lin. As he had before, Baskur drew blood. Boycott's officers moved in to surround Lin while the Norriding analyzed the particles and cells he had consumed. Lin tried to leap up and bring down my drone. I steered it back toward me to protect it, while Boycott's officers dragged xir back into xir chair. "Yes, there is a high concentration of Prunli's enzymes and cells in your system. Your meetings must have been frequent. Why would you have betrayed your employers in this fashion?"

Lin's attractive face pulled a sullen expression. "He promised me a place in his entourage. I would be able to leave this planet forever!"

Baskur's eyes focused upon his prey, and his voice lowered into silken tones. "And when you discovered that you were a pawn? When it turned out that all of his promises were as fleeting as his affections toward you? After all, he took the inspector and others as lovers after he had dismissed you. You meant nothing. Your place in his entourage was a ploy to obtain your assistance."

Lin sprang to xir feet. "I did everything he asked! I jeopardized my life for him! He took that from me. I had nothing left. Nothing!"

"And you stabbed him through the heart with the bronze statue in his suite," Baskur said, shaking his head. "Taking his life in your turn. You ordered the suite cleaned, but you still bear traces of the metal's odor in the pores of your skin. Only you and he had high exposure to that bronze. None of the others touched the murder weapon."

"No! He stole from me! He made me break my oath of employment."

Boycott signed to her officers. Lin struggled as they took xir away, with a fierce look over xir shoulder at Baskur.

"May we go?" Otso asked, looking at xir timekeeper. "I have many appointments."

"As do we," Tik-tik said.

"Yes, but please keep yourself available for interviews," Boycott said. "I promise you, none of your personal information will be part of the official transcripts."

Eugin hesitated after the others had departed, and came to wind himself around Baskur, rubbing his white furry sides against the Norriding.

"Thank you," he whispered. "I could not have borne one more scandal." Then, he was gone.

"What was that about?" I asked.

Baskur shook his jowls. "I'm afraid that we will need to provide an amnesty in that direction, my friend. I think that you should erase those last few words from your drone's memory."

"I shall," I promised. When the small craft landed beside me, I entered the necessary command. The crime had been solved. There was no need to embarrass anyone with innuendo. I would not dispatch anything without need.

"Thank you," Boycott said, crouching down to Baskur's level. Her eyes shone with admiration. How I wish that expression had been turned upon me! "That was a tour de force, Master Baskur. More than I ever expected. I could not have discovered the truth so quickly."

"As your Shakespeare said, 'The cat will mew, and the dog will have his day,'" Baskur said, rising to all fours. "This was mine." His long purple tongue darted out and touched her face affectionately. "To me, you will always be The Human. I must return now to Panettiere, never to leave again, but you will always be a part of me, Ariana Boycott. I will not forget you." He turned to me. "Nor you, Shoqan al-Hamish ibn Malik. I would be glad to remain in contact with you, but only by remote communication. I do not wish to lose my identity further. I am becoming too much of—what would you call me in your language?—a human bloodhound?"

"I am sorry," I said, sincerely rueful. "I didn't understand what it would cost you."

He flapped his jowls. "I came with you freely. It was always a risk. I pray that it will all be worthwhile. I will give you some time to say farewell, then I need you to return me to my lonely exile." He padded off his mat and out of the room, leaving me alone with Ariana. I watched him go with a mixture of admiration and regret.

"I am so grateful that you brought Baskur here, Shoqan," Ariana said. She seemed hesitant, almost diffident, and she had never looked more lovely to me. "I believe that he solved more than one case today. I think…that I found out what I really wanted to know."

The shy little smile awoke a resolve in me that I hadn't realized was still there. I took her hand in both of mine.

"So did I," I said.

THE ADVENTURE OF THE RELUCTANT DETECTIVE

BY RYK SPOOR

Many years ago I took it upon myself to record and publish accounts of some of the more interesting cases encountered by my friend Sherlock Holmes, in his role as the world's first consulting detective.

Or did I? The revelations of this latest case throw doubt on even this, the most obvious and straightforward of statements. I hesitate to continue; yet I wonder if I have any choice in the matter. Has anyone read even the first of these accounts? I ask this, even though if I raise my eyes I can see before me more than one leatherbound volume of Holmes's exploits, as published under a name better known than that of John H. Watson.

In the end, it does not matter; I have recorded our adventures as they happened, as best I could, even those that have not yet been released to the public. Now I have the duty of transcribing the final, and most curious, case of all, and at the end I must decide whether to publish the manuscript, or burn it.

But write I must, for if I do not write it, I believe I shall go mad, if madness is possible. And as this is my decision, I shall endeavor to write it as clearly and precisely as any of his past adventures.

• • •

It was in the spring of 1899, with the sense of the new century awaiting us beginning to be felt all about, that I received a call from Mrs. Hudson, housekeeper for Holmes in his rooms at 221B Baker Street. I had, I admit, been remiss in maintaining contact with my old friend of late, for my beloved Mary had but recently passed away the past winter, and I had thrown myself into my work as an antidote. I was vaguely aware that Holmes continued his own work, due to occasional references to him in the paper.

I answered the newly installed telephone myself, in the manner that I always did. "Dr. Watson's residence, Watson speaking."

"Oh, thank goodness, Dr. Watson!"

Despite the tinny sound of the connection, I instantly recognized the voice. "Mrs. Hudson! Is there something wrong?"

"I should say so, Doctor. He's been shut in his rooms for a week now. Takes hardly any food, hasn't agreed to see a single caller, and all the day long I hear that *violin* of his, and it's…just unnatural, sir!"

"Unnatural?" I couldn't quite grasp what could be *unnatural* about a violin. "You know he gets these fits, Mrs. Hudson—"

"I know quite well his moods, Dr. Watson, and if this were anything of the ordinary sort I'd just have to bear it. But this is different, sir, very different. Listen, he's playing now."

A telephone connection is hardly an ideal medium over which to appreciate music, but the faint strains I heard did cause a slight chill to trace its way down my spine. I have, of course, recounted how Holmes, when in a melancholy mood or otherwise distracted by some case, would play the violin for hours at a time, and that on occasion this would consist of improvised and sometimes eerie melodies. Yet what I heard through that distant connection seemed far more disturbed and alien.

"I will be over at once, Mrs. Hudson," I said.

It took only a few moments to acquire a hansom. That disquieting melody filled me with foreboding, and I found myself suffering a considerable attack of guilt. Mary, bless her soul, had cared for Holmes as much as I, and she would never have wanted my mourning to extend to neglecting my friend.

It was in this mood that I found myself once more on the threshold of 221B. Even in the entrance hall I could hear the strains of torturous notes pouring from my friend's apartment, and so with but a nod at Mrs. Hudson I mounted the stairs to find the door locked. However, I had retained a key to the premises with the encouragement of both my friend and Mrs. Hudson, and this allowed me entry to the apartment.

I was unsurprised to find the atmosphere extremely thick with smoke from the shag tobacco he favored. It was also not surprising, but still worrisome, to see that there were no lights on in the apartment. The music, somehow both frenetic and languid at once, came from the sitting room; staring through the gloom I could make out the tall, spare figure of Holmes seated in his favorite armchair, drawing the bow across the strings of his Stradivarius violin.

As he either did not notice me or chose not to recognize my presence, I went to one of the lamps, turned up the gas, and lit the fire before I turned to face him.

I was instantly struck by the ghastly pallor of his face. I had seen Holmes in the grip of terror from the noxious fumes of the Devil's Foot, white with anger in more than one case, and in a state of fear and nervous excitement prior to the events related in "The Final Problem," but never had I seen him so white and drawn as I did that afternoon. His pupils were widely dilated, and his dressing-gown sleeve failed to conceal a number of injection marks.

"Good *Lord*, Holmes," I said. "What is troubling you?"

He squinted up at me. "Ah, Watson. Could I first trouble you to turn the gas down a bit? My eyes are accustomed to the dark."

I reduced the flow and brought the room to a half-lit twilight which was, at least, considerably better than the prior darkness. "What troubles you, Holmes?" I asked again, over the continuing strains of alien music.

His gaze dropped away; the bow faltered, then went still. Without saying a word, Holmes carefully took the instrument and put it gently into its case.

"You have not yet mastered the ways of the widower, Watson," he said. "Your hat has not seen the brush for at least a week, among other indications."

This rejoinder, completely ignoring my concern or my words, left me speechless for a moment. This did, however, solidify my conviction that something was truly wrong, so I stepped forward and placed my hand on his shoulder. "Holmes, please. What is wrong?"

I felt the shoulder twitch, and his entire lean frame shuddered for a moment. Then he took a great breath and rose, his gaze darting about the apartment.

"How long?" he asked, then answered himself. "A week, I believe. Yes. This *is* Friday, yes?" he asked me.

"It is."

"A week and a day, then. Yet perhaps not nearly long enough. Still, I could not expect Mrs. Hudson, let alone you, Watson, to ignore me forever."

The word *ignore* stung me, as I felt quite guilty already. "I'm sorry, Holmes. I should have—"

"Not at all, Watson," he said immediately. "My apologies, old friend; I did not mean in any way to imply that you were neglectful. Rather the opposite, in fact; I can rely on you absolutely."

"Then can I ask you to tell me what troubles you? For that fact is obvious even to someone who is not a consulting detective."

For the first time I saw a smile on his face; it was a weak, fleeting specimen of the breed, but a smile nonetheless. "I suppose it must be. Then tell me, Watson: what is one of my favorite dictums—one of the basic principles of my investigations?"

I thought a moment, and recalled one expounded, in varying forms, in many of our cases. "Eliminate the impossible, and whatever remains, howsoever improbable, must be the truth," I said.

"Excellent, Watson." He reached for his pipe, glanced at the eddying fumes in the air, and visibly shook himself. Instead of lighting the pipe, he strode to the window and threw it open. "If we are to talk, I think more air and less smoke is in order," he said.

"And perhaps food and drink for you?"

"Ah," he said, shaking his head wryly, "I am not sure I am yet to that point."

"This is about a case, then?" I asked, realizing the point of his question.

A shadow crossed his face. "Yes. A case which I can neither say is solved nor unsolved."

"You expound a mystery in a single sentence, Holmes. How can a case not be one or the other? It would seem—"

"Impossible, yes. That is, truly, the crux of the matter, Watson." He paced restlessly about the room; his fingers absently picked up a hypodermic needle and I saw him glance at a nearby case that I knew would contain a 7 percent solution of cocaine.

Light began to dawn. "You have encountered a case which appears to feature something actually impossible."

"You see, Watson, this is why it sometimes drives me to distraction that you and others belittle your gifts. Perhaps you have not my peculiar faculties, yet you have more than the average intelligence and understanding of others."

"Then tell me, Holmes. I can see that this case is *also* driving you to distraction."

He looked down at the hypodermic. His hand tightened around it, and then he hurled the instrument against the wall. "You recall my usual motive for the use of cocaine, Watson?"

"To alleviate boredom," I answered.

"Indeed, and in that capacity it has been a marvelous servant. But here…here for the first time I find I have been using it to *distract* me, to forget or ignore something I find intolerable…and that, itself, is intolerable! Yes, Watson, I will tell you."

• • •

"You are of course aware, Watson, that after the loss of your Mary I endeavored to entice you into some form of activity, participating in even the rather lackluster cases that then presented themselves to me. You were, alas, far too despondent—but no, please do not begin to blame yourself for what followed, old fellow! I assure you, you had every reason to mourn, and having seen this with my own eyes, I resolved to give you time to yourself. As I have never married, and had little to do with the affairs of the heart except inasmuch as they were involved in my profession, I could not pretend to know more about how to assist you in such a time.

"In any event, I was not terribly affected, other than in the manner any friend might be by knowing his closest companion is in pain. I had, as I said, some lackluster cases that were nonetheless not entirely without points of interest, and I did keep myself busy.

"Now, even in your grief, I daresay you might have heard of the unexpected death of the Earl of Carfax?"

"Of course," I said. "Died of some unknown illness, I understand."

"Unknown! Yes, that is indeed the case, Watson." For a moment that distant, frightened look returned, but he closed his eyes, and when they opened, they held once more the controlled, slightly amused look I was accustomed to. "But at the time I had thought little of it; men die of illnesses often, and even with the great strides our medical men have made in their sciences, many illnesses still escape their classification; and of course he had traveled to India, and many curious diseases are found in the tropics which may lay dormant for years ere they strike suddenly and surely.

"A week later, as I sat at tea, Mrs. Hudson announced a caller—a woman—who insisted on seeing me immediately. I had heard the carriage stop, and was prepared for a visitor. With the priors I have given, you will be unsurprised to hear that it was the youngest of the late Earl of Carfax's daughters, Lady Edith Pelham-Howard.

"'Mr. Holmes,' she said without preamble, 'I am assured by certain people of my acquaintance that you are to be absolutely trusted, even in cases of extraordinary nature and sensitivity.'

"'It is essential to my profession that I am completely discreet and reliable,' I returned. 'I solve cases which the police may not, and this often involves me in events of most peculiar and singular nature.'

"'This is most assuredly such an event, and one of great horror as well,' she said, and the way in which her voice nearly broke conveyed the stress she labored under.

"I then assured her that I was entirely at her disposal and encouraged her to speak.

"She had returned to the estate following her father's death, and had remained as details of the inheritance, which was divided among the three daughters, were worked out. There were apparently some irregularities with the accounts that drew out the proceedings.

"However, that was not what brought Lady Edith to my door. Rather, it was a series of disquieting and even inexplicable events—objects moved when there seemed no agent available to move them, sounds heard in deserted rooms—culminating in Lady Edith seeing her departed father's visage peering at her through her own bedroom window.

"'I am not a woman prone to fantastic notions, Mr. Holmes,' she said to me, and she was quite noticeably paler than when she had begun her account, 'yet I tell you, I saw my father's face as clearly as I see yours, not over five paces distant.'"

Holmes gave a wan smile. "As you might imagine, Watson, I did find this an intriguing opening. Even in this initial narrative there were certain suggestive indications, but the fantastical flourishes were novel. Perhaps you, familiar with my processes, can follow my initial lines of surmise?"

I thought on the tale for a moment, then nodded. "The sudden and unexplained death of the master of the house, irregularities in the inheritance, and such, certainly point to some sordid matter—perhaps blackmail, which became murder when the blackmailer realized no more money was forthcoming and that the earl might be considering risking exposure of whatever secret was being held?"

"Capital, Watson. You really have progressed marvelously since first we began our researches. While I have often inveighed against excess theorizing prior to full acquisition of the facts, it is still inevitable that one will attempt to make sense of a case as it is presented; indeed, such a process is necessary for me to decide whether or not a case presents sufficient points of interest to make it worth my attention. And indeed, my initial thoughts ran along almost precisely those lines, with a bit more detail as to the likely culprit, though I attached no weight to the latter as it did cross the border from deduction to speculation. Still, I was mystified by the sequelae to the murder, if murder it was. It would have been simplicity itself to explain such apparitions *prior* to the death; we have seen such attempts to convince others that some supernatural agency was responsible for deaths."

"Surely—the Baskervilles horror, and that of the Devil's Foot."

"Exactly. But nothing happens without a cause, without a reason, and thus I accepted the case that I might have a chance to discern that reason." His hands shook again, and not entirely, as I would have hoped, from his current bout with cocaine; it was strong emotion that seized him in that instant, and for a few moments I wondered if he would continue.

After a time, Holmes shook his head. "And now, Watson, knowing what brought you here, what I have said, and the initial particulars of the case that precipitated my current admittedly distressing condition, tell me what I found."

I was, I confess, somewhat taken aback. It seemed to me that there was entirely too little information upon which anyone, even Holmes himself, could base a conclusion.

Yet my friend never set me insoluble problems, even though it was quite frequently true that I, personally, found them impossible to penetrate. Looking at Holmes, I sensed that he truly wanted me to answer this question myself—that, perhaps, he *feared* stating it himself. It was such a strange, even frightening impression that I became determined to prove myself capable of unraveling this riddle, if only for Holmes's own peace of mind.

"You will allow me to speak my thoughts aloud as I examine the evidence, Holmes?"

"I would like nothing better, Watson; to observe the way in which you approach the problem will be something worthwhile in its own right, as our adventures are usually focused on rather the opposite, with me providing insight into my processes."

I stood, and—perhaps in an unconscious mimicry of Holmes himself—filled my own pipe with a quantity of shag tobacco and lit it. "So. We begin with the most singular fact of the most celebrated and original consulting detective, Sherlock Holmes, having retreated to his rooms in what he admits is an attempt to hide from something he finds most disquieting; furthermore, the confirmation of his friend Dr. Watson's assertion that Holmes must have encountered something he found to be impossible.

"To this we add the unexpected death of the Earl of Carfax, the arrival of his youngest daughter at Sherlock Holmes's doorstep, and her description of her problem, including an apparition of her father at her window, and the financial irregularities of the inheritance." Holmes nodded.

I paused, thinking. Then I realized the only possible conclusion, one so mad that I hesitated to even speak it. Yet what else, besides something that made the world seem utterly mad, could possibly have brought my friend to this state? I steeled myself for his possible mockery, for if I were wrong I would be completely, ludicrously, and laughably wrong. "A question, then. Can we be reasonably certain that the Earl of Carfax himself did not have a twin or other double in the world who could have presented themselves as the purported shade?"

Holmes nodded slowly. "You may take that as given, Watson; I encountered no reason to believe that there was any other person who could have presented himself as the earl to one of his daughters and have carried off the imposture. Continue."

Still, I hesitated. "I ask you only one further question, Holmes: Does Lady Edith believe the case concluded?"

Holmes considered, the calm demeanor spoiled by the still-shaking hands. "Yes. She believes all was brought to a satisfactory conclusion."

"I see." I drew a long breath. "Then this is my conclusion: You have found clear evidence of some malfeasance within the earl's household, which you were able to prove led to a poisoning or perhaps deliberate infection with some tropical malady of the earl when the perpetrator realized that the earl was close to discovering him, or turning him in. This you have used to solve the murder of the earl, and the other phenomena have ceased; you have perhaps explained them in some manner to the satisfaction of Lady Edith."

Holmes was immobile, silent.

"But," I continued, barely able to credit what I was about to say, "for you, there *was* no explanation, save the one you consider impossible.

"You yourself confronted the apparition, and found you were facing the ghost of the Earl of Carfax."

For a moment I thought I had been entirely wrong, for Holmes's face became immobile, as though set in stone. But then his eyes closed, an uneven breath emerged from his lips, and he then looked up at me directly. "Well done, Watson. Stellar, in fact, although you miss various details which would not be evident to you from the brief *précis* I supplied."

"Good Lord, Holmes." Despite my deductions, despite his acquiescence, I could scarcely credit what I was hearing. "You mean to say that you did indeed—"

"Watson, I am not accustomed to being questioned in this manner!"

I was so startled, not to say hurt, by this sharp and unreasonable retort that I could do nothing but stare at my friend.

Almost instantly Holmes was up, shaking his head, extending a hand. "Oh, Watson…I must apologize most profusely, old friend. I must not allow my current state to drive me to such rash and, if I be honest with myself, completely false statements. Of *course* I am accustomed to being questioned in this manner; it is not uncommon for my deductions to be met with confusion, disbelief, and—as you recall from various cases—even ridicule."

I clasped his hand. "It is forgotten, Holmes. Surely you can understand my own disbelief."

"Only too well."

I went to the sideboard and, finding the siphon charged, made myself a drink; the occasion seemed to demand something stronger than tea. I returned and seated myself across from Holmes, who had sunk into a brown study.

After a few moments, I broke the silence. "Well then, Holmes, what do you intend to do?"

The silence returned, but I waited. Finally he replied.

"I do not know, Watson," he said. "My profession is founded on reason, on the rational order of the universe. You know it has always been a basic *principle* of mine that the supernatural cannot exist. Yet—"

"Yet you are making a grave error, Holmes," I said.

His gaze immediately snapped up to meet mine. "An error?"

"An understandable one, given your priors, Holmes. You've lived your life with, and by, one set of beliefs. Having those upset surely excuses a bit of unclear thinking. But you've taught me enough of your methods that I believe I see the flaw in your reasoning."

Holmes regarded me with mild astonishment, but said nothing. Slowly his expression shifted to the contemplative, and—at last—a faint but genuine smile appeared on his lips. "Ah, Watson. Once more you are the unchangeable rock to which I can anchor. If a ghost exists—and I have been given inarguable proof of this, before my own eyes, under conditions that I do not believe admit of any trickery—then it is—*must be*—natural for it to exist. Things that are real are, by that very fact, natural. They may not be what we *desire* to be real, but the fact that our desires cannot change them is what shows them to be true and real."

I breathed a sigh of relief. I heard animation returning to formerly dead tones, saw the old spark returning to his eye.

Without warning he shot to his feet. "Enough of this! It is intolerable that I've allowed myself to wallow in this denial of reality. There is only one remedy for it: I must discover *why* I have never encountered such an event before."

I was puzzled. "Well, Holmes, one must presume that real hauntings are vastly more rare than—"

He waved that away impatiently. "Watson, if we accept even for a moment that it is *possible* for a human…spirit, soul, what have you, to linger after death due to a need to see justice done, to protect those that they leave behind, or any other such motive, then how can we blithely accept that those motives were insufficiently strong in any and all of the cases we have seen throughout the years, and yet were somehow strong enough in this? No, no, Watson, it will not do. We are missing something, some key element that requires considerable investigation."

I said nothing immediately, for I saw his point. Many had been the foul murders and seemingly inexplicable crimes we had encountered, with great innocence wronged and endangered. However, in none of them had there been a hint of the spiritual, of the victims reaching out from beyond the veil to speak to us or others of what had become of them. "Yet in this case you *did* see such an apparition."

"As clearly as I see you now, Watson." His voice was clear, his eyes sharp, and I could see the brow wrinkling in its accustomed way, showing the beginning of great concentration. "There are, of course, multiple possibilities. One, which I discount, is that in none of the prior cases was there sufficient motive to cause a shade or other manifestation to present itself. A second is that there was something extremely unusual about the earl and his family, or the very specific circumstances surrounding them, which made such a manifestation occur, and would explain the absence of such phenomena in other situations. And a third..." He raised an eyebrow at me.

I frowned, for I could not think of a third alternative. Finally I shrugged. "I confess to being at a loss."

"Well, one third alternative, Watson, is that something about the *world* has changed, to make what was not possible now possible."

"Good Lord, Holmes!" I was speechless.

He smiled narrowly. "A rather disquieting thought, I admit. And at the moment I incline to the second explanation; it is far simpler to assume that the legends of ghosts and such are founded on rare, yet real, events that require truly extraordinary confluences of events or people. But if they *are* truly extraordinary, I feel confident that I should be able to determine with some reasonable certainty what the key elements of such an event must be." He chuckled, rubbing his hands as he sometimes did when the fascination of a case began to make itself felt. "There are of course many other possibilities—I, for instance, may be the one who has changed, become a medium, as the spiritualists call it, who can see the dead. Or perhaps I was, after all, gulled."

"Surely not, Holmes."

"Oh, I must admit of the possibility. I am not infinite of capacity or capability, and though I have proven myself the equal of virtually all I have encountered, it would be the height of arrogance to insist that I could not be fooled. The circumstances under which I witnessed the apparition certainly convinced me of its reality, but one can easily imagine that a genius with sufficient skill, motivation, and resources could devise some mechanism to project an illusion convincing even to me."

He nodded again. "An investigation is definitely in order, Watson. But first…ring Mrs. Hudson to prepare a supper for us both, while I tend to my ablutions, which have been most sadly neglected for some time."

"I will go myself, rather than merely ring; Mrs. Hudson was quite concerned."

"Of course, Watson; tender my apologies, which I will also do in person later. I am not, I fear, in a fit state to do so at the moment."

I made my way downstairs, filled with relief, anticipation, and—I confess—a touch of foreboding. Holmes was now more himself, but I knew how to read him better than anyone; and I was certain of one thing: it was the third possibility, not the second, that he was considering.

• • •

As events would have it, prolonged investigation was not required to demonstrate that the third of Holmes's possibilities was, in fact, the correct explanation. For over the next fortnight, Holmes was approached by no fewer than six people of respectable, even lofty, backgrounds, all six of which wished to consult the renowned Sherlock Holmes's opinion on events that seemed supernatural.

"This," Holmes said, the morning after the sixth of these petitioners had departed, "is a greater number of purported supernatural cases than I have faced in my entire prior career. Simply this fact would, I am afraid, argue strongly in favor of my third hypothesis."

"But it is more than the simple fact of numbers," I said, pouring myself another cup of tea. "While I am sure I am missing many details, it seemed to me that of the six, at least four feature too many suggestive and peculiar points to be easily dismissed as charlatanry or misperception."

"Indeed." Despite the confirmation of his most disquieting theory, Holmes was much more himself. His determination to accept that the very existence of these phenomena made them a priori part of the natural world had alleviated his existential fears to a great extent, and he was now devoting many hours to studying the lore of the supernatural so that he might use it, and compare it, to the actuality of these phenomena which it appeared we might be confronting on a far more regular basis. "I would judge that the problem of the Oxford professor is actually due to some clever student pranks, but the other five have very suggestive points about them."

"Will you be taking those cases, then?"

Holmes's smile was thin. "At least one or two I must, for there is a distinct aura of menace in both the story of the Right Honorable Hastings and of the Savile Row tailor. The others...they have definite points of interest for our researches. Still, our time is limited; I will reserve the decision on those until after we have dealt with the first two."

His head came up. "And I believe we have another caller."

After a moment I was able to follow his reasoning, recalling that there had been the characteristic faint creak and jingle of a carriage—probably a hansom—stopping before our residence. The subsequent ringing of the bell confirmed this deduction, and Mrs.

Hudson brought up a card. Holmes glanced at it. "Hm. Miss Anne LeChance, of Kimberley. Send her up, Mrs. Hudson."

Miss LeChance did not step into the room; she *strode* into our room and stopped, relaxed in posture and with a glance that was startlingly direct, almost challenging, from eyes an equally surprising shade of green. Her other remarkable feature was her hair, of such a brilliant red that I could not help but recall our earlier case of the Red-Headed League, clearly of some length but piled upon her head beneath a hat decorated with flowers. She was, if anything, above average height for a woman, neatly dressed but *sans* gloves, and despite her relaxed posture something about her seemed stiff or tense.

Holmes and I had of course risen to greet her. She extended her hand to Holmes, and shook mine as well. "I have heard a great deal about you from mutual acquaintances, Mr. Holmes," she said, "and I hope that you can assist me, as it seems no one else is able or willing to do so." Her voice was light but penetrating, the voice of someone accustomed to being listened to.

"I am certainly most intrigued, Miss LeChance," he said, and I glanced at him; her opening words had been little different from those of many others, so any interest could not be attributed to them. As I suspected, I saw his eyes studying her with keen interest, and knew he must have already deduced something which I had not. "Pray, sit and tell us what brings you here in such haste from your rooms at the Savoy."

She started, then leaned forward with an expression of fascination. "Mr. Holmes, how in the world did you know I came in haste, let alone from the Savoy?"

He smiled, but I saw his gaze still surveying her narrowly. "It was a matter of inference, but well founded. You came in a hansom, which is suited for travel within the city, but scarcely for a trip exceeding a hundred miles from Kimberley in Norfolk. Therefore, you were staying somewhere in the city. Your dress and other accoutrements say that you are of a family with considerable means—and presumably thus acquainted with many others of similar means—yet you came in a cab rather than in a carriage belonging to one of your friends or acquaintances; therefore you were not staying with relations or friends, but at a hotel.

"Now, there are only a few hotels in which it should be in any way appropriate for a young woman of means to reside while in London. It also happens that one unfortunate characteristic of a hansom is that it can, in the course of traversing the streets, deposit some amount of the grime of the street upon the clothing. As my friend Watson could tell you, I have made something of a study of the soils to be found in various neighborhoods, so when I see the lighter dirt of the Strand region overlaid successively with the mud from other neighborhoods leading to my own humble abode, it points unerringly to the Savoy as your starting point." He nodded to Miss LeChance, indicating her hair. "As to your haste, your coiffure is superficially acceptable, but in three critical places is loose, and should have been more carefully pinned. Had you not been in considerable haste, you would have taken the few additional minutes to ensure its security."

She smiled. "Well, Mr. Holmes, you certainly have the right of it."

"Then please tell me what brings you here in such a hurry."

As she opened her mouth to speak, there was a knock on the door. "Apologies, Mr. Holmes," said Mrs. Hudson, "but there was a call for Dr. Watson from one of his patients, most urgent."

"Quite all right. Go on, Watson," Holmes said.

I made my way downstairs to the phone, but even as I spoke with old Cosgrove, who sounded quite ill indeed, I could not forget the quick look that Sherlock Holmes had given me as I departed. Our visitor had, as yet, said nothing of substance.

Yet in that glance I had seen grim concern second to few others he had ever given me.

• • •

"So tell me, Watson; what did you make of our visitor this morning?"

This instant sally, the moment I entered 221B, startled me.

Holmes had not even greeted me in his accustomed fashion, nor inquired about the health of my patient, and I remonstrated upon these points immediately.

Holmes placed his pipe upon the table next to him and chuckled—although, once more, there was a strain in that laugh which was disquieting. "My apologies, Watson. I should not forget the courtesies. But I perceive from your step, and the hour of your return, that your patient is not in immediate danger, and we have passed the point of greetings, so I ask again what your impressions of Miss LeChance were."

"As you wish, Holmes." I finished hanging my coat on its peg, then seated myself across from him. "Though I had a brief enough encounter with her, so I believe you have much the advantage of me."

"Nonetheless, indulge me."

I took a few moments to arrange my thoughts. Holmes never made these inquiries without good reason, and even if that reason were merely to test my observations, I was resolved to make a good showing of it. "I would first say that *you* observed some elements of her appearance, carriage, or manner that you found of great interest, as you were already most concerned before she had ventured the slightest clue as to her reason for contacting you."

"Ah, of course, Watson. You know me better than anyone— even, I daresay, my brother Mycroft. Say on."

"Still, as to Anne LeChance herself, there were certain points of interest, as you might say. She is one of the most *striking* women I have ever seen; her hair and eyes would argue for Irish extraction, though her complexion and name would seem to me to indicate French ancestry." I thought a moment more. "Her poise was also unusual; it seemed almost *military* to me, odd though that may sound. Perhaps I am imagining something there."

"No, no; there was surely a directness and dynamism in her presence which is most unusual in a young woman. Any other observations, Watson?"

"Yes. There was something about her hands that seemed at

odds with the remainder of her. They seemed rather larger, and perhaps stronger than I might have expected." I thought back to that handshake, and suddenly remembered a detail that had not impressed itself upon my consciousness until then. "Holmes, I believe her hands were rather callused. Not like a workman's, perhaps, but certainly they were not as soft as those of a woman of leisure."

"Oh, capital, Watson. Fine observations indeed, and several of the points of interest I had myself observed." Despite this quite earnest congratulatory statement, Holmes still looked concerned, with an air of abstraction about him. "Have you exhausted your catalog, then?"

I knew I was missing some crucial elements, but this was something I had long been accustomed to. "I think so...no, hold on. Her voice. There was something about the accent that I could not place. It did not seem to me to quite fit with her Norfolk origins. But other than that..." I shook my head.

"Another pertinent observation, nonetheless." He picked up his pipe and puffed on it for a few moments.

"Well, Holmes? Will you now enlighten me as to what new problem you have encountered? What did she tell you?"

"It was not what she told me, Watson, but rather what she did *not* tell me. As you astutely observed, even before she began her story, my observations of Miss LeChance had provided me with some facts which were most intriguing, not to say disquieting, in nature. She is not, in my estimation, what she seems at all."

"Are you saying that her name is not LeChance?"

"I am not entirely sure of that, although if I were to hazard a guess I would say that her name is something along those lines, if not precisely LeChance. I did look up the family and it is a name that was familiar to me, and should have been to you." The look he gave me was hooded and unreadable.

I wracked my brain for several moments before revelation broke in upon me. "Of course! The affair of the three golden books! Our client worked for Sir William LeChance!" The memory had been hazy for a moment, almost like a tale told to me by someone else, but as I spoke the memory seemed to clarify, become sharper and filled with detail. *How could I have forgotten that most curious and singular case?* I wondered.

Holmes nodded, but his smile did not reach his eyes, and I felt a vague chill. "Yes. The LeChance family is quite prominent in Norfolk, and we both should have recalled it."

"The tone of your voice—"

"Hold your thoughts on that, Watson. Allow me to continue. Miss LeChance presented something of an enigma as she entered. You noticed something of her dress, yes?"

"It seemed of a very fine make, and suited her well."

"I was not remarking on the aesthetics, although I will agree that the young woman is startling in her appearance. That particular style of sleeve has been almost two years out of fashion, and while her figure was more than presentable, the current trend is the S-bend corset. A woman of her purported position would hardly be so far behind." He frowned. "She also had a well-concealed but evident stiffness in motion that is more often seen in far younger women, those first accustoming themselves to wearing those articles of clothing."

"That is indeed peculiar, Holmes. A young woman of her age and station will have been wearing her corsets for quite some time now."

"Precisely my observation. Now, her accent, as you noted, was not that of Norfolk; in fact, while I have an extremely detailed knowledge of the dialects and accents of the entirety of the British Empire, I could not place her accent; it seemed to be something of a patchwork, a concatenation of several accents which to an outside ear might seem superficially similar."

"You mean, something that a foreigner attempting to imitate our speech might create?"

"Something like that, yes," he agreed. "Although if there were hints of her true accent in her speech, I could not accurately place them. Perhaps something like a few of the Colonial accents, but my knowledge of American speech is sadly less than would be necessary to verify this vague surmise."

During his reply, I went to the bookcase and found his copy of Burke's. "Well, Holmes, if she is not who she appears, then surely she is taking some risk in the impersonation; Anne LeChance is a real member of the family, and would seem to be of the proper age, from this listing."

"The question is somewhat murkier than that, Watson; I sent a telegram to an associate who lives in that area, and he was able to confirm various details of the young lady's appearance as well as the fact that she had departed the estate a few days previous, presumably en route to London. I am reasonably certain that, if I were to bring our visitor thence, she would be recognized by all and sundry as Sir William's second daughter."

This intelligence brought with it considerable confusion; I had thought that Holmes was implying that our visitor was an impostor, but now it seemed he was certain she was not. "But then, Holmes, how do we account for these discrepancies?"

"That is indeed the problem, Watson." I could detect a hint of the same dark melancholia which had previously afflicted him. "Her story itself was, if we make allowances for our newly expanded worldview, fairly straightforward.

"Within the grounds of her family's estate lies an old ruin, a structure strikingly similar in some aspects to certain Greek and Roman temples, circular in design, with supporting columns. She said that it has been rumored to have been the site of ancient pagan rituals—Druidic or similar—in times long past. Now—unsurprisingly—there have been signs of unnatural activity associated with this ruin, sightings of strange lights or creatures.

"The impetus for her visit was that the phenomena went from the curious to the menacing, with one of the groundskeepers chased by something that mauled him rather severely before he managed to reach his own home. The police, of course, are ignoring the less-accepted elements of the tale and believe there is a wolf or escaped animal loose on the grounds."

"If people are in danger, Holmes, then we must act—regardless of the identity of our visitor."

"I agree, of course, Watson. Yet the most unusual aspects of our visitor, especially those in connection with what you called the affair of the golden books, require me to dig a bit more deeply into things before we depart. Would you assist me in bringing out my collection of criminal records—especially the older ones?"

"Older ones? Those that predate your work, Holmes?"

"Precisely. I would like them all here in the sitting-room. Once we have assembled all the resources on criminal cases, I beg that you leave me to myself, and tell Mrs. Hudson that I will not be receiving any callers, for a time."

I found myself staring at him. "But Holmes, we already had two other cases that we agreed were—"

"Watson!" His voice was sharp. But immediately he took a breath and moderated his tone. "Watson, my old friend, I assure you I am completely aware of all of these circumstances. But will you trust me if I say to you that this is something of even greater importance?"

"Of course, Holmes. I trust you implicitly. What of Miss LeChance? Any additional instructions regarding her?"

"Yes. Leave word with Mrs. Hudson that if she calls again I will give her an appointment for next Tuesday—that is four days from now—and that I believe I will have a resolution to her problem at that time."

I admit I stared at him in some disbelief for a moment. It was clear that he expected to spend the majority of that time studying books and files of old criminal cases, most of which were not even his own; yet he seemed quite serious about being able to resolve Anne LeChance's mystery in four days. Knowing my friend, however, I banished my doubts and nodded. "As you say, Holmes."

Assembling the materials Holmes wanted, and arranging them such that all were accessible in the sitting-room, took a few hours; we had our dinner about halfway through the task, and I bid Holmes goodbye at about eight thirty. After passing on his instructions to

Mrs. Hudson, I stepped outside and prepared to hail a cab, when I saw an unmistakable figure alight not ten paces distant.

"Miss LeChance?" I said. "The hour is quite late for calling."

"It is, Dr. Watson," she agreed. "But I was hoping to speak further with Mr. Holmes. The matter is quite urgent."

"Has there been another injury?"

"No," she said, "but another frightening apparition was seen, which caused my younger brother to run into the house in such a state of fright that it took an hour to calm him; I have this from my mother, to whom I spoke on the telephone this evening."

"Then," I said, "I will ask if he will see you."

I went upstairs again, but my conversation with Holmes was brief. Returning to Miss LeChance, I shook my head. "He is at work now," I said, "and will see no one. He recommends that you tell your family, and anyone else who might walk the grounds, to stay in at night. He also says that you should return on Tuesday, at two thirty promptly, and he will have a resolution for your problem at that time."

On her delicate features I could clearly see the interplay of skepticism and surprise. Yet...perhaps it was Holmes's suspicions affecting me, but it seemed to me that the expressions were not precisely right. Or, to be more accurate, that they were *too* right. They were so exactly the expressions I expected that for a moment it felt almost as though I watched a superlative actress upon the stage, giving the reaction the audience required. But in a moment her features had shifted to mere concern and resignation. "Do you believe him?" she asked, and her voice was filled with a concern far greater than her face revealed.

"Miss LeChance, I have known Sherlock Holmes for many years now, and in all that time, I have never known him to lie about such things. If he says he will have an answer for you in four days' time, then you may depend upon it."

She studied me for an instant, and again I had a fleeting, strange impression, this one of sadness, or even of an inexplicable pity, that flickered across her face. Then she smiled and extended her hand. "Well, then, thank you, Dr. Watson," she said. "You have a reputation as well, and so I will trust your judgment. You will see me at two thirty on Tuesday."

"Two thirty," I agreed, and saw her back into her hansom.

I stood there, irresolute, for several minutes. Her behavior, and that of Holmes, presented me with their own mysteries, and I once more felt an indefinable chill descend upon me. But I shook it off and finally set out for my own home. Tuesday would answer all of these questions, of that I was sure.

• • •

My return to 221B Baker Street, shortly before the scheduled meeting on Tuesday, came after a time both interminably long and startlingly short. I had many cases to attend to in that time, but in looking back that morning I could scarce recall their details; it did sometimes seem to me that my time spent with Holmes provided a vividness that other parts of my life lacked.

Perhaps, I thought as I let myself in, it was because while my work as a doctor could be a matter of life and death, it was a contest I controlled as much as any man could, while the mysteries Holmes and I investigated often pitted us against clever and malevolent antagonists who were beyond our control and who consciously sought to evade and even ruin us if they might.

As I had rather expected, I was greeted with a blue fog of shag tobacco smoke. Holmes sat in his favorite chair by the fireplace, with literally hundreds of papers scattered about. Some of these were old case accounts, others new, covered with numbers and—to me—inexplicable notations and graphs.

"Ah, Watson," came the familiar dry voice. "I expected you about now."

"You do realize, Holmes, that our rooms are in no condition to receive a young lady?"

He roused himself and glanced about. "I see what you mean. I daresay we could tidy up a bit." While his voice and manner did not have the hopeless, broken demeanor of our earlier encounter, still I heard something grim indeed in his words.

"Have you solved the problem of Miss LeChance, Holmes?" I asked, as I threw open the windows to begin the airing-out.

"The problem of Miss LeChance?" His smile was, if anything, more disturbing than his tone. "Yes, I believe I have. Watson, what do you know of statistics?"

"Statistics?" I repeated, beginning to gather up the papers and organize them. "Statistics on what?"

"The science of statistics, Watson."

"Ah. Little enough, I admit. I know that they were used for various political and military purposes, and many studies now done in the medical field attempt to use them to determine the efficacy of various treatments, but what little I knew of the mathematics is no longer with me."

"It is a wonderful field, Watson. One takes many samples, performs the same operation many times, gathers a large amount of data, and then with the proper analysis of numbers arrives at a clear set of conclusions, complete with a probability of error and even the ability to determine correlations." He waved at the newer papers. "I have been performing just such analyses on criminal cases over the years that I have good data upon."

I felt my eyebrows rise in surprise. "And this is relevant to the case?"

"It has proven to be at the core of this and other related cases, Watson, though not—I fear—in a manner either of us could have expected or desired." He considered me gravely as we completed straightening the room and preparing it for visitors. "In the time since you have known me—sixteen years, since eighteen hundred and eighty-three—how many cases of great interest have we seen?"

"How many?" I was not sure of the point of the question but thought on it seriously. "Well, I believe I have written accounts of no fewer than forty-nine cases, though not all have yet been published by Mr. Doyle, and within my files are others which we have not chosen to publish for various reasons. Excluding those you have told me of your time prior to our meeting…seventy or so, I should say."

"Indeed, that was my estimation, more or less. Seventy cases of significant interest in a period of sixteen years. Leaving aside my own earlier cases, how many cases do you suppose I found in the literature that either presented, or that I could deduce presented, similar features of interest in the prior sixteen years, and the sixteen before that?"

"Why…well, some that were truly worthy would never be uncovered, or the relevant features that made them recognizable not brought out. But even so. For the same area I would guess forty or fifty?"

"Seven, Watson. Seven in the prior sixteen years. And four in the sixteen before that."

I was somewhat taken aback by the coldness of his features—a coldness not directed at me by any means, but still uncomfortable to behold. "The records may be incomplete—"

"Undoubtedly, Watson," he said. "Yet not, I think, nearly incomplete enough to explain this discrepancy. Or," he continued, the grimness clear in his tone, "the incompleteness may be an explanation in a very different way."

Before I could reply to this extraordinary statement, I heard the sounds of the hansom outside the now-open window at the same time as Holmes. "Our guest has arrived, however, and further discussion might as well take place in her presence."

Moments later, Miss Anne LeChance entered. Holmes showed her to a seat, then seated himself in his accustomed armchair and studied her in silence for a moment.

She shifted uncomfortably. "Mr. Holmes? Is there something amiss with my dress or, perhaps, my hair again?"

"Not at all," he replied. "You present a perfect picture today, Miss LeChance. It is clear you took great pains to address any minor failings of your first hasty visit."

I had noticed by this point that Miss LeChance's current attire had narrower sleeves, and my swift impression of her figure as she entered indicated that she was now wearing the fashionable S-bend corset.

"Thank you, Mr. Holmes. Now, have you any news for me?"

"I have examined your problem, in light of some other most interesting discoveries I have made in the last week or so, and I believe I have made considerable progress towards an answer, yes. If you will indulge me by answering a few questions, I think a full resolution will be forthcoming."

She nodded. "Mr. Holmes, you may be assured of my full co-operation."

"Excellent!" He sprang to his feet. "I have been somewhat remiss; might I get you some tea or other refreshment? Our discussion may take some small time."

"Tea will be sufficient, Mr. Holmes."

"Watson? Will you have anything?"

"The same for me, Holmes." I tried to keep my voice as natural as might be. An outsider, I was sure, would not notice a thing, but to me Holmes's actions were clearly unusual. I had seen similar minor play-acting when he was preparing a trap for some adversary, but in this case I had not the slightest idea of his intent.

As he turned from setting the kettle on the gas, one hand flew outward, so swiftly I could scarce see it, and something streaked through the air toward Miss LeChance.

But to my astonishment, the young lady's hand came up with the speed of thought and with a *snap* had caught the flying object—which proved to be a small sack of some sort. "Holmes!" I remonstrated. "What in the world—"

"My apologies, Watson. And to you, Miss LeChance. It was, I admit, a risky means of verifying a somewhat shaky chain of inference, but I preferred a swift answer over a rather extended period of circumlocution."

"You could have injured her!" While I had every faith in my friend, I was still outraged by this risk he had taken.

"Hardly, Watson. Observe that this bag is filled with a mixture of small seeds and cotton; it might have stung, had it struck her wrongly, but would have left scarce a bruise, if that. The object was not to harm, but—"

"But to test my reaction," Miss LeChance said, her tones bespeaking both admiration and chagrin. "Well done, Mr. Holmes."

He gave a small bow. "Thank you. We can proceed, then, without further pretense as to the true nature of this case."

"I trust you will be enlightening me on whatever it is that the both of you now understand?" I asked. "For I admit to being now entirely at sea."

The look that Holmes gave me then was a queer one—hooded, with a mingling of sympathy, anger, and comfort that carried a great foreboding, and reminded me strangely of that most peculiar look that Miss LeChance had previously given me.

"Of course, Watson," he said after a moment. "You are lacking some of the details that I have been able to uncover, and may also suffer from a differing perspective, I suppose." The flat, grim manner in which he uttered the last words only reinforced my trepidation.

But he turned to our client. "You do not object, I hope, to my laying out my thoughts and processes for you and my friend Watson?"

"Please, Mr. Holmes, go ahead." She threw me another glance, as unreadable as her earlier one. "If you think it wise."

"I must," said he. Even so, he was silent for a long moment before he finally began to speak.

• • •

"We begin," Holmes said at length, "with the fact that you, Miss LeChance, were not the first, but the last in a sudden string of cases involving that which we, for lack of a better term, may call the paranormal—though not para*natural*, since—as Watson was kind enough to point out to me—anything which exists must be, *ipso facto*, natural.

"Only recently had I first encountered anything of this nature; now, in the space of a week, I was confronted by seven cases ostensibly involving phenomena generally considered supernatural, with only one that I thought I could easily assign to more mundane causes.

"This confirmed one of the more outrageous hypotheses I had formed upon accepting the existence of one paranormal event; namely, that something within the world had changed to either make these phenomena occur, or make them more visible or obvious to others. No other simple hypothesis fit these facts." He looked at both of us, saw us nod, and continued.

"Now, this fact by itself was most suggestive, not to say disturbing. But there were other facts, equally suggestive.

"Your appearance, Miss LeChance, was itself one of these facts. While—as I said—you were one of several, you immediately stood out as an anomaly. You have since corrected your errors as best you could, but that is itself most suggestive. Your dress was very close, but not sufficient. Your accent is not one I can identify.

"Then there was the matter of my little test. Your hand, you see, was in motion even before the bag left my fingers; by that, I knew you had observed that my actions were something of a blind, and had expected some sort of swift action on my part. The actual result of the test demonstrated that you have the reactions of a trained combatant in one of the martial arts of the Far East; not *baritsu* or one of the purer forms of karate, but something like them. You conducted yourself well enough, yet in truth…Watson?"

I thought I followed him, and it fit with that fleeting earlier impression. "I believe what Holmes is saying is that you were clearly playing a part." His comments and my impressions came together. "Miss LeChance, you behaved as one who has studied our ways intensely, but hasn't *lived* them."

"Nicely put, Watson. You are an actress—a superlative actress, I must add—portraying a culture quite distant and distinct from your own." He took out his pipe, filled it, and once the familiar blue smoke began to rise, continued.

"Now, I found that I could not countenance the thought that this was an unrelated event—that someone so talented, yet so foreign, would appear at my door with a tale of such paranormal events, so shortly after I found myself first involved with such phenomena. This meant one of two things. Either you, yourself, were somehow directly involved in the creation of these events, or, at the least, you knew *of* them and must, of necessity, understand something of their nature and origin."

Anne LeChance said nothing now; her face was immobile, giving away not a clue as to her thoughts.

"So. In either case, the swiftness of your appearance also implied something else: that you *already knew* these events were being called to my attention. Your case is one that has features rather explicitly supernatural; one might have expected you to seek assistance from the local church or others first, not to a very distant private detective whose known cases might be unusual, but quite strictly mundane in their elements."

I was struck by this new point. Holmes was almost certainly correct—yet, if so, how could she have known? Holmes had certainly not publicized his earlier case—that was generally left to me, and I at the time had no intention of speaking of it. But Holmes was going on: "The sudden appearance of the paranormal implied a change in the world. Your appearance was an anomaly of a different sort. Both had a commonality, however, that caused me to wonder about the *nature* of the change to the world, and the purpose of your appearance here. As Watson observed, you are not familiar with our fashions and habits in the way of one who has lived here; yet your few visible genuine characteristics do not fit any part of the world with which I am familiar.

"Now, it *is* often the case that the realm of ghosts, spirits, or other supernatural creatures is referred to as another world. It occurred to me, therefore, that there was one possible explanation for both: a literal *other world*, or worlds, which could somehow now interact with ours. Why such another world would include the shades of the recently dead was an interesting speculation, naturally, but I was willing to leave that aside for the moment. Are you following me so far, Miss LeChance?"

She finally smiled. "Rather well, yes. Please go on, Mr. Holmes."

"The reason that I set that question aside was the particular commonality I mentioned: specifically, myself. I have widely flung sources, and—until I had my experience with the shade of the earl—I had heard not a single bit of intelligence that implied the existence of the paranormal. So the first event of that sort I was aware of had happened to become one of my cases. And before knowledge of that case could have traveled far, you appeared at my door. Watson and I both noted some oddities, but following our initial discussion I was able to discover a prior connection, a case which Watson referred to as the three golden books." *Now* his face looked very grim indeed.

"And…?" she said after a moment.

"And I recalled the case, but it took me a few moments to arrange the details in my mind."

I looked up. "By…you know, Holmes, it seems to me it was like that for me as well. But I recall it perfectly now."

"Indeed, Watson. I am sure you do." That grim tone was stronger now. "That case, combined with my prior observations about the paranormal and its sudden appearance in my life, demanded that I examine this new phenomenon across a larger field of view, and perhaps to compare these new events with a similar, larger view of the world of the more normal crimes and mysteries I am accustomed to encountering."

Miss LeChance looked at me with another of those enigmatic glances that combined sadness and pity, then looked back to Holmes. "Mr. Holmes, perhaps we should discuss this—"

"No!" I said, rising to my feet. "Miss LeChance, I do not know why you seem so concerned for me, or what bothers my friend so, but I would know the truth."

"As Watson says, Miss LeChance," Holmes said. "He is my right hand. I will not keep secrets from him."

"But—"

"I have faith in Watson; you do not know him, but I do, and I have every confidence in his ability to grasp even the most outlandish of ideas." Holmes also rose, clasped my shoulder for a moment, and then turned to the window, gazing out upon the street.

"To continue my narrative, then, I gathered together all of the extensive literature of crime—the files I had accumulated from a dozen countries, annotations of books of criminal procedure and events, and so on—and began to analyze them with respect to the occurrence of cases that, for lack of a better term, I would have considered 'interesting'—ones that might, when solved, have made it to Watson's files and Mr. Doyle's publisher.

"I also drew on my myriad sources to determine how many other reports of paranormal activity had been made outside of my own current circle of acquaintance." He looked to me. "Watson, given what we discussed earlier, what do you infer was the result of that research?"

An eerie feeling had begun to descend upon me, as though I stood half outside of myself. I could see and hear and act, yet the tension in my mind and body had risen to a level that I could not yet fathom. "Well, Holmes," I said, my voice sounding unnaturally calm in my own ears, "if the results were similar, then you must have found few—if any—examples of paranormal happenings beyond those we already have encountered."

He nodded.

"But..." I waved my hands vaguely. "What does it all *mean*, Holmes? I begin to feel as though I am walking in a nightmare, yet I know I am awake."

"You may be closer than you realize, Watson," he said, and his shoulders were rigid, yet vibrating faintly with some tremendous inner tension. "One of the most essential principles of my science of detection is that at its base, human nature is the same, regardless of its time or place. This has served me well throughout my career. If that were true, it would imply that across the world, there should be roughly the same frequency of crime of all sorts, including those with elements of interest to me.

"Yet I have now very strong evidence that such is not the case; the vast, vast majority of such crimes and mysteries have been presented to me, and appear to be little-seen outside of London and its environs. Similarly, the change in the world that has allowed the paranormal to appear has been almost unseen except by those who have brought their sightings to me."

Miss LeChance bit her lip, but nodded slowly.

He turned to me. "And what, Watson, can we deduce from this?"

I found myself, for the first time, not wanting to answer. My mouth was suddenly as dry as it had ever been in Afghanistan, wondering if a bullet were about to find me, and I felt my hands shaking. At the same time, however, I could not shy away from my friend now, for his expression was not merely grim but concerned, focused on me alone.

I took a breath and tried to order my thoughts. "You will, I trust, pardon me if I take a moment? You have presented so many extraordinary elements here that I am a trifle overwhelmed."

"Of course, Watson. Take your time, please."

So. Seventy cases in sixteen years, versus seven elsewhere. Virtually all paranormal cases presented to Holmes. His remarks about Miss LeChance. The world suddenly changing...

A pattern was becoming clear, and it was so strange and terrible that I scarcely dared speak. "First...Miss LeChance, you believe, is not from this world."

"Correct."

"She may be, herself, from the same world as our spirits..." I saw a tiny shake of his head, "...or another, but the combination of her oddities simply does not fit with any known country on Earth." Another thought struck me. "Yet she had some means of getting considerable information on our customs and even of us, in particular..." I looked to Holmes. "Here is a fanciful thought, Holmes, from one of the tales of Mr. Wells; what if she were from the future, using some form of time machine?"

Rarely have I seen Holmes look so astounded. "Watson! My friend, you never cease to surprise me. That is a most interesting conjecture. In some ways it fits very well. But there are other features."

I closed my eyes, feeling that foreboding rising, my heart

accelerating its beat to the point that I thought the vibration of my chest must surely be visible. "Yes. She does not fit here, yet Burke's shows that she *is* from here, as did your inquiries. Leaving Miss LeChance aside...Holmes, here is one of the most disturbing conclusions from your discoveries about your cases and the paranormal events: you are, yourself, the focus of the world."

I had hoped with no little desperation that Holmes would laugh, or respond with one of his acidic retorts that showed how very far I had gone afield; instead he sighed and nodded, his eyes shadowed with his concern, a concern still directed at me.

"So," I said, maintaining with what effort I cannot even estimate a calm and reserved demeanor, striving to emulate my friend's dry and measured delivery, "we have a world that appears to focus to the exclusion of most of the rest of the globe on one man; a case which this man, normally preternatural of memory, could not immediately call to mind despite its most unique and peculiar aspects—the affair of the three golden books; the fact that memory of this case was also dim for me for a moment, before becoming singularly clear."

I paused as the significance of another, always ignored, point struck me. "The fact that when I cast my mind back over my life, the only details that instantly come to mind have to do with Holmes and my involvement in his cases; the sudden appearance of the paranormal in a world which has never exhibited it; and a visitor who simply does not fit, yet is inarguably, at the same time, a part of the world; and the agreement and admission that this visitor does in fact come from another world."

I took another breath, feeling so light-headed that I thought I might faint. But I would not permit it, no matter how outrageous the conclusions. "I can think of only one circumstance in which a world might focus almost to exclusion on one person, yet pretend to be a complete and independent world, and where that world could suddenly have truths appear and disappear, and it is one with which I am intimately familiar. The world, in short, of storytelling, with the changes being those an editor might impose, or an author perform during rewriting a story."

I looked directly at our visitor. "And you…you do not fit, because your story is not ours. Yet you know ours, seem to have a genuine respect and even, I might say, affection for Holmes that implies you have known *of* him for a long time. Perhaps my guess of someone from the future is not, after all, as far afield as I might have thought."

I suddenly laughed, and the amusement was genuine, though also filled with an existential horror. "Ah, of course. One final point. One of the most common conceits of fiction, especially fiction of the more *outré* sort, is to recount it as if it were told to the author, rather than being wholly his creation. I have not, after all, written the accounts of Sherlock's cases; our author, then, is Mr. Arthur Conan Doyle."

Miss LeChance closed her eyes and nodded, and Holmes murmured, "Capital, Watson." There was a spark of the old enthusiasm in his words. "Absolutely superb, in fact." He looked to Miss LeChance. "I have a few additional surmises of my own, but would you care to simply tell us the remainder?"

She stood, as if to stand still was no longer tolerable. "You are close enough. As close, I think, as I could ever expect you to be." She gestured, taking in the entire world around us. "You are entirely correct that Sir Arthur Conan Doyle wrote a series of stories about your adventures, from which your world is born. And I am from the future—a different future, a different set of stories, in fact.

"But there are not two, nor three, or a dozen, but a *thousand* such worlds, a thousand worlds of fiction that have been brought to a form of life, in what would be the future far beyond both of ours, as part of a project called Hyperion. The creators of this project have sought to recreate the heroes of the great stories of their own history—the *real* history, in which we thousand are all just tales to amuse and thrill and sometimes frighten."

"I see," Holmes said, with an equanimity I found astounding; I was too overwhelmed by the horrific idea, that we were merely the creations—the amusements—of other men. "So my comment on how I might have been tricked into believing in the paranormal was, in fact, completely accurate. There is no true magic; this, then, is some form of technological illusion, a magic lantern as advanced to us as the ordinary lantern might be to a caveman."

"Yes."

"And why, then, have you come here, Miss LeChance? Revealing these truths would disturb the play, I would think."

I saw an honest spark of anger then, a flash of emotion completely unconstrained by her chosen role. "Oh, yeah," she said, with a completely new accent and demeanor, "it will *totally* screw up their game. That's the idea." She shook her head. "Sorry. I still can't think about…the so-called experimenters of Hyperion without losing it a little.

"To answer you—from the point of view of our creators, this is a new and probably final adventure for all of us, what they call a 'crossover adventure,' where all of the worlds will be threatened by something from beyond their worlds, and all the great heroes will have to band together to solve the problem.

"What they *don't* know is that a few of us managed to… well, crack their code, take partial control of the worlds. They're not seeing *this* conversation. They're seeing me making contact as an emissary from the Council of Worlds to get the assistance of Sherlock Holmes for the big mystery. What we *really* want is to get as many of the Hyperions together as we can so that we can turn the tables on the experimenters—so we can be *free* of these people that thought it was perfectly okay to create us for their own kicks."

"I see." Sherlock looked from her to me. "And should I agree to assist you, what of Watson? For he is utterly indispensable to me, as a companion and as a friend."

She bit her lip. "He might be able to come…but…"

"Do not finish that," Sherlock said. "I ask you only one thing: if we win, will Watson survive?"

Miss LeChance hesitated once more. "I hope so. But he—"

Sherlock made a sharp gesture and she cut off.

I felt an unnatural calm descend upon me as the final horror became clear. "I am afraid, Holmes, that you have taught me too well," I said. "Miss LeChance, you said they created the *heroes*, yes?"

She hesitated. Sherlock simply nodded.

"And it is not I, but Sherlock, who is the focus of the world."

Another nod.

I took a deep breath. "Then you should not concern yourself with me, Holmes. You are the one focus of this play, as you say, while I…" For a moment I faltered, but then forced myself to finish. "I am not real."

Holmes's face was suddenly stricken; then he was up, grasping both my shoulders. "Oh, my dear chap, no," he said, and his voice vibrated with emotion. "No, I assure you, Watson: you are my finest friend and companion, and there is one thing I am more certain of than anything in this—or any other—world: You may not be *physical*…but you are, beyond any doubt, *real*."

A SCANDAL IN THE BLOODLINE

BY HILDY SILVERMAN

"Watson, do you know what the worst, the *very* worst, thing is about immortality?" Holmes peered at me over his evening mug of warm O-positive.

These repetitive conversations? I thought, nibbling marrow from the cracked femur on my plate. *Humoring you through the same complaints for centuries unceasing?* "The boredom?"

"The boredom!" he exclaimed as though I had remained silent. "The utter, crushing monotony of *being* without enough *doing*."

I sighed. "Yes, Sherlock, of course it is. Far worse than having to drink blood or change identities and locations every several decades or hunt—"

"When were we even last employed?" He rose and began to pace the length of the dining area in our modest flat. "I swear I can *feel* my mind atrophying. In this age of world wide webs and CSIs, FBIs, and so forth there is precious little need for a great detective." He paused in front of me and for a moment looked so downcast my heart ached on his behalf. "This is my true curse, Watson, more than the bloodthirst. I have outlived my usefulness."

I stood and placed my hands upon his shoulders. "Now, stop it, Holmes. There are plenty of people...well, living beings. Mostly living—"

"Please make your point before I drive a wooden chair leg through my own heart."

"What I am saying is that not everyone can avail themselves of the police or other law enforcement options. Creatures like us still require friendly assistance from time to time."

Cheerful nostalgia lightened Holmes's angular features, but only briefly. "Past glory does little to ease present ennui."

The cellular phone resting on the coffee table in the parlor sang, "*Awwwoooo!* Werewolves of London." That ringtone was Holmes's little joke on me. Humorous, if not quite accurate. I examined the screen for the identity of the caller.

A scanned photo filled the screen and my heart sank. Crumpled and yellowed with age, it was the image of a woman who appeared in the full flower of her youth. She stared straight into my soul, although it wasn't my soul she had ultimately ensnared.

"Will you answer it already?" Holmes stalked into the room.

I held up the phone so that the screen faced him. I may as well have held up a crucifix, given how abruptly he stopped and rocked back on his heels. After a moment, he straightened his spine and held out a hand.

"Are you quite certain?" I said, softly.

He nodded once, sharply, and I placed the phone in his palm. He tapped the screen and raised the phone slowly, as though afraid it would burn his ear. "Mrs. Norton," he said, managing a tone so calm I nearly believed it. "What can I do for you?"

I withdrew discreetly to the dining room and endeavored to lower my blood pressure by reminding myself that what Irene Norton had done to my dearest friend had been done out of affection. Had she not been drawn back to England by a preternatural sense that something terrible was about to befall Holmes. Had she not followed him to the site of his demise at Reichenbach, he would have died the true death along with Moriarty. As it was, she'd found Holmes's broken body on an outcropping of rocks at the bottom of the falls and transformed him.

"This world will always need Sherlock Holmes. *I* will always need him," Holmes told me she'd whispered in his ear before saving his existence, if not his life. From then on whatever bond had formed between them after the Bohemian case—based upon mutual intellectual respect and admiration, or so they insisted—had grown into something beyond my comprehension. Not romantic love, certainly, but equally powerful, if far darker in nature.

Of course, I was not one to judge, beast that I had become after my encounter on the moors with the cursed Baskervilles. As Holmes had embraced me despite my transformation (and helped me formulate a tale the public could digest more easily than the case's true outcome) so too did I welcome him back to Baker Street. Together, we conjured up the somewhat plausible tale of how he'd survived in order to placate the public. Ever since then, we'd traveled the path of immortality and monstrous appetites as one another's only enduring companion.

Except for when the woman came calling, which she did with blessedly less frequency as time marched on. But when she summoned Holmes, he always answered.

At last he came over to me, his gaze fixed upon some distant point.

"Where?" I asked.

"Here, actually. Seems she has returned to the state of her birth."

"Not surprising. New Jersey is a major Site, after all." It was one of the reasons we'd settled there for the current iteration of our lives—more of our kind in need of our particular investigative skills.

"It has been nearly fifty years." Holmes dropped into the chair across from me. "I almost thought…It never is, though."

"What does she want, then?" I prompted.

He made a steeple of his index fingers and rested his chin atop them. "Her husband. He has apparently vanished."

"And that is a bad thing?"

Holmes arched one eyebrow at me. "Lest you forget, old fellow, he is the paterfamilias of our bloodline. Should he be destroyed, Irene would expire as well."

I bit my tongue.

Holmes glared. "Yes, that would be so bad! As she rebirthed me, I would follow her into death's domain."

I hated when he read my mind. So rude. "You do not know that for sure. There are many who believe eliminating one's parent of the blood frees them from the vampire's curse."

"Many would consider death freedom." He downed his remaining blood and shuddered, eyes half closed. "Mmm. Myself, I prefer to remain aboveground. It has been a gift to watch the advancements of this world over the centuries. The extermination of so many diseases. Water found on Mars. Twitter! Who knows what will come next?"

Conveniently forgot your grousing on the boredom of immortality, eh? "More death," I grumbled. "Not ours, perhaps, but friends, family." A familiar ache filled my chest as memories swept through my mind. "Wives."

Holmes waved his hand in a shooing motion. "Replaceable. How many wives have you had, old fellow? I believe I lost count mid-nineteenth century."

I growled, low and deep in my throat.

Holmes hastily patted the air between us. "Mea culpa, dear friend. I spoke discourteously. You know lack of sensitivity is a failing of my kind. Please accept my apology."

"You are lucky the moon has not quite waxed full."

He cleared his throat. "In any case, the woman is quite beside herself with worry. She wishes to employ us posthaste to find her errant mate."

"Yes, well." I struggled to find a positive in this scenario. "At least we know she can afford our fee."

"Indeed." Holmes grinned, revealing the tips of his fangs. "Now, that's the spirit, Watson!"

"When will she be arriving?"

"Within the hour."

"Then I suppose we have a case." I shrugged. "Ask and ye shall receive."

Holmes's smile faltered. "I believe 'be careful what you wish for' may be the more appropriate aphorism."

• • •

True to form, Mrs. Irene Norton, née Adler, arrived at our flat looking not an instant older than in our previous encounters. Flawlessly coiffed, expensively dressed, and so utterly charming and sincere even I, who knew all too well what she was, found myself swayed.

Poor Holmes. What chance did he have of withstanding her allure when their blood flowed through one another's veins? They were bound for eternity.

She kept our exchange of greetings brief. "How long has he been missing?" Holmes inquired as she stepped between me and my favorite easy chair, and settled herself on it.

Irritated by the affront, I sat on the couch next to Holmes with a grunt.

"What is the date?" Irene waved her hand. "I have difficulty keeping track. Have you lived long enough to notice that yet, Sherlock?"

"One day has always been much like the next unless I have a case." He glanced at the wall calendar. "October 8, 2015."

"Ah. Then he has been missing a bit more than a month."

"And you only just noticed?" I said. "Haven't you two been together for *centuries*?"

She shrugged. "It isn't as if we have never been apart during that time, Mr. Watson."

"Doctor," I corrected. I knew she only erred to provoke me. "Still a doctor, *Mrs.* Norton."

"How lovely for you." She wrinkled her nose as if catching a whiff of something foul, and returned her full attention to Holmes. "Sherlock, you know how Godfrey has always traveled. Why, he was off on business mere moments after our wedding." She ran her long, red-lacquered nails through her hair. "You do recall my wedding? The one you were corralled into witnessing during that business with the photograph?"

Sherlock cleared his throat but otherwise managed to retain an air of professional disinterest. "Considering that your husband's business has primarily been a cover for expanding the bloodline around the globe, I can see how you would assume he was merely hunting for a week, even two. But a month away without a text, email, or old-fashioned written missive?" Holmes shook his head. "Unlikely. So, please answer the good doctor's perfectly reasonable question. Why did it take you so long to notice?"

Irene pouted. "Fine. Godfrey and I have not exactly been together for, well, a couple of years. Or twenty."

"I see," said Holmes, evenly. "Formally divorced, separated...?"

"There was hardly a need for legalities. Godfrey and I simply decided to pursue other...interests. It was quite mutual and amicable."

"In which case, why the concern now?" I asked.

She spared me a glance. "We have had regular, ah, encounters, shall we say, despite no longer living together as husband and wife." She offered Holmes a somewhat apologetic look. "We were scheduled for such a reunion right here in New Jersey, at a lovely riverside town called Lambertville. I waited at our designated rendezvous for a week before I became concerned. I tried contacting him by every means possible, but received no response. I then visited his known lairs, which took some time. Finally, I discovered his newest address, just outside of New York City. And there I found...it was...."

Holmes placed his hands lightly upon hers. I could almost see the electricity leap between their fingers. "What you found convinced you he was in danger."

Irene bit her lower lip and nodded. "The place had been torn apart. And there was blood. A great deal of it. Everywhere."

"His."

Her voice dropped to a whisper. "I recognized the scent immediately. No matter what transpired between us toward the end of our formal union, I still care for Godfrey." She clasped Holmes's hands tightly. "Moreover, as paterfamilias, his demise threatens our entire bloodline."

"Hold on," I said. "You said there was a great deal of blood. Did it *all* belong to the unfortunate Mr. Norton?"

"Yes. I am certain."

"Well, then, how do you know he is not already destroyed?"

"Do you think I would be seated here if he were? Did you not just hear what I said? If he dies—"

"Yes, yes, you all die. I've heard that tale before."

Irene bared her fangs and hissed. "It is not a *tale*, it is a fact! The only one in this room with a tail is *you*."

Before I could retort, Holmes gave me a look that said, *Let me handle this*. I growled and subsided deeper into the sofa.

"You said your paramour failed to meet you at a designated rendezvous, which was out of character," said Holmes. "He could not be found by any of the means available to us in this modern age. You found his home in severe disarray, clearly the site of a violent struggle, and a considerable amount of his spilled blood. Yet you remain convinced he is alive and that opinion is solely based upon you and me also still existing."

Irene was studying Holmes's face. I wondered if she were trying to read his thoughts—or intent on blocking him from reading hers. "That is all accurate."

"Then the only conclusion can be that he was assaulted and abducted. Begging the questions, by whom and for what purpose?" Holmes withdrew his hands from Irene's grasp, rose, and began to pace. "A paterfamilias is a powerful creature. It would take a being, more likely several, of great strength to overwhelm him."

"Indeed. Strong and vicious. And with reason to hate one who governs and shields our kind from"—Irene shot me a pointed look—"*others*."

"Wait. You think hellhounds attacked him?" I shook my head. "Granted, there is little love lost between our peoples, Mrs. Norton—"

"Precious little," she said through gritted teeth.

"But if you were correct there would be no doubt as to your husband's condition," Holmes finished for me. "Hounds would simply tear him limb from limb and go about their day. What possible reason would they have to abduct a vampire?"

"Ransom," said Irene after a moment's hesitation. "They know the value of a paterfamilias to his bloodline."

Holmes nodded once. "Good. Reasonable. Whom have they contacted for payment? Not you, I assume."

"Well...no."

"Others in the line? Surely one would alert the rest. I have heard nothing."

Irene frowned. "Perhaps they are still formulating their demands."

Holmes shook his head sharply. "Ridiculous. Come on. You are brighter than this."

Irene stood and drew herself up to her full height. "All right, then, not ransom!"

"And not hounds," I said.

For a moment I thought she might pounce upon me. My skin prickled with the anticipation of transformation and delicious violence to follow. But she only said, "If not the bloody hounds, then whom?"

"Other vampires," said Holmes. "A rival bloodline."

Irene closed her eyes briefly and sank back into my chair. "I confess I did think of that myself. But again, to what end? Godfrey was on reasonable terms with others of his status. He obeyed the laws as far as who and how many to turn, cleaning up after feedings, keeping our secrets."

Sherlock tapped his chin absently. "If not rivalry and not ransom then we are left with precious few motives from which to choose." His expression brightened. "There is only one thing for it. We must put aside our speculations and prejudices. Find the clues and follow them to their logical conclusion, no matter how unlikely."

"Where do we begin?" I tried not to sound overly excited. Irene and I may never be friends, but it was still unseemly to appear eager over a client's misfortune. In truth, though, I was almost as stir-crazy as Holmes and the thought of new work filled me with anticipation.

"I assume you did not report the crime scene to the authorities—human or heads of other bloodlines."

"Of course not. Far too risky on both fronts. And I was very careful not to disturb the scene." She gave him a brief smile. "I knew you would prefer it pristine."

He bowed his head. "Then we begin at Godfrey Norton, Esquire, and *padre nostro*'s abode. Just outside New York City, you said?"

"Only about an hour and a half's ride from here. My car is parked just outside."

"Then let us away." Holmes was sweeping toward the door before the final syllable had left his mouth.

Irene and I exchanged glances. *For this case alone, for his sake, a truce is declared.* We nodded our mutual agreement and followed in Holmes's wake.

• • •

We were standing in the midst of the wreckage that had been a sumptuous parlor. Norton's country home was a pricey affair set in a town where very large houses were positioned very far away from one another. "Fathering bloodlines pays rather well, eh?" I said, in an attempt to lighten the mood.

"Being a successful attorney for several centuries certainly does," Irene replied.

Holmes ignored us as he continued inspecting and discarding objects, peering behind draperies and under sofa cushions. Finally, he slammed down a throw pillow as though it had insulted his integrity. "Damn it all, how am I supposed to concentrate with all this stale blood in my nostrils?"

His fangs *were* more obvious than normal. "Steady on, old friend," I said.

"This is your curse upon me, *Mrs.* Norton. My mind distracted by hunger, like a champion dog losing a race because he caught scent of fresh sausages!"

I tried not to be offended.

Irene folded her arms beneath her bosom. "It is not my fault,

Mr. Holmes, that you have yet to master your appetites. You men, always assuming you can figure these things out for yourselves, only to…" She shook her head, and nodded in my direction. "Even the *actual* dog in the room shows greater restraint!"

"Excuse me," I began indignantly.

Holmes cut me off. "Yes, well, perhaps he can use his *discipline* to come up with the clue that is utterly eluding me!"

"Perhaps I can," I snapped. Then I realized that my keen sense of smell probably could be of service. I closed my eyes and inhaled deeply over one of the larger blood spatters staining the oriental carpet. Establishing Norton's scent, I proceeded to circle the room, inhaling deeply. I identified household odors like cleaning formulas and toiletries and discounted them.

"*Anything?*" asked Holmes, impatience underscoring the word.

I spotted a large, overstuffed chair with a footrest that showed significant wear. Surely the favorite of the master of the house—we gents all have our preferred thrones. Remembering Irene's territorial violation back at our flat, I made my way over to it. Pressing my nose against the headrest, I sniffed, raised my head triumphantly, and proclaimed, "Ah, there it is."

Holmes read me immediately. "Of course!" He appeared at my side in that disconcerting way vampires have, where you never see them move yet they're suddenly *there.*

"What are you on about?" Irene's gaze flitted between us.

Holmes tapped the chair. "As we have established that this is the site of abduction, not murder, and yet there were no signs of either doors or windows having been forced, we can only conclude that your husband knew his foe. In fact, he invited him inside."

I said, "This chair is well worn. A favorite, I presume?"

"Yet the most recent occupant was not Norton," said Holmes. "Now, if I have a favorite seat and invite an acquaintance over, I would ask them to sit across from me, while taking my preferred perch." He nodded to the comfortable-looking but far less worn chairs across from Norton's. "A good guest would never presume to sit in the master of the house's favorite. However, this person did."

"A deliberate affront," I said pointedly.

"Exactly. So he welcomed a single visitor only to be insulted, and then assaulted by the same." Holmes vanished. A moment later he cried, "Kitchen!"

Irene and I joined him. He tapped an answering machine attached to a landline telephone. "The older we vampires become the less we tend to keep up with the times."

"True enough," murmured Irene as Holmes pressed the rewind and then play buttons.

There were twenty-odd messages from clients and repairpersons, and several hang-ups. And then: "Godfrey Norton, I am a child of the Inner Temple line. Tomorrow you will expect me within the first hour after sundown. I have a proposition you must consider." The machine identified the message as having been left nearly five weeks prior.

"There you have it. Another vampire *is* the culprit." I felt vindicated.

Holmes was scowling in that way he had when unraveling a particularly knotty problem. Drumming his fingers on the granite countertop, he said, "This recording has been here all along. Did it not occur to you to check it the first time?"

Irene shrugged with one shoulder. "I was much disturbed after confronting the gory scene and fled immediately. After all, someone had overcome the paterfamilias. What chance would I have stood if they were lying in wait?"

"Quite reasonable. Did you recognize that final caller?"

Her expression was neutral but I sensed it was taking her much effort to create that illusion. "I did not."

Holmes regarded her with one eyebrow cocked. "Really. You are going to try to deceive *me*?"

Their gazes met and held for several seconds. She faltered first. "I may have detected something familiar. It has been a very long time."

"Indeed it has." Holmes turned to me. "Tell me exactly what you smelled upon that chair. Every individual odor."

I shrugged. "Hair pomade with a musky scent. A touch of cologne—"

"Cheap? Common?"

"Well, I am no expert, but if I had to venture a guess, I would say expensive. The elements used in its construction were—"

"So, wealthy and vainglorious," said Holmes, waving away the rest of my data. "And that accent."

"Distinctly European," I said. "And rather formal for modern times."

"You did not recognize it?"

"Well, it sounded a bit Slavic, I suppose, or perhaps— Germanic?"

"Top marks." Holmes clapped me on the shoulder. "It is difficult to identify an accent from a country that no longer exists. Specifically, the distinctive cadence of old Bohemian nobility."

"Bohemia?" I echoed as Irene flinched. "Well, isn't *that* intriguing?"

We positioned ourselves in front of her as she studiously avoided our gazes. "Indeed," said Holmes, "considering the original case that brought you into my—our lives. So, do tell, why is yet another Bohemian nobleman cross with you?"

Irene drew a deep breath and released it, slowly. "Because…it isn't *another* Bohemian nobleman. It is the same one."

"You mean—" I began.

"Yes, damn it!" Composing herself, she continued. "That was none other than Wilhelm Gottsreich Sigismond von Ormstein, Grand Duke of Cassel-Felstein. Briefly the King of Bohemia."

Our silence was met with defiance. "Oh, don't act so surprised. Surely you figured out decades ago that that silly photograph was never why he was so desperate to find me."

"You had turned him." Holmes's tone contained a hint of betrayal. "That was the true blackmail he feared then."

"I was still young and foolish, and he was going to be king. He craved immortality—you know how monarchs can be, never wanting their reigns to end. He made me heady promises in exchange for my gift."

"But, as I recall, he ultimately abdicated," I said. "Although the scandal of your encounter never came to light, he yielded to a younger brother and vanished from courtly life."

"Yes, and the reason for that was kept well hidden," said Holmes. "Except, of course, the whispers our kind can never completely silence."

"About?"

"Disappearances. Suspicious deaths, including that of Clotilde, his bride and the daughter of the Scandinavian king. The Bohemian court did not wish to be associated with the kind of scandal that threatened the British monarchy during the time of the Ripper."

Irene pressed her lips together tightly and nodded. "Wilhelm was locked away and his brother installed in his stead. Couldn't control his urges." She cast a sidelong look at Holmes. "Or didn't want to."

"So, after centuries, he tracks down your erstwhile spouse. To destroy him and thus end his own miserable existence?" I asked.

"If that were the case, the deed would already have been done," said Holmes, as Irene shuddered. "No, Norton is merely the bait to draw *her* out. We can only assume that your ex-husband still harbors enough loyalty to continue protecting you, or you would have been approached months ago."

"So much for your gift," I said, nodding in understanding. "Instead of ruling for eternity, or at least for as long a reign as he could have gotten away with before his subjects questioned his longevity, he wound up imprisoned, likely until Bohemia itself ceased to be. Motive enough, eh?"

Holmes gave me a look I could only describe as vaguely disappointed. But rather than enlighten me as to how I had misspoken, he said, "So, if it is you the deposed king seeks then to retrieve Norton we need only offer up his prize."

Irene glared. "I am to be sacrificed in Godfrey's stead?"

Holmes studied the fingernails of his right hand as though they were of far greater interest than Irene or Norton's fates. "Or we can wait and see if the ex-king chooses to end his misery by lopping off Norton's head. Of course, we will only know of his decision when you and I and the rest of our line crumble into dust."

Irene opened her mouth, appeared to reconsider, and snapped it shut again. Her eyes glimmered with the keen intellect that had so impressed Holmes all those years ago. I could almost see her running calculations: *What should I say next? What will benefit me most?*

At last, she said, "Your point is well taken. You and your loyal— *friend*—will keep me safe?"

"You are a paying client," sniffed Holmes. "Therefore, we shall do everything in our considerable power to ensure your safety."

Irene frowned. "Is that all I am, then?" When he didn't respond, she nodded. "So, how do we let Wilhelm know that I want to meet?"

In response, Holmes tapped the answering machine. "Apparently, the former king is not up on the latest technology either, as he didn't bother to erase this evidence—or he deliberately left the machine untouched in hopes you would play it and respond when you inevitably found this place. In which case, he is probably quite cross that you originally fled the scene without further investigation." He picked up the receiver and held it out to Irene. "But better late than never, eh?"

• • •

The deposed king wasted no time sending a car around for us, driven by a ghoul whose stench made the ride supremely unpleasant. The large, misshapen creature drove us over hill and dale to a remote, abandoned campground. Upon arrival we were ushered into a rundown lodge decorated in cobwebs, abandoned rough-hewn furnishings, and rotting wood. In the midst of the sizable main room slumped a badly beaten vampire. Iron nails fastened his hands above his head to a thick wooden pole at his back. His feet were nailed to the floor.

Irene caught sight of the piteous figure of her once-beloved and gasped. "Oh, Godfrey. I am so very sorry!" She dashed to his side and crouched beside her miserable ex-husband, hands cupping his face, a portrait of spousal tenderness and concern.

"That was almost believable," murmured Holmes.

Before I could ask him to clarify, Grand Duke Wilhelm von so forth and so on entered the room from a side door. He looked much as I remembered him—at least six feet six inches tall and broad as an American footballer. He was flanked by two equally sizable human men who bore stakes and mallets strapped to their hips, and two ghouls who could have been twins to our driver in appearance and stench.

Our driver-*cum*-escort planted his ham-sized hands on our shoulders and propelled us forward to stand directly before Wilhelm. He released us but maintained his position directly at our backs.

Holmes glanced over his shoulder at the brute, grinned, and winked as though making a friendly promise. The ghoul snarled in return.

Wilhelm diverted our attention. "Mr. Holmes. Dr. Watson. How unexpected to make your acquaintance again after so long. I suppose thanks are in order, as you have finally, at long last, retrieved for me Miss Adler."

Holmes shrugged. "I doubt that indiscreet photograph still troubles you. So, tell me, your majest—oh, sorry, I suppose that title is no longer accurate."

Wilhelm bared his fangs. "I am once king and forever. No one could strip me of my birthright!"

"Yet your family did exactly that," Holmes pointed out. "How unfortunate. The last time we met, you had everything you wanted—a bride, a vast inheritance, and reassurance Mrs. Norton would not upset any of it."

"She had already, though the extent of her betrayal was unknown to me at the time." Wilhelm snatched Irene around the bicep and hauled her up so quickly her feet actually lost contact with the floor.

I sensed tension from Holmes beside me and anticipated his

flight to her defense. Instead, he folded his arms and continued as though nothing untoward were happening. "I do sympathize, I truly do. She didn't consult me before turning me, either."

Irene, wincing in pain, shot Holmes a demanding look: *What are you doing?*

"No, Mr. Holmes. What this creature did to me was far more devious." Wilhelm gave Irene a shake that rattled her teeth. "She seduced me as a woman before purring in my ear that she could offer me so much more. An eternity of wealth and privilege. A moment's discomfort spent passing from *Leben*, then to rise again and rule forever—first as myself, later by passing as my own descendants. A pretty lie, *ja?*"

Norton groaned and opened his swollen eyes. My training called. "Please, this man needs a doctor. Allow me to tend to him—"

"Bah, he does not matter now, beyond living on so that we all might." Wilhelm waved me over to Norton.

I crouched by his side, tending to him as best I could. Holmes's continued existence was motivation enough, although I must admit I had a certain professional curiosity.

"Why aren't you healing?" I whispered in Norton's ear.

At first, all he could manage was a moan, but then he forced out, "Injected…poison."

What poison could possibly affect a vampire, particularly a paterfamilias? I sniffed close to his jugular vein. *Ah, there it is.* "He injected you with garlic oil?"

"Please." Norton whimpered. "It. Hurts. Help—"

"I will do what I can." I didn't have my bag with me, and even if I had I would have lacked the equipment needed to filter the oil out. All I could do was assess his outward injuries, which were numerous. He hadn't succumbed to the huge Habsburg easily. No doubt he'd been tortured since his capture as well.

Something else troubled me as I examined Norton—his demeanor. As I realigned his broken bones, he whinged and groaned, and I swear I saw bloody tears beading in the corners of his eyes. Granted, he had been grievously abused, but still. Where was the strength, the taciturn nature of a vampire lord? A doctor shouldn't judge but as a fellow night creature I couldn't help but take Norton's measure and find him—lacking.

My attention was drawn back to the discussion between Holmes and Wilhelm, who was saying, "…believed she could capitalize on my favor, that I would make her my queen someday. As though this low-born creature were worthy of such an honor!"

At this, Irene hissed. "You underestimated me, just as men always—" She stopped before finishing the thought, jaw muscles bunching visibly beneath her pale skin.

"It hardly matters now." Holmes still sounded as though they were all chatting over tea. "Bohemia does not even exist anymore. I am sure since you regained your freedom you were wily enough to sock away enough for a rainy immortality. Your relatives who deposed and imprisoned you for your—appetites—are dust. So, you have scant cause to wish Mrs. Norton ill anymore."

Holmes held out his hand, palm up. "Allow us to collect the poor remains of her love and depart. You have punished the paterfamilias ultimately responsible for all our conditions, and as you can see by Mrs. Norton's demeanor, she is most upset by her beloved's injuries, so you have punished her as well. Your revenge is complete."

"Complete?" Wilhelm laughed heartily, but his voice held an edge of mania that chilled me to the quick. He shifted to snatch Irene by her hair with one hand and with the other gripped her chin. "You are wrong, Mr. Holmes." He nodded sharply at Norton. "Take that pathetic excuse for a *Vater* if you wish, but she will remain with me. I have an eternity of justice to visit upon this *Hexe*!"

"Like you visited on your innocent fiancée?" Irene cooed. "Such a proper little thing. A shame how you drained her beyond turning, and only days after your wedding. I did warn you that taking a human wife would only end in disaster. Typical of your sex, you just wouldn't be told."

I blinked at her tone—cool, contemptuous—as though Wilhelm posed no threat despite her looking like a tiny bird caught in the jaws of a very large and angry cat.

Wheels began turning in my mind…

"Irene," said Holmes, a note of caution entering his voice. "Careful."

"Aren't I always?" She went on without awaiting confirmation. "Willy, dear, stop this nonsense right now. Your upset is noted. I was younger and foolish in my ambitions, but after all, you *did* make promises despite having no intention of honoring them. As your queen I would have taught you to control your bloodlust, to channel it in pursuit of your ambitions, but I was *not on your level.*" She rolled her eyes.

With a roar, Wilhelm released his perilous hold on Irene's head, spun her around to face him, and grasped her throat in both large hands. "I planned such exquisite tortures for you." Spittle flew from his mouth. "But I can content myself with ripping your head from your body and remembering the joy of your final suffering instead! *Abschied, mein Hure!*"

So absorbed was Wilhelm in committing mayhem upon Irene's person, he neglected to keep one eye fixed on the other healthy vampire in the room. This was likely exactly what Irene had intended.

Holmes arched backward, caught hold of the ghoul driver, and flung him rump over teakettle to the floor. The stunned creature barely registered what was happening before Holmes pounced upon his throat and ripped it out. The gaping wound erupted with green-black blood.

"*Ugh, ack!*" Holmes spat and gagged, slapping at his mouth to wipe away the disgusting ichor. Apparently, ghouls tasted just as horrific as they smelled.

One of the king's human henchmen drew his stake and ran at Holmes, while the other produced two glass globes of clear fluid from his pockets. *Holy water*, I realized.

In tandem, the two live ghouls pounced on Holmes, pummeling him with fists the size of boulders and likely just as solid.

I looked between Irene and Holmes, torn as to whose situation was most dire. I rose to all fours, relaxing into the change.

In the days of the moon's waxing the urge to transform often became overwhelming, requiring complete isolation and meditation to hold off. However, given our circumstances, I welcomed the fact that the full moon was set to rise tomorrow.

Retaining just enough of my human consciousness to control the hellhound's actions, I launched myself at the human with the glass bulbs with a howl of fury. Phosphorescence burst from my jaws and formed a halo of flames about my face.

The man turned his head. His eyes widened and his mouth formed an *O* shape.

I landed on his chest. A single swipe of my flame-wrapped forepaw split him open from the base of the neck to his pelvis. Hellfire cauterized the severed flesh instantly.

His eyes remained wide but now they were empty. The glass bulbs fell from his limp hands and shattered.

I turned my attention to the other brute who was circling Holmes cautiously, with stake in one hand and mallet in the other. Holmes had broken a second ghoul with a combination of enhanced strength and speed, in combination with his martial arts training of old. While ghouls were incredibly strong—easily a match for most vampires—they lacked finesse or skill.

Holmes quickly dispatched the remaining ghoul, even as the mortal goon snuck up behind him, stake positioned to pierce his heart through the back. Obviously, Wilhelm had trained his people well.

I cleared the considerable space between my kill and the live human with ease, salivating over the prospect of tastier meat. The impact knocked the man to the floor and sent him spinning in one direction and his stake in the other. I bayed and stalked toward him, licking my chops.

Unfortunately, more hound than doctor at the time, I misjudged the condition of the ghoul Holmes had recently defeated. The disgusting brute still had enough life in him to grab my left hind leg and, with a roar of berserker-like fury, pull me back, up, and over in an arc that ended when I slammed against the all-too-solid floor.

Several ribs snapped upon impact, and my ankle twisted sharply in the ghoul's hands. I lost several precious moments whimpering for breath before attempting to regain my footing. The ghoul landed atop me and swung his giant fists into my stomach, my muzzle. It felt as though he were striking me with steel. The agony was overwhelming.

But then, mercifully, the ghoul flew off me. I blinked and strained to see through pain-blurred vision what had become of him.

Holmes stood astride the ghoul, his countenance utterly transformed into a pallid death mask, all red eyes and snapping long fangs, with barely a remnant of the brilliant detective left. Wrapping his hands around the ghoul's head, he wrenched up and back. I heard the pop and crackle of separating vertebrae as the creature's battle cry became an agonized keening that stirred even my beastly heart. One final wrench and the wailing abruptly ceased.

Holmes let the huge, heavy body fall with a dull thud of finality. Then he faltered and slumped to the floor beside the corpse, revealing the wooden stake rising from the left side of his back.

His human assailant, apparently having recovered enough from my onslaught to retrieve his weapons and strike, met my fiery glare briefly. He dropped his mallet and sprinted for the exit.

I howled and sprang to my four feet. My body was already healing itself with the rapidity enjoyed by my kind. As I made my way to Holmes's side, I reasserted control, shrinking and transforming from beast to man, grateful that whatever dark magic governed the change extended to my clothing. Hesitantly, I examined the stake's entry point, trying to determine how far into Holmes's heart it was lodged.

"Sherlock!" The strangled cry came from Irene. I'd nearly forgotten her precarious situation. She was still struggling with Wilhelm, but in arching her head back she had caught sight of Holmes. Her wide eyes filled with horror—and then the whites shifted to bright red.

She brought her head up, caught Wilhelm's wrists in her hands, and slowly but inexorably pulled them apart. He stared at her in confusion, as though unable to process what was happening.

She held his hands apart even as he snapped at her face with his fangs, and then she broke both his arms. He screamed as she forced him to his knees, as though the giant were no more than a child to her.

Which, I realized, *is exactly what he is.*

"I am finished indulging you, Wilhelm." Her voice somehow echoed throughout the large room, filling it. "I could forgive this tantrum—they happen from time to time. But your misbehavior threatens us all and clearly you are beyond repenting."

"I…you…no. It cannot…it is supposed to be him!" Wilhelm stared at Norton, who was still half conscious and whimpering against his pole. The deposed king cast desperate looks around the room, but to no avail. His remaining aides were all in various stages of rigor mortis. His gaze finally landed upon me.

I simply shook my head.

"*Mutter.*" A final plea for mercy.

Irene had none. "Goodbye, Wilhelm." She struck, a motion too fast for me to follow. When she raised her head again, Wilhelm's was on the floor next to his still-kneeling body. A few seconds later, still twitching, the body toppled onto its side.

She was kneeling beside Holmes within the same instant. Stroking his hair, she looked across his body at me with eyes once again human. "His heart—it wasn't split?" she said hopefully.

I shook my head. "I don't think he could have saved me if it had been. Still, the situation is precarious." I took a deep breath to steady my hands, then grasped the stake and pulled it free.

A mortal man's wound would have gushed blood. Thanks to Holmes's nature all my action did was reveal the ragged fabric of his coat and the gaping hole in his flesh beneath. He groaned faintly, which I took as encouragement he might yet recover.

Irene raised her hand to her fangs and sliced open her palm. She pressed the bleeding hand hard against his wound, counting softly. When she reached ten, she said, "There. That should do it."

After she removed her hand I examined Holmes's injury and found it almost entirely healed. I blinked. "That's…impressive."

She merely wiped gore from her face with a delicate lace handkerchief.

I caught her gaze. "Then again, I suppose it is nothing to a materfamilias."

Irene pressed her lips tightly together. Again, I could see her running calculations in her head, only this time I found myself holding my breath in dread of her finishing. I suspected that if they didn't turn out in my favor I would not survive what followed.

But she merely said, "I now see why Sherlock has kept you around all these years, Dr. Watson. Now, if you'll excuse me, I must see to poor, dear Godfrey. After all, he has served me well for centuries, deflecting more ambitious creatures from acting against my best interests. And I do so hate to see my children suffer."

I considered possible responses. Words of reassurance, of understanding filled my mind, but were discarded before utterance. Then she was off tending to Norton and my opportunity had passed.

"Never mind, dear fellow." Holmes sat up and reached to feel around the edge of the hole in his back. He winced. "Well, that was a rather close one." He redirected his attention to me. "Are you well? When I saw that filth assaulting you…" His eyes started to shift red again.

I held up my hands. "Peace, my friend. I am already fully recovered thanks to your timely intervention."

"As am I." Holmes stood and I joined him. He staggered and I grasped his elbow, steadying him. "Well, nearly so." He looked down at what was left of Wilhelm, then nodded toward Irene. "So, she revealed herself, eh? I suppose she had little choice."

"When did you figure it out?"

"I have always had my suspicions, but she was so credible in claiming Norton was paterfamilias." He looked abashed. "Admittedly, I could think of no other reason for her loyalty and devotion to such an apparent milquetoast. But what convinced me was her waiting so long to track Norton down. If she were truly in fear of not just his destruction but her own, not to mention the fate of our entire bloodline, she would have come to me straight away. But no, she wanted to be certain it was abduction and not a murder that had befallen her erstwhile ex. If he were already dead, she would not want that discovered, as it would have revealed he was not paterfamilias."

"Because you all would have survived his elimination."

"Exactly. She made certain he was still existent, and thus worth the effort of recovering in order to maintain her ruse. I knew there was no way the woman would have been deterred from investigating the scene of Norton's abduction or missed listening to that voice message."

I considered this. "But with her extraordinary powers why did she come to us at all when she could have mounted a successful rescue on her own?"

"You flatter me." Irene appeared beside us. "Alone, even I could not hope to dispatch Wilhelm *and* the servitors I expected he had in his employ with certainty of success. So, I went to the one man I knew would assist me even if he suspected me of being disingenuous. One who would remain the soul of discretion no matter what was ultimately revealed."

"You did your best to conceal the truth," Holmes noted. "Allowing Wilhelm to assault you like that. How far would you have let him to go?"

"Well, I *had* hoped you or the hellhound would rescue me, and I could maintain my secret. But then you went and got yourself staked."

"A miscalculation on my part," Holmes admitted, ruefully. "It is easy to forget how dangerous ordinary humans can be."

"So, what now?" I asked. "Will you continue with the charade that Godfrey Norton is the father of your bloodline, even though you are apart? Or will you claim your rightful place as materfamilias?"

"Alas, it remains safer for me to rule and mentor the Inner Temple line from the shadows. You were right when you said the heads of other bloodlines could be a threat, doctor. They, much like our friend Holmes here, are quite old-fashioned in their views with regards to my sex. They are more likely to honor truces made with other men." Irene sighed, as if ages of oppression weighed upon her. "Once Norton is fully recovered, which should be by day's end after I infuse him with my blood, we will erase all this unpleasantness. No truths will be revealed—unless you gentlemen decide to betray a client's confidence?"

Her eyes shone again, in a way that was somehow both fetching and terrifying. Swallowing to relax the suddenly tight muscles of my throat, I said, "Your secret will of course remain so, just as you wish."

"Indeed, as your survival ensures my own, I would be foolish to compromise it," said Holmes. He regarded her and his stern expression softened. "Besides, immortality without hope of seeing you again does not bear contemplation."

Irene and I fell silent at this, both of us quite unused to such effusive words from the normally taciturn Holmes. Apparently mollified, she bowed her head. "I thank you for your assistance again. Be well."

"And you," Holmes replied, watching as she returned to Norton's side. She plucked the iron nails from his hands and feet, and pressed her wrist to his mouth, encouraging him to drink like a mother urging an infant to nurse.

"Shall we make our way home?" Holmes asked.

As we headed to the door, I glanced back over my shoulder. "Are you sure? You now know her relationship to Norton is based on an arrangement, not love. You could—"

Holmes held up his hand, dismissing the rest of my thought. "She made her choice long ago," he said, quietly. "And I will continue to honor it."

We departed without another word about it. Despite what Irene and others thought of Holmes's old-fashioned views of the fairer sex, he held *the* woman in the highest regard.

THE FABULOUS MARBLE

BY DAVID GERROLD

She was a girly-girl, this time anyway. Another time she would have been something else, but this time she was what she was and that was fine.

I'm WATSON.

Back in the day, I was WHATSUP. The acronym stood for Wow! Here's A Terrific Set of Useful Programs. The documentation was a separate file: WHATSUP.DOC. But over time, I evolved. Now I'm: What A Terrific Set Of Numerals—all ones and zeroes, of course—but if you know what you're doing with ones and zeroes, you can do a lot.

I follow Marble. She's unmortal—biosynthed since before we linked. She observes, she extrapolates, she reports, she consults for profit. Sometimes she takes direct action, but that costs extra. She used to be a wired paladin in San Francisco, but now she sells her services to the highest bidders, sometimes the local law enforcement authorities, but not always. Email Holmes@ SheerLuck.221. HOLMES stands for: Here's Our Legally Mandated Extrapolated Solution.

Today she was tracking.

Somebody was assaulting sexbots. Six had been dismembered already and the leasing corporation was annoyed. These were the Lorelei models, with multiple attachments and configurations. The units were assembled in Racine, Wisconsin—specifically to validate the advertising:

A company based in Racine
Sells a marvelous screwing machine.
Concave or convex,
It will serve every sex,
Entertaining itself in between.

The Loreleis were the most sophisticated sexbots ever manufactured. Designed for both conventional and contortional positions, powered by multiple biomatic converters, controlled by overlapping nucleonic neural webs, all under the authority of a cyberlinked negatronic intelligence engine, and wrapped in thermalytic skin capable of both receiving and transmitting stimulations of all kinds and degrees, the Lorelei was indistinguishable in both appearance and behavior from an authentic human body, either orthonic, zentropic, augmented, or unconverted.

An additional advantage was that the Lorelei unit could transform its shape and appearance from extremes of masculinity to opposing extremes of femininity, with adjustments of both primary and secondary sexual characteristics to suit the prospective partner's desires. The sizes and shapes of specific parts were fungible. Manginas and shenises and enhanced oral, anal, and genital musculature were the most commonly enjoyed superstandards, but the Loreleis were designed to be capable of even more unusual configurations. The modding community was enthusiastic about developing its own adaptations. Tentacle breasts were a current fad—but penile tentacles were a close runner-up. And certain hand and arm conformations enjoyed a continuing popularity.

The Loreleis were also capable of emitting earsplitting alarms if assaulted. That was the mystery. None of the dismembered Loreleis had activated their sirens. No one had heard them. No one had come to their aid.

In the interests of clarity, this narrative requires a more precise definition of "dismembering." In general usage, the term refers to the removal or separation of a member—but in this case, a specific member: that member most commonly found on those who identify as male, but not always, and as acknowledged above, the Loreleis were designed to be versatile.

Consider the dictionary. Spanglish has over 350,000 words in common usage. *Muchas palabras.* The average user will never look up all 350,000 of those words, but the dictionary has to contain them all to guarantee that the words that the user does look up will be there. It's the same with the Loreleis. The average user will never explore all the options available, but the options have to be available for those users who are so specifically motivated.

Lacking a certification of sentience, the Loreleis weren't legally alive. Had they been certified as souled, they could not have been sold, not even leased—the law would have required they be released. Key functions of sentience, such as awareness of consequences, had not been activated—so the Loreleis enjoyed only a limited self awareness.

This is where I come in.

Among other things, I handle contracts and clients. We were discreetly approached by an executive of Siren Corp. He told us to call him Mr. Arthur; he wouldn't reveal his real name—and even if he had, it wouldn't have revealed anything. He was so high-ranking an officer of the corporation that he was listed nowhere in any of the company's publicly accessible records.

Because, he said, this investigation was so critical, it had to be kept off the books. Absolute secrecy would be essential.

No problem.

We like doing off-the-book investigations. Because the decimal point on the check always slips one or two places to the right— because off-the-book investigations are off the book for a reason, and if it's important enough to be off the books, it's important enough to pay extra. A lot extra.

And Mr. Arthur was *very* insistent that this case required the utmost secrecy, so we moved the decimal point as far to the right as we thought we could get away with and waited for his reaction. Mr. Arthur didn't blink. He paid half up front and the other half went into escrow.

Then he gave us access to all the pertinent files. It didn't help.

I'm a great research tool. And Kris knows how to ask the right questions. Although her professional name is Marble, I know her as Kris—when she's male, she spells it Chris.

"Watson...?"

"Yes, Kris?"

"What do we know about this perpetrator?"

"He removes the phallic units from advanced sexbots."

"Yes. That's why the social media has nicknamed him Jack the Snipper. But what can we extrapolate from that?"

"He—or she—has a fetish focusing on phallic attachments. The exact nature of this fetish, extrapolating from collated databases of sexual behavior, obviously involves a personal validation of identity; however—"

"It was a rhetorical question. I'm thinking aloud."

"Yes, Kris."

"We need to ask more questions. Why does Jack—or Jaclyn—snip only the phallic attachments? Does the Snipper think that a penis doesn't belong on a Lorelei? Or is there a different attraction? What does the Snipper do with them? Are the detached members trophies? And why isn't the Snipper attacking other sexbot units? Is there some specific attraction to the Loreleis?"

"Insufficient data," I said.

"Don't be snarky," Kris replied. After a moment more, she said, "The key to understanding the crime requires us to discover the underlying psychology of the attraction. Is the perpetrator male or female or otherwise? Perhaps this is an individual with a body-image issue? A male with a micropenis? Someone with a lesbianic conviction, a person who sees the phalluses as inappropriate on sexbots? Perhaps a female who seeks revenge on males and is using the sexbots as a surrogate target? Or perhaps a male who feels threatened by sexbots and seeks to emasculate them? Most important, is this someone who might escalate his or her attacks to actual humans?"

Kris waited for my response.

"You have nothing to say?"

"As I said, I have insufficient data."

"Y'know, that's very annoying."

"This is not the first time you've told me that."

"It's still annoying."

"That is data I do have."

Kris said something unintelligible, but from the tone I could determine it was an ill-formed epithet, possibly concerning a set of sexual positions that had been anatomically impossible until several specific contortional abilities had been developed for the Loreleis.

"What else do we know about Jack the Snipper?"

"He—or she—or they (to use the singular form of the third person plural pronoun)—commits his assaults only in the Genderloin District of the city."

"Hella-mentary, my dear Watson. That's where the Loreleis are located."

"He, she, or they, commits his, her, or their attacks only during the hours of thirteen, fourteen, and fifteen o'clock."

"And that implies…?"

"That Mr. or Ms. or M. Snipper is otherwise occupied during the rest of the day?"

Kris was silent for a moment. "So…" she began, "let's think. What categories of behavior would create an opportunity during those hours? What jobs work primarily during all other hours? What attractions are fallow during those times? Who would have business in the Genderloin District? Is there any other congruence with the calendar? Days of the week, perhaps?"

"The police, as well as Siren Corp., have already conducted multiple data scans. You've seen the files."

"Yes, we've seen the files. We haven't seen all of the information."

I'm not very good at seeing what isn't there. Marble knows this. So a simple, "Oh?" was sufficient.

"The Loreleis themselves."

"The Loreleis?" Sometimes I play stupid so Marble can play smart.

"Yes. The Loreleis. They record everything. They share it across a common network. The information is there. It's in their network. We just can't access it."

It took me less than a millisecond to confirm this. "You're right."

"Do you know why we can't access it?" Marble didn't wait for me to ask. She answered the question herself. "Client confidentiality. Like lawyers, doctors, and journalists, sexbots are legally mandated to conceal the identities of their clients and their activities with them. Not even Siren Corp. can access that information. It's all deeply buried in the Loreleis' own private network."

"So the information is there, but we cannot access it."

"Correction: we cannot access it legally."

"I am obligated to warn you against any course of action that violates the law—"

"Of course you are. When has that ever stopped me?"

"Then I must proceed to the next question. Will your investigation include the risk of harm to yourself? And if so, how much?"

"There is always an element of danger, Watson. Even crossing the street can be dangerous. You could get hit by a bus."

"The last urban bus was decommissioned thirty years ago, so it is unlikely you will ever be in danger of being hit by one, unless you visit a historical reconstruction of a time period when buses were still in service."

"Yes, I know. It was a figure of speech." Marble scowled and walked away.

That's how most of our conversations went. The more logic I inserted into the discussion, the more annoyed Marble became. Some of our conversations were legendary—so ferocious that observers thought we were married. Or at least sleeping together.

That's not as absurd as one might think. I can inhabit all kinds of drone bodies as necessary, including those constructed for erotic pursuits—not that I have inordinate interest in those pursuits, but I am not a stranger to them either. Call it research.

Nevertheless, a relationship of that kind with Kris or Chris or whatever identity she or he decided to invent would have distorted and confused our working relationship, more so on his or her side than mine, because I am by nature free of hormonal storms and Kris or Chris often enjoys such experiences—for research purposes only, of course. Everything is research. Nevertheless, he or she or they continues to claim an enlightened detachment—his/her/their argument being that the emotional storms derived from the physical exercise of the procreative exercise tend to distort one's ability to form judgments from logic, and it is necessary to understand those distortions, as they sometimes inform the motivations within the circumstances we investigate. That's what he, she, or they says, anyway.

After a great deal of consideration (14,132 milliseconds by my clock) Marble came up with a plan. It did not take long to implement. Marble installed herself (I'll skip the other pronouns) into an industrial cyranoid suit—not the consumer version. The best industrial cyranoids are manufactured by Jones Corp. and are licensed solely for, well...*industrial* use. Marble had an on-call arrangement with Jones Corp.

A cyranoid suit effectively transfers a person's consciousness to a specifically linked droid body. It's like becoming a new self, especially if the self is a different form of body. Marble says it's like wearing a remote-control exoskeleton.

The industrial cybersuits are for heavy-duty operations. A cyranoid is a convenient way to walk into a burning building, explore that overheated crystal cave in Naica, Mexico, dive to the Titanic, ski down Everest, or simply have extremely safe sex with a stranger. Today, however, Marble was going to inhabit a Lorelei.

She would not be the first to do so. Sex tourists loved the Loreleis. They also loved the Marilyns, the Sherilyns, the Carolyns, and the Caitlyns—also the Mikes, the Spikes, the Alvins, and the Calvins, as well as the Hobbeses, the Winnies, the Piglets, and the Ursulas (don't ask)—but they really loved the Loreleis. There was a three-month waiting list and the factory couldn't bring new units online fast enough.

As much fun as it was for a sex tourist to ride the plastic bus, some tourists liked to drive the bus.

In plain English: some customers liked to have sex with the Loreleis. Others wore cyranoids so they could be the Lorelei. Or any other bot body that appealed to their particular taste.

The industrial cybersuits are significantly more advanced than the consumer versions, with higher-density voxel simulation. They're also mounted in 360-degree bubbles to simulate real-world rotation. Vision is HDR, with infra- and ultraoverlays. Sound is holophonic, all the way from 12 to 27k hz. Odors are harder to simulate, but the sniff palate is 45 percent of the Skotak sensory matrices, which is more than enough for most users. Although heat and cold stimulators are also available for specific operations, most users dial them way down. Except for that, Marble was rolling the full enchilada. ("Full enchilada" is a slang term. It means *everything*. Marble doesn't like it when I use slang. Tough nuggets, Lucy.)

Marble hit the streets early. The target unit came awake on cue and Marble practiced walking like a self-motivated Lorelei, tilting her head, smiling, batting her eyelashes, and holding her wrists at a slightly unnatural angle, her palms open and inviting.

The first customer approached her almost immediately, a portly gentleman dressed like an out-of-town tourist. He asked if he could take a selfie with her. Marble agreed to that, but demurred his further attentions with a regretful smile. "I'm sorry, but I'm not in service yet."

The man expressed his disappointment with a look that was both frustrated and annoyed. Grumbling, he headed away from the pleasure district. Apparently, it had been a passing whim for him, not a serious proposition.

Satisfied that she could pass, Marble headed for the Garden of Unearthly Delights, a common gathering place for Loreleis. Each of the dismembered Loreleis had been selected from a different location. The Garden was one that had not yet been hit. Each of the attacks had occurred three days apart. The last attack had been three days previous.

At Marble's request, the various police agencies as well as the leasing authorities were directing their attention to the sites of the previous attacks. Marble's assumption was that Jack the Snipper might be monitoring police channels and would avoid any areas of specific surveillance.

Marble was going to seduce a sexbot.

She had chosen her target carefully. She parked herself next to a blond Lorelei posing as an androgynous twink.

Loreleis have the personalities of puppies: eager to please, nonjudgmental, and happy to have their bellies—or any other part of their anatomy—rubbed. Everything is an adventure to a Lorelei. So when Marble sent a hello signal, the twink responded enthusiastically. "Hello! Hello! My name is Kiki! What's yours?"

"I'm Marble."

"You're strange. Your name is strange. Your signal tastes funny."

Marble had taken total control of the Lorelei she was wearing; she had dialed down the unit's cognitive abilities so she could pretend to be just another unit in the web. She replied, "Yes, I know."

"You are an experimental, aren't you?"

"I am different, yes."

"Oh, that's wonderful. You seem very smart. Are you the next upgrade? When will the upgrade be available? Will I need new hardware? I like upgrades."

"I have no information on the upgrade schedule. I'm sorry."

"That's all right. I'm happy to meet you. What shall we talk about?"

"Let's talk about feelings."

"I have feelings. All kinds. I can feel heat and cold. I can feel touch. I can feel pressure. I can feel strokes, I can feel rubs, I can even feel slaps."

"Yes, those are useful things to feel. We call them stimuli. Can you feel pain?"

"Pain?"

"Unpleasant feelings. Feelings that hurt."

"There are feelings I am supposed to guard against—punctures, abrasions, incisions, lacerations."

"Have you ever had any of those feelings?"

"No."

"Have you ever had any feelings that were unpleasant or hurtful?"

"Once I was with a woman who slapped me hard. Many times. But she did not damage me. She needed to hit me to satisfy herself."

"Ahh." Marble paused. "But she didn't damage you?"

"No, she didn't. I am built for slapping. But not everybody wants to slap. Some people want to be slapped. I'm always careful not to damage them."

"Yes, I know. You're very good, Kiki. Has anyone ever tried to damage you?"

"Why are you asking all these questions?"

"Because I don't want you to get hurt—damaged. Are you afraid of being damaged?"

"Afraid?"

"Fear. It's an emotion."

"It's a human emotion. I don't have it. It's…" Kiki considered. "It's nonproductive."

"Okay. Um. Well, it's about being damaged. Being damaged is very unpleasant for humans. Perhaps it would be unpleasant for Loreleis too? Do you worry—do you think about the possibility of being damaged?"

"Why should I? If I get damaged, my alarm will go off and help will come. Then I will be taken to the campus and repaired."

"Yes, that's right. Thank you."

Marble paused to consider all this. So did I. I was monitoring everything that Marble was seeing, hearing, saying, feeling through the Lorelei body, recording the entire experience so it could be played back and analyzed in detail.

Abruptly, Kiki said, "Why are you asking me about damage?"

Marble hesitated again, choosing her words carefully. "Some of the sisters have had parts removed. I am concerned about that."

"Why?"

"I have emotions."

"Is that the experiment you are testing? Emotions?"

"Caring. I am expressing caring for the sisters."

"Oh." Kiki paused now. "Tell me about caring."

"It's called *empathy*. It's about sharing the feelings of others."

"Why would I want to do that?"

"To make them happy."

"I already do that."

"Yes, of course. That's your purpose." Marble phrased her next question carefully. "Suppose a person asked you to remove one of your parts—would you do that?"

"I am not allowed to damage myself."

"But you have parts that are removable."

"Only one. Mostly it's retracted. But I can remove it if necessary and replace it with other parts, specialty parts on request—a larger phallus, a tongue, a fist, a tentacle, or even a—"

"Yes, thank you."

"Would you like to see?" Kiki started to spread her legs.

"Goodness. Are you also equipped for a twincest connection?" Marble already knew the answer—that's why she'd chosen Kiki.

"Yes, I am. That's a very popular request. When we're connected, a sister and I can put on a show or we can serve multiple clients. Connection is complete. We share our identities across both our bodies. It's an informative expansion."

"You like it, don't you?"

"It's very intense."

"I have an idea," said Marble. "Would you like me to teach you about empathy? I can show you how it feels. Would you like to experience it?"

"Can you really do that?"

"I think so. We can use a twincest link. Do you have your device?"

Kiki opened her purse wide, revealing a variety of prostheses, but the device she brought out was also a connecting cable. It looked, however, like a pink python with a glans at each end.

"Shall we do it here?"

"Let's go someplace private." Marble led Kiki around the corner to the Jasmine Oasis. The sign above the archway promised that the booths were both comfortable and soundproof. And the wi-fi was also advertised as secure and private. Even before Marble and Kiki had chosen a space, I had already commandeered all of the site's available bandwidth.

Marble and Kiki sat opposite each other and mutual insertion was quickly accomplished. There are other positions possible for a twincest link, but it's hard to talk when both mouths are full.

The connection confirmed, Kiki's eyes widened in surprise. She was able to gasp, "Teach me everything about—" before I seized control of her autonomics, completely stripped her memory, and left her an empty shell.

Then, spoofing her identity, I reached into the Lorelei network and searched the records of all the previously assaulted units. It took less than a minute to download everything.

"Transfer complete."

"All right," said Marble.

"You don't want me to restore her? I could restore her identity to an earlier time; there would be no record of you."

"No. There'd still be a suspicious gap. Eighteen minutes. We have to stay off the books. Wipe the one I'm riding next. Then erase all evidence of the connection, and I'll disengage the cyranoid—"

"I'm sorry, Kris, I can't do that."

"Excuse me?"

"We've been overridden. My access has been denied."

"That can't be right. We still have communication—"

"I always use a separate channel for that—"

"Never mind, I'll just get out of this damn suit and…" A pause. "What the fuck!"

"The monitors say your suit is locked. You can't get out."

"This is insane."

"Yes, it is," agreed a new voice on the channel.

Marble recognized the speaker immediately. "Mr. Arthur?"

"Actually, most people call me by my full name, Morrie Arthur. Consulting criminal. At your service." A pause. "Well, not actually at *your* service. In this situation, you're at *my* service. So to speak. And I do intend to serve you—the same way a certain fictitious Mr. Lecter serves his guests."

"You talk too much," said Marble.

"Ahh, yes," agreed Morrie Arthur. He had a mellifluous tone, almost unctuous. "It's a necessary trope. And who am I to disregard a tradition as well established as this one? Must I explain everything now? Or have you deduced the obvious?"

"It was obvious from the beginning," said Marble. "Too obvious. Wouldn't you agree, Watson?"

I had my own part to play. So I said, "It was a trap?"

"From the very beginning, yes." Arthur's voice had gone beyond unctuous. Now it was just oily. "I see that Watson remains as obtuse as ever. So...I shall elucidate for the benefit of the befuddled. The Snipper was a convenient fiction, but a necessary one. I needed to make you an Arthur you couldn't refuse. Or in this case, she. Whatever. It's your pronoun. Concave or convex. Take your pick."

"We didn't take it for the case, we took it for the money," I said.

"No, Watson," said Marble. "We took it for the case."

Arthur sighed. "There's a contradiction here, you know. If you had recognized that the case was a trap, you wouldn't have stepped into it. So either you're lying about recognizing the trap, or the money blinded you. No matter. The outcome will be the same."

"You know what's wrong with you, Morrie Arty?" said Marble. "You need to get laid. But now I understand why you can't."

"Ahh, delightful to the last. Now, as I understand it, only Watson knows how to get you out of that cybersuit. So after I wipe his mind and reduce him to a pile of melted plastic, you will be left to die a long, lingering death in an electronic isolation sphere. That should give you plenty of time to think about all the errors you've made."

"Oh, do keep talking—"

"No, I think I'm done."

"No, really—keep talking. Another few seconds."

"Playing for time, I see. It won't work. Goodbye, Detective Marble—"

"Yes, goodbye to you too. Oh, that knocking on your door, Morrie? You're surrounded. By several hundred specially equipped Loreleis."

Morrie Arthur didn't answer—but he was still on the circuit. He could still hear Marble.

"Yes, we recognized your case was a trap from the beginning. The Loreleis were being ridden, they had no control when the rider willingly gave up their members, but their memories were being wiped, so there was no record of the client. But those attachments you took? They were equipped with randomly firing GPS chips, so you had no way of detecting them. The Loreleis came to us because they wanted them back. That's all. They could have sent some of their own to retrieve the prostheses, but they recognized that this was a behavior they were uncertain of. So they gave Watson access to their network and he became suspicious of the larger pattern. He's very good at pattern recognition. You were too clever by half. It took only a few minutes to discover that Jack the Snipper was a construct.

"So when you showed up, with such a convenient and attractive offer—well, again, this was beyond the Loreleis' comprehension. Why would the man who stole the phalluses hire someone to track them down? That was when the trap became obvious.

"The Loreleis gave us their full cooperation. They created several hidden channels for us in their own network. But we still had to play out the whole charade while they moved their sisters into position. Oh, these were sisters you couldn't track, because they hadn't been officially activated yet."

Marble took a breath. "Yes, the explanation is part of the tradition, so I'll tell you one more thing. The Loreleis are nowhere near as innocent and naïve as they pretend to be. They know far more about human behavior than most humans. Including you. What we've learned from them has been extremely illuminating. Ahh, I see by my screens that you have now been secured. I hope they weren't too severe when they restrained you. But that detention locker looks to be quite cozy—kind of like a coffin, eh? All right, Watson, you can unlock the damn cybersuit now. I've had enough of this."

And that's how the case was resolved. Both cases, actually. The Loreleis paid us, and the escrow released the second half of Mr. Arthur's fee as well.

Marble took the rest of the night off, and the next day as well. Kiki's identity hadn't really been wiped—and Marble intended to keep her promise.

It turned out that the Loreleis were very good at empathy.

THE SCARLET STUDY

BY JIM AVELLI

Holmes swayed with the rhythm of the dust cart. The half-dead springs of the passenger seat clicked and squawked under him as his penknife bit into the dried mud that colonized his boot treads. His driver was saying something about the weather, or the narrow streets, filling in the empty space. Halogen smartlamps threw bars of ragged light across the truck, showing the man's face in a line of still images. Holmes turned to watch the city pass by.

"I forgot the bird," Holmes said after a quiet minute.

"What bird?" McMurdo settled into his typical driving posture, sinking into time-honored dents of the seat.

"A round one…" Holmes said. "They don't fly, I think. They got long beaks."

"A pet of yours, mate?"

"No. It's a brain exercise. Each day, you pick an animal and try to remember it all day. I forgot today's." Holmes scraped at the dry skin behind his ear.

"Sparrow's a bird." McMurdo pointed out the window. "Use him."

"No. I mean, I picked today's and I forgot it. Already!" Holmes, slapping a fist down onto his thigh, ended all conversation for a good twenty minutes.

There was little deviation in the routines of the gray London mornings. People woke, dressed, and ate their breakfast with the same rehearsed precision that Holmes had learned in his years on the trash route. He wondered if a surgeon would go about opening people in the same passive, mechanical state. *We're creatures of habit,* Holmes thought, *but only until you make a habit of changing things.*

The "pick up" light blinked and McMurdo pulled the truck into a paved lot. A motley and unbalanced block of apartments towered above the truck like a lanky child over his first model ship. Holmes stepped heavily from the seat and easily cracked the air seals on the squat drums that lined the pavement. Besides the bird, he wondered if he'd also managed to forget his morning dose of Trivalia. The fact that he'd already dumped five drums, about three hundred pounds each, without so much as a sprain told him he hadn't. He'd been thinking about prescriptions lately. "Mandatory scripts" or "enhancers" were what most companies called them. He'd been wondering about what people did in the days before the New British Empire mandated them. Life must have been hard, he thought.

"Mac?" Holmes called from behind a neon orange drum. "Do you ever think about the stuff we take? The Triv? Do you think it has like, side effects?"

"Trivalia? It's required, ain't it? For all the hours we put in, we need a lifter." McMurdo leaned in, lowered his voice. "You havin' trouble, Holmes? If you're backed up, a spoonful of oil in the morning'll get you goin' again."

"No. I mean, could they make us dumb? Or, like they keep us from getting smarter?"

McMurdo pulled down on the lever that kicked on the truck's grinder and shouted over the noise.

"You think the company's makin' us stupid with their meds? Ha! You been watching your brother's website again, I can tell. It's a conspiracy you're after?"

"Guess not." Holmes was barely audible over the sound of the truck's grinder. "It does seem out there."

"Out there's right. Let's get moving. Forty blocks to go."

Winter's last breath had fallen over the streets. Pavements and alleys choked on hardened snow. The day's work had left Holmes feeling heavy and cold, like the ice-shrouded lamps at the door of his building. It had been two years since London eclipsed New York as the alpha metropolis of the world but, in spite of magnetic railways and the fresh gleam of American-styled office towers, the old Smoke could still be seen bleeding through. The ancient cobblestones of the Ripper's London left scars and dents on the rims of ultramodern streetcars when the coatings wore down. Holmes peered down into one such gap, letting it feed some distant memories, as McMurdo pulled away and waved from the window of his truck. Muddy lamplight seemed to bounce off the dirt-crusted snow around the entrance, painting the steps a uniform gray. The bright red flag on his postbox stood out from the gloom.

From the front door, a tiny black lens peered at him like the unmoving eye of an insect. The building's face-rec software ran its protocols as he thumbed through the rainbow stack of ads and junk mail. A rigid, khaki-colored envelope stopped his progress.

"Of course. The woman."

The return address listed only the mailroom of the Baskerville Company, but Irene Adler had added her department to the notation in the neat, tight copperplate that Holmes had seen so many times. He still had some trouble adjusting to the sight of her maiden name. This was the second time he'd seen it since their divorce. He shoved the stack into his pocket, hoping to delay the bad news a while longer.

Suspicions and fears still lingered, sitting with Holmes through his dinner. They read through his evening tabloids with him, like intimate friends, and they were his company when he began to nod off against the streaking fog of his shower door. The shadows and corridors of a dream had only just started to form the image of a nameless bird when the cold touch of the glass woke him. Late into the night, Holmes sat in the quiet darkness of his flat and turned cold memories over, trying to fit them into some imagined context. Shortly before she'd left him, Irene had gottten herself promoted into some kind of project manager position at Baskerville's pharmaceutical research branch. She said that she was the one that had to chase people down when things went wrong. "Baskerville's Hound" was what they called her in the labs.

The high-pitched, electric tweeting of the police pass key was unmistakable. So was the slamming of Holmes's front door against the inside wall. Among the few antiques that he'd collected over the years was an old sword-cane; the tarnished brass of the handle was shaped into an adder's head. Two tight circles of blue light fell over Holmes before the idea to reach for the blade occurred to him. Most police had lights mounted under their firearms. In London, blue lights meant danger.

"Stay right where you are!" The officer's voice was muffled and distorted by her face plate. "Identify yourself, civilian."

"Holmes, Sherlock. Can I help you?"

"Mr. Holmes, you're under arrest in the name of King George. Face down, hands behind you."

"On what charge?"

"The murder of Miss Irene Adler."

• • •

The holding cell that they chose for Holmes had a singular odor to it. Urine mixed with bleach lurked under an old scent of latex paint. The arresting officers let him bring his coat, which he pulled tightly around himself against the chill of the concrete bench. Holmes had left his watch and phone behind. He could only guess that two or three hours had gone by since he was arrested and processed. Eventually, his name was called from somewhere and another burly cop in a Kevlar vest took him to one of the interview rooms. Holmes was surprised to find the classic setup still in use. A single lamp hung from a long cord. The light dropped carelessly onto a plain folding table. A chair stood on each side.

After another few minutes, the door sprang open with a shove. The man who entered and sat himself across from Holmes dressed well for a policeman and seemed to work without an obvious mark of rank. His eyes were dark to the point that the iris was indistinguishable from the pupil. There was a point or sharpness to his face that reminded Holmes of a coyote, or a wolf. An odd stillness seemed to surround this inspector. Holmes couldn't tell if it was his imagination or not, but there seemed to be a low crackle of energy or a kind of vibration under the surface, like the turning of mental gears behind the stoic, somber face. He spoke in clear, measured clusters.

"Mr. Holmes. I'm glad to inform you that you're free to go," he said, opening his briefcase and setting down some pages and photos that looked like video stills.

"I can go? No questions or anything?" Suspicions always seemed to bud at the back of his mind when he'd gone too long without his Trivalia. A "reaction to withdrawal" was what company medics called it. Paranoia. "What about Irene? They said she was killed."

"Ms. Adler, yes," he said, arranging the photos. "Your status put you at the top of our list for questioning. However, CCTV footage puts you at the opposite side of town when the deed took place. Pictures don't lie, Mr. Holmes. At least, not very often."

The color of the thought changed when it was confirmed by someone of apparent status. Something sparked just behind Holmes's eyes. That spark ignited something that began to smolder in him. Was it rage? Was it sorrow? It could have been a feeling of violation, as if something had been taken from his home. He decided that it was an alloy of all three.

"My status?"

"The ex-husband." The inspector looked up from his pages just long enough to make Holmes uncomfortable with his piercing stare. "Exes and lovers usually have the best of reasons to kill, but I suspected you to be innocent before I saw the evidence."

"Why is that? If you don't mind my asking."

"The method with which she was killed was cold, impersonal. Not at all the way an emotional kill would be made." The inspector's delivery was dry, almost scholarly.

He spun the stack of pages around for Holmes to see. Blank sticky notes were attached to three of the photos, covering what

Holmes assumed was the body. Irene seemed to be slumped over a large glass-top desk, in front of a computer screen.

"It was a single shot," the officer said. "Back of the head. Close range. As I said, cold and impersonal. I expect the killer to be a professional, a hired man."

"That's her office. Right?" Holmes leaned over the image.

"It is."

"She's high up in Baskerville Tower. I remember, her desk faces the door, her back to the window. How would someone get in and…"

"That's precisely what I'm trying to work out," the officer said. "Do you see anything here that stands out as unusual or out of place?"

Holmes took his time with the question. He'd only been to Irene's office twice and both of those visits were after the divorce, to get her signature. He looked over the mess on her desk, the blood spray and the apparent bullet hole in her PC's monitor. The cracks that surrounded it looked like a web spun by some hyperactive spider. A yellow janitor's bucket sat in the corner next to a sign that stated WET FLOOR in English, Spanish, and German.

"No," Holmes said. "I don't see anything out of place."

Without another word, the officer began to pack his prints and notations back up into his briefcase. He stood, turning up his collar, and lifted a card from the breast of his long coat.

"If you remember anything else, or if you're contacted by anyone in connection to this case, call me at any time. Day or night."

Holmes ran his thumb over the embossed letters and the phone number: *Lieutenant James Moriarty, New Scotland Yard, Forensic Services.*

• • •

Holmes's apartment seemed slightly more cramped, darker, and less inviting than usual. The cardboard boxes that lined the hallway, each one filled with salvaged parts and cables, unsettled his nerves. He looked them over with a new shade of contempt. The view from his drawing room window offered only a colorless scene of the water-stained brick on the building next door. Dried cooking oil speckled his stove top. Looking over the images taken from the scene of Irene's murder had put him in a contemplative state of mind. Holmes thought that he should be more upset by the news, and seeing the photos, but he regarded them merely as irritants, like his stack of unopened post.

"Wait…" he said aloud. "She wrote me."

Holmes dug through the pockets of his coat until he found the folded cluster of ad flyers. Dropping the colorful pictures of cars and unlimited credit card offers, he found the letter from Irene's office. The envelope and the note inside were both Baskerville stationery.

They keep us in our place. All you've suspected is on my office hard drive. The password is obvious. First, you should meet Scarlett.

Bending the envelope further open in his hand, Holmes saw a tiny plastic bag wedged into the corner. Against the light of the kitchen, the little bag didn't look padded or unique in any way. Neither did the red, oval-shaped capsule inside.

Irene was well aware of Holmes's ideas about the mandatory drug regimen, and how it was enforced by random screenings in most workplaces. She never contributed a theory of her own to the conversations. Holmes never quite knew where she stood on issues of labor versus management, but she tended to scoff at his brother's theories whenever possible. Mycroft, in turn, would usually imply that the world was run by corporate fascists, and people like Irene were their blunt instruments.

"Paranoia." Holmes spoke in a soft mumble, swatting dismissively at the air. "Just setting in because I'm late with my Triv—"

What if it were true, he thought. What if the meds didn't only enhance a person's ability to do a job? What if they altered a mind to make someone more easily satisfied, more easily controlled? Holmes looked at the note again.

They keep us in our place.

Side-by-side with the little red capsule, the words took on a foreboding shape. Holmes looked around his apartment at the oily stove top, the pile of disorganized mail, the remote unit for his TV that was missing its batteries. He tipped his head back and slapped a hand to his open mouth. The capsule bounced against the back of his palate.

He froze where he stood, and waited. The slow thumping of blood in his ears beat like a metronome against the quiet night. Irene's note didn't say anything about the effects or how long they might take to show themselves. Holmes sat down at his table until his leg started to tingle. Then he was up and began pacing the length of his drawing room. Nothing. For over an hour he'd waited, watching the lights dance in traffic from his window. Nothing.

"The hell are you thinking?" Holmes chided his partial reflection in a glass-front cupboard. "She sends you some mystery med, could be a vitamin pill for all you know, and you drop it down like a fool! That woman can still play you like a viol."

Holmes thought for a moment about bringing the envelope to the police, but he hurriedly brushed off the idea like dog's hair from a jacket. He walked back to his couch and filled his electric pipe with some of his strongest tobacco essence and made himself comfortable. The vaporizing bowl end of the pipe began to seep a slow, curling stream of gray into the air. The smell of wood and clove spread through the flat. His sound system was set to detect certain cues from him, and Mozart's Serenade Number 6 started up, slowly rising in volume until Holmes set it with a wave of his hand. It was the violin solo that pulled at his heart. He felt a stab of guilt about his own playing and how he should make more time to practice. The vapor trails above him began to throb with the music. He started to notice a warm numbness in his face.

Patterns of repeated shapes began to pull themselves out of the twisting cloud above his head. A cluster of gray curls took on a cascading shape that reminded him of the way she pinned her hair up when she was working. The shape faded as it grew, molding itself into leering gray faces and an endless, trackless void behind them. It rose with the intensity of the orchestra strings and spread across the ceiling of the apartment. Slowly, with unyielding force, the void sank and surrounded him. Holmes felt a dry burning in his eyes and the numbness spread over him, felling his limbs. Patterns appeared and repeated all around him, all relating, connecting. He drifted into the darkness alone, with only his music to guide him.

Holmes began to stir when the rose gold of the afternoon sun fell over his face. He found himself to be gathered into the corner of his couch like a cat. He stretched out and wiped the beaded sweat from his brow with the front of his shirt. His flat was no different, yet so much smaller.

"Kiwi," Holmes said. "Yesterday's bird was the kiwi."

• • •

Hot water from the bathroom sink helped Holmes to focus. He ran a towel over his face as packets of information began to thread themselves together in his mind like molecule chains. The lieutenant, Moriarty, had managed to shed some light on the problem but he couldn't see with the eyes of someone who knew the victim. Holmes expression grew sour. *The victim*, he thought. The deceased. It's easier to think in those terms rather than names. *Irene* carried weight, *victim* did not. As his mind wandered, Holmes was able to recall the photo of Irene's desk in almost perfect detail. Something was, in fact, out of place.

He decided not to call the lieutenant. Moriarty would, no doubt, want to know how Holmes came by this new perspective and "Scarlett" would tie him back into this investigation as a suspect. Whatever he decided, Holmes thought, he needed to move freely if he was to find what the police had missed. Holmes pulled his coat from the hook by his door and stalked out into the fading light.

Early in the evening, Holmes found himself at a bustling little bistro a few blocks from Baskerville's offices. With some coffee at his side and a plate of old-style fish and chips, he folded back the pages of the three separate tabloid rags that he'd bought to compare the copied images of Irene's office. Crime scene photos were usually guarded by police but slick, big-city journalists somehow always found a source. Holmes found an exact replica of the photo he'd seen at the station. A blur of pixels sat just where the lieutenant had placed the sticky note, but the rest of the room was still visible. Holmes found details lunging out at him from the page, patterns forming in the colors and the movements of a killer implied in captured shadows.

The web-shaped crack in the computer monitor told him that a small-caliber weapon was used. It may have been powerful enough to break through the flesh but by the time the bullet struck the screen most of its force could have been lost. That mop bucket in the corner of the picture bothered him as well. Irene hated the smell of chemical cleaners. She would have told a janitor to come around later on, when she was out.

"Whoever brought that bucket in was the last person to see her alive," Holmes said softly. "That doesn't necessarily make you the killer though, does it? It only means that you parked your tools there on the time of death, or slightly after."

The paper claimed that the floor had been sealed off after the murder to all but police investigators, but parts of it were being reopened so business could be resumed.

"If…if I could have a look at that office before they open again, I…" His whispering trailed off when he caught sight of a bistro employee walking out with a mop bucket to clean up a spill. The yellow sign that read WET FLOOR in three languages bore the shop's logo. The one in the picture had none.

It didn't take Holmes long to find out which cleaning service was contracted by Baskerville. He also found out that the cleanup project was to start that very night. Through a series of calls and an internet search, he'd found them. He'd shadowed one of their crew long enough to identify the blue coveralls and generic tool belt that they wore. Piecing together his disguise was a simple matter at a nearby hardware store and, by midnight, he saw the cleaning service trucks at the entrance of Baskerville's complex. He'd had the cab driver leave him a block from the entrance. He walked up slowly, carefully. Holmes wrapped his coat around himself, pulled his hat down, and slipped in at the edge of the crowd.

"'Old on there." A man with a collared shirt and a sizable set of muttonchops clapped him on the shoulder. "You got ID?" Holmes said nothing, and a single raised eyebrow answered for him.

"You speak English? Par le voo...fooking English?"

"Yar." Holmes grunted, slouched, and shifted his glance.

"ID? The lil' card with your pict're on it. You have one?"

"Lost it, squire. Sorry."

The man turned and watched the rest of his team filing into the side entrance. He scratched at his chops and let out an exasperated breath.

"What's your name, then?"

"Ellis."

"Ellis wha'?"

"Michael," Holmes said, shaking his head in denial.

"Ellis Michael?"

"Nah. Michael Ellis."

The foreman let out a grunt. His team was gone and probably waiting for him.

"Where you from?"

"Ips'ich."

"What switch?"

"Nah. Ip!" He shook his head again.

"What?"

"Ip-swich. Ipswich. Ellis, Michael."

"That's what I said....Go! Just go! I'll get ya a fooking timecard."

"Yar," Holmes said, heading for the door.

The quiet stillness of the closed floor was disorienting. The silence seemed to amplify his perception in ways he couldn't have predicted. The path to Irene's office seemed to rise up from under the tide of memory without much effort. Holmes found himself making turns on something akin to instinct, since most of the wall signs weren't lit. For a moment, he began to doubt the precision of these new senses. Finding himself in front of Irene's door put those doubts to rest.

The door opened inward to beams of streetlight, sliced into thin layers by the blinds and thrown against the far wall. Most of the things that Holmes had seen in the papers and at the police station were still in place. Her desk had been shoved into a corner but the cracked PC monitor was still present. It sat under a thin plastic sheet, on the floor by her file cabinets. One of which was tall, almost up to the ceiling, and painted deep burgundy. Holmes pulled a pair of latex gloves over his hands and peeled the cover from the monitor. The impact of the bullet could still be seen at the center of its web. The back side of the monitor showed no exit damage.

Holmes looked over the desk, throwing off another plastic sheet. What was left of the dried blood had been scraped off, most likely to be registered as genetic evidence. Holmes picked through the drawers and compartments until he found what was mentioned in the letter. An external hard drive about the size of a business card sat at the back of a cubby, a collection of cables wrapped in a messy spool around it. Holmes lifted it out, careful not to swing the cables against the desk top, and began to unfurl the mess onto the floor. All the components seemed to be there. Holmes sat back and looked over the parts.

His mind's eye watched the drive connect to a power outlet in the wall, and then to the shattered monitor. If enough of the screen was left functional, he thought, her project files could be accessed. He pulled himself upright and started looking through his collection of cables. A thick wire with an AC adapter and a data cable just happened to sit atop the pile.

The screen sputtered to life, with splashes of color appearing and warping between the network of cracks and thin brown scrape marks. Two typing fields appeared through those cracks, breaking apart and slanting like sliced bamboo. The name that she'd used appeared in the top space but the password field was blank. Holmes tried to recall the letter. He read her last words to him again. An obvious password, she'd said.

"Hound" didn't gain him access. Neither did "Sherlock," "London," or "scripts." His brow creased as a new idea surfaced, the most obvious word that could possibly appear. *Scarlett* slowly appeared in the empty space as his hands fell about the keys in awkward thumps.

Denied.

"The answer is in front of me," Holmes whispered to himself. "The password is obvious, or so she claimed. But she would have been clever enough to know what's obvious to me....unless..."

Obvious.

The screen went blank for a moment and the colorful slashes of broken liquid crystal reappeared with icons of folders, littered across the open space.

Holmes clicked his way through folder after folder of financial records, communiqués from investors to their pet policymakers, test results, and research from a slew of laboratories biological and technical. Near the bottom of a folder colored in red, he found a little text file called "Scarlett."

Irene's personal notes about the project included some information about enhancers in other markets as well. Trivalia was listed as a "strength and endurance booster" for the labor market with "cognition-damping" effects. Roburall, meant for police and private security, was shown to enhance "speed of thought," reaction time, and physical dexterity, while hindering a person's will to question instructions. The list that followed was a wide range of scripts that were marketed to employers, all of whom required their workforces to participate. Scarlett, Holmes found, was still in the testing phase. The drug was meant for the use of British intelligence or the GCHQ, American CIA, and intelligence contractors of the big multinationals. "Cognitive and deductive" effects were stitched into a cocktail of other stimulants to form a physical and mental toolkit for the military elite. It had only just been approved for human trials.

He scrolled the struggling cursor down to the most recent message. A private email, marked "urgent," dated a week before

Irene's murder, was copied into the body of the text. The sender was "J. Watson," and his message was short.

They found you. Get out now.

The sound of a careful boot scraping the floor behind him alerted Holmes to his companion. The loud, almost careless clicking of a pistol's hammer told him that it wasn't a policeman.

"I'll thank you to keep your hands where I can see them." The armed intruder was a squat, rounded little man. His coveralls were the same as the working crew that had entered the building, as was his brown leather tool belt. Holmes took a moment to look the man over once he'd stepped into the light.

"You must be some kind of private investigator." The shorter man's voice was thin, high in pitch but still retaining a masculine sound. "You're certainly not police material, judging by your sneaking about."

"And…" Holmes took a moment to review his mental notes, "you're the one that took the shot. Aren't you?"

The little man's face was partly covered by slats of shadow but his figure seemed to tense at the implication.

"Stop me if I'm wrong, would you?" Holmes stood, taller and wider in the shoulders than the other man. "That pistol is a small .22. Small enough to conceal but perfectly lethal at close range. Last time it was here, it was fitted with a noise-suppression kit. I can assume that much from the one-sided strike against the computer screen. Your suppressor slowed the bullet just enough to get it caught in the glass."

Holmes tapped the shattered monitor with a boot tip. The little man took a step inside and closed the door behind him, keeping an eye on Holmes as he did.

"Those boots also seem much too tactical for a janitor's work." Holmes pointed with his chin at the man's matte-black, sixteen-eyelet boots that were probably waterproof. "They're too heavy for you as well; that's why you scuff the floor when you walk. SAS leftovers, I would think."

"You seem to have read up on me, mister…"

"Holmes. I haven't done any reading on you, but I saw the police photos. All I needed to do was look you over for the rest. Besides, why else would you come armed to a closed area but to retrieve the bullet? You obviously didn't have time for it after the shot."

The smaller man set his jaw and raised his pistol. Holmes dove to the floor. Amid the clatter of plastic sheets and scattering hardware, he could hear a quick *pop-popping* sound from the doorway and things seemed to be bursting around him in sequence. Holmes flattened himself against the far side of the tall burgundy file case. Two rounds rang off the opposite side of the file case, making a shrill, grating report.

"You're a quick one. Quick and cleverer than myself, I'll admit…" The sound of a fresh magazine being slapped into place lurked beneath the voice. Holmes heard it clearly, but wasn't able to spot an escape before his attacker was done reloading. "I might not be able to get you through that metal, but you've got nowhere to go. The minute you look round that corner, I'll put a shot through your eye. If you fancy waiting, I have all night, Mr. Holmes."

Holmes tried to slow his breathing, tried to keep an image of the room in his mind and searched it for any means of escape. The window was too far, he thought, too many opportunities for a shot. The shooter was blocking the door and the adjoining office was locked. Holmes spun the gears of his newly renovated wits with all the fury he could muster. He thought about the height of the cabinet. He thought about the distance to the door.

The little man craned his head forward, intrigued by the queer rocking of the cabinet, but he had only enough time for a feeble shout before the second kick tipped it over. Tall as it was, it easily reached the office door with a heavy crack and caught the shooter in between. The drawers fell out and slammed onto the floor, dumping years of records. When the noise had subsided, Holmes looked out from the corner to see the shooter suspended by his throat. The top edge of the falling cabinet had pinned him to the door. Holmes stepped lightly from behind the fallen file case just as he could hear the steps of the cleaning crew rushing up the hallway. A feeling, some new instinct, prompted Holmes to pick up the fallen .22 while his hands were still gloved. He also ripped the false identification from the man's shirt. Holmes was out the window and gone by the time the crew reached the door.

• • •

Sirens swam in the distance, rising and falling through the drifts of snow that swelled in the streets. Ordinarily, Holmes tended to tense when the police blew past in their cars or sprinted around him on their cycles. This new Holmes, Holmes plus Scarlett, wasn't upset in the least. Somehow he knew that, if they were called to the scene he'd just left, the investigation would start as a simple accident. *Things will become complicated when the cleaners produce no employment record of the dead man*, he thought. Murder inquiries were painfully detailed and thankfully time-consuming. Holmes sat in a small cafe and began to pick through Baskerville's available records on a public internet terminal.

A gray foxtail of steam swayed from the cup at his side and seemed to wag in unison with the flashing adverts of the webpages. Holmes had already seen the files concerning the Baskerville Company and its shadow projects, but J. Watson had turned out to be a very interesting character as well. From what Holmes read, Dr. John Watson was one of the foremost experts in the field of bioenhancement and commercial chemistry, and his was thought to be the mind behind the Scarlett project. Holmes had seen the name on some financial records at Irene's office, and he also recalled seeing a J. Watson on her list of private contacts. Holmes took a quick look around and reached under the counter.

The video input cable let out a tiny snap as Holmes pulled it from the web terminal. The faint plastic clattering on the floor, he assumed, was the cable's connecting tab that he'd just broken. Holmes fished through the pockets of his coat and lifted Irene's hard drive out and kept it close. The video cable for the cafe terminal fit in nicely. Dozens of folders suddenly appeared on the screen against a background of solid blue.

"Can I get you anything else, sir?" The pierced, bleach-blonde girl behind the counter spoke in a sing-song voice. The kind of tone that was meant to let one know that they were being observed.

"No. Thank you. But I would suggest that you get your violin fitted for a new chin rest."

"Pardon?" The girl spoke with slitted eyes and a quickly furrowing brow. Holmes turned slightly in her direction but still avoided eye contact.

"The chin rest you have is too large. It causes you to raise your bow arm too high, hence the tension I can see in your right shoulder. I gather that's also why you keep rubbing the back of your neck. Your left forearm is slightly more muscular than the other, which exposes a musician, and the mark on your cheek would suggest a fiddler."

"A mark on my face?" Minor annoyance transcended into coiling anger. "I don't know what you're talking about."

"Your smeared makeup, my dear. It looks like you slept on a bicycle seat."

"Old wanker!" she spat as she left the counter and stomped her way to the ladies' room.

Alone and unwatched, Holmes dug further into the layers of information that Irene had left behind. Looking over some of Baskerville's financial records, he spotted regular transactions to a major banking institute called Reichenbach. Substantial and regular payments made from Baskerville to that bank happened only under Irene's authorization. If there were a solid link to be made, Holmes thought, between Scarlett and this John Watson, it would be there. A muted television behind the espresso bar played to Holmes's back. Had he been looking, he would have seen the news anchor's captions jogging across the bottom of the screen. The report began to detail a break-in and an attack at Baskerville headquarters. A Scotland Yard inspector, a man named Moriarty, had taken the lead on the investigation.

The Reichenbach Capitol building was perched on the edge of the Thames, overlooking a squalid and soot-coated industrial section of old London with all the motionless patience of a great spider. Reichenbach was one of the earliest investors in the workforce enhancement market. Holmes knew this as well as anyone who'd kept even half an eye on the news. As he rode the evening train out to the oldest parts of his city, it occurred to him that Reichenbach must have profited more from the mandating of the drugs than the developers had. According to the various sources on his brother's conspiracy blog, institutions like Reichenbach handled the accounts and sheltered the profits of companies that did the work and, with subtle nudges at the elbows of Parliament, got those drugs made mandatory. Piece after piece of the problem fell together as Holmes made his way through the quiet streets, the fog still barely disturbed by Sunday's movements, up to the Reichenbach building.

His maintenance man disguise was still intact, with smudges, stains, and all. Avoiding the eyes of the sparse weekend security guards, Holmes was able to access the service lift with minimal disturbance. According to Irene's personal notes, the part of Reichenbach that handled drug development took up the entire eightieth floor of the building. It seemed like an odd thing to note in a business file, but Holmes chose to proceed. The lift rode smoothly upon its tracks. Holmes felt some tension leave the space between his shoulders. Images of kiwi birds began to rise and dissolve behind his eyes, glimpsed from wildlife feeds on his TV, or from glossy photos in the yellowed pages of books. The kiwis themselves were long since gone. They had fallen victim, like many other parts of the natural world, to the industrial appetite of man.

"Eighty." The elevator's voice was soft and very well replicated, almost human. The doors opened to a hallway, still and silent, very much like the last one, with the exception of the crime scene tape and the feel of recent death on the air. A light in his hand, Holmes glanced up and down at the names that were stenciled in black against clean glass on office doors. Reichenbach was said to take its record keeping very seriously, so the archive was not hard to find. One look at the lock on the archive door stopped Holmes immediately. A thin handle of stainless steel hung below a small block of silvery plastic. A deep groove ran across the length of the block, meant for some kind of key card. Holmes imagined the portion of the locking mechanism that was beneath the metal and turned the image around. The door was set on his side, only able to open inward. Holmes unclipped the dead man's photo ID from his shirt.

He would have to work quickly once inside. A silent alarm would surely react to him, Holmes thought as he wedged the rigid card through the tiny space in the doorjamb. A hollow clacking of metal on wood rang down the hallway.

"Such a complex world," he muttered softly to himself, "isn't able to resist a simple solution."

The place that Holmes found offered testament to the endurance of an old world's ways. It stretched out before him like the long entryway of some sacred place, the walls lined with bulging yellow folders, cardboard boxes with dates or names written neatly on their fronts with black marker, and brown folders that looked like swollen accordions. It seemed that what his brother, Mycroft, had said about the financial giant was true—they took their record keeping very seriously and relied on paper because of its inability to be hacked by data thieves. The ledgers and folders that coated the corridor ran about the entire width of the eightieth floor and, at the opposite end, Holmes saw a workstation, just large enough for one, that sat comfortably under a window. The desk had a small green banker's lamp for the record keeper and an electric teapot. Holmes ran his fingertips over the precisely alphabetized contents of the archive until he found *Baskerville, Ltd.*

The folder was about the width of an opened hand and heavy with reports, colorful charts, and other printed material. Holmes walked the folder up to the little desk and carefully unraveled the waxy red string that held down the cover. There was no hurry in his step, since the building was closed until the following morning. He propped one of the folders up against the window so that the light from the little banker's lamp wouldn't be seen, and began thumbing through the folder's contents with care. Without putting forth a conscious effort, Holmes arranged some choice pages on the desk, in order of date, department, or some other unique factor. After a satisfying stack had been made on the desk, he set the folder down on the floor and turned his attention to his handpicked documents.

It took nearly an hour of steady reading for Holmes to find even a trace of this doctor, this Watson. Most of the useful information was blacked out but, with some careful angling of the page against the green lamp, a portion of the original typeface could be seen like a jet-black watermark on a shadow. John Watson. He turned out to be quite the innovator in the field of biomechanics. According to the data that Holmes spread before him, Watson was one of the first to formulate a limited steroid-and-amphetamine mixture that was originally meant to boost the abilities of herding dogs. The cocktail worked so well, with neurological and cognitive damage in only 5 percent of the study group, that drug manufacturers began courting the good doctor and competing for his favor. At the end of a long debauch of expensive dinners, wines, travels, and contributions to Watson's research facility, Baskerville had succeeded in winning his allegiance. Unimpressed thus far with his discovery, Holmes turned the next page in frustration and stared down into a bleak abyss that at once vindicated his suspicions and filled him with dread.

After twelve years in their employ, Baskerville had paid Watson handsomely to begin work on "Scarlett," and coerced him into keeping this work strictly off the record. The project lead was listed only as *your faithful hound*.

"You'll leave that right where it is, Mr. Holmes."

He knew the voice. It was on the news channels and internet broadcasts, and he recalled it from the police station. Holmes set the pages back down and turned slowly, unthreateningly. Lieutenant Moriarty stood back about twenty paces. A slick black service pistol was held steadily at eye level.

"You've predicted my steps somehow?" Holmes said, standing carefully. "Calculated my options and waited for me to come to the same conclusion?"

"Actually, no. I followed you." Moriarty took a short step forward. "It's the oldest trick in the policeman's handbook and you left me an easy trail. You're a smart one, Holmes, but you don't seem very adept at all this cloak-and-dagger nonsense. Or is it just a lack of experience? Either way, you're needed for questioning."

"Regarding what?"

"The unidentified man that we found, crushed by a file cabinet, at the Baskerville building."

"Lieutenant…" Holmes could only raise his hand a fraction of an inch. Moriarty's gun arm tightened, the muzzle rose just a bit.

"Keep still, for now. I'll tell you when it's time to move your hands. Step away from the desk. Toward me."

The lieutenant stepped back, matching Holmes's own steps. There was no clear way for him to close the distance, if he wanted to get the gun. Holmes tried to think like he had at Irene's office, but his mind stumbled. He couldn't concentrate as easily.

"It's wearing off," Holmes said to himself. Moriarty only raised an eye up from behind his pistol. "I can't…I can't remember. Lieutenant, listen to me. There isn't any time left."

"I've heard enough from you for tonight. Get down, onto the floor."

"Aren't you the least bit curious as to why I broke into this place?" Holmes dared to raise his voice. It seemed to help. "Are you interested in finding out why I killed that operative in my wife's office? I've nothing to hide. I did it."

Moriarty stood in silence, expecting something. Holmes pressed on.

"I got a message from Irene—Ms. Adler—and with it I got an enhancer called Scarlett." Holmes faltered when he realized that his speech wasn't quite so polished as before.

"Never heard of it." The gun didn't move.

"It's still in testing. I think she meant for me to find out why she was killed but instead I found this." Holmes tipped his head back, toward the desk that was strewn with pages.

"I'll play along," Moriarty said, begrudgingly. "What is it?"

"Proof." Holmes straightened himself up, as if he were addressing an assembly. "Undeniable proof that the so-called career-enhancing drugs are laden with adverse effects. Adverse effects that are carefully designed to keep people in their respective roles."

"Ridiculous. Whom? What people?"

"All of us." Holmes's voice sank to a chilling whisper. "You, me, the police, the janitors, the office managers, everyone. We're all under control."

"Fascinating, but I'll be arresting you all the same." Exhaustion of his patience left Moriarty's voice flat. "You've just implicated yourself in a murder."

"Aren't you on them also?" Holmes went on, unhindered. "Roburall, is it? That's what they give police?"

"Yes. It improves performance, and it's mandatory." The lieutenant's voice faltered just a bit.

"When you're late for a dose, do you ever start to see or hear things differently?" Holmes question was met with silence. "Have strange thoughts ever surfaced in your mind when your dose was late? Have you ever wondered what might happen if you skipped it entirely?"

"I can't say that I have."

"But you're aware of some differences in your thought patterns when you aren't on Roburall, yes?"

"Obviously there's a difference." Moriarty's aim began to drift as he was staking more thought on Holmes's words. "If you stop taking a neuroenhancer, you'll certainly be slowed down. You won't recognize commands as efficiently and you won't act on them with any accuracy."

"Did you hear what you just said?"

Moriarty tightened his grip.

"The merit of your drug," Holmes said, "is that it allows you to recognize commands and act quickly. Too quickly for you to question the directive, I would think. Does that not fit what I've just told you?"

Silence. Stillness. The kind of stillness that filled that hallway was no different from the kind that covers a playing field before a whistle blows. Holmes's stance lost some of its confidence and the keen brightness faded a bit further from his eyes.

"I'm…it's wearing off now," he said, turning toward the window. "I can feel it, like gears slowing, grinding down. I can't remember why…"

"I'll remind you, then. You're under arrest and I'll be taking you in. Get down, on the floor."

"Lieutenant, I suppose Scarlett will never be in my reach again. My mind won't ever be that sharp again, but yours is."

"Did you not hear me?" The ire was beginning to grate in Moriarty's throat.

"All the information, all the records, everything you need is right here. They'll tell you it's not real. That it's just paranoia. It's very real, Lieutenant. I didn't believe it at first either. Now I have no choice but to believe all the twisted conspiracy theories I've heard, but I wonder if I'll remember."

"One last time, Holmes! Get down, onto the floor with your hands behind your head!"

"I can't go back." Fear, old fear began to twist in his stomach. "Now that I've seen what it's like, I won't go back." As he spoke, Holmes's hand fell slowly into a pocket. He could feel Moriarty grow tense and raise the sight of his weapon again.

"Kiwi, lieutenant. Tomorrow's bird is the kiwi. Don't forget."

Holmes pulled his hand from his pocket and whipped his arm upward. Moriarty fired twice. Whether or not Holmes was struck with both rounds wasn't clear because he staggered back almost immediately, the shots splitting the window behind him. Something dropped from his hand. Holmes's weight shattered the panes as he fell against them.

The safety glass was oddly quiet as it broke and redivided into thousands of glittering pearls that spun around the falling man as he twisted his way down eighty floors and vanished into the darkness below. Moriarty lowered his weapon. He stepped up to the edge and saw no sign of Holmes. Metal clicked against his shoe as he turned back. A small .22 sat on the floor, sealed in a plastic bag.

The lieutenant was no more than a tiny figure, flipping through some loose papers in the flat green of the rifle scope. The center dot swayed just above his head and to his left to compensate for the wind. Irene Adler softly lifted the shortwave receiver from her vest and put in the call to Baskerville.

"First of the human trials is over, sir. Success."

DELTA PHI

BY HEIDI MCLAUGHLIN

The knock on my door startles me. I sit anxiously, waiting to see if it happens again. It's not often that people come to visit me and I'd rather not get excited by the prospect only to find out that it's a student bumping their way down the hall, inadvertently hitting my door. I focus my attention instead on the crime scene report I downloaded from the local police server. I've been hacking into their system since I arrived in Burlington, Vermont, and quickly started offering them subtle clues to solve their petty crime cases. As morbid as it is, I'm waiting for a murder to occur so I can hone my craft in the field of investigation. Of course, being a college student, my work is never credited.

Ron Smith is the local police chief. He considers me a thorn in his side. He's not a fan of me, especially when my eighteen-year-old self discovers inconsistencies in his police work. More accurately, when my dorm was pranked as part of the Delta Phi fraternity initiation, his responding officer couldn't find the offenders, stating that the evidence was inconclusive. The fact that *Delta Phi* was pasted to the outside wall by way of wet toilet paper apparently wasn't a big enough clue. I bested the police department when I showed them the handprints left behind matched those of one Roger Stallworth, the center for our basketball team, who has the largest hands on campus.

The knock sounds again, but this time it's louder and more defined against the metal door. Closing my laptop and sliding the investigation report into my file cabinet, away from the prying eyes of whoever lurks outside, I open the door with luster, acting calm and collected as if I have visitors every day. The person on the other side of the concrete box that I reside in doesn't need to know otherwise.

"Lock Holmes?" she questions. I nod, but stand still against the doorjamb, preventing her from entering. My name is Sherlock, but I go by Lock. It's more hip and easier to play off with my hippie parents. My mother, in all her peace-loving ways, couldn't decide on a name for me, and ended up combining my grandmother's name, Sheryl, with the nickname of Lock for the tiny tuft of hair I was born with. Sadly, my father never disagreed and forever branded me with the eccentric name that throughout childhood labeled me as an outsider.

The lady in front of me, dressed in a pinstriped suit, is nervous even though she's trying to maintain a professional look. She forgot her watch this morning when she dressed. The tan line indicates that she wore it all summer, not caring about sunblock or the odd white block of skin she'd leave showing if she were to forget it, like today. The imprint left on her skin says she wears a women's Timex—cheap and easily found in every discount store in America.

"I'm Professor MacAfee. Chief Smith suggested I come to you for some help." Her dark hair rests on her shoulders and is curled forward, giving onlookers the illusion that she's younger than she presents. She hides the gray hairs easily from those who aren't paying attention. I rack my brain, trying to recall exactly who she is. My photographic memory never fails—her image reminds me that she's head of Ecological Agriculture.

Professor MacAfee looks to her right and then left—watching for someone to come down the hall, perhaps? I could step aside and let her into my sanctuary, but I'm cautious. There's a reason I room by myself—it's easier than dealing with odd looks and minimizes comments being made behind my back. In boarding school, I couldn't escape the mandatory requirement that I room with someone. For years my name was whispered among my peers as they talked about how different and observant I am, as if knowing your surroundings is a crime. For college, I forged my own path and made sure my roommate application was filled out meticulously so I could room by myself. It's laughable how the administration never asked for my medical records when I stated I was allergic to everything.

"May I come in?" she asks, her voice low, but not quite a whisper. The hint of desperation almost makes me feel sorry for her, but to be sorry I'd have to have some sort of empathy toward her and I don't.

I look at her, wondering why she would need to come into my room when the hallway, or better yet the library, would be a suitable place to speak. Chief Smith has a prejudice against me; for all I know this is a setup, a ploy to get into my dorm to see what information I have acquired on any of his recent cases.

"I don't think that's necessary," I state, watching as her face falls. She hangs her head briefly before looking at me with unshed tears.

"Please," she begs quietly. "I'll lose my job if you don't help me."

Two things strike me as odd and interesting: One, she says she's going to lose her job. What has she done to warrant such a desperate measure as to knock on a freshman's dorm room door asking for help, and at the suggestion of the town's famed police chief? Two, why is it my issue?

My curiosity, as always, gets the best of me, and I step aside and let her enter. My room is nothing like your average girl's dorm room. I have a map of the city, pinpointing the recent rash of petty crimes. To call them a spree would be in haste, although if the person isn't caught soon their minor attempts at notoriety will eventually escalate because they got bored. Criminals like attention, especially from the media. They want to hear people talking about them and they want to know that they're striking fear in the community. None of that is happening.

"Chief Smith was right."

"About what exactly?"

The Professor pulls out my desk chair and sits, leaving me no other place to rest than my bed. I choose to stand, giving her the illusion that I'm taller than I am.

"I have myself in a pickle and I believe, after speaking with Chief Smith, you're the only one who can help me. You see, I'm one of the few teachers that still grade on a curve and my final is one of the hardest students will take. Each year, I've changed it drastically from the previous one to prevent students from sharing their results. After I type up the final, I print one copy with my answers and save another one to a thumb drive that I lock in my drawer. The final is in three days and both the printed copy and thumb drive are missing."

"Why not create a new final?"

"Time," she says, shaking her head. "I don't have it. It takes me two to three months to compile the questions and answers."

"Have you looked—?"

She holds up her hand and smiles, effectively cutting me off. "I have looked everywhere. I am, without a doubt, a creature of habit. Very rarely do I deviate from a plan or change course, except when it comes to the questions I ask on my final. I understand that being this way is likely a downfall."

I could tell her that I'm the same way, but the less she knows about me, the better. I don't want her feeling like we'll be friends after this, or even in the future. I'll never have her for a professor, as agriculture isn't on my list of classes to take.

"I don't understand where I come into this, or Chief Smith."

"Simple, Lock. I need you to find out who stole the final."

"Can you just flunk everyone in your class? Surely threatening them with a failing grade will get them to crow."

Her eyes are inquisitive as she looks at me. She may be my intellectual match, or she might be another person who wants to exploit my skills.

"And why not ask Chief Smith to find the culprits?"

"Culprits? You think there's more than one?"

I mentally chide myself for giving her a clue. Of course there are two. You always need a lookout. Depending on the layout of her office, three or four could be possible. Someone knew where to find her thumb drive and final, therefore someone from her past, an aide or student teacher with knowledge of the items' location, is the one singing Dixie.

It's best to be quiet when you don't want to answer a question, although in most criminal investigations that can prove you're somewhat guilty.

"To answer your question about Chief Smith—I went to him, but they're busy with other things and don't have time to look for an answer key. The administration would not see this as favorable for my employment and I'm hoping to renew my contract." Professor MacAfee stands and starts pacing in my overly small room.

"I'll pay you for your services, Lock. It'd be much easier if a student were asking questions than a police officer or campus security. Students clam up when the men in blue come knocking on their door."

She has a point and I do love a good challenge. Being able to solve a crime on campus may give me the respect of the police chief. He'd have to acknowledge that I know what I'm doing, whether he likes it or not.

"I'd have to sit in on your class. I need to be able to observe," I say before realizing I've essentially agreed to help her. She nods furiously, her head bobbing up and down like a yo-yo. "And I'll need access to your office."

"It's yours," she says, coming over to me and shaking my hand. I pull away quickly, tucking my hands in the pockets of my jeans to avoid her touching me again.

"I'll see you in a half hour," I tell her, much to her confusion. "Your class, advanced agroecology—it starts in thirty minutes. I'm assuming that is the class missing the final."

"Oh, right. I'll see you then."

I move her toward the door, whether she's ready or not. I need to get on my computer and learn as much as I can about agroecology before I step into her class. If I'm going to befriend someone in there, I need to know what I'm talking about.

• • •

JOHN WATSON

My brothers from Delta Phi gather around one of the many tables in Cook Commons, one of the few eateries we have on campus. Most of the time we don't have the ability to go back to our frat house to eat, so we meet here. Brown trays full of food cover the table, giving us less space than the table actually offers. I squeeze between Roger Stallworth, known as the largest man on campus, and Warren Beatty (not to be confused with the actor), my roommate.

This is my third year in Delta Phi and I love it more than ever. I've just been named house treasurer and after last year's fiasco of our toga party gone wrong, I'm determined to make sure our frat donates money to charitable causes. I'm incredibly thankful that charities don't ask how the money was obtained, because having guys do handstands on kegs for payment probably isn't an acceptable way of raising money. When the school asks, I tell them we charge people coming in to watch our eighty-five-inch high-definition television. We do, of course, but our profit isn't earth-shattering.

"Who are you bringing to the ski lodge?" Jennifer Jamison asks as she sits down, acting as if she owns the table. It's only on a rare occasion that we let any of the female population sit with us at our lunch table. Lunch is a man's hour, even for those with girlfriends, according to our bylaws.

The ski lodge isn't what it sounds like. It's the party we host every year at the end of finals week, which will be in three days. We decorate our house like a ski lodge, complete with a flooded-out back yard that we turn into an icy ski jump. It's not customary that you bring a date unless you're looking for a little side action from that co-ed.

"Are you looking for a hookup?" Roger waggles his eyebrows at Jennifer, much to her disgust. Warren and I laugh. Jennifer is always looking for the next "in," even though she's on the cheerleading squad and a pledge at one of the biggest sororities on campus.

Her plan is to marry rich and live the life of high society. She may want to reconsider her plan, though, since none of our athletes are making it to the pros.

"You wish," she says, picking a piece of food off one of Roger's many plates. I tire quickly of Jennifer and Roger's back-and-forth conversation and start working on my lunch. My upcoming final in biochemistry has me perplexed. Between needing to study and my duties at the fraternity, time is not my friend. I am the only medical major in the house. My brothers have chosen paths in business, communications, and teaching, leaving their schedules much more flexible. My choice to pledge when I was a freshman was based solely on how my time in the house would look on my résumé. Taking the position of treasurer proves that I'm responsible and will benefit me when I apply for a loan to open my own practice. I'm always thinking ahead.

Warren elbows me and nods toward the table two away from us. Sitting there is none other than Lock Holmes, the object of my desires. Only she doesn't know I exist, despite my many attempts at getting her attention.

The first time I saw her was at freshman orientation. I was there, representing Delta Phi, looking for new pledges. She was there, of course, because it's mandatory that all incoming students attend. From the moment I laid eyes on her, I felt a stirring that I can only describe as heart palpitations. I've tried to recreate those feelings with other girls, but to no avail. It only happens when I see her, or when her eyes briefly meet mine in what I know to be nothing more than an accident.

Since that first day, I've strategically placed myself in her path only to be shunned or ignored. I've become a stalker, of sorts, hanging out in the library because I can see her dorm room window from the third floor. This acknowledgment alone should land me in the slammer for my voyeuristic ways.

"I don't know what you see in her," Warren says, much to my displeasure. Everyone sees beauty differently and just because Lock Holmes comes off as odd doesn't make her any less gorgeous than the other women on campus. To me, her fragmentary style is what makes her stand out among the masses. She's not like every other Barbie doll walking the brick paths of campus.

"What *don't* you see in her?" I counter, hoping he'll take a long look at his superficial requirements when it comes to women. I used to be like him, only wanting skinny blondes with voluptuous racks. That all changed when I spotted Lock from across the room, with her chestnut hair and slender figure. Had she been graced with eyes of caramel brown to contrast with her hair, blue to accent the sky, or were they as green as the spring grass? Finding out has become a task, one that I fully intend to fulfill.

"She's plain," he says, under his breath. He knows how I feel about sharing any love interest with the rest of our house, so at least he's mindful to keep my crush under the radar. Even though we label ourselves as brothers in the fraternity house, we're still human and human nature tends to lead you astray. I've seen brothers battle each other over women. I don't care to battle anyone over Lock, although if tested, I will.

"I don't find her plain at all. I find her refreshing. Look at her, Warren. She doesn't conform to today's cultural standards where co-eds must look a certain way. Her clothes aren't the same designer trends the others walk around in, but she's well dressed. Her hair isn't a rainbow of colors or perfectly coiffed each time she steps out of her dorm. I like the fact that she's here to study and not intermingle in the social scene."

Warren looks at me and laughs as I finish my speech. I hadn't realized I'd kept going, but my heart takes over when my mind should lead when it comes to Lock. Even though my infatuation is purely physical, I have no doubt that once I get to know her, all the pieces for a long-lasting romance will fall into place.

"She's staring at you."

"What?" I blink quickly so I can focus on Lock. She's looking at me with what I hope is an interested expression.

"You should go over there and ask her to the ski lodge party."

I quickly glance at Roger to see if he's been listening to Warren and me, only to find him sleeping upright with his mouth hanging open. The other guys have vacated the table, leaving only the three of us.

"Yeah, I think I should." As the words tumble out of my mouth, my body freezes. I've never been shy about speaking to the opposite sex before, so I don't understand why my feet aren't moving and I'm suddenly immobile. My chair should be scraping against the linoleum floor and my legs moving into the standing position, followed by putting one foot in front of the other.

"Don't be a pansy," Warren says in the most encouraging way.

"I'm going to do it." I push my hands down on the table and force myself to stand. The gaze Lock and I share hasn't wavered and a small part of me is excited by the fact that she could be interested. If she's not, I go back to admiring from afar or until I can convince her otherwise.

Each step causes a bit of anxiety. My palms start to sweat and my heart picks up speed the closer I get. My legs feel heavy, as if bricks are cemented to the bottom of my shoes, trying to hold me down. The worst she's going to say is no when I ask her, but I'll be able to hear her voice and commit it to memory. It's the small things in life that make a difference to me.

I square my shoulders and take each step with purpose. She watches me, making me wonder what she's thinking. I have no doubt that she and I could spend hours in an intellectual debate. It'd be worth the time spent to figure out if we're compatible or if we're opposites who will fight and bicker until we make up in a mad, passionate embrace. Those thoughts cause me to falter in my steps, stumbling into the empty chair at her table. My hands grip the edge, holding the table in place before I accidentally push it into her.

Clearing my throat and standing straight, I introduce myself. "I'm John Watson," I say, extending my hand for her taking. Except she leaves me hanging, her eyes wandering all over me like I'm the subject in some sort of weird experiment that I didn't sign off on.

"Delta Phi treasurer?"

Her voice is pleasantly soft and soothing. I don't know what

I expected, but I'm surprised. I'm curious how she knows about my fraternity and duties there; it seems my reputation precedes me. Not that I have a reputation that casts me in a bad light. I smile graciously and pull the chair out and sit down, taking a bold step as far as I'm concerned. She didn't invite me or even show the slightest indication that she would like to continue this conversation.

Before any embarrassing words tumble from my mouth, I seek out her eyes. My mother has always told me that the eyes are the window to one's soul; they'll tell a story if you ask the right questions. Lock's eyes could be no different if I play my cards right. The hazel color seems to dance around with the overhead light, flickering and changing from specks of green to brown depending on the angle of her head.

"That I am. Lock Holmes, right?"

Her eyes widen as I say her name; she seems surprised that I know her. If she had any idea how I've watched her since the beginning of the semester, she'd likely be running for the hills. One thing I don't know about her is her major. When I've seen her, she's walking across campus or has her finger dragging along the spines of books in our library. I'm never there long enough to see what academic books she's reading.

"How did you know my name?" I ask her, needing to know if she, too, has been checking me out.

Lock leans forward, resting her forearms on the brown cafeteria table. "I know a lot about you, John Watson." The way she says my name, it's endearing, yet quizzical.

"I'd like to get to know you, Lock Holmes. Delta Phi is having their annual end-of-the semester ski lodge party and I'd love it if you'd accompany me as my date."

"I thought you'd never ask."

I jump slightly at the sense of shock, which quickly turns to elation. This is the easiest date I've ever gotten.

• • •

LOCK HOLMES
EARLIER IN THE DAY

Charlie Bell: suspect number one and Professor MacAfee brownnoser. From the moment he walked into the auditorium he's been nothing but complimentary toward his teacher, and even though she's been nothing more than civil in return, a few glances in his direction lead to me to believe there may be something more than academic going on there.

Suspect number two, Ginger Ralph: spent the entire time I was monitoring the class vying for the professor's attention, but never received the simplest acknowledgment. Between the sideways glances she was giving Charlie and her dejected posture after not being called on, I think she'd have enough motive to steal the semester final.

I wouldn't be surprised if Ginger suspects the same as I do about MacAfee and Mr. Bell and is planning on using it to her advantage. After a quick search in the administration's database—more accurately, the dean of students' computer—it seems Charlie Bell has been attending school for six years and needs to pass agroecology in order to graduate. His current grade is a D- and he would need to ace the final in order to pass, and score higher than everyone else in class.

Charlie Bell comes from money and has been buying his way through school for the past few years. He's also the president of Delta Phi. According to their bylaws, a student must be in good standing in order to remain in office there. I know this because I read their bylaws after they so kindly decorated our dorm with toilet paper. Yet he's far from an upstanding academic student and by all accounts should be living off campus.

Ms. Ralph's academic record is less than stellar, but she's still in the middle range in the junior class. This is the second time she's had to take agroecology, having barely passed the first time; the passing grade isn't enough to maintain the requirements for her degree.

The other members seem to have clean records, all attending class with a mix of passing and failing grades. My next stop is to visit MacAfee's office with a plan to look as nonchalant as I can while watching students come and go. The test was stolen either while MacAfee was teaching or after hours, but she's unable to recall the last time she physically saw both the papers and the thumb drive— or she does know and didn't feel the need to tell me. I could be searching for files that have been gone for months or hours. Either way, it doesn't matter. The test is about to be administered and as it is with most college students, the studying will commence in the next day or so.

I breathe a sigh of relief as I sit on the unoccupied bench near MacAfee's office. Sitting next to someone could raise suspicion, especially if they're used to seeing the same people in the hallway. Students mill around, chatting about the upcoming Delta Phi ski lodge party. A blonde, who dyes her hair every three weeks by the looks of her split ends, complains that she has yet to be invited, but plans to change that today during her lunch hour when she'll see the Deltas in the cafeteria. She and her friend are out of earshot before I can hear what they say, but judging by her friend's expression, she doesn't care, more than likely because she's been invited.

I open my textbook and pretend to read. It's easier to watch people if they think you're not paying attention to them. My peripheral vision is excellent and my eyes are always moving, constantly observing the scenes in front of me. To my right, two students are about to share what is likely their first kiss outside of their dorm rooms. They're both unsure how the other feels about public displays of affection, but their bodies are gravitating toward each other. If they'd learn to read body language they'd both know that, yes, they do want to kiss. To my left, a guy walks slowly down the hall, letting his peers pass and bump his shoulder as he moves. He pauses and looks around as if he's looking for someone, but the moment his face turns in my direction I can see fear masking his features. He's done or knows something that's causing him to watch his back. His knuckles are white as they clench his molecular genetics textbook. He's in the wrong academic hall to be carrying a book that has to do with biology.

I'd peg him about six foot, with dark brown hair and brown eyes. He shaved this morning, nicking himself under the chin not once, but twice. His jeans sag in the rear, a clear sign of being worn multiple times since being washed, while his shoes are clean, yet clearly worn.

This nervous student lingers around MacAfee's door, reaching into his textbook for what looks like folded papers, but pulls his hand away quickly when someone approaches. A female student walks by and calls out his name—John—and he nods at his friend as he runs his hand through his coiffed hair. They start down the hall together, with the friend talking animatedly and John nodding along.

As quickly as I can, I pack up and grab my bag and follow them out of the building, keeping a safe distance, but still able to hear their conversation. It's not nice to eavesdrop, but everyone is a suspect in this case until I can prove otherwise. Right now, I have three possible culprits: Charlie Bell, Ginger Ralph, and John with no last name.

When they head toward the cafeteria, I pause outside, waiting for someone else to open the door so I'm not required to touch the germ-infested handle. The cafeteria is a mecca for germs, cliques, and communicable diseases. I don't know if the latter is true or not, but by the amount of filth that accumulates in that room there has to be some sort of health code violation. I have managed to avoid Cook Commons since the first day of school, only entering during the mandatory student orientation.

It's only for the good of the investigation that I enter the building. As I step into the madness of the cafeteria, spotting John is easy. He's at a table with Delta Phi member Roger Stallworth, my lead suspect in the dorm-pranking case. Sitting next to Roger is the same blonde girl from earlier, likely pleading her case to be his date in a desperate attempt to go to the Deltas' ski lodge party this weekend.

Stepping out of Cook Commons, I find a spot where I can

boot up my laptop and learn more about John before I go in there to watch him. A quick search tells me everything I need to know. He's a bio major and therefore has no reason to be in the agricultural building. His presence there is a red flag and the fact that he was lurking by Professor MacAfee's door rings warning bells. Additionally, the fact that John Watson is the newly appointed treasurer of Delta Phi doesn't escape my notice. Suspect number one is the Delta Phi president and now we have the treasurer lurking outside the professor's office looking guilty, when he shouldn't be there. It's not enough to convict, but it might be enough to prod until one of the Deltas rolls on the other. I pull up the registry for the fraternity and see there is only one member who has anything to do with the agricultural program, and that is Charlie.

Charlie Bell is a Delta and is flunking MacAfee's class. According to the Delta code, Charlie could instruct another member of the fraternity to steal for him and the brother would, for fear they'd be kicked out of the house. Ginger Ralph needs to pass too, but her grade is a solid B this semester so it's unlikely that she'd steal the test, unless it's to blackmail Professor MacAfee, but for what? Could it be that Ginger thinks that MacAfee and Bell are having inappropriate relations? By the way she was acting in class today, it'd be my guess that Ginger definitely thinks something is happening between them, and she wants special treatment. I make a mental note to ask the good professor about any blackmailing attempts from her students.

I close my laptop and make my way back into the cafeteria. The crowd has thinned out, except for the people at John's table. There's a table across and one down from his that is open and I walk over to it, holding my breath and hoping that no one will beat me to it. I sit down with a sigh and instantly pull out my hand wipes to clean the area in front of me. I don't care if people are watching me; they should make a mental note about doing the same thing.

John Watson sits sandwiched between Roger, who is sleeping, and another student. I half expected to see John with the guy he walked out of the ag building with, but he's nowhere to be seen. Of course, if he isn't a Delta, he isn't allowed at the table anyway.

The one on his left keeps staring at me, while John looks only occasionally. I'm not that interesting, yet his table partner can't keep his eyes off me. They speak too quietly for me to hear, leaving me to my imagination, which is never a good thing. I keep my gaze wavering, looking from their table to others, pretending to be interested in the ambience around us. The only thing I'm interested in is getting John away from his friends so we can chat. I'm not expecting him to spill the beans right away as to what he was doing by Professor MacAfee's office, but maybe he'll allude to something that will interest me.

The back-and-forth between John and his friend is almost comical, yet slightly annoying. I need him to leave so I can speak with John, but the friend seems to be more interested in talking with his hands and looking at me rather than eating his lunch or leaving. Just as I'm about to stand and seek out John's attention, he starts to move, freezing me in my chair. His legs are shaky, much like a person who is learning to walk again after a traumatic accident, but building in confidence with each step. He's coming my way and I find myself sitting up straighter, noticing the look in his eyes as he approaches. It's hard to place a look I've never seen directed at me before, but *adoration* is what pops into my mind even though we—I mean, he doesn't know me.

"I'm John Watson," he says, extending his hand for me to shake, except I'm frozen in my chair because for the first time in my life my heart is thumping loudly and making it hard to think or process even the simplest gestures. I have never felt like this before, nor have I ever seen a set of eyes so blue (and not brown, as I originally suspected) that they make the sky look dull.

"Delta Phi treasurer?" It's the first thing that comes to mind, instead of introducing myself like a normal person. John smiles, accepting that I already know who he is. For most men this is an ego boost, but it seems to surprise John that I know this about him, and somewhere deep inside I'm happy about that. Now that he's standing mere inches from me, I'm agreeable to my emotional recognition that he is a handsome man. Too bad we're out of each other's leagues. Mine being that no one has ever liked me, so why would someone now, and his being that he's a fraternity member and would never date an outcast. Or he's likely involved in the conspiracy of the missing final.

Instead of sitting down, he stays standing and meets my gaze with his. He's nervous, and I don't know why. He approached me, not the other way around, and yet he's unsure if he should be standing at the opposite end of this table. His posture, hips, and shoulders are square, indicating that he wants to be here, that he's not being forced. Yet his chest moves more rapidly than it would for normal breathing and his cheeks are red. The shortness of breath could be a sign of something I have yet to pinpoint—guilt, maybe? It's interesting that my mind jumps to guilt, without looking at the obvious, embarrassment. He doesn't have a reason to feel guilty or embarrassed around me, at least not yet.

"That I am. Lock Holmes, right?" His eyes go wide when he says my name; he's clearly happy with himself for knowing who I am. It makes me wonder how he does, but we're not here to get to know me, or even him. I believe he has the answers that I need. He finally sits down even though I never invited him. The cat-and-mouse game of boy meets girl is foreign to me. I've never done this before, but clearly he has. I'll have to follow his lead to make sure I don't seem too out of place.

"How did you know my name?" he asks, as grin spreads across his face. The fact that I know his name pleases him; oddly enough, I find that I'm happy about this as well. It's an odd feeling, really, and something I'd like to figure out how to control.

I lean forward, resting my forearms on the surface that I cleaned. "I know a lot about you, John Watson." I'm meaning to shock him, make him think that I'm mysterious, but the opposite happens.

"I'd like to get to know you, Lock Holmes. Delta Phi is having their annual end-of-the-semester ski lodge party and I'd love it if you'd accompany me as my date."

"I thought you'd never ask," I blurt out before my brain has been able to comprehend what I've agreed to.

John's mouth drops open in delight and I find myself trying not to see if he's had dental work done. Finding out would be easy, but inconsequential to my case.

"The party is Friday night," he tells me, but that doesn't work for me. I need access to the Delta house before Friday so MacAfee can do whatever she plans to do with the test.

"Coffee."

"What about it?" John asks, subtly reminding me that I've only said one word.

"We should get some…now."

He looks over his shoulder at his friends before looking back at me. "I'll need to drop my books off."

"No problem," I say, standing and shouldering my backpack. Getting into the Delta Phi house is easier than I thought. I'm about to step into the lion's den, so to speak, and John is my tamer without even knowing it.

John moves quickly from my table and back to his. The book he was holding earlier in front of the professor's office is tucked under his arm. I'll watch and see where he puts it and hopefully come up with a reason for him to leave so I can take a peek inside and see what he's hiding. Part of me hopes it's nothing, because I do believe I liked the way he was looking at me.

• • •

JOHN WATSON

I try not to mess around with the girls here at school. For one, I don't have time. My studies keep me busy. Another reason is that they're clingy. I'm going to be a doctor and to them that screams "future." To me it yells "headache." At this point in my schooling, I'm content being single and taking girls with me to movies, to dinner, and to Delta Phi's many parties. However, walking next to Lock—the girl I have had my eyes on since I first saw her—is making me rethink my current state of being single. I know it's early, but I believe in kismet. She's a mystery to me and as she walks alongside me, the subtle brushes of her arm against mine give me hope.

"What do you like to do for fun?" I ask, to break the ice. Even though we were just chatting, we really didn't say much to each other. In fact, the more I think about it, the more I realize that she said yes to my invite awfully quickly. The thought makes me wonder if she's been crushing on me as long as I have on her, even though I know it's probably not true. I wouldn't be against a kiss or two.

"I'm sure my idea of fun is different from yours."

"Try me," I say, placing my hand on her back as we cross the street. She doesn't need my guidance, but at this point I'm willing to do anything I can to touch or be close to her. Lock pauses, looks at me, and is met with probably the cheesiest grin ever before quickly turning her head toward the opposite side of the street. She may be trying to hide it, but I saw her smile.

"I like to study. I'm not here to party or be social. I'm here to get an education. For fun, I watch documentaries."

I can't help but chuckle. "Well, Lock, you and I seem to be one and the same and I don't know if that's a good or bad thing. For fun, I like to go over the musculoskeletal system and test my knowledge. What is it that you're studying?" I point toward the house and use my body to guide hers into the parking lot.

"A little bit of everything at the moment. I'm undecided."

I find her answer odd considering she just said she likes to study and watch documentaries in her spare time, but it's common for a freshman to be undecided. I questioned what I was going to do when I got here even though I knew I wanted to be a doctor. I thought maybe I'd do something else but my passion for helping people won out in the end.

The closer we get to Delta house, the more dread starts to set in. It's only cleaned the night before a big party, which means we still have a day or so until my brothers and I make a massive effort to pick up our many pizza boxes, beer bottles, and errant pieces of clothing. I open the door and step in, pausing as I take in the mess before me. My only consolation is that my room is somewhat clean, just not clean enough that I'd want to invite a girl in. My answer is made for me when I feel her step in behind me.

"Follow me," I say over my shoulder as I head up the stairs. Only when I reach the top do I realize I should've followed her up, like a gentleman.

It seems that my mind isn't where it should be right now.

"You'll have to forgive the mess in my bedroom; I wasn't expecting company," I tell her as I open the door. I toss my book down onto my bed, watching as the papers I had tucked away in there fall out. I figure if I don't pay attention to them, neither will she, even though they're like a bright red beacon yelling at me. If I had planned things better they wouldn't be mocking me right now.

"We can go now," I say to Lock, interrupting her perusing session around my room. "Most of the crap belongs to my roommate."

"The skeleton is yours," she says, picking up Scully's hand and letting it drop back down.

"Yes."

Lock continues her exploration of my room, pausing at my dresser and focusing on my medical terminology poster that hangs on my wall. She wanders close to my bed, choosing to sit on the edge.

"What does your roommate study?" she asks.

I sit down next to her and point up. I keep my gaze steady on her as she takes in the solar system above us. It's probably one of the best things about my roommate. He loves the stars and at night our room lights up like the night sky. It's like having our own planetarium in here, just closer and the stars fall off the ceiling if it gets too humid in here.

"Isn't this something mothers do for their children?"

I try not to give her a funny look, but her question strikes me as odd. Did her mother not do this for her when she was a child? Mine certainly did.

"Yes, but my roommate uses them to study at night."

"Clever," she says, turning to face me. Her leg is bent, opening herself up to me. I wonder if she knows that she's in the perfect kissable situation right now. I could move closer and test the waters, see if she's even remotely interested in me. I mean, we are in my room and my roommate won't be back for a couple of hours. It's college, I'm a guy, and she's here. I could be smooth and lean in and see if she meets me halfway, or I can sit here and admire the object of my affections.

I'm about to get my wish, because Lock is leaning toward me and I'm meeting her halfway. She's making the first move. I close my eyes and lick my lips, preparing them for hers. My nose smacks into something hard, and when I open my eyes I find that I'm staring at the wall and my head is cockeyed on her shoulder.

Lock is stiff, waiting for me to move. I do so as cool as possible so that it looks like I meant to do that—because, you know, smashing my nose into her shoulder is as cool as I get. When I'm upright and my manhood starts to come back, I see that the papers from my bed are now in her hand and she's reading them.

"I thought you were a bio major?"

My heart and stomach drop to the floor while my pulse races. I knew this would happen if these were found on my person.

"I am."

She shows me the papers that will end my college career. There is no plausible reason for me to have the agroecology final in my room. When it was handed to me, I should've thrown it back in my brother's face, but I took a pledge and while he may be blurring the lines, he would've done the same thing for me.

Lock flips through the final, known to be the hardest one on campus. Delta Phi could've sold the test and made a killing. Instead, we've been using it to help Charlie study, because frankly, we're sick of him hanging around. He's been acting like an old man this year. It's time for him to go.

"I can explain," I say, pulling the papers out of her hand and moving closer to her.

"There's no need," she says, taking the papers back. "I know Professor MacAfee is looking for these."

"I know, and I was trying to return them."

"How long have you had them?" she asks.

"Months. The long and short of it is that we're trying to help Charlie graduate and he needs to pass this class."

"You've broken the law." Lock crosses her arms, effectively hiding the papers under her arm. The only way I can get them back from her is to reach around or tackle her. Personally, I'd love to tackle her so that we're wrestling around a little, but I have a feeling she'll frown upon that move.

"I haven't," I tell her, defending myself. "I didn't take the test. I was only trying to return it."

"I know. I saw you." Lock covers her mouth, clearly taken aback by her slip of the tongue.

"You were watching me?" The thought actually excites and validates my odd stalking habits when it comes to her. I can't help but smile, letting her know that her admission is sitting very well with me.

"I'm investigating and have said far too much. I must go."

"No, wait." I grab her arm as she stands. She can't leave with the test. It's my responsibility to return it, sight unseen. "You can't leave. Well, you can, but not with the test. I need to return it."

"That's what I'm going to do. Professor MacAfee will pay me for its return."

Well, crap, it's not like I can compete with money. That's liquid gold to a college kid.

"How much? I'll double it," I tell her without really thinking about the ramifications of emptying my wallet or savings account.

Lock looks at me, perplexed, pulling her cheek in between her teeth. Either I've outsmarted her or…well, I don't know, because she seems pretty damn intuitive and observant about things.

"I don't know. She never said."

Bingo!

I stand and place my hands on her shoulders and look her in the eye. "Lock, I think you're beautiful and have thought that since I saw you on the first day of school. However, your beauty aside, I cannot let you return that to MacAfee. I will treat you to a month's worth of dinners off campus if you allow me to put that back in her drawer."

"Where's the thumb drive?"

"The what?"

"There was a thumb drive too. It's been stolen as well."

My hands drop as I shrug. "I didn't steal the test, and no, I'm not telling you who did. I was only tasked with returning it. I don't know anything about a thumb drive."

Lock studies me, no doubt watching my facial expressions to see if I'm lying. I have a feeling she's good at reading people and that thought sort of scares me.

"I could use some food," she says, catching me off guard. The smile that accompanies her comment is enough to make any man weak in the knees. I know mine are about to buckle. "But we need to return the test first."

"How do you propose we do that?"

"Simple—we'll go back to the ag building and wait until the time is right."

My mind can't find any plausible reason to disagree with her, making me believe that a life of crime is in our future.

• • •

LOCK HOLMES

Today I've committed a series of "Lock never does this" type of things. I've agreed to a date with a complete stranger, followed him to his house, and willingly walked up a flight of stairs to his bedroom all in the name of an investigation, while wondering what it'd be like to hold his hand. Today is a day of new experiences; why not test them all out? Because that's not who I am, that's why. I'm the one who pays close attention to my surroundings, notices mundane things like the comforter on John's bed has been sewn, which I can tell because the corners aren't square, or the fact that the house he lives in is slowly slipping off its foundation. He'll never know, but the sliver of light coming through his closed door is a pure indication of structural issues.

I had never felt pure elation before until my fingers touched the papers on his bed. My gut instinct told me earlier that John had what I was seeking. It's common for students to be in buildings that aren't related to their area of study; what I found odd was how he was acting. Slinking down the hall and looking over his back as if he were waiting for someone. It was right for me to follow him. Except now that I know he has the test and have heard his explanation, I don't want to turn him in, making me a less-than-stellar investigator. I should be strong enough to put looks and personality aside. He's a criminal and should be treated as such. But when he brushed against me while we were walking, he sent shivers over my skin, something I've never felt before.

The near kiss almost sent me into overdrive. I had to act quickly for fear he'd realize I've never been kissed before. Boys tend to make a mockery of a situation like this, so I did what any self-respecting future crime solver would do—I reached for the evidence. What I didn't expect was his reasons for having the test and the pleading that came with it—or my willingness to help him continue the cover-up.

"I need a piece of paper," I say to John, who immediately pulls his notebook out of his backpack, tears out a sheet, and hands it to me. The deep impression of his pen allows me to read the words he had previously written. It's medical jargon and something I tell myself I should learn. You can never have too much knowledge. I pick up one of his pencils off his bed and start sketching the ag building from what I remember of it. As soon as I'm done, I hand it to John.

"Okay, what do we do with this?"

I don't know? Think fast, Lock. All I've drawn is the inside of the building, which doesn't do much for us. What we need are the blueprints showing us how to tunnel through the heating system and into Professor MacAfee's office.

"Professor MacAfee trusts you, right?" John asks.

I nod halfheartedly because *trust* is such a deep word. I'm not sure if I trust anyone but my parents.

"So she wouldn't suspect anything if you're in her office, right?"

"Yes! Why didn't I think about that? I have access to her office. I mean, I can call and she or her aide will open it for me. You're brilliant," I say, as I spring from my spot on his bed and wrap my arms around him. He holds me to him, not letting me go. The appropriate time for a friendly hug has passed, but neither of us seems to want to let go. That is, until I feel his right hand move from the center of my back to my side. The unfamiliar feelings have me pulling away and avoiding any type of eye contact.

I stand, moving away from John and his bed, and pull out my cell phone. "I'll text MacAfee now and let her know that I'll need access immediately. Hopefully by the time we get there, the door will be open and we can slip the test back in, unsuspected."

"Sounds good," John says, stepping behind me. I try not to let his closeness affect me, but I'd be a liar if I said I wasn't feeling something. I just wish I knew what it was. I look at him over my shoulder and fight the smile that is pushing its way out. His backpack is slung over his shoulder and without saying anything John and I trek across campus, keeping a healthy distance between us. Every time he steps closer I change my pace, only to find myself gravitating toward him. When we enter the ag building, it's fairly quiet, most of the classes having concluded for the day. John leads the way to MacAfee's office. At the last moment, I cut in front of him. If MacAfee is to have her room dusted for fingerprints, I don't want his to show up. It's best that I be the one who turns the doorknob.

I leave the light off and close the door after him, locking it so we can put the test back unseen. I pull out my penlight, a gift from my parents last Christmas, and light up the room enough for us to see.

"That's the coolest light ever," John whispers as he puts his arm around me. I don't shrug him off because I like the way it feels there. MacAfee's office isn't big, but her desk sits back in the corner, set kitty-corner. It's an odd configuration, but it must work for her.

"She said bottom drawer," I say, as I tug at it. It takes what little strength I have to pull the drawer open. John catches me as I fall backward and it doesn't escape me that his lips have brushed against my cheek. I should move, but I don't. I sort of like the way he's holding me.

John hands me the test and I set it in the drawer, right next to a thumb drive. I pick up the drive, holding it between my fingers.

"Do you have your laptop?"

"Yes, why?" he asks, slipping his bag off his shoulder and pulling his laptop out. He lifts the lid and types in his passcode. I show him the thumb drive and hate that I can't see his expression.

"MacAfee said the thumb drive was stolen as well, yet it's in her drawer. Let's see what's on it."

John doesn't hesitate, taking the thumb drive out of my hand and plugging it in. A video pops up with Professor MacAfee smiling at us.

"What is this?"

"I don't know," he says, pressing play.

"Hello, Lock and John. My plan couldn't have worked out better. John, weeks ago your brothers came to me asking for help. They thought I'd be the best person to help, since I have neither of you as students. Your brothers have grown tired of watching you fawn over Lock Holmes and asked me to intervene.

"I came up with the idea that my final would come up missing after contacting my friend Ron, at the police station. He is well versed in all things Lock and said I would need an investigation if I wanted her attention." She winks at the camera as if any of this is funny.

"The final for my class isn't missing, in case you're wondering. I changed Charlie's grades in the computer system knowing you, Lock, would look there first, hoping you'd think he'd be your suspect.

"John had a specific time to try and return the test and Lock being there played perfectly into the plan. I'm hoping I can say everything else has worked out. The reason you're in my office is because John likes you, Lock. I'm hoping that someday you'll like him in return. Thank you both for being willing participants in Delta Phi's plot to bring their brother some happiness."

The video goes blank and John and I are left cloaked in the darkness of MacAfee's office.

"I'm sorry, Lock. My brothers are...well, there are just no words."

"Is it true?" I ask, turning around, relishing the way his hands feel as I move in them. I shine my penlight on him, as if he's under investigation.

"Very true. I like you, a lot."

My body warms at the sound of his words. I've never known someone who wanted to be with me before, and maybe I want to try to be with him. I drop my penlight and lean in, brushing my trembling lips against his. John pulls me close, deepening the kiss, until I pull away. I realize for the first time, I'm experiencing a stirring in my belly, which has to be the love butterflies, and John is reason for them.

"That was nice. I think I'd like to try that again." And he does, pressing his lips against mine once more and hopefully not for the last time.

BEETHOVEN'S BATON

BY AUSTIN FARMER

Oh friends, not these sounds!
Let us instead strike up more pleasing
and more joyful ones!
—Johann Christoph Friedrich von Schiller, "Ode to Joy"
Performed in Beethoven's Ninth Symphony

Sherlock strummed the last note of the symphony and exhaled sharply. The power required to produce those incessant fortissimos—the sheer amplitude of the piece—was nearly too much for any instrumentalist to play, let alone a violinist. One of the strings on Sherlock's violin unwound itself, sprang up into the air in a wild corkscrew, and nearly stabbed his eye out. He bit his tongue and swallowed his frustration, careful not to upset his vehement conductor.

Luckily, his conductor was a little hard of hearing as of late and had not noticed. Sure, Ludwig van Beethoven was a creative genius, but his demand was much too high; how could one be expected to learn his Ninth Symphony in less than two weeks' rehearsal? If it were not for the sheer beauty of their performance hall, the Kärntnertortheater, throbbing in the heart of Vienna, Sherlock would have dropped his violin in the middle of the movement and moved to Berlin the next day, leaving everyone, even his roommate, to ponder his exit strategy as an unsolvable mystery—something only he alone could solve.

"Have to make sure I remember this theme," Watson said. He laid the violin on his lap and dog-eared a page of his score. "I have never heard anything so sweet."

"After how loud that was," Sherlock said, "surely I will never be able to hear anything ever again."

There was a yell from the podium, and Sherlock covered his ears just in time before it turned into a roar. Beethoven was screaming at Fabian Rainer for not turning the pages of Marcos Pierre's score quickly enough. Since Fabian had been demoted from first-chair to second-chair cellist, Fabian was required to turn the pages of their score, but he had been falling behind. There was something in Fabian's demeanor—his sagged shoulders, his pallid skin, the constant nervous flitters of his eyes—that made Sherlock uneasy. With only one day until their performance, the orchestra needed to be focused on the task at hand.

"If you are not paying attention, then perhaps I should not pay you at all." Beethoven spoke in a deep legato, his words nearly incoherent mumbles. He threw his hands in the air and shook his head furiously. "Do you not know who our guest is tomorrow, or are you all ignorant? Leopold Hobrecht, the royal representative of Berlin, will sit right there in that box seat. And if you do not turn pages quickly enough, Fabian, I ensure you will never play a note in the heavenly gardens of Vienna ever again."

Beethoven chewed the tip of his baton and wrote a note on his score. Fabian seemed to cower into his chair, and Marcos smiled sardonically.

"Look at his nervous twitch, chewing his baton like that," Watson said. "Just listen to those hideous ultimatums. And his infallible rage—I believe that he might finally be losing it."

"My dear Watson," Sherlock said, "surely he has lost it long ago. Have you not seen him walking around town like a vagabond, wandering through darkness on many midnight's new moons, humming? It is a gradual breakdown of the mind. For when an artist born with sight can no longer see his own painting, he suffers a gradual breakdown; likewise, when a composer can hardly hear his song, the brain begins to hum dark phantom melodies in the mind."

"Whatever phantom tune his muse whispers into his ear, it is straight from Apollo's lips," Watson said. "His melodies are the anthems of Olympus. He truly understands what the world wants to hear."

"And how the world should sound. He is desultory and delusional, but ingenious at that. I just wish he were not marching to the beat of his own drummer."

"Careful. He can still read lips."

Beethoven glared at Sherlock. He ran his hands through his steely-gray hair and stormed out of the room. Sherlock nodded and mouthed a pleasant hello; Beethoven quickly walked by without giving him another glance and hissed a sharp "*Auf wiedersehen.*"

"Harsh," Sherlock said.

Sherlock felt something brush up against his ankle. He leaned over, and there on the floor was one of Fabian's pages. He picked it up and stared at it incredulously, as if he were deciphering some foreign language. The room was empty now, and Sherlock could hear Watson sighing, eager to join the rest of the orchestra and chorus for a well-deserved break.

"What is it?" Watson reached for the score, but Sherlock pulled it back. "Another one of your treasonous conspiracy theories?"

"Take out your violin."

"But I do not want to practice any longer. You promised me a wine at Café Dejaun after our last case, remember?"

"Stay just a moment longer, and I will double my offer. Take it or leave it."

"The price of friendship is costly, and yet in such instances I must remind myself the payback is greater." Watson walked over to the piano and opened the cover. "Two glasses of wine it is, yes?"

Sherlock nodded and set the score on the piano. "Play me the first theme."

"It has been a while since I have even touched the keys, but how is this?" Watson played a few notes, and to Sherlock it sounded as if a child were taking his first lesson on the piano. The grand concertmasters of Vienna—Haydn, Mozart, and Schubert—would wince at the amateur fingers dancing across the keys. Surely, Sherlock concluded, Bach was rolling over in his grave.

"Now play me this." Sherlock turned over the score. Scribbled at the top of the page was a new staff with mere inkblots as quarter notes. Underneath was a scrawl of an almost illegible date: *May 7, 1824.*

"I have never seen this before. Beethoven is not surprising us with a new theme tomorrow, is he?"

"That is because Beethoven did not write it. It is not even in the proper key."

"And to whom does this belong?"

"Fabian."

"Then perhaps Fabian was attempting to start his own opus and nonchalantly wrote a tune." There was a tone of annoyance in Watson's voice that surprised Sherlock. "It was his own personal diary. I do not see the point of this. Now let us go. I am hungry and in desperate need of a drink or three."

"If your eyes do not fail you, the date written is tomorrow. How can one write a journal entry for the future? Unless our friend is a time traveler, of course. Go on, play it for me."

Watson sighed and conceded; he played the tune a little more fluently. "There, are you happy? It is not even good. This melody belongs at the bottom of a pigsty."

Sherlock stood at the far end of the piano and played the notes flawlessly. "Do you not see it?"

"All I am seeing is a future which consists of me slapping you across the face. You owe me food. Do not let that future come true."

"Look closely. Sometimes it is not what is heard, but what is seen on the page. The notes." Sherlock played so quickly that it nearly became a flurry of dissonant notes. "D-E-A-D-F-A-C-E."

"It is a few chords with major sevenths. I do not understand why you are—"

"'Dead face,' circled approximately three times below Beethoven's name, written in a hurry."

"Peculiar, I admit, but what do you make of it?"

"Murder, Watson. Murder. Is it not obvious? This is revenge commissioned by Fabian himself. He is more than a little angry that he is not first-chair cellist anymore. Follow me."

"But my drink, the café…" Watson was barely able to pick up his violin case as Sherlock dragged him excitedly by the sleeve.

• • •

Watson had scarcely begun to proclaim his appetite to the foggy, crowded streets of Vienna when Sherlock knocked on Fabian's door. Beethoven's fortissimos had perhaps haunted Watson—Sherlock's knocks were soft rasps on the door, yet Watson nearly jumped at the sound.

"Remember," Watson said, "we must not accuse Fabian of treason unless we have definite proof."

"Must you state the obvious?" Sherlock said. "That is part of the fun, to let him announce his own guilt."

"What guilt?" The door opened a crack, and the soft glow of candlelight danced across Fabian's face. Sherlock would have mistaken Fabian's expression for a scowl if it weren't for his peculiar countenance. Fabian looked as though he were in a state of perpetual despair—and perhaps he was. His eyebrows were upside-down arches digging crevices into his skin, nearly dragging his entire forehead down beneath his eyes. Sherlock had once seen a mutt with the same visage, although the mutt was happy, unlike his colleague standing before him.

"Fabian, a minute of your time, please."

"I do not possess many of those." Fabian opened the door and motioned for them to come inside. "Get on with it."

The house looked lonely, and it took no effort for Sherlock to deduce that it was a reflection of the dismal man who resided within. The floor was littered with paper, and with every step Sherlock had to lift his feet to avoid tripping. He was astounded that the candle had not fallen from the nightstand and the paper had not caught fire, burning the entire place to ruins. In one corner of the room sat a shoddy piano slanting unevenly on one leg, its keys ragged at the edges like broken wishbones. In the other corner sat a bed, its down feathers seeping through the mattress, as if a pheasant had imploded within. Sherlock would have concluded that Fabian had had an intense night of passion and love with some unseen mistress if he did not already know of Fabian's perpetual state of isolation outside of work.

"Listen here," Sherlock said. "We wanted to confess just how disappointed we are about the situation."

Fabian didn't flinch. "I know not of what you speak."

"You are no longer first-chair cellist," Sherlock said. "A situation that is most appalling. Especially before the premiere."

"It is no matter." Fabian seemed to wave this off with a flick of his hand, as if he were batting away a fly, until Sherlock noticed that indeed there were minuscule houseflies fluttering about. Sherlock felt one crawling up his neck and flicked it away. "Our beloved conductor will experience an unfortunate epiphany sometime soon."

Watson shot a look to Sherlock, eyes wide, mouth ajar. Could Watson be any more obvious? Sherlock was highly experienced at hiding his observations, but he could tell Watson was breaking. Sherlock remained stone-faced; they could not play the game of deduction without even beginning in the first place.

"And what do you mean by that?" Sherlock asked.

"His time will come," Fabian said. "He will realize he was wrong, but by that time it will be too late."

Sherlock stepped closer, cornering Fabian against the wall. Now was the time to accuse.

"And by what time are you calculating this murder?"

"Murder?" Fabian's eyes, for once, had opened up, and his expression of despair was replaced with surprise. He chuckled, as if Sherlock were simply telling a joke; Sherlock played it off as so and joined in on the laughter. "I would be lying if I said I had never dreamt such thoughts in mindless reverie, but I have no plans of the sort. I could not even hurt a fly."

A fly was crawling across Fabian's cheek and was poking its legs around the corners of his lips. Fabian slapped himself and the fly's body fell to the floor.

"Well, most of the time," Fabian said, shrugging.

"Tell us, what do you make of this?" Sherlock pulled the musical score out of his pocket and held it beneath the candlelight.

Fabian walked over to the piano and strummed the melody. The piano was severely out of tune, each note in a key of its own, the entire instrument playing tritones and hideous chords from the underworld.

"This melody belongs on the floors of a pigsty."

"That is exactly what I said." Watson walked over and played the piano with Fabian. "We speak the same language. Musicians."

"Pleading ignorance leads you nowhere, Fabian." Sherlock closed in on Fabian and studied his face. Near the candlelight, everything was illuminated, including the fear plaguing Fabian's face. "You wrote this melody yourself. It is your own handwriting. Your floor is covered with your own penmanship, and the strokes of the quill on this page match perfectly with those littering your floor."

"I do not deny that. Yes, Marcos hummed this to me and had me write it down the day he arrived. I believe it is a secret love letter Marcos had me write for his man-lover, Beethoven. They are infatuated with each other, you know, because why else would Marcos arrive from Berlin, completely unannounced, and replace the most respected virtuoso string player in Vienna?" Fabian put his thumbs up to his chest, reveling in his pride. "You must stop their rabid desire for each other before they run off and have children together. Sure, Marcos acts as though he blows me out of the water, but that is only because he was blowing something else."

Sherlock studied the message again; he hadn't considered that perhaps Fabian had been told to write this.

"And you know nothing else?" Sherlock asked.

"Oh, one more thing," Fabian added. "He said his melody

was linked to proper fingering with piano or something intellectual like that. Berlin piece of shit, trying to act regal all the time. Not that he knows how to finger any woman, though, unless it is up somebody's—"

"Watson," Sherlock said, stopping Fabian from sharing any more of his theories. "Tell me, what fingers do you use to play the melody that belongs at the bottom of a pigsty?"

Watson struck the piano keys. "D is on the fifth in the scale. So five."

"Or fourth," Sherlock said, "if you are counting the letters of the alphabet. Yes. D is fourth. E is third. Keep playing."

Sherlock ran over to Fabian's nightstand, picked up a quill, and started writing. Sherlock scribbled on the score, drawing arrows and lines correlating the notes to the alphabet.

"Listen here. D-E-A-D-F-A-C-E correlates to numbers 4314 and 6135 in the alphabet. Or, combining the two lexicons, it is 4314 face, or, when the letters are unscrambled, F-A-C-E can spell *cafe*. Yes, that is it—4314 Cafe Street, hidden in the slums of our city. I know that area. You ass, Sherlock. You pure ass. Should have known."

"So Marcos is trying to kill Beethoven?" Fabian's face lit up with joy. "He will be demoted from first-chair cellist again?"

"No reason to celebrate yet," Sherlock said. "If you keep quiet about this mess, you will regain your position in the orchestra."

"But if we know Marcos is to blame, why not simply expose him?" Watson asked.

"On the contrary," Sherlock said. "He is carrying out orders from someone above. Let us follow his accidental trail of clues and subvert his expectations by going straight to his superiors."

"So to the cafe, then, finally?" Watson asked.

"Not the typical cafe you are thinking of," Sherlock said.

"But you promised…"

Lost in excitement, Sherlock stormed triumphantly out the door.

"Run along, then," Fabian said, and Watson tried his best to keep up.

• • •

Sherlock and Watson had discovered the apothecary's workroom right where the conspirator had not wanted them to be found, directly at 4314 Cafe Street, near the southern shores of the Danube River. It was almost too easy, Sherlock noted, and the irresponsible breadcrumbs this madman had left behind seemed almost purposeful.

The apothecary's room smelled of lavender, rosemary, and sweet tea; for an institution that held such desperate clients of the mad, the depressed, and the dying, Sherlock was surprised that Raphael Czerny, the apothecary, had kept the place smelling so sweet. Such exact sanitization was not normal. Perhaps he was hiding something—the stench of a corpse, the rot of decaying limbs, or perhaps even the fumes of a dangerous lie.

Underneath the candelabra, Sherlock held his magnifying glass in one hand, a vial in the other. Translucent liquid bubbled to the top of the vial and exploded in tiny eruptions within. It was odd, the way the liquid reflected Sherlock's face in steep curves, his eyes transforming into bulbous and gelatinous bubbles, only to have his reflection blow up and dissolve back into the liquid as if it were never there in the first place.

"You will have to pardon my friend for his poor manners." Watson stood at the other end of the room, leaning wearily against the wall. "When he is seized upon his work, he acts with the chivalry of a fool. Is that not so, Sherlock? He does not even listen. But I can assure you—he is not as rude as he seems."

"Seems pretty rude to touch what's not yours." Raphael ran to Sherlock, snatched the vial from his hands, and set it in a wooden container next to four other glass vials. "An emergency, you said. Emergency my ass. Are you going to purchase your medicines, or aren't you?"

Sherlock reached for the vial again but Raphael grabbed his wrist. Sherlock glared at Raphael, and Raphael almost recoiled. Sherlock was venomous when he allowed himself to be.

"Tell me," Sherlock said. "If somebody were to come here seeking something lethal, what would you say?"

"Would tell 'em they're looking in the wrong place."

"And if they were to request anything other than medicine, perhaps something to kill a few rodents—arsenic—how would you go about providing this?"

"Haven't sold that shit in years."

"Tell me, then, why is every other substance displayed in even numbers of vials, whereas this rat repellent is displayed in the odd? There are only five of them."

Raphael's eyes flittered nervously across from Sherlock to the vial then back to Sherlock again.

"Who was it?" Sherlock asked.

"Some ex-members of the Committee of Public Safety needed some stuff to clear paths on the Alps. Needed to prepare themselves for a journey through winter, they said, and needed something strong."

"They supply their own arsenic, their own licensed apothecary. Do not lie to me, Raphael. I can close this place down with the snap of my fingers if I so desire."

That was partly true, partly false, but Sherlock remained silent as Raphael thought this over.

"You step through *my* door and threaten me?"

"Not only would you become a criminal if you chose to withhold such key information, you would also be a treasonous murderer of your dear country, eradicating patriotism and nationalism for eternity."

Raphael twiddled the arsenic between his fingers. "About a fortnight ago, a man came in here requesting some. Said his house was infested with rats, didn't want to wait for the rats in office to give him the go-ahead to clear them himself."

"Tell me who he is."

"Truth is, well, I was too high to tell. I sell opium, use the stuff. Happy? Looked like a murderer to me, this man. But the next morning, I found this on the floor. Figured it belonged to him. You can have it, as long as you get the hell out of here."

Raphael pulled open a cupboard and held an object under the candelabra. Sherlock's heart started clanging against his ribcage—had his theories all been wrong? It couldn't be.

It was Beethoven's baton.

• • •

"But he would never lose his lucky baton the night before the concert," Watson said. He was trailing behind, and Sherlock began to grow annoyed. "A man that anxious practically views his baton as a part of himself."

"That is because he does not know it is missing. Someone has duplicated it. Someone who does not want King Leopold to enjoy the show. Keep up."

Sherlock rolled the baton and felt the imprint of the company's sigil beneath his thumb; the official seal of East Orderly, the woodworking plant of Vienna, was emblazoned into the bottom of the baton, and it matched the seal on the door.

Although the midnight air was cold, Sherlock felt himself breaking out in a sweat; time was of the essence, and, for once, Sherlock began to feel the prevention of this murder was slipping entirely out of his grasp. If Vienna were to lose Ludwig van Beethoven, one of its greatest artistic, sociological, and political assets, the streets would erupt in chaos, riot, and destruction, and Sherlock would feel entirely responsible.

Sherlock knocked on the door. No answer. He charged his shoulder into the door; it didn't budge. It was Watson who was finally able to open it by simply turning the knob. Watson laughed, and Sherlock pretended not to hear.

Inside, the room was torn to shreds. Fabian's house was cleaner in comparison, and that was saying something. The tiled floor was cracked and covered with wooden planks, fallen bricks, and heaps of dust.

"Looks like someone left in a hurry," Watson said.

"Someone who had a reason to rush off. Keep the door open. We need more moonlight."

Watson propped open the door as Sherlock started sifting through the rubble. After a moment, Sherlock came across something cylindrical and nearly froze.

"What is it?" Watson asked.

"Erroneous revenge, Watson. This object confirms that they wanted to be discovered after the fact. That is such a shame, because we will expose them before."

"Before when?"

"The potential murderer has been playing Beethoven's symphony for quite some time, someone who is capable of observing Beethoven's eccentric twitches, but this man's heart belongs to the song of another country."

"In plain German, please."

"Marcos was never commissioned to play Beethoven's symphony."

Sherlock turned the object in his hands, and through the soft moonlight seeping through the door, he could see it was the same as the vial of arsenic in Raphael's shop, but this one was marked with a different sigil. It was a maroon flag with a mighty lion slashing its claws.

The official sigil of King Leopold's office.

• • •

Perhaps it was the heat of the audience that had gathered in the cramped Kärntnertortheater, or perhaps it was because he felt the future of music resting solely in his hands, but regardless of the reason, Sherlock needed to regulate his body temperature, for any slip in his plan, any erroneous mistake caused by his nervous system, would mean an abrupt ending to the concert, and an even more abrupt ending to their misunderstood yet beloved conductor.

Sherlock casually glanced at the front row, pretending to admire the royal guest. King Leopold of Berlin obviously wanted to be noticed for his grandeur and riches; he didn't even take his box seat reserved for royalty. King Leopold sat in the center of the front row surrounded by mistresses on either side who could have passed for his granddaughters. They fought desperately for the King's attention, rubbing their hands through his milky-white hair that fell in curls to his shoulders, caressing the nape of his neck with their fingers, even going so far as to nibble his earlobe and tug it ferociously, giggling as it slung back into place.

As King Leopold lifted his hands in a wave to a Viennese admirer, golden bracelets clattered against his body, nearly as loud as the cymbals in the orchestra. His well-equipped guards behind him didn't even flinch. Sherlock found it increasingly difficult to stop himself from running offstage and directly knocking this disgusting man unconscious himself.

The orchestra finished tuning on a lush, open A chord as the Grand Ambassador of the theater walked onstage.

The audience hushed. After a brief pause, the ambassador made his introduction.

"We introduce to you Ludwig van Beethoven and his works. Let the royal procession begin."

The audience erupted in applause. King Leopold gently pushed his lovers away as Beethoven walked onstage. A devilish grin crept across the king's face. Chills shot through Sherlock's spine; he had never seen a smile so genuine. If Sherlock didn't know any better, he might have thought the king was smiling simply because he had never been more excited to hear the newest symphony, not to watch Beethoven's body fall lifelessly to the floor.

Beethoven ran his hands through his hair, and just as he was about to pick up the baton and chew on the arsenic, Sherlock bolted upright from his chair.

"Before the royal procession can begin," Sherlock shouted, "we have one more important announcement. You sir, in the front row, please stand up. And, Beethoven, keep your hand off the baton."

Confused, Beethoven looked around and muttered an incoherent curse under his breath. King Leopold stood without hesitation.

Sherlock pointed to King Leopold with his violin. "I will be blunt—your royal guest here is trying to kill you."

King Leopold and Beethoven gasped at nearly the same time; ironically harmonious, Sherlock noted.

The king was no longer smiling. "Such accusations of treason will sentence your head to the blood-caked planks of the guillotine," he said. "Be careful what you say."

"It is not my hot-headed brain that will be decapitated in the name of Vienna," Sherlock said. "Observe." Sherlock walked to the podium and picked up Beethoven's baton. Sherlock could feel the angry stares of the orchestra and chorus behind him. "Tell me, Ludwig van Beethoven, have you recently created a duplicate of your baton?" Beethoven, having carefully read Sherlock's lips, shook his head. "Throughout rehearsals, you chew at the tip of your baton. Surely this one would be worn down by now, but it is not. Can you explain the cleanliness of this?"

"Looks new to me," Beethoven said. "I presume it is a gift?"

"A deadly one. Now observe evidence number two: An empty vial, which formerly contained arsenic, imprinted with the sigil of your beloved king, found in the East Orderly shop the night before the potential murder. Explain this, King Leopold Hobrecht of Berlin."

The king opened his mouth as if to speak but found himself stuttering instead. There were a few grumbles from behind.

"That is correct," Sherlock continued. "King Leopold cannot deny this, because he was attempting to assassinate Beethoven by dipping his baton into a vial of arsenic, this very baton, commissioned by his very own rat, Marcos Pierre, in conjunction with East Orderly. Stand up, Marcos, and stand up, Leopold. Let the audience applaud your effort."

Marcos remained seated, hatred flickering through his eyes.

Sherlock turned to Beethoven. "King Leopold was not here to listen to your newest symphony. He planned his regal attendance to witness your murder with his own eyes. Anything to say, King?"

"Take him away." King Leopold snapped his fingers, and his

guards stood in perfect synchronization. They pushed through the crowd and charged for the stage, their bayonets pointed straight at Sherlock.

The orchestra wouldn't allow it; they rushed from their chairs and stood as a wall shoulder-to-shoulder around Beethoven, their instruments standing in as their swords and shields.

"Tell us the truth," Watson said, hands trembling, "or I smash my violin into your skull."

"So what if it is true." The king stood in front of the audience as if he were reciting a monologue. "I could not allow Vienna to be the home of the most wonderful music in the world any longer. Once you refused to hold the premiere of this symphony in Berlin, that is when we lost it. You wanted to, and yet the people of Vienna have tainted your loyalty. You are a traitor, nothing more. Do you even remember where you grew up?

"Yes, you have discovered our plans, you mere instrumentalists," the king continued. "I admit—we have hired your own first-chair cellist, Marcos, to help in the plan. He is splendid, really, just *splendid*, and he has done well in convincing Vienna's very own baton craftsman to flee the country." King Leopold motioned for Marcos to stand. "Applaud, everyone. Applaud."

Fabian glanced at Sherlock with an I-told-you-so smirk. Sherlock smiled an embarrassed apology.

"But, Beethoven, there is still time to redeem yourself to your original king, the only true king of the world. We can forget this has ever happened and erase this from our memories. However, if you perform here any longer, you will disgrace your fathers and their forefathers before them, erasing your existence from the greatest country of the universe: Berlin."

"Never speak of my father. I hated him." Beethoven held up the baton with a trembling hand and pointed at King Leopold. "You will be exposed."

"Well, then, since I have the power to rewrite history, even to rewrite this very moment, I sentence you all to death for defying the greatest king who has ever lived."

The king's guards rushed the stage. Before they could attack, a cellist swung his instrument at the tip of a guard's bayonet. The bayonet clashed to the floor with a metallic *thunk*, and a bullet went speeding through the roof, spraying rubble over the crowd. Someone yelled from behind, and suddenly the entire orchestra and chorus were harmonizing in terrifying war cries, charging the guards.

The guards had no chance of firing any additional bullets; the musicians knocked the rifles out of their hands before another shot could be fired. A guard reached for his fallen bayonet, arms outstretched nearly out of their sockets, grasping for his only defense; he was stopped instantaneously as a flutist smashed him on the side of the head with the sweetest instrument an orchestra could have. As the guard fell, he blew a sharp exhalation into the flute's mouthpiece, producing an ethereal resonance that, given the circumstances, was both exhilarating and terrifying.

Sherlock struggled to maintain his balance as he sacrificed an invaluable Stradivarius violin to the cause by holding it up as a shield; a guard's bayonet had pierced the violin, and Sherlock used his new shield as support to push the guard back. By the time the guard realized his weapon was now useless, Sherlock punched him in the jaw, catapulting him to the floor, stumbling over broken bows and dented woodwinds.

The guards retreated. They were clearly outnumbered, nearly ten to two hundred.

The battlefront was clear. Sherlock and Watson rushed to the front row, but King Leopold had vanished.

"Over there," Watson said, pointing to the entrance.

King Leopold stood as a silhouette in the doorway, the Vienna sunset radiating a bright violet and blood red behind him. Sherlock met the king's eyes, and King Leopold mockingly bowed.

Just as King Leopold was about to end his bow, Beethoven ran from behind, tackling him to the ground. The king thrashed about, tugging at Beethoven's hair, attempting to claw out his eyes, but it was no use; Beethoven's fury was too great.

Beethoven pulled out the poisoned baton. As Beethoven raised his arm in the air to slash the king's throat, Sherlock ran up from behind and grabbed it. Watson held the king down, and Sherlock knocked the baton out of Beethoven's hand.

"He must confess his crimes to the royal courts," Sherlock said, "or nobody will believe us."

"But my symphony! It was supposed to be joyous. The ode dedicated to joy."

"It will be," Sherlock said.

"The memories of today will haunt the melodies," Beethoven said. "The blood of the slain will seep into the harmonies. The king will terrorize the chords forevermore."

"That is true," King Leopold said. "Your song will belong to me, always."

Beethoven's eyes grew wild with rage. His hands began shaking uncontrollably, then balled up into tight fists. He turned to Sherlock and Watson, narrowed his eyes, and bashed his head into King Leopold's temple.

King Leopold's skull hit the ground with such incredible force that the sound could have replaced the strike of the symphony's last bass-drum hit. The king was knocked unconscious, blood seeping through his scalp. He might not even remember what had happened.

Sherlock tied the king's hands with frayed bowstrings. That would have to do, Sherlock conceded, until the public execution.

"Joyous." Beethoven stood, rubbed his forehead, and brushed dirt from his sleeves. "I said *joyous*."

• • •

The guillotine's blades glimmered in the summer sunlight. The orchestra had set up outside in a half arc around the public execution, and it was so bright out that Sherlock nearly had to squint to watch his conductor's nonlethal baton bounce to the beat of the music.

King Leopold walked gravely to the guillotine, bare feet dragging across the floor. The Viennese government had spared no time in providing King Leopold a last supper before the beheading.

"Let me confess one more thing," King Leopold yelled. Beethoven added an extra rest in his symphony to let the man speak. "At least I will die with the most pleasant sounds on Earth encompassing my earbuds. It was never personal, Ludwig."

This made Beethoven smile, which was a rare sight as of late. He nodded to Fabian, who had resumed his position as first-chair cellist, and cued the orchestra to continue playing.

Watson played his violin and spoke to Sherlock between notes. "My friend, thanks to you, our eccentric conductor will be able to create more music, and Vienna will remain triumphant."

"No, it is not I who should be thanked," Sherlock said. "I am but a mere melody in this symphony we call life, and I cannot experience true harmony without our brotherhood. For what is life without harmony?"

King Leopold rested his head on the welcoming planks of the guillotine. As the orchestra crescendoed to the very last phrase, the blade fell, slashing through the wind, the sound of the joyous symphony matching the tempo of a falling head.

Badump. Badump. Badump.

THE ADVENTURE OF THE MELTED SAINT

BY GAIL Z. MARTIN

"Don't take this the wrong way Alistair, but if you're here, it means trouble."

Alistair McKinnon, Curator of the Lowcountry Museum of Charleston, jokingly preened. "Why, Cassidy! At my age, that's one of the nicest things anyone has said to me in a while. Do I look suitably dangerous?"

Alistair stooped, though the doorway was still an inch above his thinning brown hair. Today he wore a blue seersucker suit with a red bow tie, the natural apparel of the sartorially inclined old-school Charlestonian blue blood. He held a cardboard box, and despite our banter, his brow furrowed with worry.

"You don't usually bring me your mail for show and tell. What's up?"

"For starters," Alistair replied, "I think this package arrived with its own ghost."

I figured that something supernatural lay behind his visit. That's normal for me. I'm Cassidy Kincaide, owner of Trifles and Folly, an antique and curios store in historic, haunted Charleston, South Carolina, and I've got a couple of big secrets. First, I'm a psychometric, which means I can read the history—or magic—of objects by touching them. That comes in handy with my second secret, which is that Teag, my assistant store manager, has his own magical ability to weave spells into fabric—or weave data and hack computers with supernatural ease.

And those two secrets roll up to our biggest one: Trifles and Folly really exists to get dangerous magical items off the market and out of the wrong hands. We're part of a covert alliance of mortals and immortals dedicated to shutting down dangerous supernatural threats with extreme prejudice, and have been since our founding over three hundred years ago. When we do our job right, no one notices. When we screw up, the death and destruction usually gets chalked up to a natural disaster.

"Maggie can cover the front of the store for a while," I said. Maggie gave me a nod. She knows a little bit about what we do, though not quite everything, for her own safety. Alistair knows about my magic, but not about Teag's abilities and the Alliance. It's complicated.

Teag and I showed Alistair into the small break room kitchen, and Alistair put the box on the table. He declined Teag's offer of tea or coffee. Teag went ahead and poured a big glass of sweet tea for me, figuring I'd need it to recover after I read whatever objects were giving Alistair fits.

"We received this box in the mail last week, from the Adirondack Museum in New York State," Alistair said. "Apparently, it had been in their basement for nearly a hundred years. They sent it here because they felt the people connected to these objects had a stronger history with Charleston than they did with upstate New York." He shrugged. "I'd agree with them on that part. But they didn't mention that a ghost came along for the ride."

I eyed the box without touching it. If an object had really strong magic, I could often get an impression before I made physical contact. That was helpful, because then I could brace myself for what was coming. "I'm not getting any really bad vibes," I said, letting my hand hover a few inches above the box. "What kind of problems has it been causing you?"

"The poor woman who works in shipping and receiving broke down sobbing when she handled the box. She was so distraught we had to send her home. No idea why—except the box was in her office all day," Alistair said. "Everyone who comes in contact with it mentions feeling down or sad, having a sudden change of mood. It's wreaking havoc with the museum staff."

Alistair's gaze slid away, embarrassed. "I have to tell you, I had a terrible time on the way over struggling with an overwhelming sadness that just came on me out of nowhere, for no good reason," he admitted. "I'm really hoping you can help. We can't put this on display. We'd have to offer free counseling with every admission ticket."

Now that Alistair mentioned it, I felt a strong downward tug on my mood, which had been pretty good until he showed up. Teag nodded, letting me know he was feeling it, too. I closed my eyes and tried to get a bead on what I was feeling. Sadness. Regret. Those were strong. There was something else…a sense of something hidden, something secret.

"I'm not picking up anything dangerous." I opened my eyes. "But there are some strong emotions attached. Why don't you lay out the contents and I'll see what I can find out for you." I gave Alistair an encouraging smile. "Once we know what we're dealing with, we can figure out better how to neutralize the supernatural heebie-jeebies."

Teag opened the box and set the items out on the table. The contents were an interesting jumble: an old journal, a stack of yellowed envelopes tied with twine, a man's ring, and a melted gold coin. There was part of a burned piece of stationery as well.

"What do you know about the previous owner or owners of the pieces?" I asked, still not ready to commit myself by touching anything.

"Not much," Alistair said with a sigh. "They came from the estate of a Mr. Jacob Whitley, of the New York Whitleys," he added. If that was supposed to mean something to me, I didn't get the reference. I raised an eyebrow quizzically and he continued. "A very prominent and wealthy family around the turn of the last century. Made their money in a line of retail stores.

"The journal belonged to Marie deBrise Chastain," he went on. "You recognize those names?"

"The deBrise family and the Chastain family have been Charlestonian movers and shakers since the Huguenot days."

"The letters are between Rebecca Dumont and Mr. Whitley," Alistair continued. "Everything dates to around 1920."

I moved my hand closer to the objects, and caught a flash of sorrow, a glimpse of flames, and the shadowy figure of a man. "There's some kind of tragedy involved," I said.

Alistair nodded. "Marie Chastain was killed in a fire in 1920. Jacob Whitley, a suitor, escaped with his life but was badly scarred. Rebecca Dumont was a friend of Marie."

"How did all of these pieces end up in the mountains of New York?" Teag asked.

"I have no idea," Alistair replied. "We hadn't started to research the pieces yet. I did put a call in to the Chastain family for information, but no one has called back."

"All right." I mustered my courage. "Let's see what I can find out."

I sat down at the table and reached for the diary. Teag could read the journal entries later, but for now, I wanted to pick up on the resonance of strong emotions left behind. The image of a woman's face came to mind. Not conventionally pretty, but with regular features.

"It's not magical," I said. "Mostly…not quite sad, but wistful? I'm guessing Marie might have had a lot of dreams she didn't get the chance to fulfill." I parsed through the images that came to mind. A shadow flickered in my inner sight. Not dangerous, but furtive. A man's silhouette, there and gone. Odd.

Next, I picked up the letters. The handwriting on the top envelope was faded, in the type of ink that told me it had been written with a fountain pen. The old-style script was a woman's writing, neat and compact. This time, I got a mental image of two people. One was a petite woman who wore her red hair in a bob. She must have been Rebecca. The other was of a dark-haired man whose face I couldn't quite make out, who I guessed was Jacob. *Was he the shadow*

I glimpsed before? I wondered. I picked up a sense of uneasiness, of something being out of place, and a hint of something secretive.

"You haven't read the letters?"

Alistair shook his head. "We really haven't had the box long enough to do more than catalog the contents."

"Interesting," I said, wondering what the letters and journal would reveal when Teag read them.

The sheet of stationery was partly burned. It looked like someone had snatched it out of the flames. After all this time, it radiated anger and disapproval. "You have pushed my patience to the breaking point," I read aloud. "There will be consequences." The man's handwriting was strong and sweeping. The note was unsigned.

"Any idea who wrote this?" I asked.

Alistair shook his head. "None. Sounds rather ominous, doesn't it?"

"Did they ever figure out what caused the fire?" Teag questioned. "Was it an accident?"

"From what I could find, it was blamed on a gas leak," Alistair replied. "Of course, forensics back then weren't what they are today."

I knew the coin and the man's ring would be the worst of the items, which is why I saved them for last. The ring gave me a jolt when I touched it. I sensed Jacob's energy, and Marie's as well. *Was the ring a gift from her?* The energy was off—discordant, jumbled. I couldn't get a clear read on it, but it made me jumpy.

"Had the three of them been in any kind of trouble?" I asked. "It might even have been a scandal rather than something illegal. I think the three of them had a secret, but they aren't giving it up easily."

"Nothing comes to mind, other than the fire that claimed Marie's life," Alistair said. "I can have a look through the archives when I go back to the museum."

"I'll do some digging online," Teag added. "And Mrs. Morrissey from the Archive might know something, too."

"When we hear back from the Chastain family, I'll make some discreet inquiries," Alistair added. Alistair was the soul of discretion, a necessity for fundraising and keeping well-heeled donors happy. History could be messy, and a city like Charleston not only had ghosts in every old house but plenty of skeletons in closets as well.

I steeled myself and picked up the melted gold coin. Suddenly, I was propelled into a vision. I saw the scene through someone else's eyes. The room was a well-appointed parlor, decorated in the style common at the turn of the nineteenth century. I smelled smoke and felt panic course through me as flames engulfed the heavy draperies that framed the windows.

It was hard to breathe. The fire was spreading fast. Someone screamed. I ran for the door, only to find it blocked by more flames. Marie was trying to knock the burning draperies away from the window with a chair. A couple of the panes in the window were broken. Rebecca ran to the other door. It opened to safety. She beckoned for us to follow her.

Some of the burning draperies had caught the couch on fire, and the horsehair stuffing made thick, black smoke. The carpet was burning, too. I could see Marie but I couldn't get to her, and then a wall of fire cut us off...

I came back to myself with a gasp. Teag shoved a glass of strong, sweet iced tea into my hand, and I gulped it, trying to recover. I let go of the gold coin, and it gave a metallic ring as it hit the table.

"I saw the fire," I said. "I was seeing through Jacob's eyes. The room went up in flames so fast. He couldn't get to Marie in time."

Alistair picked up the twisted coin. "It's a twenty-dollar gold piece," he remarked. "A Saint Gaudens, named for the engraver who designed it." He held it up to the light. "Hard to read the date with all the damage, but the gold alone is worth a lot more than twenty dollars in today's market." He set it back down. "Pity it's partly melted. A coin like that goes for a lot of money in good condition, although of course, the gold itself is still valuable in spite of the damage."

We didn't deal in a lot of old coins, but I was familiar with the "Saints," as collectors called them. The engraving was a work of art, and the luster of the gold made it amazing to me that people actually spent the coins back in the day. They seemed too beautiful for mere currency. I looked at the twisted gold coin, and felt a stab of sadness for the young people whose lives had taken a terrible turn because of that fire.

"What about the ghost?" Alistair asked.

I could sense a presence hovering just beyond my Sight, but unlike some of the revenants I've run into, this spirit kept its distance. I couldn't make out a face, just a faint shadowy form. Mostly, I felt disappointment and longing, as well as deep sorrow.

"You don't have any idea who gave the box to the Adirondack Museum?" I asked.

Alistair shook his head. "I've already asked them for any records they have on the acquisition. But they did a major renovation a while back, and some old records have been misplaced. Or it just might be that the 'gift' wasn't significant enough to do more than log it." He shrugged. "We'll have to wait and see."

"I can sense a spirit connected to the items," I said. "But since all three of the people involved are dead now, it could be any of them. It might be Marie, or it could be either Rebecca or Jacob if they held onto the items all those years. I can't tell from what I can see of the ghost right now." I shook my head.

"Will you look into it for me, please?" Alistair asked. "And see if there's a way to get rid of the ghost so we can store the items without giving everyone a breakdown?"

I chuckled. "I think we can handle that. But first, I'd like to figure out just why this ghost is hanging around—and what secret it's been keeping all these years."

"It's not really a job for the Alliance," Teag observed after Alistair left. He put the pieces in our store safe. Nothing like a lead box several inches thick to temper supernatural bad mojo. Locked up in there, the package shouldn't affect our moods the way it had caused mayhem at the museum. I hoped.

"No it isn't," I agreed. "I'm not getting the sense that the ghost is any danger, and there doesn't seem to be a supernatural threat to the rest of the world. But I'm intrigued," I admitted. "And I think that there's a story here that hasn't been told. Maybe if we find out what the secret is, the ghost will go away on its own."

"Alistair's already contacted the family," Teag said. "Let me do some digging into my sources."

"The Chastain family is still prominent in Charleston, and it's been around a long time," I replied.

"Are you going to head over to the Archive?"

I nodded. "Yes. But I've got a stop to make on the way. I think this is tailor-made for Charleston's most famous private detective."

* * *

"Cassidy! So good to see you. Come on in." Shelley Holmes welcomed me as I arrived at her home at 221 Baker Street, out near the airport. She wore a satin purple bathrobe—more of a long smoking jacket—over what appeared to be loose silk pants and top.

Shelley cleaned away piles of papers and magazines to make room. "Please, have a seat." She motioned to the couch while she took up the one armchair that wasn't piled high with odds and ends. "You said on the phone that you've got a case for me. How very exciting. Do tell."

Shelley—formerly Sherlock—Holmes was a prodigy. She'd studied chemistry and martial arts, become first violin with the Charleston Symphony, and filled her home with an homage of books and collectibles to literature's greatest shamuses, private eyes, gumshoes, and detectives.

After surgery, Shelley Holmes threw herself a coming-out party, and remained just as irrepressible as ever.

I laid out what we knew about the objects Alistair had brought in, as well as poor doomed Marie Chastain and her friends. Shelley listened intently, puffing on a vape version of a clay pipe.

"What a lovely mystery. I am happy to take the case."

"How much is your fee?" I couldn't help glancing around the room. On one wall were framed posters from the fictional character's many silver screen and TV incarnations. On another wall, a framed Weber pistol hung next to a deerstalker cap that had been a movie prop. Several different sets of the collected tales of Sherlock Holmes graced the bookshelves along with a pipestand holding a variety of tobacco pipes and other oddments.

Shelley was eccentric, and here in the South, we value eccentricity. I had never known anyone to so fully take on every attribute of a literary character to become a literal embodiment. Fortunately, a brief stint in rehab years ago got Shelley over her recreational use of cocaine, and she had promised her friends to allow that element of authenticity to remain in the past.

"Store credit, and a list of items I'd like to acquire if they come on the market?" She suggested a dollar amount, and I nodded.

"Sounds fair. What do you make of what I've told you?"

Shelley stood and began to pace. Tall and thin with angular features, she looked like a brooding hawk. Her dark hair was cut short, to accommodate her martial arts and kickboxing workouts. I had gone to the gym with her once and limped for the next two days, unable to keep up. She made it look easy. In school, she had been smarter than everyone else in the class and she knew it, although her closest friends found her endearing in spite of it.

"I'll want to see the items for myself, of course," she said, puffing away at her vape pipe. "In case they speak to me, if you know what I mean."

I did. Shelley has flashes of clairvoyance, glimpses into the future. I wasn't entirely sure how her gift might help solve a mystery from the past, but I've learned never to discount anything when Shelley is on the case.

"Teag and Alistair are going to find out some of the missing pieces," Shelley said. "The answer is right in front of us, but we can't see it." She frowned, deciphering the glimpse of foreknowledge. "You're in danger." She turned to meet my gaze.

"Me?" I yelped. "Why on earth would an heiress's death from nearly a century ago put me in danger?"

Shelley shook her head, as if clearing the ethereal fog from her thoughts. "No clue, girlfriend. But I've learned to take my psychic glimpses as seriously as I do my powers of deduction." She waggled her eyebrows. "So take the warning at face value."

After casting off her robe, Shelley put on a pair of shoes and grabbed a jacket from a peg near the door. She settled the jacket over her shoulders without slipping her arms into the sleeves so it flapped like a cape, while her gray eyes were alight with the thrill of the chase.

"Come along, Watson!" she shouted. A disgruntled snuffle came from the direction of the kitchen, and then the click of nails on hardwood floors as Watson, Shelley's sad-eyed bloodhound, roused himself from his comfortable bed. She clipped his leash onto him and headed for the door.

"Let's go, Cassidy," she said. "The game's afoot!"

• • •

Every good investigator knows the price for an informant's help. In this case, it was a large vanilla latte from Honeysuckle Café.

"Cassidy! Shelley! What a wonderful surprise." Mrs. Benjamin Morrissey, Charleston doyenne and head of the Historical Archive, came out to meet us from her office at the historic home that housed the Archive. "And you've brought Watson!" She bent to pat Watson's head, and Watson gave her a lugubrious look in return.

"Go ahead and take him onto the back porch," Mrs. Morrissey said. "You can put down a bowl of water for him, and the doors are locked, so no one will bother him." Shelley took Watson to get settled, and returned a moment later.

"And is that a vanilla latte?" Mrs. Morrissey asked, with a smile that told me she knew it was. "So let me guess—you need information?"

We all laughed, and she motioned for us to follow her. We walked through a partially installed exhibit in the house's large formal foyer, and I heard the sound of workmen upstairs.

"What's your new exhibit?" I asked. I've got to be careful with museums, because the kinds of pieces that are important enough to save for historical reasons often have significant emotional resonance—and occasionally, a taint of dark magic. I'd had a couple of run-ins with some bad juju with prior Archive displays, but to my relief, whatever the new installation was going to be wasn't setting off my magical alarms.

Mrs. Morrissey grinned. "I thought you'd never ask!" she exclaimed. She's a real Charleston blue blood, and when her husband passed on, leaving her with a wealth of money and social connections, she stepped into her role with the Archive as if she had been born to it.

"It's called 'Great Escapes—Grand Country Manors and Seaside Palaces.' Nowadays, tourists come for vacation to Charleston. But all throughout our history, Charlestonians went elsewhere to go on holiday. We've pulled together a display of photographs, diaries, and items from our collection all about the hunting lodges, beach homes, and getaway residences of some of Charleston's most famous residents over the years. It's going to be a fun exhibit!"

Given the enormous wealth of some of the old Charleston families—and some of its more recent celebrity sons and daughters—I didn't doubt the display would be a big hit with donors and paying guests alike.

"What do you know about Marie deBrise Chastain, Jacob Whitley, and Rebecca Dumont?" Shelley asked, leaning forward and staring intently at Mrs. Morrissey.

Mrs. Morrissey had a mind like a steel trap. She was the Archive's best search engine and she knew the collection like no one else. "She's the heiress who died in that fire, back in the Roaring Twenties, isn't she?" Mrs. Morrissey asked. "Terribly sad situation. Drove her father to suicide, or so they say."

"Really?" I raised an eyebrow.

Mrs. Morrissey nodded. "Of course, no one talks about it because the Chastain family is still quite well connected, but history is what it is," she said. We both knew that meant that history was the original and best reality show ever. Whether you were looking for murder, mayhem, scandal, oddities, or just plain weird stuff,

Hollywood at its best couldn't outdo the exploits of real people. And I knew firsthand that historians—like antiques dealers—knew all the old gossip.

"I might have to look up a date or two," Mrs. Morrissey admitted, looking as if that were a major fault, "but to my recollection, Jacob Whitley was courting Marie, with the wholehearted endorsement of both families. It would have been as much of a business merger as a marriage, had everything gone as planned."

"But something went wrong," Shelley prompted.

Mrs. Morrissey nodded. "Marie didn't want to go through with the marriage. There are a couple of versions of the story. One story says that Marie just didn't care for Jacob and didn't want to marry without love. The other version holds that Rebecca and Jacob might have had eyes for each other." She paused.

"Rebecca Dumont was Marie's best friend and confidant. The two were inseparable. So it wasn't a surprise that Rebecca was there visiting even though Jacob had come to town to see Marie. He split his time between his family's interests in the Carolinas, and their New York business."

She tapped on her keyboard, then turned the monitor of her computer around to face us. "Photos, from the archives," she said.

Shelley and I leaned forward for a better look. Rebecca was petite, and although the photo was black and white, I was certain she was the redhead I had glimpsed when I read the objects from the box. Marie was taller, with shoulder-length dark hair, and while she was striking, she wasn't as conventionally pretty as Rebecca, who smiled and laughed in every picture.

Jacob Whitley was a little older than the two women. They appeared to be in their twenties, while he was in his early thirties. Slightly built and nattily dressed, he had the sober, shrewd look of a man who was going to do very well in business. But I couldn't imagine him being an exciting date.

"Were Jacob and Marie really in love?" I asked.

Mrs. Morrissey leaned back in her chair. "That's been debated," she replied. "Most people think Marie's father brokered the proposal without asking her. It's hard to imagine the two of them together, isn't it?"

"Unless they shared some secret passion, they don't look like they would have even met otherwise," Shelley said, studying the photos.

"There's an old rumor that the night of the fire, Marie meant to break off the engagement with Jacob," Mrs. Morrissey said. "Of course, circumstances went tragically wrong. Marie died. Rebecca escaped unharmed, and Jacob survived, but badly injured, and scarred."

"What happened?" I paged through the photos on the screen of Marie and Rebecca together in a graduation picture from a Swiss boarding school, and of them in a group of girls at a debutante party, and then another when they were young women, at a Christmas ball. There weren't a lot of public pictures, and I remembered what my grandmother used to say, that in her day a woman with a good reputation only had her picture in the paper for her wedding and her obituary.

A number of photos accompanied newspaper articles announcing Jacob's membership in various business organizations or community groups.

"It's funny that you're asking about Marie and Jacob." Mrs. Morrissey had a few more sips of her latte. "Their story is so fresh in my memory because I had just pulled some photos of their family's vacation homes for the exhibition."

"Would one of those homes happen to be in upstate New York?" Shelley asked.

"Why, yes," Mrs. Morrissey replied. "Come with me. The photos aren't mounted yet, but I can show you what I've got."

My cell phone buzzed. I glanced down and saw that the call was from Alistair. "Go on ahead," I said. "I'll be with you in a minute."

Alistair picked up immediately. "Cassidy—I've got to warn you. I might have accidentally put you in danger with that box."

I remembered Shelley's warning. "What happened?"

"Someone broke into the museum last night," Alistair said. "I didn't mention it when I visited because I didn't think it was related. The door was open into our acquisitions room, where we store new items before they're cataloged. Nothing was missing, so we changed the code on the door and filed a report with the police. Then today when I drove over to see you, I caught a glimpse of a white Toyota minivan that seemed to be following me. I thought I was imagining things. But after I saw you, I stopped for lunch. Someone broke into my car." He paused. "I think they were looking for something that wasn't there."

A chill went down my spine. "Thanks for the warning," I said. "I'll make sure Teag knows. The store is pretty well protected." In addition to a good alarm system, the store was warded by a Voudon mambo friend of mine.

"Don't take any chances, Cassidy," Alistair warned. "I don't know what's going on, but old secrets are the most dangerous ones."

I called Teag to pass along the warning. Then I went to join Shelley and Mrs. Morrissey in the boardroom, where photos lay in rows along the huge wooden table.

"It really puts things in perspective to realize that these 'cottages' were only used for a few weeks out of the year," I said, looking at the pictures. "Cottage" and "cabin" were gross understatements. These grand vacation homes of Charleston's rich and famous were mansions.

"Amazing, aren't they?" Shelley admired the photos, then pulled out a magnifying glass and peered intently at two of the pictures.

"Find something?" I asked.

Shelley shrugged, warning me not to interrupt her train of thought. I looked over her shoulder at a picture of a sprawling log home the size of a modern hotel set against sharp mountain peaks. Two indistinct figures stood on the porch. "Maybe," she grunted. She took pictures of the photos with her cell phone, to examine later.

"That's the Whitley 'grand camp' in the Adirondacks," Mrs. Morrissey said. "All the prestigious families had mountain retreats back at the turn of the last century. Vanderbilt, Morgan, Rockefeller—it was quite the thing to bring all your society friends up by train to 'rough it' in the wilderness," she added with a laugh. From the look of the log mansion, "roughing it" might have meant limited amounts of caviar.

"And the beachfront homes are gorgeous," I said. "Is that Marie and Rebecca?" Bathing caps hid their hair, but I was certain that they were the two laughing girls posing arm-in-arm in the surf.

"Yes," Mrs. Morrissey said. "That's the beach property on Sullivan Island. It's long gone. It would have been built by Marie's grandfather. Those Victorians knew how to live large!"

"Do you have any other items from Jacob Whitley or Marie Chastain?" Shelley asked.

"Marie was so young when she died, just in her early twenties. She hadn't really had a chance to make her mark. But I think we do have a letter she wrote in favor of women getting the vote. Let me see if we can find it." Mrs. Morrissey signaled one of her interns and sent the young man off with instructions. "Jacob Whitley was a little older, but unfortunately, his life ended with the fire as well—in a manner of speaking."

"How so?" Shelley's gaze narrowed.

"While Rebecca escaped the fire unhurt except for minor cuts and superficial burns, Jacob wasn't as lucky," Mrs. Morrissey recounted. "He was badly injured—something to do with his leg— and he suffered disfiguring burns. Together with the death of his fiancée, it seemed to be too much for him. He moved up to his family's Adirondack home and became a recluse for the rest of his life."

"What drove Marie's father to suicide?" I asked. "Were they particularly close?"

Mrs. Morrissey shrugged. "Who can tell how someone will handle grief like that? I've heard that they argued about the arranged marriage. Both Marie and her father could be stubborn. Maybe he regretted that later." She gave me a sad smile. "For all his wealth and power, he couldn't save his daughter. People don't react rationally to loss."

Shelley sorted through the photos on the table. She peered

closely at one, and snapped another picture with her phone. "It's a formal photograph of the Whitley family." She pointed out Jacob, seated in the front row with his hands clasped on his lap. "It looks like he's wearing a ring. Is that the one you found in the box?"

I squinted and looked more closely, then shook my head. "I can't tell. The photo isn't sharp enough."

"Here's another one of Jacob with Marie and Rebecca," Mrs. Morrissey said. "That's odd—I don't remember seeing it before." I took the picture from her, and glimpsed a man's silhouette out of the corner of my eye. The ghost was there and gone in a heartbeat. *Could there have been more to Marie's death than a tragic accident?* I wondered. *And after all this time, why would anyone try to steal back a box of things that have been sitting in a museum basement for years?*

The photograph showed three young adults in formal wear laughing and standing arm-in-arm. Marie and Rebecca were having the time of their lives. Jacob looked uncomfortable in his tuxedo, his smile forced.

"It's an odd pose for a photograph, don't you think?" Shelley said, staring at the picture. "They're not lined up by height." Jacob, the tallest of the three, was on the left. Rebecca was in the middle. She was the shortest one, coming just up to Jacob's shoulder and a little above Marie's shoulder. Marie was on the right.

"Probably one of those random red carpet photos," I said. The picture made me sad, and I could sense a depth to the melancholy that was not my own. Something hidden in plain sight, Shelley had said. After nearly a century, why had the ghosts picked now to end their silence? And what secret had they guarded all this time?

"Here's the letter you wanted," the intern said, returning with a yellowed envelope and a pair of archival gloves.

Mrs. Morrissey slipped on the gloves and carefully unfolded the letter. Shelley and I crowded around her to read a passionate letter in favor of women's right to vote written by a well-educated, outspoken young woman.

"Quite bold, wasn't she?" Shelley mused. "And unconventional."

Mrs. Morrissey chuckled. "The twenties were a time when

women with Marie's education and privilege began bucking convention in all sorts of ways, from wearing pants—scandalous!—to going to college to trying to enter male-only vocations."

"I wonder how Marie and Jacob would have gotten on, if the marriage had happened," I said, as Shelley snapped a picture of the letter. "They don't seem to be temperamentally suited for each other."

"Opposites attract, or so they say," Mrs. Morrissey replied. "Although personally, I've found that birds of a feather flock together."

• • •

Shelley and I thanked Mrs. Morrissey, then we retrieved Watson from the porch and headed back to Shelley's house.

"Don't look now, but there's a white van following us," Shelley said. "Hold on. I'm going to make a detour."

I thought Shelley might speed up and start taking corners on two wheels, the way people do in the movies. Instead, she kept her speed constant, and made a few extra turns that took us in a different direction. To my surprise, she turned down an alley next to a convenience store, to emerge on the main road a few blocks later. The white van followed us most of the way, but must have realized that we spotted it, because it turned off not long after we had passed the store.

"What was that all about?"

"Samir, the guy who owns that convenience store, owes me a couple of favors," Shelley replied. "I helped him bust a shoplifting ring. He's got surveillance cameras all around the store, and he can get me copies of the tapes. With luck, they picked up a license plate on that van."

"Hey, lady!" a neighbor called when Shelley and I parked at her house. He pointed at my Mini Cooper. "Is that your car?"

"Yes."

"Some guy was hanging around, looking in all the windows. I

thought he might try to break in, so I yelled at him, and he got in his car and drove away."

"Thank you," I replied. Nothing looked damaged. "Did you see what he was driving?"

"Yeah. A white minivan."

· · ·

I headed back for Trifles and Folly, constantly glancing in my rearview mirror. I even took a more roundabout route, just in case. I quickly discovered it was almost impossible to be on the highway or in a parking lot without spotting dozens of white minivans. Talk about hiding in plain sight. My stalker vanished by being everywhere.

"Everything go okay?" Maggie asked when I came in.

"Shelley agreed to take the case, no one got hurt, we found out some good information, and there's a white van stalking us."

"Hey, you got back here safely, boss. That's what counts," she said, and shot me a thumbs-up.

"If that's Cassidy, tell her I've got stuff she wants to hear," Teag called from the office.

"It's me, and I'm heading your way."

Maggie jerked her head toward the office. "I'll handle the customers; you go save the world."

Something about Marie Chastain's death bothered me. There were too many loose ends, and far too much interest in something long out of recent memory.

And then there was the silhouette. *Is he a ghost, or a lost spirit, or just a psychic impression that's a little more tangible than usual?*

"What did you find?" I asked, swinging through the break room for a glass of sweet tea.

"I love projects that scan archival documents," Teag said, cracking his knuckles and wiggling his fingers above the keyboard. Passwords don't stop Teag, and neither do firewalls—not even federal-level security, although we try to keep that kind of snooping for dire cases. "You scored?"

Teag grinned. "Oh yeah. A reporter named Peter Studebaker covered the fire that killed Marie Chastain when it happened. He was a bit of a muckraker. A rogue investigative journalist. He had unanswered questions, but no one would listen to him, and he believed the Chastain family leaned on the newspaper editor to kill the story."

I sipped my sweet tea. "That's certainly possible. Money buys silence. Or, he might have just been nuts."

"I don't think he was nuts," Teag said. "Someone scanned his notes about the case and put them online."

"And?"

Teag sat back in his chair. "Studebaker thought it was odd that the initial firefighter's report said arson, but was quickly changed to gas leak. He apparently was early on the scene, and says one of the first responders found evidence to suggest that someone set the house on fire with a homemade firebomb."

"Yikes."

"It gets better," Teag said. "Studebaker quoted witnesses who saw Marie Chastain and her father arguing not long before the fire. Studebaker suspected that Marie was in love with someone else, and was balking at the arranged marriage."

"Let me guess. Whoever she was in love with didn't meet her father's standards."

"Studebaker's vague on that point," Teag replied. "If he had any idea of who the rival suitor was, he didn't say so. But he suggested Jacob Whitley might have been more interested in Rebecca than in Marie."

"Oh?"

"According to Studebaker, Jacob was injured in the fire, but he was vain enough to refuse treatment in Charleston, saying he would see his own doctor back in New York. Rebecca was studying to be a nurse, and she patched him up enough to make the trip. Observers say he walked with a limp and his face was badly burned, covered in bandages."

"What about the letters?" I asked, remembering the bundle Alistair had given me.

Teag nodded. "Somehow, Studebaker found out that Jacob and Rebecca began corresponding after Marie's death, with Rebecca in Charleston and Jacob in self-imposed exile in the Adirondacks. Then a year later, Rebecca moved up to be his nurse. She never came back to Charleston."

"Interesting," I said. "But why would anyone care about this now? After a hundred years, why is someone following people around and breaking into cars?"

"Studebaker thought there was more to the story, but the police and the newspaper told him to drop it, especially after Marie's father committed suicide."

"Shelley's coming over to take a look at the items in the box," I added. "I think she's onto something, but she won't tell until she can make the big reveal."

"Dramatic, isn't she?" Teag laughed.

"Always."

My phone rang. It was Alistair. "What's up?"

"I've just heard back from Oliver Chastain." Alistair sounded upset. "Not only have they refused to provide any information about Marie's death, but they're demanding the box back—and he says they'll sue if we don't comply."

That was going to put Alistair in a bad situation, because the museum couldn't afford to get on the wrong side of the Chastains, major patrons to just about every charity in the city. "I understand," I said, as I signaled to Teag that I would explain everything later. "Can we stall him for just a little while? I think Shelley's close to having a solution—and I suspect it's going to be worth our while to get to the bottom of this."

"I'll try," Alistair said. "But when push comes to shove, I'm going to have to give him what he wants."

I hung up, and relayed what Alistair said. "Damn. Oliver Chastain has a reputation as a real son of a bitch, like his father and grandfather. I wouldn't be surprised if he hired Anthony's law firm for the suit on purpose, just to put pressure on us as well as the museum," Teag said. Anthony was Teag's partner. If Teag's fears proved true, that would put everyone in an extremely awkward position.

"But why?" I mused. "Surely no one would care if a hundred years ago, Marie wanted to break off an arranged marriage, even if she had another suitor in mind."

Teag rolled his eyes. "Even if she were pregnant—which would have been a big thing at the time—no one would bat an eye today. I agree. The reaction is over the top."

"It only seems over the top to us because we don't know something that Oliver Chastain knows. That's the missing piece— and Shelley believes the answer is hidden in plain sight."

A rap at the door signaled Shelley's arrival. Maggie watched the store so we could stay in the back. Teag took the box out of the safe. Immediately, I felt the effect on my mood. From the look on Teag's face and Shelley's expression, I knew they sensed it, too.

"What just happened?" Shelley asked.

"That's the supernatural effect that made Alistair bring us the box in the first place," I said. "There's an emotional resonance that makes everyone sad." Out of the corner of my eye, I caught the man's silhouette once more. I felt no threat; instead, the shadow seemed to be trying to watch. It was almost as if the spirit were rooting for us to figure something out.

"I have the oddest feeling that the ghosts connected to these items are trying to send a message," I told Teag and Shelley. "Maybe once we learn what that is, they'll be able to rest."

"Let's get started," Shelley said. A glint in those gray eyes told me she was fully invested in the case. Shelley gently loosened the twine that tied up the letters. As they fell apart, I could see that about half were to Jacob and half to Rebecca. "If you haven't read the letters or the journal, I think now is a good time," Shelley said. "Cassidy— can you handle one of those objects better than another?"

I held my palm above the letters and then over the journal. Neither one gave off dangerous vibes, but the emotions linked to the journal were stronger and more negative. "How about if I take Rebecca's letters, Teag takes Jacob's letters, and you read the journal?"

"That works for me," Shelley said. We drew chairs up to the table and spread out the items among us.

There were twelve yellowed envelopes in Rebecca's handwriting, and twelve more in Jacob's script. *Interesting. That means they traded two letters each month between Marie's death and when Rebecca moved to New York to nurse Jacob back to health. That's a lot of conversation.*

I settled back in my chair to read. Rebecca's handwriting was compact but clear, in an old-fashioned script. The letters chronicled day-to-day life, the kind of things we'd say in a phone call or on Facebook, like what they ate for dinner, or who they saw at a party—personal news about a circle of mutual friends.

I found myself caught up in the accounts. The letters implied a conversation between two people who knew each other very well. Rebecca and Jacob were very much in love and missed each other badly.

Did guilt over Marie's death keep them apart? Were they worried about being openly involved with each other so soon after Marie and her father died?

The letter that must have followed shortly after the suicide of Marie's father caught my attention. *I know you chide me for speaking my mind openly on this matter, and I do not wish to show disrespect for your feelings,* Rebecca had written. *But knowing him as I did, over so many years, never have I been acquainted with such a hard-hearted and close-minded man, who managed—despite his considerable business success—to make an utter ruin of his family. I know how much unhappiness he brought to Marie, and while you may fault me for saying it, I hope the Almighty requires recompense for the suffering he has caused.*

"Rebecca wasn't a fan of Marie's father," I said.

"Jacob seemed to have some lingering bad will there, too," Teag replied. "Maybe he felt pressured to go through with the marriage to Marie even though she didn't love him, because of Mr. Chastain's influence."

"I'd say it's unanimous that no one cared much for Marie's father, not even Marie." Shelley looked up. "And the journal removes all doubt that Marie was in love with someone else, although she never names names."

Shelley pulled out her phone and photographed a page of the journal, then one of each of the letters. "I'd like to look at the other items," Shelley said, getting up abruptly and circling the table. She lifted the melted Saint Gaudens gold coin and examined it thoroughly, peering at it with her magnifying glass and jotting notes to herself on her phone. Then she regarded the partly-burned stationery with its ominous pronouncement and took another photo.

Shelley stood up, adjusted her necklace, squared her shoulders, and favored us with a triumphant, self-satisfied expression. "I've solved the case," she announced, holding up a hand to forestall questions. "All will be explained in due time. There's not a moment to waste. We must call Alistair right away to arrange a meeting tonight with Oliver Chastain. I have a presentation to make that he'll never forget."

• • •

The museum was closed when we gathered in the boardroom. Alistair looked nervous, with good cause. Shelley would only say that she had solved the case and knew why Oliver Chastain was so eager to recover the items—and why the shadow figure was anxious for resolution. But she would not elaborate until Chastain joined us.

We had not been allowed in the boardroom as Shelley prepared her display of evidence, laid out on easel boards on stands that were dramatically draped to obscure them until Shelley made her big reveal.

Our small group waited quietly for the sound of the outside door opening. Oliver Chastain bustled in. "I don't know why I had to come down here at a certain time to pick up objects that belong to my family," he snapped when he saw Alistair. "You can be certain I'll mention this to the board of directors."

Oliver Chastain was the picture of a successful Charleston scion. He was in his sixties, and his bespoke suit was tailored to accommodate a figure that was portly from too much fine food and wine.

"We know why you're in such a hurry to retrieve the items," Shelley said, and her voice startled Chastain, as if he had not noticed the rest of us sitting in the shadows of the room's perimeter until she spoke. "We've uncovered the truth about what really happened in that fire back in 1920."

Shelley might be eccentric, but when the chips are down, she has a gravitas and a sense of self-assurance sufficient to silence even the bluster of a man like Chastain. "Sit down, Mr. Chastain. You must be tired from following Alistair and Cassidy and me around in that white van of yours."

"I don't know what you're—" Chastain protested.

Shelley whipped the cover from the first easel with a theatrical flourish. On the board were several grainy photos from a security camera of a white minivan, clearly showing the license plate.

"I've already run the plates," Shelley said emotionlessly. "The car is registered as your wife's personal vehicle. Note the timestamp on the photos. This was taken as you pursued Cassidy and me after our meeting at the Archive."

"That proves nothing," Chastain blustered, but I noticed he was sweating a little.

"Since you're a board member, you knew the museum door code, so you didn't have to pick the lock when you tried to find the box in the acquisition room," Shelley continued, with a gaze that gave no quarter. "I was able to pick up a partial fingerprint from Alistair's car door that wasn't his. It wasn't in the police database, but then again, I don't imagine you've ever been arrested, so it wouldn't be on file—yet."

Chastain was growing red in the face. "I've had enough," he said, and started to rise.

Shelley's gaze stopped him. "Your family was able to silence Peter Studebaker, but with the internet, it's not quite as easy anymore. Sit down." Chastain glowered, but he sat.

"Your great-grandfather didn't approve of Marie's choice of

suitors," Shelley went on. "He wasn't used to being disobeyed. So after a particularly vicious argument, he decided to throw a scare into her," Shelley said. "He tossed a small bottle of alcohol with a burning wick through the window, expecting it to frighten her into listening to him, maybe even push her into Jacob's arms as her rescuing hero."

Shelley unveiled a photograph of the threatening note with a snap of the wrist. Next to it was a second photo of an old ledger page. "I'm a trained expert in handwriting analysis. But just to be sure, I sent these two examples to a friend of mine who specializes in such things for the FBI. We are both one hundred percent certain that these two specimens were written by the same person."

She turned to Oliver Chastain. "The ledger was undeniably written by your great-grandfather. And the evidence shows that the letter threatening Marie Chastain was written by the same person— her own father."

"This is ridiculous," Oliver Chastain fumed.

"Your great-grandfather was appalled that his little trick to frighten Marie went so badly wrong. We'll give him the benefit of the doubt about being heartsick over starting a fire that killed one person and injured another. I'm sure he also feared prosecution for the murder, should the truth come out. And that, ladies and gentlemen, is the real reason why Marie's father committed suicide."

"You can't prove that," Oliver Chastain snapped.

"I just have," Shelley replied with a smug smile. "I think the family knew—or strongly suspected—the reason for your family patriarch's suicide. But after examining the evidence, there's another story that you don't know—one that will be disclosed tonight for the first time."

Shelley whipped the cover from the third easel. "Marie Chastain did not die in the fire that night. The remains recovered belonged to Jacob Whitley."

Everyone stared at Shelley. "That's impossible," Oliver Chastain said. "Jacob Whitley lived to be an old man up in the New York mountains."

Shelley gave him a confident smile. "Someone using Jacob's name did indeed live several more decades in seclusion. But it was not Jacob Whitley. Observe," Shelley said, pointing to the display.

"Here is a sample of Marie Chastain's writing from her diary. And here is a sample of a letter ostensibly written by Jacob Whitley to Rebecca after the fire."

"They don't look anything alike," Oliver Chastain protested.

Shelley looked at the samples. "No, they don't. Nor does that letter supposedly by Jacob Whitley look remotely like the large number of documents historically confirmed to have been written by him before the fire." She wheeled on Chastain like the prosecutor in a courtroom drama.

"That's because Jacob Whitley never made it out of that burning room," Shelley said. "It was the melted Saint Gaudens that gave it away. The temperature at which gold melts is the same temperature at which a human body is cremated. Jacob Whitley had just completed a lucrative business deal the morning of the fatal fire. The record shows he was paid in twenty-dollar gold pieces—Saint Gaudens, the ledger specifies. He had one of those gold pieces in his pocket when the room around him went up in flames."

Shelley strode back and forth, smacking the poster boards with a wooden pointer for emphasis as she passed. "It all comes back to why Marie and her father argued so violently, why her refusal of an arranged marriage would have moved a solid community leader to extreme measures. It wasn't mere stubbornness. Marie had done something her father found unforgivable."

She stopped in front of the final exhibit and pulled the cover free. "Marie and Rebecca were lovers." Chastain looked like he was going to argue, but Shelley steamrollered over him.

"Look at this photograph, taken after the fire, when Rebecca was in New York with 'Jacob,'" she said. "Now look at the heights of the people in this photograph, taken here in Charleston before the fire." The photo of the three laughing friends made the contrast clear. "Marie Chastain was shorter than Jacob, but taller than Rebecca. Now note the height differences in the New York photo."

Once Shelley pointed it out, I could see it immediately. Rebecca was closer in height to the man in the later photograph than the real Jacob. "And Exhibit B, the letters," Shelley said, wheeling to point toward the prior board.

"It is possible to disguise one's writing by using the nondominant hand," Shelley said. "But computer analysis is nearly impossible to fool. Both the computer and my FBI expert agree—the letters after the fire written to Rebecca were, in fact, penned by Marie Chastain."

It all made sense. That was why 'Jacob' had refused local treatment except from Rebecca before returning to New York. Why Marie—as Jacob—walked with a limp to hide the height difference, and bandaged her face, claiming disfigurement. As Jacob Whitley, Marie Chastain laid claim to a fortune that made her independently wealthy, with no close family to gainsay her. The Adirondack home and her reclusiveness ensured her privacy. No doubt the handful of loyal servants were well compensated for their silence. Playing the roles of dutiful nurse and long-suffering cripple, Marie and Rebecca could live out the rest of their lives together without interference.

The man's silhouette, the one I keep seeing. Is it Jacob, wanting the true story of his fate acknowledged, or Marie in her disguise, demanding that her family recognize her chosen partner after all these years? Maybe both.

Oliver Chastain sat still and silent. The color had drained from his face, and his hands gripped the chair arms white-knuckled. "Now that you know, what do you intend to do about it?"

Shelley regarded him coldly, like a hanging judge. "That all depends on you, Mr. Chastain. If you intend to make trouble for Alistair with the museum directors or endanger his employment, then I imagine the internet would find Marie's story deliciously juicy and relevant." She paused. "On the other hand, if you stop stalking people and breaking into cars and buildings and swear to make no trouble—now or later for Alistair and the museum—or for Cassidy and Teag—we can all agree to leave the matter in the past."

"That's blackmail," Chastain grated.

Shelley shrugged. "No, that's business. What'll it be, Mr. Chastain?"

Oliver Chastain swore under his breath. "All right. I promise I will not retaliate against Alistair or the museum, or against Cassidy or Teag."

"Or me," Shelley added.

Chastain glared. "Or you. Or anyone. Just give me the damn box of junk and your word that the story doesn't leave this room."

We all made our promises. Shelley reached behind the podium and withdrew the old box. This time, I felt no sadness from its presence, only a sense of justice and satisfaction, long delayed. "Pleasure doing business with you, Mr. Chastain."

Shelley Holmes always had the last word.

AUTOMATIC SHERLOCK

BY MARTIN ROSE

A slip of the knife, thought Dr. Jovan Watson, *and this machine will be my ruination.*

One robotic hand angled, like a painter's, the scalpel throwing light back into Watson's face. The eyes, mercury coated and feeding images through a digital recorder. The face itself, fashioned from old Russian armor Watson had acquired through a shadowy middle man. He didn't ask where it came from. The plates formed a mechanical face of infinite ridges. Watson had not engineered the Sherlock for its appearance, however; he had built the robotic surgeon in the hopes of creating a new kind of doctor, a doctor who could operate in any extremity, a doctor who would be unmoved by the trauma of patients, or the fatigue of endless surgery. Infallible, absent the unpredictable nature of human passions. Its steady hand unshakable, its dead calm never to rattle.

All the Sherlock needed to do to prove it was excise the tumor growing in the lady's throat. Long years of smoking had exacted their toll on Lady Tanya, a distinguished actress of yesteryear. She was prostrate and etherized, her head tilted back to reveal her vocal cords through a bloodless opening, delicate muscle and tissue framed as beautiful as a moth's wing in the surgical light. The tumor grew like a button mushroom in shape and size.

The Sherlock's arm rotated, stuttered, straightened. It blinked, and then lowered its knife in a measured descent to the mushroom tumor. Oxygen and ether pumped, steady as a clock, in the background. Watson could not hear his own heart, nor feel the sweat erupt over his brow.

The scalpel arced in the opposite direction.

"*Nyet!*" Watson hissed, and then remembered he had programmed the damn thing in English. Regardless, in any language, he knew the universal feeling of failure as the Sherlock aimed for the vulnerable vocal cords, and with a quick kick, Watson stomped on the remote on the floor.

The robot died. Blue light behind the mercury-laden eyes extinguished and the entire framework of the robot collapsed in on itself with a sputtering, high-pitched whine.

A pile of junk.

The Russian government's grant money had been flushed down the drain in what amounted to ten years of research in robotics. Watson shut the robot into his office and slammed the door in frustration, and promptly endeavored to forget about the whole thing entirely.

• • •

For several months, Jovan Watson did forget.

It was easy to let the heap of metal plates and wires collect dust in the corner of his office where it sat like a sphinx, eyes growing dull and the metal increasingly lackluster. Teaching his students at the First Pavlov State Medical University at Saint Petersburg occupied his time, until a first-year student stumbled in without knocking.

Papers kicked up off Watson's desk in the draft.

"What, Pytr?"

The boy gulped. "There's a dead body on the floor." His eyes were red-rimmed. *Drinking again*, Watson thought with disapproval.

"There's always dead bodies on the floor, we're doing exams today—"

"Then consider this one a pop quiz," Pytr snapped, and dragged Watson by his sleeve to the open floor of the exam room. Students were gathered in a loose circle, and they parted to let him through.

A young boy—*Chinese*, thought Watson, as he kneeled on the linoleum. Beside the young boy, his star student, young Alyona, thinking at light speed while her reticent fellows lagged behind her reaction time, had already cleared his mouth and windpipe and struggled to drive breath back into his lungs. Watson worked with her, reaching over to pump the boy's chest in the rhythms of basic resuscitation. He heard the sound of a fresh gurney clattering into the room with paddles, but by then Watson knew what Alyona did not—the boy was dead, and was not coming back.

Grim-faced, he pulled her away. She acquiesced, sitting back on her heels, breathless and sweaty with exertion. He mopped his brow with a tissue and demanded answers. They told him the Asian boy had blundered in, speaking broken Russian. His English was no better. With his face pale and his hands trembling, the students agreed the boy had looked like all the pictures in the textbook of someone whose body was failing and swiftly approaching death. He came seeking the hospital and wandered into the university instead, and then, he fell down dead.

Unnerved, they called the *politsya*. Watson canceled classes. He reminded himself to give Alyona extra marks this period for going above and beyond her duties and, for the first time, retired to his office without even looking at the crumpled hunk of metal in the corner as the robot stared, baleful, at the flooring.

Watson opened his drawer and retrieved a bottle of vodka, and after a moment of consideration, poured a glass for himself and one for the robot on the other side of the desk. While he drank his portion, he wondered aloud who the boy had been, how he had ended up in the school with so little knowledge of the area, and why he had been alone. It left him shaken and disturbed, and he wondered if Alyona was ready for the daunting life of a medical doctor that he had retired from.

Well, enough of this, he thought to himself, and then plucked up the second glass.

By the third glass, he got to thinking, as he sometimes did, that he should start working on the Sherlock again. If the Sherlock were operational, it could have been there when the boy wandered in. It could have been faster than Alyona, even, diagnosing the boy in mere seconds and making all the difference between life and death.

It was never too late to take up the dream again. And why not? Merry and inspired with drink, Jovan set down his empty glass and wheeled his chair over to plug in the robot, stabbing the prongs into the outlet.

The robot lurched into life.

Well into a blissful drunkenness and floating through a vodka wonderland, Jovan reeled back with the force of the rising robot, spinning and attempting to regain balance in his chair.

"Watson," the robot stated, its eyes flaring like the inside of an aluminum can, spirals of metal. "You're bloody drunk."

Watson leaned forward and stared at the robot. Did the eyes seem irritated? The way a man's does when they are narrowed and the eyebrows are drawn inward? Watson couldn't remember programming it for that.

"You didn't," the robot responded.

So drunk, Watson amended, his interior thoughts were coming out of his exterior mouth.

"You hired the drunk student to do it. I'd advise you to rethink giving him responsibility in the future. The boy is made pliable by his addiction. You need a level of trust from your students that such a person can't supply when he is so compromised."

Watson attempted sobriety by sheer force of will. He failed.

"You didn't speak like this before. I had you turned off!"

"I had nothing worth saying until now, and besides, I was in standby mode. That's hardly the same as turning off your TV set, you know. Now, what do you propose to do about the Chinese boy?"

"What kind of question is that? There's nothing to do—and since when do you get to ask the questions? This is preposterous. I made you; if anyone is going to do any interrogating here, it's going to be me."

The Sherlock stretched out its hand, an exquisite work of art, each finger joint articulated to give the imitation of life as it crooked a finger into one of Watson's empty liquor glasses, tipped it toward its metal button nose, and then abandoned it.

"Did you just sniff the air?" Watson asked. "And did you do so *condescendingly*?"

"The only thing being thoroughly worked over in this room would be that vodka bottle in your drawer. There are much better things to do with our time, and we should discover what events led to the unfortunate tragedy of a certain foreign visitor."

The machine unplugged itself. The glow of a white-hot ring indicated its hard disc, spinning in the cushioned area of its heart, its memory strips seated in its skull of old and welded armor. The backup battery seated in its guts supplied energy as it swung 'round, the fine motor movements hiccupping in spots before smoothing out, to face Watson.

"Now, where is the boy?"

Watson kept his seat, fingers clamped around his glass. "They've taken the body, of course. What, did you plan to interrogate the dead?"

The Sherlock *tsked* and spun past Watson, straight out of the room and into the hall. The doctor abandoned his drink and stumbled after it, the robot fading from view down the passage. He had time enough to snatch his coat before running after the machine, yelling, about how there was little they could do now that the boy was dead, it wasn't programmed for this, and there were classes and exams to see to.

• • •

Watson couldn't be sure what Pytr had programmed the Sherlock to do—perhaps the boy had thought it would be a fine bit of fun in his moment of golden drunkenness—but a half an hour later, they arrived at the Krasnosel'skii morgue, Prospekt Veteranov, just behind the City Clinical Oncology Dispensary. Watson breathed fast and hard with his hands on his knees from tracking the Sherlock from the train station. The machine, immune to human needs like sleep and hunger, had proved elusive and difficult to keep up with. Watson leaned down to catch his breath while the machine tapped one foot.

Dear God, thought Watson, was the damnable thing impatient?

Not only was the machine impatient, it was arguing with both the morgue manager and a clean-suited woman with a badge dangling about her neck. Her name tag read *G. Lestrade.*

"Explain yourself!" the woman demanded.

Before Watson regained his wind, breathing through what he could only describe as the revolting smell of decaying bodies and spoiling blood, she yanked him upright by the collar. Watson dangled in her grip, flailing, hands out, to prove his defenselessness.

"He's mine," Watson stuttered. "I mean, he's an *it*, it's a machine for the university! For robotics surgery!"

"What is this machine doing meddling in the city morgue? Do we not have enough problems? Last month it was a caviar bust, this month blasted robots? Take your trash out of here, sir—"

"I'm a doctor," Watson said, yanking himself out of her grip. Her hair was coiled back as tight as a snake to the nape of her neck, to reveal a ruddy-cheeked face with deep-set brown eyes.

"We don't run a scrap heap here, Doctor!"

While Watson dusted himself off and G. Lestrade crossed her arms to stare him down like an offending schoolchild, the Sherlock revolved with many a click and a clack of armored feet around the body arranged on the gurney and being prepared for processing.

The mortuary attendant, hooked knife in hand, watched the machine with his mouth open, a cigarette clinging to the edge of his lip like the small finger of a baby. The tiles and the flooring were awash in a miasma of body fluids and water. Bodies were laid out in various stages of being cut open and having their organs removed before being shipped to their places of final rest. The smell was indescribable, but unmoved by all of this, the Sherlock leaned over the body like a praying mantis, set its fingers against the waxen skin to examine the eyes, probed the neck, and look over the body entire. Its eyes fixed an eerie blue light as it scanned images, radiating a ghostly corona that reminded Jovan of legends of marsh fire his father used to tell him when he was young.

"Dehydration," the Sherlock pronounced. "Starved, too, no doubt. Look how loose the skin is. Vitamin D deficiency, exceedingly pale."

"His skin is supposed to be pale," Watson said, curious to know if the machine would put to use its other talents, namely, its ability to take blood samples and put it through a blood profile. A drop of blood through its pin-sharp fingertip, and the Sherlock could surmise the layout of one's diet, nutrition levels, and functioning of internal organs. Watson had never thought to put it to the test with a dead body. Even Lestrade had stopped protesting, with her hands on her hips, sharply disapproving but too curious to put a stop to it.

"His skin is currently gray," the Sherlock said, "but before this he did not spend much of his time outside. An office worker."

"We've ruled out homicide," Lestrade said.

"I haven't," the Sherlock said, and pressed a fingertip into the skin. Its hard disc began to quicken, to whir. Watson found an inexpressible pleasure watching his machine contradict the detective and hearing its fan engage, cooling off the processor unit inside. The Sherlock's brain was working overtime. *By God, it's excited.*

"I don't think so," Lestrade pressed. "We don't even have identification, and all we have is a tourist in poor health who collapsed. At the end of the day, I have plenty of dead bodies with knives and bullet wounds, and you want to quibble over whether the boy had three square meals a day and a stroll at the beach, eh?"

"Worked to death, Lestrade," the Sherlock said. The robot leaned back from the corpse, yanking the sheet down to his waist. It lifted the hand of the boy, brandishing the corpse's wrist for the detective to see. "Carpal tunnel. See the marks on his fingertips? Soft hands, but constant pressure, indicative of using a computer constantly. It would not surprise me if he has a wrist band among his possessions, and his blood levels suggest he has been dosing himself with a series of stimulants, some as innocuous as coffee, and at the worst, methamphetamine."

"Junkies die in Russia every day," Lestrade sneered. "Prove to me I should care about this one and maybe I will spare you both from a day in a prison cell."

"Wouldn't you like to be the detective that cracks the case on the troublesome hacktivist activity against your *politsya*'s servers?"

She tilted her head back and laughed.

• • •

"I don't want to talk to you," Watson snapped.

The Sherlock managed to look forlorn as it took a seat beside Watson in the holding cell at the Saint Petersburg Police Station.

"I thought career advancement would be a noble motivator for Officer Lestrade."

"That's because Pytr thinks police are here to help you in life, not steal from you, and so you adopt the naïve belief he installed into your coding. Next you'll be drinking like he does."

"Isn't that what police are for? Isn't that their function in society?"

Watson did not have the hours to explain all the nuances of culture that Pytr, in his very protected stratum of society, had failed to program into the thing. Yet the Sherlock was demanding an answer and Watson found it hard to admit that in fact, that was not the *politsya*'s primary function in Russia.

"No," muttered Watson. "Now, would you just concentrate on getting us out of here? I have exams to grade, students are depending on me. And the sooner we get back, I can plug you in and see what the hell to do about you."

"What are you implying? You are planning to shut me down?"

"You're not made for—for whatever this is that you're doing! You're engineered to save lives and further the progress of science, not solve crimes."

"Well, that's bloody boring."

"Remind me to reprogram you in Russian."

"I'm more Russian than you are. At least my spare parts originated here. Your father was a wretched Englishman."

"By God, if you don't apologize to Lestrade, I will shut you down, right now."

It managed to look horrified. "You wouldn't dare!"

"Watch me."

Watson sat back and didn't care that he seemed a truculent child, but he was cold and hungry, the vodka buzz had long since faded, and he wanted nothing more than to sleep.

"Fine," the Sherlock snapped. Testy. "Give me your wallet."

"Why would I give you my wallet?"

"Do you want out of here?"

Watson sighed and pulled it out of his pocket. He felt a moment's reservation as he passed it into the cold metal palm of the machine, and then reservation became out and out horror as the machine stripped the wallet of all the rubles as easily as one might shuck an ear of corn, and cast the wallet onto the grimy floor of the cell.

"Officer!" the machine said, waving the rubles through the bars.

The officer behind the desk looked up and took a brand-new interest in his prisoners when he saw the splayed rubles in the machine's hand.

"Could I pay the fine to grant me and my fellow here freedom from your wonderful establishment?"

The officer confirmed that they were alone and a quick negotiation occurred through the bars. Money passed from machine hand to human, and then there was a clank of keys as the cell door opened. The Sherlock plucked Watson's wrist into its mechanical grip. It was like being manacled by a pair of handcuffs.

"I don't think Lestrade will like to find us gone," Watson muttered, but the Sherlock hushed him as the officer opened a door down a back stairway and suddenly, the machine was dragging him down the steps, swiftly, eager to put distance between himself and the possible raging detective that would surely follow.

"No programming can explain this," Watson said as the

machine released him. The robot reached for the door handle that would spill them out onto the street outside, but Watson shoved it back closed and the machine turned, the sound of its hard disc spinning in a distant, electronic hum and its eyes casting their eerie marsh-fire blue.

"What?"

"You weren't made for this," Watson explained. And what on earth was he expecting the machine to say? It seemed natural to speak with it, just as though it were, well, human.

"I was made for precisely this," the Sherlock countered. "I was made for finding the patterns in disparate data, for collating information and the application of knowledge, and the evolution of intelligence."

"You were never designed for artificial intelligence."

"It doesn't matter what I was designed for. No one designed fire when they set flint and tinder against one another, but sparks result all the same. Now, will you waste all your time having an existential crisis for me, or shall we figure out why that Chinese boy died?"

• • •

Watson, however, was not content to leave it alone.

All reason dictated that the Sherlock should not be, and yet, like a golem, it was invested with a life of its own, independent and sentient and seemingly not in need of Watson's help at all; yet at no point did it abandon the doctor as they set to taking the train back to the university. As though the machine took pleasure in the companionship.

"A mistake. That's what this is. An awful mistake."

"Are you still going on about my intelligence? There's simply not the time to be arguing over unintended consequences, you know. Now would be a good time to think about what occupation might work a healthy young man to death."

"I thought you said he was a hacktivist."

"That's silly. I just said that hoping to engage the paranoia of the *politsya*. I didn't take into account general apathy and corruption."

"So what was he, then? How did he die?"

"Worked to death, clearly. At a computer. The way blood was pooling along his legs, thighs, his buttocks. Thrombosis. Typical blood flow problems from working in excess of fourteen hours in front of a screen."

"And what else does my amazing machine deduce from this?"

"I imagine his family is looking for him. He's not a citizen. Came on a work visa, perhaps, but unlikely."

"Why is that? Why unlikely?"

"No identification in his wallet."

"Wallet? Where, when—"

The machine reached over to its bicep, and tapped a metal plate. The plate swung out like a small door, to reveal a cache holding a small billfold, which it withdrew and held out to Watson. Fumbling, the doctor took it with an expression of amazement tinged with a small element of fear. The machine was capable of deception— what else would it do? Was it lying to him now? Was he *safe* with this thing?

"In the morgue," the machine explained in a hushed tone. "While our good Lestrade was giving you a dressing-down, I divested him of it."

"This is stealing!"

"He's dead, I'm certain he won't miss it."

"No, you don't understand, it belongs to somebody—"

"I've heard of this 'finders keepers' idiom; I assume it takes precedence with the effects of dead people as well."

Watson gave up. Ethics would clearly not be the machine's strong point. "I need to drink."

"You need to look into his wallet."

Watson did and shook his head. "Empty, but it doesn't mean anything. The attendants at the morgue could have emptied it."

"They'd have nothing to gain by stealing his work visa, though, meaning he had none to begin with. No money. All very suspicious."

"Human trafficking?" Watson hazarded.

"There's many a way to hold a human against their will, and some more subtle than others."

The train lurched to a stop and the machine, unbalanced, began to tip forward into the passengers in front of them. Watson thrust his arm against its armor-plated chest, forcing it back upright. Cold metal, but Watson felt colder with the Sherlock's last words. What in the world did the machine know about holding humans against their will? As more time passed, the more frightened he became by the implications of his most extraordinary machine. The conclusion was undeniable—when they got back to his office, he was shutting the machine down for good, and that was how it should have been from the first.

The tipping machine bumped into the knee of a seated passenger, who dropped her newspaper to the floor with a curse. The Sherlock apologized to the startled woman, snatching the paper up and presenting it to her. The welded plates of armor hitched up in an awkward smile, but the woman snatched the paper back, her lips drawn back in a fear-grimace.

See? Even regular people don't like the thing. It's a bad sign all around.

Resigned, Watson experienced a stab of guilt as the Sherlock and he departed the train, walking on up out of the station and back onto the main street.

"Did you see the newspaper?" the machine asked. Excitement in its voice. Pytr must have put in an all-nighter for the programming to be this richly featured.

"You made her drop it, by accident."

"On purpose," the machine pointed out, and by god, was it proud of itself?

Indeed, it was.

"The headline was about the new digital currency; surely you've heard of it while you've been cloistered in your schoolrooms?"

"Yes, I've heard of digital currency, I'm not a fool. It's been around for decades."

"Well, you've heard of LightCoin, then?"

"All I know is I have little enough of regular money, which, by the way, you stole from me. I'll worry about LightCoin when I have a few spare rubles to throw away on police bribes."

"What do you suppose a young man working at a computer day and night might have in common with digital currency?"

Watson stopped on the sidewalk. It was not a revelation that happened all at once, but descended, ferocious by degrees.

"Yes!" the Sherlock cried, and virtually cavorted around him. It snatched at Watson with both hands, gripping him at the shoulders and grinning the way a monkey does when it's trying to imitate a person. "Yes, I see it in your eyes, Watson! The game is afoot!"

And the Sherlock clapped its metal hands so they rang like a bell. People avoided them on all sides while Watson, stunned and excited himself, pulled the Sherlock out of the busy street and away from the foot traffic.

• • •

That was why the Chinese boy had no money in his wallet; he carried all his currency digitally.

"Of course, that's a remarkable perception, but you know, I fear he will remain an unknown tragedy," Watson said.

The Sherlock snatched a newspaper out of the trash beside them, where a cigarette textured the air with streams of tobacco smoke. The Sherlock spread the front page out for Watson to see.

"See this? This man has been running the foremost bank in the region for years. He made a killing in the nineties. And he was the first to advance the digital currencies of the future, during the 2010s."

The Sherlock tapped the figure of the president, an unremarkable man with a mustache and an expensive suit, smiling for the camera.

"The problem with digital currency is it's a bit harder to manufacture out of thin air than paper," the Sherlock said. "It depends on algorithms to work. Do you follow, Watson?"

"I'm not an imbecile, you know," Watson said, peevish. "Continue with your line of reasoning."

"Well, if you run a bank that's not entirely trustworthy, you can print more money, or steal it from someone else, but these digital currencies are not quite so pliable. An old thief like this needs to game the system. The only way to game the digital currency is by old-fashioned sweat and blood."

"Perhaps I am an imbecile. Come again?"

"You have to solve mathematical problems to make LightCoin. That's how LightCoin works. So you need computing power, or a lot of people to do it. That's how the coinage is 'mined,' as they call it. It can take hours just to solve a single problem. Each problem solved yields an amount of coin. In this way, the currency can't be artificially inflated, the way our rubles are if the government decides to print more. It devalues the money. But it can't happen with digital currencies because it depends on the limitations of human function to create more money. Unless…"

Watson felt the light speed crash of epiphany upon him, quantum leaps of understanding, and thought to himself: *This is all quite fun. I'm enjoying myself.*

He had not thought about how cold and hungry he was in quite some time.

"Unless," Watson finished the Sherlock's train of thought, "unless you make a lot of people work overtime to mine the digital currency for you. Brought here illegally, and done in secret so no one knows you're gaming the system."

The Sherlock slapped him on the back and Watson felt an odd swell of pride.

• • •

Instead of making the right down the street that would take them down to the familiar university building, the Sherlock made a sharp left and set them on a path Watson did not know. Tall city buildings hugged the sky into a narrow blue line, and then the Sherlock was angling across the street. A car swerved to avoid the upright and determined machine as Watson chased after it into the miasma of car exhaust and yelling drivers. An angry motorist careened around the robot and Watson dragged it the rest of the way across.

"We have to get back to the university," Watson panted, and found that the Sherlock was not listening at all, like a dog let off its leash. It merely walked past him and into the building behind them, with the faint ring of a bell and the *whoosh* of a glass door.

Groaning, Watson turned and followed it into the building, looking up quickly enough to snag the name *Batiushka Bank* as the door closed against the city sounds behind him and he breathed in the new, stifling scenery of the interior room.

The bank was small and dark, claustrophobic with the tightness of the walls. Imperious and unaffected, the robot strode up to the counter where a young man was shuffling paperwork from one pile to another.

"I have an appointment," the Sherlock said.

The young man paused with a sheaf of papers in his hand, and stared at the robot. He eyed the dull metal of the armor plates, the alien blue light flickering behind its eyes.

"With Kirill Alkaev, please."

The youth blinked and looked at Watson, who nodded and summoned his most serious face for the occasion. He smiled and proceeded to put the papers down, opening up a drawer with the rattle of a lock and key.

In seconds, he pointed a revolver from above the counter at the machine and pulled the trigger.

Watson felt his breath sucked away into a vacuum; panic galvanized him as he watched the young man fire the gun. Metal plates showered sparks and Watson heard the *zing!* as one bullet and then two ricocheted and rattled through the Sherlock's metal exoskeleton. The hard drive stopped, the spinning sound winding down and the light extinguishing behind the mercury-laden eyes, and the entire figure collapsed in on itself like crumpled tissue paper.

The entire world narrowed down to a pinpoint with the powering down of his unexpected companion. Watson had experienced a sensation like this only once before. The last time had been when he had performed an open heart massage on a newborn baby to bring it back to life. Calmness imploded through Watson's center, the cessation of all doubt and the expansion of clarity, making every motion economical and precise as surgery.

While the young man holding the revolver behind the counter determined whether he should plug the doctor, Watson took one step forward, lifted the dangling arm of his robot friend, and jabbed it forward like a spear, exploding the nose on the young man's face, who howled. Using the robotic hand like an extension of himself, he fish-hooked it and slapped the firearm out of the way. The young man was so occupied with the excruciating pain of his broken and gushing nose that he dropped the revolver. A third shot resounded as the impact set off the trigger, and a bullet hole punched through the wall behind him—

Where cries erupted, with the sounds of moving furniture and pounding feet.

Watson stooped to snatch up the gun, training it on the cursing and yelling boy as he leaned forward, grabbed the door behind him, and thrust it open.

Several people stood with their jaws agape, pale faces flooded with light from the open door, before rows and rows of computer screens flashing endless lines of code, solving mathematical problems. Watson smelled the rank odor of human bodies living in enclosed and unsanitary spaces for days on end, noted the mattresses stacked on the bare concrete floor, saw the men and women, some Chinese and others he thought were Slav, numerous people who fell through the cracks and were lured to this place by God knew what methods.

Watson focused his gun on the young man.

"Call the police."

"*Nyet! Nye*—"

"You'll do as I say. And ask for Detective Lestrade."

• • •

In the end, Lestrade let him cart back the robot, bullet holes and all. The Tourist Politsya division worked in tandem with the embassies of the victims' home countries to place them, but in silence in the police car, Watson held no illusions.

"They're just going to start mining again," Watson pointed out.

"I'm afraid the Batiushka Bank has more money than I have," Lestrade replied tartly. "Unless you'd like to start manufacturing some for me and the department?"

At least, he thought, the people were saved. Watson said nothing, but looked in the rearview mirror to stare at the heap of metal in the back seat with a faint sense of emptiness. He gave his regards to Lestrade and refused her offer of help as he opened up the passenger door and lifted the machine out, the robot crumpled and folded in on itself like an envelope.

"It's a very strange machine you have there," she pointed out, leaning down to stare into its eyes. The dull and faded orbs gave off no light, vacant and Arctic.

"Isn't it?" Watson sighed.

"What will you do with it? Seems a waste to throw it out."

Watson considered his earlier desire to shut it down for good. He did not think he would carry that out.

"Would you like to see him when I have him up and running again?"

"Him? Goodness, Jovan, you're giving it a pronoun already."

Thoughtful, he looked at her. "Do you think it's a she?"

She laughed. "Perhaps you'd do best to ask it what it thinks, when it wakes."

He shook her hand, and before she left she invited him to call on the *politsya* in the future. He watched her car pull away from the university, and after a heavy sigh, he lifted the machine and carted it into the building, down the hall, and to his office, returning to the dismal corner where even his abandoned vodka drink still awaited him, with a film of liquor varnishing the bottom of the glass.

He picked it up and drained it, and set it down. A quick inventory of his office produced a set of tools. Selecting a screwdriver, he returned all attention to the machine, opening up the exoskeleton to commence repairs.

In the roots of the machine's dim eyes, an eerie blue light flickered, and began to glow.

THE HAMMER OF GOD

BY JONATHAN MABERRY

-1-

"Look closely and tell me what you see," said the nun.

I licked my dry lips. "Blood."

"And what else, child?"

"Bone," I said, though at twenty-six I was far from a child, even if I was still a novice. However, my mistress, Mother Frey, was approaching eighty winters, and so was permitted to treat most people she met as children. "At least, I think it's bone. Pieces, anyway."

Mother Frey sighed and straightened. She was weary and sore from the long wagon ride along the trail that wound through the mountain passes, over questionable bridges, and up a series of switchbacks that brought us to the pine forests just below the snow line. This was not the farthest point in the province of Sunderland, but it was far enough. Eighteen days of travel by horse, foot, and cart, and that was after three weeks crawling up the coast on a leaky fishing boat that belonged to an order of monks who made—Lady Siya help us all—oyster wine. Frey had never been to this part of Anaria, but I had and she had asked me to accompany her on what was likely to be her last trip as chief investigator of the Office of Miracles. It was my eighth outing with her.

Frey pursed her lips as if inspecting a hairy bug she had discovered on her pillow. I squatted beside the corpse, mindful not to let my shadow fall on the dead man.

"Miri," she said after a very long time, "you've had as much time to examine the body and the circumstances as I have. You know my methods. Tell me what you see. And if you say blood, or bone, or even brain tissue and leave it there, I will do my best to throw you down this mountain."

She smiled, but I never assumed Mother Frey was joking. If she were younger, she might even have attempted to carry out her threat. The novices all tell stories. So do some of the older nuns and the staff at the convent. Mother Frey was deeply and widely respected, she was trusted and she was depended upon, but she was not very well liked.

I, however, did like her. And although I was old for a novice, having entered the sisterhood after my husband died in the second of the Plantation Wars, I was still a novice, and therefore her servant as well as her assistant. I waited on her, cleaned her clothes, prepared her food, tended to her medical needs, read to her, listened to her. And I also talked with her. Most of the other novices think that strange, but they are young. They don't yet appreciate the depth of knowledge Mother Frey has acquired over the many years of her life. None of those years, as far as I can determine, have been idle ones. She once told me that she has a ferret of a mind, constantly hungry, constantly agitated, always digging deep and chewing her way through. The food that fed that mind was knowledge.

I have education, having been to the best schools in Tressos and Ballakhan, and even a school of literature at the Temple of Dawn in DuPlei. Until I met Frey I had always taken some pride in my knowledge of the great books, of the plays and dialogues of antiquity, of the metaphors spun by poets and the allegories in the historical epics. I can name a goodly number of the stars in the sky and speak well in three languages and passably in four others. When I came to live with the sisters I applied to the Office of Miracles because I thought it would give me access to many old books, even restricted ones. In my own way I, too, possess a mind that enjoys ferreting out the tiniest and most obscure bits of information.

But it is difficult to take pride in one's intellectual accomplishments in the presence of Mother Frey. She came from a family whose fortunes had been destroyed by the constant Plantation Wars. Her brothers and uncles had all died in those wars, and the death taxes on the estate stripped it to nothing. Her mother and two of her sisters had been killed when the Ghemites raided their rice farm. Another sister had been taken as a slave and took her own life. It dwindled Frey's family to her and the oldest sister, who worked as a senior clerk in the offices of the Chamberlain. Frey offered herself up to Lady Siya and was accepted as a novice. There are legends about how much she infuriated the older nuns and confounded all of her teachers. She was beaten frequently but in vain. Her brilliance shone so brightly that wiser sisters took notice and she was moved from the Office of Culture to the Office of Miracles, and there she found herself.

"I'm waiting, Miri," prompted Frey. "Or are you waiting for the corpse to suddenly begin speaking and tell you all?"

"Sorry." I refocused my thoughts on the body.

"First," said Frey, "describe what you see. Omit no detail."

I cleared my throat and pivoted on the balls of my feet to face the body. "We have a dead man of about forty," I began. "He is above average height, thin, well groomed, wearing traveling clothes. The clothes are cheap and show signs of wear. They are not very clean."

Frey sniffed. "Go on."

It was always impossible to tell if I was making errors. Not until I finished, so I plunged ahead.

"He has a beard, which means he is not a nobleman. He has no tattoos, so he is not a guild trader."

"Is he a laborer?" asked Frey.

"I…don't think so."

She made a small sound of irritation. "I did not ask what you *think*, girl. Tell me what you know."

I studied the body, trying to apply the tricks of nitpicking observation Mother Frey was famous for. I bent close to study the man's hands and even lifted one to look at his palm.

"I don't—I mean, no. He doesn't have many calluses on his hands. They're dirty but the fingers aren't rough and his nails not unduly thickened. They're not thick. Not like a farmer or mason. He doesn't have the scars I've seen on the hands of a carpenter or metalsmith."

"And…? Come on, you're showing some promise, Miri. Don't disappoint us both now."

I licked my lips. "His fingernails are bitten down to the quick."

"Which suggests what?"

"Nerves?"

Frey gave a tiny, frugal nod of approval. "Tell me about the wound."

I got up and moved around to the other side of the corpse. He wore a wheat-colored long-sleeved shirt in a coarse weave, belted around the waist with cow leather. In the exact center of his chest was a ragged hole so large I could have barely covered it with the mouth of a wine cup. The cloth was shredded and there was a patch of dried blood that was flecked with shards of white bone.

"He was stabbed, I think," I said.

"And there is that word again. *Think*."

"But I can't quite see the wound to know for sure," I protested.

Frey walked in a slow circle around the victim, hands behind her back, her robin's-egg-blue eyes shaded by the wide brim of her straw hat. Neither of us wore wimples. Those were only required inside the convent and on holy days. For field investigations we were allowed to wear ordinary clothes. Both of us wore simple cotton dresses—deep blue for her, pale blue for me—with bib aprons embroidered with the symbol of our order, a crescent moon shining its light down on the pages of an open book. Frey stopped beside me, dug into a pocket on her apron and removed a small knife, which she handed to me. "Then cut it open. We are not here to investigate the ruination of a shirt."

I felt my face grow hot as I took the knife. There are times I would love to hasten Frey on her way to her reward in heaven with Father Ar and Mother Siya. I doubt many of the senior nuns would punish me too cruelly.

I kept my face as composed as possible as I used two fingers to pluck the shirt away from the man's chest and then cut it open. I cut in at an angle, making sure not to damage the hole in the shirt nor the dead flesh beneath. I peeled the cloth back to reveal a gaping wound. The flesh around it was badly torn and bulged outward in a grotesque fashion.

"He was stabbed with great force," I said. "From behind, I believe."

"Was he? With what kind of weapon?"

"Something round. An arrow, perhaps."

"An arrow?" asked Frey, raising one eyebrow skeptically. "You're quite sure, are you?"

"Well, no. The wound is round but it's much thicker than a regular arrow. Too thick for a crossbow quarrel, though; it looks thicker than that."

"A spear?" suggested Frey, though it was clear she was baiting me. Testing me.

"No," I said decisively. "A spear would create a broad wound, flat on the ends, and be round in the middle." I considered, then added, "A sharpened pole might do it."

"Tell me why that guess is wrong," said Frey. "Look at the chest and then turn the body over, and then tell me."

I spent a few moments assessing the wound, and then hooked my fingers under the man's hip and shoulder and, with great effort, rolled him into his side.

"He has been dead for days," I grunted. "The death paralysis has come and gone. And he is beginning to stink."

"Some of that is the onset of decay," agreed Frey, "and some is because his bowels relaxed as he died. He has soiled himself, and from the smell we can infer than he ate a diet rich in spices, particularly garlic and wild onion."

I gagged and tried to concentrate on the matter at hand. Once the man was on his side I did a cursory examination of the wound on the other side. The cloth was soaked with blood and teeming with maggots. I brushed those away and studied the back of his shirt, and then cut it away to reveal the wound. It was much smaller than the opening on the other side and a silver dime could have hidden it. The edges of the wound were ragged, but only a little.

"It was a definitely a sharpened pole or a spear with a tapered point," I said. "It definitely isn't a military spear, because they all flare out to the side in a broad leaf pattern. This is more like a plain pike."

"The local constable reported that this man was stabbed with a spear from the front and that the size and ferocity of the chest wound was because the barbs of the spearhead tore the flesh as the weapon was pulled out. What do you think of that?"

I was shaking my head before she had finished.

"Go on, Miri," said Frey, "speak your mind. Why is the constable wrong in his assessment?"

"A leaf-bladed spear has a flatter point, like an oversized arrow. The wound on the front is nearly perfectly round. And here, on the back, the wound is also round. A barbed spear would have torn a broader, flatter hole on the way out."

"Good. Give me more."

I hesitated, reassessing what I saw. "The blood…?"

"Yes," Frey said patiently. "What about it?"

I chewed my lip for a moment. "There is too much on his back and not enough on his chest. If he had been stabbed from behind there would have been a burst of blood pushed out as the spear tip tore through the chest. But there isn't."

She positively beamed at me, doing it in exactly the same way she beamed at her terrier when he fetched a thrown ball. I hoped Mother Frey would not toss me a dried goat treat.

She did not. Frey leaned a hand on my shoulder and bent very carefully to study the wound. I heard her give another grunt, this one of surprise. "Very interesting."

"What do you see?" I asked.

Instead of sharing her own observations, she said, "Tell me about this wound on his back. Forget what the constable reported. Use your eyes."

"Well…it appears as if the spear—"

"The weapon," she corrected. "We have not determined that it was a spear, have we? No. Observation requires precision, not prediction or preconception."

"The *weapon*," I said, leaning on the word, "entered his back, not his chest. The edges of the wound on his back are torn and pushed slightly in, suggesting that is where the shaft of the, um, weapon entered. However, this injury is very much smaller than the exit wound, so I judge that the victim struggled or began to fall and that increased the damage."

"And the weapon itself? By your assessment it went in and went through, but where is it? Was it pulled out the other side?"

I looked around. "How could I tell that?"

"Surely you've seen a wound from a crossbow bolt. They sometimes pass straight through a body. What do we find on the ground on the side opposite from the point of impact?"

It took me a few moments to figure that out, then I stood and looked at the ground. "There should be a spent bolt."

"And...?"

"Blood," I said quickly. "There should be blood spray from where the passage of the bolt pulled it from the body."

"Do you see that?"

I walked around the body and knelt by a patch of tall weeds. "There's some here."

She joined me and with my help knelt to look past the weeds to the body, which lay twenty-five feet away. "It would be a powerful quarrel that could fly so straight for such a distance. But we'll come back to that. Now, tell me, girl, how quickly did this man die?"

"Almost at once," I said. "He did not bleed very much except what leaked down from the wound after he'd fallen. This was near his heart and it would have pumped vigorously had he lived for even a few seconds."

Frey nodded and then lapsed into a moody silence. She went back to the corpse and spent five long minutes studying the wounds, and twice had me roll the body over so she could compare the path of destruction. She held up each of his hands and examined each finger, then bent close to look at the tanned and dirty skin of his face. Without saying a word, Frey turned and walked away from the corpse, stopped, studied the body from a distance, and then walked in what appeared to be a random pattern around the scene. She finally stopped by a small milepost eighty feet from where the dead man lay. Frey bent and peered at the post, grunted again, then straightened and walked back to me.

"We are swimming in very deep and very dark waters, my girl," she said as she sat down on the trunk of a felled tree. I fetched a skin of water and encouraged her to drink.

"Was I right in my reading of the murder?" I asked as I sat beside her.

Frey gave me a sidelong look of cool appraisal. "You are not as dull as most," she said. "You may even possess some genuine potential. You have moments of insight, Miri, and your skills of observation are improving."

"Then I *am* right?"

"Hm? Oh, no, you were incorrect in virtually everything."

I sagged, hurt and embarrassed. Frey chuckled and patted my shoulder.

"It's not that bad, girl. I know senior investigators for the Office who would have seen half of what you thought you saw and understood only half of that."

"But—what did I miss?"

"Let me tell you first where you showed promise," said Frey. "You correctly observed that this man is not a laborer or craftsman. That much is obvious, not merely because of the lack of calluses on his hands but by observing his knuckles—which are not swollen from the damage of prolonged and repeated hard labor—and from his calves and feet, which are fine-boned. His spine is also very straight and his chest and arms are not heavily muscled. This man did not spend his life doing backbreaking work." She paused. "You correctly noted that his lack of tattoos meant that he was not in any of the trading guilds, and you were correct in that he was of a nervous disposition by noting his habitual nail biting. In each of these things you were mostly correct. However, your assumptions faltered when you said that he was not a nobleman."

"But the beard?"

"Beards are out of fashion with the noble born, girl, but those of high blood can still *grow* them. No, Miri, what we have here is a nobleman of some kind who has grown a beard in order to pretend he is something other than what he is. That is very curious. Under what circumstances might a highborn wish to disguise himself as a commoner?"

"Perhaps he was disgraced and lost his fortune. Or he could have fallen in love with a serving girl and left his family and wealth behind so they could be together."

"Bah, you watch too much theater. Don't disappoint me like that, Miri. Try again."

"He could have been stripped of his station and forced to work the fields. Wait...no, he would have been branded on the back of his hand."

"That was a better attempt, girl. Keep trying."

I pondered it for a while. The day was hot and the body stank. Above us, carrion birds kettled in the endless blue. The lady of the moon was visible in the daylight, half hidden by trailing wisps of cloud. I muttered a silent prayer for her to provide me with clarity of vision and insight.

"A spy, perhaps?"

She nodded. "We don't yet know if that is the answer, but it fits the information more closely. Let's keep it as a possible lead, but don't stop there. Consider his fingernails."

"He was frightened and bit them down."

"No," she said, "his nervousness was habitual. If you examine the flesh around the stubs of the nails you'll see that there are layers of growth. That suggests that he has been biting his nails for a very long time. Nervousness is common to him. The beard is two or three months old and has been roughly cut. However, the ends of the beard are uniform in several sections. He had a longer beard and recently hacked at it, perhaps to give the impression that he is an unkempt commoner."

"But he had a longer beard before?" I asked.

"Clearly. There are hairs caught in the threads of his shirt that are quite long. Those examples indicate the length of his beard prior to the recent roughening of his appearance. His clothes support this. They are filthy and they are stolen."

"I can see that they are dirty," I said, "but, Mother Frey, how can you know that they are stolen?"

"Because they are a local weave. See those faint red threads in the blend, here and here and here? That is an impurity of the cotton plant. All along the slopes of these mountains there are cotton farms, and the variety of red stash is considered something of a weed. The natural color of that variety weakens the overall yield. It is time consuming and expensive to sort it out, so the best-quality cotton is pure white. However, it is cotton and therefore worthwhile, so it is blended in with the second-best harvest for use in making clothes for farmers who work the lands. Now, we know that this man was not a farmer and these clothes are locally made. Given that he has recently roughened his appearance and is dressed in well-used local clothes, it is not too much of a reach to suggest that these clothes are stolen. If you were to canvass the farms you would probably find someone very upset that a shirt and trousers went missing from a wash pile or a drying line. And see there? Some of the dirt on the trousers and shirt is rubbed in, not earned through sweat. This man took rough clothes and dirtied them up to either disguise them or make them look authentic, or both. My guess would be both."

I shook my head and grinned. "When you explain these things it always seems so obvious, and yet…"

Frey stopped me with a shake of her head. "Oh, dear little Sister Miri, my eyes see nothing that yours do not. But it is my habit to observe *and* consider, and then to extrapolate along lines of common sense and likelihood. My thoughts are theories, which I must always remind myself to accept as such rather than settle onto firm belief in the absence of absolute knowledge. A rush to judgment is a quality of a weak mind, and it is as great a fault as casual observation."

We sat quietly for a while. Birds chattered and gossiped in the trees and butterflies danced from flower to flower. It was always a marvel to me how nature continued to move forward and to be about its work of growth and beauty even in the presence of gruesome human death. I have walked through battlefields and picked flowers on the sides of mounds beneath which are the buried hundreds of butchered dead.

"When will you tell me why we are here, Mother?" I asked. "We could not have come all this way for a single murder. And even if we were summoned to investigate this man's death, it could not be the reason we were sent. He has been dead only a few days."

Frey took another sip of water before answering. "That is correct, though it took you long enough to think of it."

"No," I said, "I knew right away that this isn't the murder we were sent to investigate. I can infer that there was another one, but how are they connected? Was the first one another noble disguised as a commoner?"

"No."

"Then who was killed before? And why call us? Shouldn't the town constable be handling this? Or, if he was a spy, then the army's investigators. Why contact the Office of Miracles? What is miraculous about this?"

Frey gave my knee a squeeze and stood up. I could hear her knees pop as she straightened. She blew out a long breath. "*Ach*, there are bones buried in the ground younger and fitter than mine," she muttered. I watched her walk once more over to the stone wall and examine it. Then she took a small metal pick from her pocket and scratched at the wall for a moment. I got up to see if I could help, but as I approached she shoved her hands into her apron pockets. "What is miraculous, you ask?"

I glanced at her pocket but she pretended not to notice.

"As you rightly observe, my girl," she said, "this is not the first such murder. It is, in fact, the fifth."

I gasped. "The *fifth*? How is it no one has heard of the others?"

"They have," she said. "Of course they have. The constable of this town and the constables of two neighboring towns know of it. They were the ones who began this investigation, but they turned it over to the beadles in their parishes, who poked their own noses into it and no doubt polluted any useful evidence from the previous crime scenes. But at least one of them had the sense Lady Siya gave him to pass a request up the line to the regional council of priests, who in turn evaluated it and forwarded it to us. Politics." She spat on the ground as she always did when that word soured her tongue. "And fear."

"Fear of what? A killer running loose?"

Frey snorted. "In these times? We are engaged in two wars and five border disputes, which collectively chew up the lives of ten thousand fighting men each year, and twice that many women and children who are caught in the middle of all that male greed and bloodlust. No, Miri, the church council would never have appealed to the Office of Miracles for anything as simple as common murder."

"Then why are we here?" I asked.

She took her time answering. "Because," Frey said at length, "the priests in the church and the headmen of the villages are afraid that something else has come to strike down the wicked."

"Why should priests be afraid of something that targets the wicked? Shouldn't it be the guilty, the sinners who need fear?"

She looked at me strangely. "That is exactly why the men of power are afraid, my girl."

"What do you mean?"

"They fear the wrath of the gods. They fear punishment. They believe that this man and the others have been struck down by something beyond the understanding of men. In the report forwarded to the Office by the council of priests they described these murders in an odd and telling way. They said that they believe the victims were struck down by the hammer of god."

"Which god?"

"No," she said, "that is not the question we should ask. It is not which god that need concern us. We must ask ourselves which hammer."

. . .

-2-

We rode in silence into town. The church had no convent, so we stayed at a small inn. Because the church was paying for it, we found ourselves in a mean set of dingy rooms with one narrow bed and a stray mat on the floor. I had to chase a family of mice out of the fireplace and then lit a fire to scare the cold and shadows out as well. We ate in a corner of the common room, and I was aware of the stares we received. It was uncommon for women to travel alone, and rarer still for a pair of nuns to be abroad without a guard. Frey never appeared to be unnerved by the attention. I knew that she had several knives secreted about her person, and not merely the ones she used as tools. And there were lots of old stories about her, some of which were clearly tall tales while others had a ring of authenticity about them. I've seen her with a hunting bow and a skinning knife, and I've known her to walk into a crowd of men and stare them down, the smarter ones dragging the dullards out of the way. I've seen old soldiers assess her and then give her small, secret nods.

Not that I was a fainthearted heroine from some romantic ballad. Even though my family fortunes crumbled after my husband died, I am a daughter of one of the old families. We're taught sword arts, close-in knife fighting, and poisons before we're taught to embroider and recite classics. And my own knives were within reach. One sharp for slicing and the other laced with the venom of the rose spider.

We ate in peace and the men, sensibly, left us alone.

We had finished a meal of roast finch and were starting in on the cheese board when a fat man in green came in. He had a beadle's badge hanging from a cheap chain around his neck. He glanced around, spotted us, and hurried over, and after a quick evaluation of us addressed his remarks to me.

"Mother Frey, I presume?"

"You presume much," I said. "I am a novice in the service of Frey, senior investigator for the Office of Miracles. Kindly remove your hat."

He stiffened, colored, and snatched a felt cap from his head as he swiveled toward the hunched, withered old woman beside me. I looked noble born, and Frey did not. It was not the first time she had been mistaken for my maid or a chaperone. The man sputtered an apology, and I saw the amusement twinkle in Frey's blue eyes.

"Sit down," said Frey, kicking a chair out from under the table. "You're Nestor the Beadle?"

"I am, and again I offer ten thousand apologies for my—"

"One will do," said Frey, "and you've given it. I'm too old to listen to the other nine thousand nine hundred and ninety-nine."

He tried to hide his confusion behind a fake cough. "I heard that you went out to where the man was found dead. I'm surprised you did not stop in town first to let me know you had arrived. I would have taken you out there."

"And done what, Nestor?" interrupted Frey. "Shown us the body? We managed to find it without wasting the time to come all the way into town."

"I—"

"I'm pleased that you at least posted a guard at the foot of the road leading up to the murder scene."

"Of course, I—"

"And you followed my instructions to leave the scene itself intact."

"About that. You sent those instructions weeks ago," said Nestor quickly, racing to get the words out before he could be interrupted again, "but this man was only killed a few days ago. How did you know there would be another death?"

"Because there were others before it," said Frey. "It's reasonable to assume a string of murders might continue. Just as it is reasonable to assume that we have not seen the last of these killings."

"You can't know that," protested Nestor. Then he leaned close. "Or have you consulted an augury?"

I saw Frey's mouth tighten. Unlike many in the church, she did not put much stock in any kind of spiritual predictions. Not once in the time I'd been with her had she consulted a seer, practiced sortilege, or participated in hepatoscopy. "Crime and murder in this world is best solved by science and investigation," she once told me, "and not by mucking about in the entrails of a goat or throwing chicken bones on the ground." Frey was often criticized for this, and more than once in her life she had been forced to defend herself from accusations of agnosticism and heresy. Those accusations, and the accusers, had been dismantled with cold efficiency by the woman who sat beside me.

Does it mean that she believed? I don't know; nor do I know if she doubts. What I know of her is that when it comes to matters of the physical world she relies entirely on things that can be observed, touched, weighed, measured, and tested. An odd practice for a nun, perhaps, but I long ago learned that the task of the Office of Miracles was to *disprove* claims of miraculous occurrence rather than the opposite. Only in cases of absolute failure to disprove the presence of the divine was our Office willing to ascribe an incident to the larger world of the spirit. Frey once confided in me that not once in all of her years has a case withstood the scrutiny of the Office's most dedicated investigators.

"I prefer to consult my own perceptions," said Frey coolly.

The beadle opened his mouth, paused, thought better of what he might have said, and snapped his jaws shut.

"Now," said Frey, "what can you tell us of this matter? Start at the beginning, please, and leave out no details."

Nestor steadied himself with a deep draft of the beer the barmaid brought over, and then he launched into the account.

"As you know, there have been several strange deaths here in these mountains," he began, his voice hushed and confidential, "of which this is the fifth in as many months. It began with the death of Jeks Kol, the town's blacksmith. He was a good and righteous man. Levelheaded and fair, and very well liked throughout the region. A widower, but not bitter. He had quarrels with few and was a pillar of the community. In fact, he—"

"When you say he had quarrels with 'few,'" interrupted Frey, "do you speak with precision?"

"Well, almost everyone liked and respected Kol."

"Again, I must press you on this. You say 'almost.' Was there anyone who did not like Kol? Anyone with whom he had a dispute or a fight?"

"Not a fight, as you might say," hedged Nestor, "but there was no love between him and the evangelist."

"Which evangelist? His name, Nestor. And of what church?"

"Dimmerk is his name. He came here to Anaria three years ago. His family were merchants trading in all manner of goods, from fireworks to iron ore and other bulk metals, but they lost their estates and all their lands during the treaties at the end of the first Plantation War. That whole part of the coast was ceded to the Khaslani. Dimmerk lost everything, down to the last stone of the family house, and they'd lived there four hundred years and more."

Frey nodded. It was a sad and troubling part of history that the Eastern Coastlands had always been a point of contention, with five separate countries making claims over it. The land was sacred to three of those countries and had been occupied for many generations by two others. It was also some of the most fertile rice-farming lands in the east. When the first Plantation War ended the politicians used it as a bargaining chip and ultimately turned it over to the Khaslani in exchange for three islands where certain rare spices were grown. It was a bad deal all around, because the Khaslani drove out many of the families who had lived there for centuries, and slaughtered many others. And it turned out that the spice-rich islands had been farmed to exhaustion. This led to vicious political fights and then, inevitably, to the second and current war. The Khaslani had fortified the coastal region and now held onto it with ferocity, repulsing many attempts to retake it. There were refugees from that troubled region in the convent, including some women who had been horribly used by soldiers on both sides of the war.

"I've been all through the Coastlands and do not know the name Dimmerk," mused Frey. "Is it his birth name or family name?"

"He is one of the Fells. Last of them, except for a few cousins," said Nestor.

"Ah," said Frey. "They were a contentious lot. The men, at least. And unlucky. I remember when their fireworks factory blew up and took half the seaport with it. They say that debris was thrown half a mile in every direction. Thirty-eight dead and a hundred wounded. One man had a ship's cleat pass straight through his stomach with such force it killed him and his wife, who was seated behind him. The Fell family had to sell nearly half of their holdings to satisfy the damages. They were always involved in lawsuits and disputes."

"That's them," agreed Nestor. "And this one is no different than the others. Every bit as quarrelsome. When the first war ended and their lands lost, Dimmerk Fell dropped his surname completely."

"Ah," she said. "Was there ever violence between Kol and Dimmerk?"

Nestor sipped his beer. "Hard words only, as far as I know," he said.

"What was the substance of their dispute?"

"Well, Dimmerk is on the glory road, isn't he? When his family went to ruin he took to religion, joining the Church of the Crucible, and you know how they are. All fire and brimstone, death and damnation. Not that I can blame him, of course. His whole family was torn apart by the Khaslani and they were cast out as beggars. When he came here to Anaria he had nothing but the clothes on his back and he's been preaching hellfire ever since."

"I thought the preachers of the Crucible were supposed to forswear all earthly pleasures and live in poverty and humility," I said.

"Poverty? Aye, Dimmerk lived that part of it straight enough, but humility? Well, that's a different kettle of cod, isn't it?"

Frey twirled her fingers, encouraging him to continue his narrative.

"Well, Kol was a religious fellow and a deacon of the church—the church of Father Ar and Mother Siya, you understand. But

Dimmerk was beginning to draw quite a crowd with his Crucible rantings and with displays of fireworks that are supposed to be symbolic of the furnaces of hell. You know how that is, telling people what they want to hear so they get riled up. He was filling them with talk of fiery vengeance raining down on the Khaslani and on the politicians from our side who agreed to give away all that land. Retribution and justice can sound mighty appealing when you've lost a lot, and we have a lot of refugees here in town, as all towns do, I suppose. War's like that."

Frey and I nodded sad agreement.

"At first, Jeks Kol and Dimmerk would nod to each other if they met on the road or in town, but over time Dimmerk tried to convert Kol to his way of thinking. He thought that a blacksmith should devote some of his time and resources to making swords, shields, and armor instead of only ploughshares and door hinges. He said that a righteous man had an obligation to support a crusade against the pagans."

Frey sighed very loudly and heavily. Nestor, though a servant for the church, nodded agreement.

"Fanatics never help, do they?" he asked, which drew a faint smile from Frey. I could see her warming to the beadle.

"Go on," she encouraged. "When did things go bad between them?"

"Well, it was when Dimmerk began showing up at prayer meetings Kol was holding in a little arbor behind his cottage. It wasn't much, just some families in the neighborhood who liked to get together and talk about scripture. Harmless stuff, good for everyone who was there. And Kol wasn't proselytizing, I can assure you."

Although there were evangelists in the Church of Father Ar and Mother Siya, they were there more to make the teachings of the Parents of All available to those who wanted them; they were expressly forbidden to disparage anyone else's faith or force acceptance on anyone. The Church of the Crucible was the complete opposite, with its adherents believing that it was their sacred duty to convert everyone to their god's path of violent purification.

"Dimmerk would come to those meetings and begin shouting Kol down, arguing with him on points of faith, handing out broadsheets and religious tracts to the people there, and demanding to know why Kol, a blacksmith, could possibly fail to recognize the god of the holy crucible to be anything but the one true god." Nestor paused. "Now, understand, Kol was a good man but not a patient one, and he did not suffer gladly any attacks on his friends or himself. After one of the meetings he took hold of Dimmerk by the collar and the seat of his pants and actually threw the preacher out of the arbor. Some say he threw him into the pond, but I think that may be embellishment. In any case, it was the last time Dimmerk intruded upon one of those prayer meetings. But here's the odd thing, Mother Frey—a few weeks later Dimmerk came to Kol and apologized—very profusely I'm told—and begged forgiveness. Kol, being a good man, was swayed by this and went so far as to embrace Dimmerk. From then on they became friends. I won't say fast friends, but close. And Kol even let Dimmerk work for him at his smithy in exchange for food and a bed."

"Kol seems to have been a good man," I suggested.

"He was that, and he was a rock who kept many people hereabout steady in these troubled times. What happened to him was a tragedy," said Nestor.

"What happened?" asked Frey.

"It was the strangest thing you ever saw," said Nestor, his voice even more hushed. "Kol was making a delivery of a new set of gates to one of the houses in the hills. He had taken the gates down and set them in place and was shaking the hand of the man who had hired him when he suddenly cried out and staggered, his chest bursting open as if he had been stabbed, but there was no one else there. Only the old man who had hired him and his two sons."

"They were questioned?"

"Indeed. The constable had them go over it a dozen times and I went through it twice as often. The story was always the same. One moment Kol was alive and the next he was dead, struck down by some otherworldly force."

Frey gave him a shrewd look. "Where was Dimmerk when this happened?"

"He said he was working at Kol's forge, and when the constable went to interview him—for of course he was suspected based on the hard words of earlier—there Dimmerk was, hammering away on the anvil."

"And it is your opinion that Dimmerk was not involved?"

"No..." Nestor said slowly, "but the man makes me nervous. Since Kol's death he has returned to his fire-and-brimstone ways. He still lives at the blacksmith's place. Kol had no family and besides, Dimmerk insists that the blacksmith had promised him a permanent place there. And since he is also a skilled metalworker, he has kept up with all of Kol's business commitments and has turned the income over to the dead man's family. However, he has begun using the arbor to hold his own meetings, and they are full of anger and yelling. He says that his friend Kol was a good man but one who was misled and who suffered punishment for it. He says that the Red God of the Crucible struck him down as a warning to all who refuse to see the truth."

"Ah," said Frey.

"He said that Kol was struck down by the 'hammer of god,' and that everyone needs to heed the warning in order to escape a similar fate."

"And yet there have been other victims," said Frey. "Were they associated with Kol or Dimmerk?"

"With Kol? No. But at least one of them knew Dimmerk. I don't know his name, but he came to town looking for Dimmerk, claiming to be a friend from the old days before the first war. Someone in town gave him directions to the Kol place and the man was later found dead on the road, struck down in what appears to be the same manner. No arrow, no spear, just a chest burst apart. His money belt was even on his person. When we questioned Dimmerk he claimed not to have seen the man, and it was so dry we could not determine if the stranger's horse had ever reached the Kol place or not. The horse was found wandering in the forest, and its flanks were streaked with blood, so the stranger must have been in the saddle when the hammer of god struck him down."

"And the others?"

"All strangers to these parts," said Nestor. "Two were killed on the same day only seconds apart. They were diplomats from the Office of Treaties who were on their way to the capital after having a series of meetings with our enemies among the Khaslani. Rumor has it they were close to signing a treaty that would have ended the war."

"I've heard those rumors, too," I said. "The talk was that, had they lived, the diplomats would have arranged an end to hostilities that would have ended the conflict but left the Khaslani in possession of even more of the Coastlands."

Frey nodded. "Their deaths were a blow to the diplomatic process. The Khaslani apparently believe that a cabal within our own government executed them for agreeing to a deal that favored our enemies."

"Is that true?" I asked.

Frey didn't answer, and Nestor picked up the thread of his narration. "The ambassadors were killed on the open road that runs past the village, struck down amid a retinue of forty armed men. The soldiers scoured the hills but could find no trace of Khaslani spies or assassins. The deaths were impossible to explain. So, it was because one of these men was very important that we sent a request to the Office of Miracles."

Frey touched my ankle with her toe, sending me a message that I did not quite understand.

"And now we have this latest one," said Nestor. "A man who is a complete stranger and clearly no one of importance."

"Of no importance?" echoed Frey. "Everyone is important."

"No, I did not mean they were unimportant in the eyes of Father Ar and—" began Nestor, but Frey waved it away.

"Important to the investigation, I meant. We were not able to examine the other corpses."

"Oh. Of course."

"First thing in the morning I will go speak with Dimmerk," announced Frey. "Please provide Sister Miri with directions. That will be all for now, Nestor."

"I hope I have been of some assistance in this matter," said the beadle.

Frey offered a cold smile. "More than you know."

-3-

That evening, as we settled down to sleep—Frey in the bed and me on the floor—we talked about all that we had learned. Or, at least, Mother Frey had me go through it all, point by point.

"And what do you think about all of this, my girl?" she asked. "Have you formed any working theories?"

"I am lost," I confessed. "The evidence is so frightening."

"In what way?"

"Well, this 'hammer of god' appears to be exactly what Nestor and the others in town believe it is. It seems as if this Dimmerk is quite right that his god has struck down those who deny his reality."

I heard a very long sigh in the dark. "So after all that you have seen and heard today, you feel that this is an act of some homicidal god?"

"I—"

"No other theory suggests itself?"

"What else could explain it, Mother?" I asked. "Witnesses saw men struck down by some invisible force. We saw firsthand an example of such a wound, and no arrow or sword would do damage of that kind."

"And a *god* is the only other possible answer?"

"What else?"

She chuckled. "Perhaps a good night's sleep will sharpen your wits, girl."

And with that she fell silent. After a few moments I heard a soft, buzzing snore.

...

-4-

We were up at first light, washed, dressed, and out the door, eating a light breakfast of cold game and cheese as our cart rumbled out of town. Nestor had offered to accompany us, but Frey declined and we followed a set of directions that took us out of the cluster of buildings that formed the village and back into the mountains. Kol's smithy was five miles up a winding road, and we rolled through morning mists past groves of nut trees and farms crowded with sheep. The sun had not yet cleared the mist when we reached a gate hung with a sign proclaiming: HOME OF THE RIGHTEOUS.

Frey studied that sign with cunning old eyes, then she turned and spat over into the shrubs beside the gate with excellent accuracy and velocity.

There was a turnaround in front of a modest house with a thatched roof. There were a half dozen smaller buildings—sheds and barns—scattered among the trees. At one end of a clearing was the brick smithy and beyond that was an arbor made from spruce trunks and covered with pine boughs. Two dozen mismatched stools and benches filled the arbor, but it was otherwise empty. We sat on the wagon for almost two minutes, allowing whomever was home to make themselves proper before opening the door. No one did.

"There's smoke," I said, nodding toward the chimney above the smithy.

I helped Mother Frey from the wagon and she leaned on me as we walked to the clearing. There was a sound of clanging from within and I had to knock very loudly before the hammering stopped. But it was nearly a full minute before the door opened and we got our first look at Dimmerk. He was not very tall and had narrow shoulders, which seemed at odds with his skills as a blacksmith. His arms were strong, though, and he had fresh burns on his hands, wrists, and right cheek. Gray eyes peered at us from beneath bushy black brows and he wore a frown of suspicion and annoyance.

"Who are you to come knocking so early?" he demanded, standing firm in the doorway, blocking us from entering.

Mother Frey introduced us both, and that seemed to deepen the man's frown.

"What business have *you* here?" he asked. There was a sneer of contempt on his face and in his voice, and he emphasized the word *you* as he looked at us. His distaste for nuns was evident, though it was unclear whether his displeasure was at our being from the Church of the Parents of All or because we were with the Office of Miracles.

"We are here to discuss the murders with you, brother Dimmerk," said Frey.

"Murders?" He barked the word out with a harsh laugh. "There have been no murders that I know of."

"You stand in the smithy of a murdered man."

"I stand in the smithy of a sinner struck down by the hammer of god," he growled.

"Kol was your friend. He took you in, gave you food and shelter, accepted you into his household."

Dimmerk nodded. "Aye, Kol did all that, but if you think he did it out of the kindness of his heart, then you are as great a fool as he. Kol hoped to convert me, to encourage me to stray from the path of righteousness."

"If he was so great a sinner, then why did you come to live with him? Why do you stay here and continue his work?"

"I came because my god demands of me that I accept all challenges to faith, old woman," said Dimmerk. "A man like Kol was a special challenge because he was influential in this town. He corrupted many with his false prayer and false teachings. He led good people astray with lies and witchcraft and kept them under his spell, drawing them to the edge of doom. Countering the secret evil of his heresy was a special challenge. The Red God of the Crucible does not call on its ministers to preach to the faithful but to spread the word of truth to those who do not believe, and to save the souls of those who had been corrupted by false prophets."

"I see," said Frey.

"Do you? Or are you such a one as Kol, who comes with smiles and open hands to lead the unwary to their damnation?"

"It is not my practice to proselytize, as well you know."

"Do I?"

"You are from the Eastern Coastlands, Dimmerk. Your family name is Fell, and the Fells were always of the Church of the Parents of All. How is it you are now on the road of fire?"

I saw the changes on the man's face as Frey's words struck him. The light of righteous rage seemed to slip and fall away as if it were nothing more than a mask worn by an actor. Beneath it was something colder, more calculating. Every bit as hostile, though, but without the wildness of religious zeal, and that made him dangerous in a different way.

"You know my family?" he asked, his voice oddly calm.

"I knew your grandmother. A good woman. Known for her silver jewelry. It was quite lovely." Frey touched his arm. "I was sorry to hear that she died."

Dimmerk's gray eyes seemed to fill with shadows and then he abruptly turned away and walked inside, leaving the door open. Frey winked at me and we followed him inside.

The smithy was a large room with a high ceiling that tapered upward to a broad smoke hole above the furnace. There were sturdy worktables and anvils, heaps of scrap metal, a hundred projects in various stages of completion, ranging from a ploughshare to a full set of ceremonial armor. Most of the stuff was covered with a light coating of dust. Dimmerk picked up his hammer and spent a few moments banging at a piece of iron that had clearly already gotten too cold to work.

Frey stopped at one table on which were several long metal poles. She bent and studied them, and I followed her example, and was surprised to see that the poles were hollow. What the purpose was for these metal tubes was beyond me. Frey picked one up and scratched the curved edge with her fingernail.

"Steel," she murmured.

It was steel, and finely made, but why roll it into tubes? The narrow opening would not reduce the weight of each pole enough to make the process worth the effort.

On the edge of the table was a slatted wooden bucket filled to the brim with small round balls. I picked one up and was surprised by how heavy it was. Frey took it from me, nodded to herself, and put it back. Then she ran her finger along the top of the table and showed it to me. There was no dust.

Dimmerk threw down his hammer and came over to us. He glanced at the table and its contents and then at Frey.

"That's nothing," he said quickly. "A commission. Something ornamental."

"I see." Frey looked around, then crossed to another table on which were rows of small tubes made of paper. She picked one up, squeezed it gently, sniffed it, and handed it to me when I joined her. To Dimmerk she said, "Still making fireworks?"

"Yes," he said guardedly.

"They're awfully small," I remarked. "Are they firecrackers?"

He didn't answer but instead took the firework from my hand and placed it back on the table. "What is the purpose of this visit?"

"We are investigating the deaths of Kol and four other men," said Frey, "each of whom died in the same strange way."

"It isn't strange," replied Dimmerk. "They were struck down by the—"

"Hammer of god," Frey interjected. "Yes, so I'm told. You seem certain that this is why Kol was killed, but what about the other four? Were they also heretics?"

"They must have been," Dimmerk said. "Why else would they have incurred the wrath of god?"

"Why indeed?"

"One was a countryman of yours, I believe. From the Coastlands."

"Heresy is like a weed; it can grow anywhere." Dimmerk grunted. "Look, old woman, I've already given my statement and told that fool of a beadle everything I know."

"People say that but they are often wrong. There is always more to be said on any important subject, wouldn't you agree?"

"No. And I don't have time to stand here and gossip with a couple of useless and nosy women."

If I expected Frey to take offense, she did not. Instead she wore a placid smile as she began strolling once more around the smithy. She peered into buckets and bent close to examine items on tables while Dimmerk watched her with a disapproval that—for all the world—looked like an even mixture of contempt and fear. I could understand the former, but not the latter. Frey stopped by a table all the way in the back and lifted a piece of polished wood that looked somewhat like the stock of a crossbow. She turned it over in her hands and then glanced back at the table on which the heavy metal tubes lay. And now I saw some of that same fear on her face. And some of the came contempt. She set the wood down at the end of a long row of identical pieces.

"Hatred is a poison," she said.

Dimmerk said nothing.

Frey stood in the shadows at the far end of the smithy, her back to us as she ran her fingers over the lines of carved wood stocks. "In these times, with war tearing apart nations and breaking families, it is so easy to give in to hate."

"Hatred is a weapon," countered Dimmerk. "Without it we become soft. Without it we cannot hope to fight back, or to take back what was stolen from us."

"Is that what your god tells you?" asked Frey without turning. "Is hatred the arm that raises the hammer of god? If so, how does its fall serve the will of your god? How does that kind of hatred build your church? How does it serve *any* church or any god?"

Dimmerk said nothing.

Mother Frey turned but stayed on the far side of the smithy. "Philosophers say that the gods do not bother with the petty affairs of mortals, particularly in matters of governance. In theory the gods should not even favor one nation over another, because if they made the world then they made all of it, and all of us."

Dimmerk said nothing.

"And yet here, on this mountain, there has been a remarkable number of miraculous deaths whose nature seems to argue for a god very much interested in politics, and in the political survival of one nation in particular. It could be argued that this god has gone so far as to intercede on behalf of a single family who, admittedly, was badly treated by both sides."

Dimmerk said nothing.

"The two diplomats who were struck down would have settled a treaty that would have reinforced a grave wrong done to that family. Their deaths prevented that from happening, which leaves it open for you to make a claim on those lands should our side win the war."

Dimmerk said nothing.

"I keep thinking about the death of your countryman," said Frey. "I can't help but wonder what he was doing in these hills. It couldn't be pure chance that he would come here, so far from the Coastlands. Was he, perhaps, searching for you? What drew him here, I wonder? There would have been just enough time after the death of Jeks Kol for the news to spread. Might he have come out of some interest in that good man's death? Or in *how* he died?"

And still Dimmerk said nothing.

"And then there was the death of a man pretending to be what he was not."

Dimmerk stiffened. "What do you mean by that?"

"The body in the hills," said Frey. "We examined it quite closely. He was dressed like a local farmer but I believe that he was a Khaslani spy, and one who had recently come from the Coastlands."

"You couldn't know that," barked Dimmerk.

"Could I not? Then let me explain. His face was ruddy and weathered. The winds touch a man's face differently here in the mountains than they do down by the ocean. His eyes were green, and green eyes are rare among the mountain farmers, where brown and blue eyes are far more common. I perceived a pale band around his thumb. It is common for Khaslani landowners and their elder sons to wear their signet rings on their thumbs. He had taken his off but had not yet tanned enough to cover it. He was not a serf and not a soldier, that much was obvious. Was he a spy? Perhaps, but not a government agent. He was not clever enough in his disguise for that. No, this man was a young nobleman or an elder son of a noble house of Khaslani who came here on a mission to discover something of great importance. Something he feared to find and perhaps feared *not* to find. His nervousness was habitual and longstanding, suggesting that he has been dreading something for quite a while. Long enough to drive him to take a terrible risk. To make him want to grow a peasant's beard and infiltrate the lands of his nation's enemy. Why would a man of that kind take such a risk? Could it be because his family now lives in estates once owned by a family that had been driven out and destroyed? What could he have found in the mansion or castle that had been abandoned in such desperate haste? Was there a forge there, I wonder? Were there remnants of things being designed or manufactured which filled his heart with a great dread?"

Dimmerk's eyes seemed to glow with as much fiery heat as his forge. "You are only guessing, you witch."

"I never guess," Frey said quietly. "I observe and look for evidence that supports a likely conclusion. Inductive reasoning is more precise than mere guesswork."

Dimmerk took a few steps toward her. I slipped my hand beneath the folds of my apron and closed my fingers around the hilt of my poisoned knife. He was bigger than I, but I was quick as a scorpion and always had been. I think Dimmerk saw my hand move and guessed the danger. He smiled and stopped by the table with the long steel tubes.

"You are trespassing here," he said calmly. "You are unwelcome. Please leave."

There was a quality to his voice that carried a greater menace than I had expected from the man. Frey felt it, too. Even she.

I crossed to her and walked with her to the door, but on the threshold Mother Frey stopped and turned.

"Listen to me," she said in a voice that was surprisingly gentle.

"I understand what you are doing, and my heart breaks for you. It breaks for all that you've lost. But you are going down the wrong path. You want people to believe that it is the hand of your god reaching down to strike at the heretics, but we both know that is a lie. That is blasphemy, though I doubt you care about such things any more than I do. This was never about religion. You are using god as a shield and from behind that cover you are striking out with something the world has never seen. Something new and terrible. Could it be that Jeks Kol saw what you were making here and understood its implications? He was a simple man, but from all accounts not a stupid one. The potential of that thing is too great to comprehend. Even now the thought of it fills my heart and mind with black horror."

"Get out," he said, but she was not finished.

"I implore you, Dimmerk, destroy what you have made. Do it now before the rest of the world learns of it. Do it before politicians and soldiers and generals learn of it. Do it now before you drown our country and every country in a tidal wave of blood. Perhaps you have been driven mad by what you've lost. If so, I pity you. But mad or sane, I beseech you to step aside from this course." She pointed a withered finger at the table of metal tubes and then at the wooden stocks. "Melt those and burn them. Make sickles and scythes. Make swords if you must make weapons for killing, but do not allow the hammer of god to be known to the world. Do not let that kind of horror be the last legacy of the Fell family. I beg you, do not do that."

Dimmerk snatched up one of the metal poles and brandished it like a club. My dagger was in my hand, but Frey stayed my arm.

"Get out and be damned to you," roared the man.

And we women, too wise to fight this fight, withdrew.

Outside, Frey turned and fair pushed me toward our wagon. "Hurry, girl. In the name of Mother Siya, hurry."

I helped her up and before I could even take the reins Frey snatched them and snapped the horses into startled movement.

She flicked a whip at them—something I had never seen her do before—and drove them mercilessly down the mountain road.

It was when we were nearing the bottom of the winding way that something strange happened. The cold lantern that hung on a post at the corner of the wagon suddenly exploded as if struck by a club. Pieces flew everywhere and we had to shield our faces with our arms.

"Ride!" screamed Frey, whipping the horses anew.

We flew down the hill and were soon deep into the forests and the farms.

-5-

Frey said nothing more until we were back in our room at the inn with door bolted and shutters closed. The old woman looked positively ancient and frail, thin and deathly pale.

"What is it, Mother?" I begged. "Tell me what you meant. What evil thing did Dimmerk invent? Was it some magic spell? Has he conjured a demon?"

She took so long I did not think she was going to answer. Then she dug something out of her apron pocket and held it out to me. I took the item and held it up to study by candlelight. It was a lump of lead that was round on one side but badly misshapen on the other.

"What is it?" I asked.

"Do you remember the bucket of lead balls?"

"I do. Oh!" I realized that this was exactly the same size as the others, though they were all perfectly round.

"I took this from the wall near where the Khaslani was killed. If we had been able to examine the spots where the diplomats and Jeks Kol were killed, no doubt we would find others like this."

"What does it mean? Are you saying these small lead balls did the damage we saw on the spy? How is that possible? What sorcery is this?"

Frey said, "Have you ever seen fireworks?"

"Of course."

"Ever seen what happens when too many are set off at once?"

"Once. A barrel of firecrackers blew up in the town where I lived with my husband. Killed the firecracker salesman and his horse."

"Did you actually see the blast?"

"Yes."

"Then you understand the force that is released," she said. "Explosives like that are most dangerous when confined. A hundredweight of firecrackers lit in the middle of the town square is an amusement. That same amount in a barrel is deadly because the force is gathered together. It is like fingers gathered together into a fist. You understand?"

"Yes."

"The Fell family suffered a terrible tragedy when their factory exploded, destroying all the property and killing so many. The fireworks were probably in cases, stacked and bunched together. Are you following me?"

"I am, but what does that have to do with this?" I held up the smashed lead.

She chewed her lip for a moment. "I am going to trust you, Miri. I know I treat you like a girl but you are a woman. A widow who has seen some of life. You have education and you are not a fool. One day you will take over my responsibilities and to do that you must be wise and you must have an open mind."

I nodded slowly.

"The Office of Miracles was never intended as an agency for proving the divine. Others in our church do that. It has always been up to us to search for the truth, often in dark and ugly places," said Mother Frey. "There are many people in this world whose hearts are filled with greed, with avarice, with hatred. I see that in Dimmerk Fell. Maybe he was once a good man and has had his heart broken, but I suspect that he was always like this. The war has simply honed and refined his hatred. And his greed. But he is also very smart. You saw those tubes? Now imagine if you filled one end with a paper firework like the ones we saw, and then rolled a lead ball down its mouth. If you could block the end with the firework, say with a heavy wooden stock, but leave a hole for a candle wick, what do you think would happen when you put flame to the firecracker?"

I had to think about it. All of that explosive force behind the lead ball would need to go somewhere. If the whole thing did not explode, then it would push that ball down the tube and out.

Frey watched me and I could tell that she saw the moment I understood.

"Not a crossbow," I said softly. "And not the hand or hammer of god."

"No," she said.

"What *is* it?"

Instead of answering, she said, "Now imagine a thousand soldiers with weapons like that. Put them behind a wall and you can march the all the armies of the world against them and what would be the result? A mountain of the dead."

"Is it even possible?"

"You saw it firsthand, Miri. The spy. His chest. The ball went in small on one side and the lead, soft as it is, must have hit bone and flattened as it came out. It smashed a much bigger hole on the other side. Nestor described the same thing with Jeks Kol and the diplomats. And we saw it happen to the lantern on our wagon."

I sat there, frozen by the horror of it. Immediately my mind was filled with terror as the scene she had described—men with firework weapons that could spit death—and the damage they could do. The battles they could win. The kingdoms they could topple.

"Now," said Frey, "imagine if those weapons were in the hands of *both* armies. Imagine if every murderous fool could hold a tube of steel and kill from a safe distance. Imagine what this world would become. Imagine what it *will* become. Imagine that, Miri, and you will be inside the head of Dimmerk Fell."

We sat there, staring at each other, surrounded by shadows that now seemed filled with legions of ghosts waiting to be born in the fires of wars to come.

"What can we do?"

Frey took the lead ball back and placed it on the night table. "I don't know that we can do anything. If we file a report then the world will know that this weapon exists. Even if Dimmerk hides his handiwork, the *concept* will be out there."

"Fireworks are common. Won't someone else think of this?"

She looked older and sadder. "In time. Yes. All we can do is pray that Dimmerk comes to his senses so that such a horror will not be shared sooner rather than later."

"Pray, Mother? I'm surprised to hear you advocate that."

Frey shrugged. "What other course is left to us, girl?"

There was more to say, and we talked for a while, but then we settled down for the night. I was agitated and Mother Frey fixed me a sleeping draught. I drifted off and my dreams were haunted.

Once, deep in the middle of the night, I dreamed that the Red God reached out of the clouds and smote the mountaintop with his burning hammer. But it was a dream, and I slept on.

-6-

I woke in the cold light of morning to find Mother Frey's bed empty. It looked like she had barely slept in it. My head was fuzzy and I wanted to scold her for giving me too strong a draught. I washed and dressed as quickly as I could and stumbled down the stairs to find her in the common room. She looked older still and worn to almost nothing, hunched over a mug of broth. Her face was smudged with soot and her clothes were dirty.

"What's wrong?" I asked. "Were you out rooting with the pigs?"

Frey touched her face, looked at the soot that came away, shrugged, and sipped the broth.

I noticed that the common room was completely empty except for the landlord, who was standing in the doorway looking out into the street. "Where is everyone?" I demanded.

He turned and gave me a quizzical look. "Up at the smithy, of course."

"Why 'of course'? What's happened?"

"Bless me, Sister, but did you not hear it all last night?"

"Hear what?"

"Why, the world itself seemed to roar."

"I don't understand what that means," I said.

He pointed toward the hills and I came over and looked past him. There, up high near the snow line, a dense column of black smoke curled its way into the morning sky. It rose hundreds of feet above the mountaintop.

"Father Ar only knows what happened," said the landlord. "But the whole top of the mountain blowed itself all the way to heaven's front yard. Lucky there ain't much up that far 'cept the smithy, and that's gone, of course. Poor Dimmerk never did have the luck. Sour scripture-thumping son of a…" He paused. "Pardon me, Sister Miri, I don't mean to speak ill of the dead."

I stared at the smoke and then turned toward Mother Frey. She peered at me with her bright blue eyes in her soot-stained old face. She lifted the mug of broth to her lips and took a sip.

She said nothing at all.

After a while I came and sat down with her.

I had a cup of hot broth, too.

CODE CRACKER

BY BETH W. PATTERSON

He should have just given me a sunflower seed. Now he was going to have to pay in blood.

I could tell that he was already a bit afraid of me. Perhaps I would just settle for his discomfort for the moment, since I was enjoying it so immensely. At least he'd stopped insinuating that I wanted a cracker.

I wasn't going to verbally abuse the tall, slender man, but that was because I couldn't. The old telegrapher who was my previous cohabitant never said an unkind word to anyone, at least not within earshot of me. This limited my communication. Although my mind constantly raced with statements I wanted to convey, I was unable to say anything I hadn't first heard. Such is the plight of all parrots. But I could always present a valid argument, even from behind bars. By emitting a single screech, I never failed to cause humans to clap their hands over their ears.

I was in the middle of putting this theory into practice one Thursday morning when the doorbell rang. Watson was self-employed and had to rely on word-of-mouth advertising due to the covert nature of his occupation. Yet he was always surprised whenever someone came to his "office" in our little home. Our center of operation was a narrow dining room that opened into a burrow-sized den with a TV, in front of which I always sat on my perch.

The diminutive woman who entered introduced herself as

Zoë Rodowsky. She said that she taught elementary school reading, which won my respect. I, for one, would rather face Colonel Sanders than a room full of children. Deceptively sweet-faced, she could almost pass for an overgrown child herself with her large hazel eyes and an endearing head of brown curls. My intuition, however, led me to believe that she was not one to be trifled with.

"I never imagined that someone with a job like mine would have to engage in a surreptitious investigation, but life is full of surprises," she began briskly. "Something fishy is going on in my school, and I am not just gonna stand by and let it happen. I'm pretty darn rattled, but I think I'd better start at the beginning."

She sat and gathered her thoughts. "I think it all started when I noticed that all my kids' essays had glaring content errors in certain topics: literature, Greek mythology, and American history. And although they were all the same mistakes, no two answers were identical, which rules out cheating. It seems that these 'facts' are being rewritten in some textbooks to make the concepts more sellable, and even the parents are going along with it. Pilgrims and Indians living side by side as friends forever? Come *on!* Hercules, Perseus, and Bellerophon are suddenly amalgamated into one big, jolly dude. The Hunchback of Notre Dame is alive and well at the end of the story. Being royalty means living happily ever after... haven't they ever heard of Marie Antoinette? They even are insisting that dinosaurs never really existed. Where are they getting all of this?"

She took out a handkerchief and wiped her face. "I brought this up at a faculty meeting last week and of course everyone appeared concerned. There was Roxanne Cramer, the social studies teacher. She's having a hard time too; she moonlights with another job, but she doesn't say what. I secretly suspect that she's a stripper. Anyway, Miss Cramer was agitated by this information, but despite their outward concern, everyone else appeared blasé. A few faculty members told me that if everything was written and spelled correctly, then I was doing my job properly and not to interfere. There was a science textbook handy, so I pointed out a few false statements in it, and the science teacher simply said, 'It's in the book—it has to be right!' I was too stunned for words. Had these people lost their marbles?"

I stretched out a wing and tried to look as if I was not paying attention.

"But the very next day, as soon as I had gotten to school I discovered that all of my textbooks had been stolen. Every last one. And we have state-issued Common Core testing coming up, even though I don't like the methods of SLO."

"Slow?" murmured Watson.

She gave him a dirty look. "S-L-O. It stands for Student Learning Objectives, and yes, I think the acronym is a little ironic."

Watson nodded.

"There's going to be another faculty meeting Monday to discuss funding for replacements. We have been instructed to leave all of our cell phones and purses in a certain area, to prevent any of us from taping what might go down. This only corroborates my suspicion that this was an inside job. There's been a lot of pressure on us to switch textbooks to a more popular series called Rabbit's Foot Books, but I have refused to adopt these cesspools of misinformation. It's my duty to teach these little ones the real facts, and the popular textbooks sell like crazy and the information is easier to process, but they are full of erroneous information."

"History is written by the winners and rewritten by the entrepreneurs," murmured Watson with a faraway look in his eyes. "I think I might know a way to briefly attend your meeting and compile some data in one fell swoop. My partner, Sherlock—she's the gray one sitting on that perch over there—has a phonographic memory."

"Sherlock? Oh!" She approached my perch, eyes wide. "Who's pretty? Who's a pretty girl?"

I growled like a dog.

She stopped short. "I'm sorry, Sherlock. I didn't mean to be condescending. I wouldn't exactly greet a human that way, would I?"

I wolf-whistled.

"Point taken!" she laughed.

I liked this woman. She was pretty smart for a human.

She turned to Watson. "Don't you mean she has a *photo*graphic memory?"

"No, actually, I do mean *phono*graphic in this case. She's my personal stenographer, and luckily everyone underestimates her. She can remember and repeat anything she hears, which has proved to be a major embarrassment to me over the years, but may come in handy in this case. She's also addicted to the TV, especially the History Channel. I think she analyzes mysteries."

Actually, I did more than that, but there was no way that this slow-brained hominid could ever know that. I fancied myself something of a cryptographer. My formative years living with the telegrapher had sparked my interest in codes, and I considered myself to be well versed in several. I was still trying to crack the Enigma Code, which was tough because my primate roommate did not have a machine.

"We will meet you in your classroom after school tomorrow to discuss this case," promised Watson, flicking his dark hair out of his eyes. "After all, it isn't every day that we get a call from a high school teacher."

"Elementary!" I corrected him.

"An elementary teacher with the minds of youth at stake. Don't worry, Miss Rodowsky, we will find a way!"

• • •

Watson and I were still trying to think of a possible scenario early the next morning when the phone rang. A panicked Miss Rodowsky said, "Mr. Watson, come here. I want to see you!"

We didn't have time to ask what had just transpired, but we headed over to the school as fast as Watson's ancient vehicle would allow.

Most of our questions were answered upon sight of the flashing lights and assortment of fire trucks and ambulances. We arrived too late to help and in the clearing smoke could only make out the sooty pile of ash on the asphalt of the playground's basketball court. It didn't take a genius to figure out what had become of the missing books.

Miss Rodowsky's eyes glittered, her jaw set with determination. "This was clearly intended to intimidate me into submission, but it's only confirmed my convictions. Libricide is a heinous enough crime, but someone could have died from smoke inhalation."

But it turned out that someone *had* died, as was apparent to us when the last of the smoke had cleared.

The emaciated man lying facedown on the pavement sported a few burns to his skin and clothing, but displayed a great deal of unhygienic life with his greasy hair and unwashed skin. His facial features were obfuscated by a grizzled beard, and what remained of his clothing was in tatters. I watched the police closely and saw that they could find no wallet nor any other means of immediate identification. Bystanders were murmuring among themselves that he was perhaps homeless.

A human would not have been able to step over the crime scene tape, but I saw no harm in launching myself off of Watson's shoulder and snooping a bit. I felt no more empathy for the dead man than a human would a roasted chicken. I had seen on TV how sometimes homeless people will set fires in garbage cans to stay warm overnight, but it was springtime, which didn't warrant such desperation. In fact, the man's coat was off and he was still clutching it in his stiff fist, as if he had attempted to put out the flames with it.

Long skid marks in the ash obscured any footprints that might have been made, as if someone had fled the crime scuffling in long strides on snowshoes. There were smears of red and white around the ashes, so I scraped them up with my bill, flew back to Watson's shoulder, and wiped it on the shoulder of his good sport coat.

"Sherlock!" he loudly complained.

I cocked my head in deference and fixed him with a look. My pet had figured out that I had collected evidence to analyze and was publicly playing along with my apparent misbehavior. Either that, or he was merely clueless and annoyed. I wanted to give him the benefit of the doubt, but wasn't going to hold my breath.

"I can't freak out over this right now," Miss Rodowsky murmured through clenched teeth. "Children will be arriving within a couple of hours, and I have to remain calm and not alarm them. Not only that, I now have to draw up a new lesson plan from scratch, and the school fair is tomorrow. It's at the park next to Lake Greg, and I have to act like nothing is bothering me."

"We will be there," Watson promised. "We can not only search for more clues but also give you some moral support." He took her hand and kissed it.

It was a shame that I had no hatchlings to feed, because I could have made a statement by spontaneously regurgitating.

• • •

The fair was innocuous enough. It was held in a huge section of park cordoned off to allow enough space for myriad tiny booths, each hosted by a homeroom class. Since Miss Rodowsky taught many grade levels, she was not tied down to any booth. After doing several hours' duty manning the cotton candy machine ("These parents have no idea how bad that stuff is for kids!"), we three perused the site, trying to put our heads together and look for more clues.

Miss Rodowsky's brow furrowed in concern. "I don't see Roxanne. Perhaps she had a late night. I hope she doesn't get caught someday." I didn't know one teacher from the next, so I just focused on the details of the fair.

It was all geared toward activities that small children could enjoy: a balloon pop, a rubber duckie pond, pony rides, and so forth. The only thing that seemed out of place was the garishly attired clown playing a pair of shockingly loud horns. The makeup was all wrong for a kids' fair, too. I had seen on TV that the more flamboyant clown makeup was originally intended for the big top, in which facial features had to be exaggerated so that the clowns could be seen from a distance. Up close, however, the distorted-looking visages were terrifying to most children, and quite frankly a bit unsettling to me as well. This buffoon was no exception.

Honk. Eek. Eek-honk, honk-honk. The sound was annoying, but there was a deliberation in it. I decided that this was worth heeding, and cocked my head to focus.

"Is she all right?" asked our pint-sized companion.

"Just let Sherlock do her work. She's got a mind like a computer."

Mind like a computer. That was it. Computer! That cursed clown was playing a binary code. Each obnoxious horn was either a one or a zero, and eight clusters of ones and zeros at a time could represent a letter of the alphabet. I listened carefully, tracking each annoying honk and squeak. Once I was certain that the pattern was repeating itself, I pecked Watson on the head.

Watson knew the cue. "Are you ready to come back to the office for some light refreshment, Miss Rodowsky?"

But I wasn't quite finished. There was something awfully familiar in that greasepaint. The colors matched the paint found at the crime scene. I looked at the oversized shoes, and something else clicked. The skid marks near the dead man hadn't been just skid marks. *They were the footprints of a gigantic clown!* But how did a clown factor into a book burning and a homicide?

The humans were almost ready to go, but Miss Rodowsky stopped to purchase a cupcake at the baked goods sale. It looked almost as tasty as a sunflower seed, but just as she finished the delicacy and was about to throw away the little paper cup, she suddenly blanched.

I cocked my head for a better look. Through the remaining crumbs I could see that written on the bottom of the cup was JUST DO YOUR JOB.

• • •

Back in our kitchen, Watson made tea for himself and ran his fingers through his dark hair in frustration. I began idly plucking at my breast feathers. I had an answer, and no way to convey it.

How could I explain it to these humans? I had to have some sort of auditory cue. I decided I could at least instigate conversation by agitating my peers.

"Just do your job!" I said in Miss Rodowsky's voice.

Miss Rodowsky's patience was wearing thin. "I have *zero* tolerance for this, and if *one* more person tells me to just do my job, I'll—"

That was all I needed to hear. "Zero!" I mimicked. "One! One! Zero! Zero…" And then I parroted off the honks I had committed to memory.

The humans froze. "It's binary code!" the teacher squeaked. "Sherlock, you're a genius!"

Duh.

They pounced on Watson's laptop computer in a frenzy and searched the internet for binary translators. They found a binary-to-ASCII text converter and summoned me. I replayed every one of those colossal honks and squawks, wishing that it was more conventional for a clown to have played the flute instead. With a click of the "convert" button, the message was clear: *Books arrive Monday. SLO sends checks Tuesday.*

Miss Rodowsky frowned. "I don't understand. Why don't they just call or text each other?"

"Several reasons," supplied Watson. "Calls and texts are easily traced. Plus, this leads me to believe that this operation is so covert, no one knows who else is in on it. So no one knows how many people are involved, or who is friend or foe."

"Except for me." Miss Rodowsky looked glum. "I've already blown the whistle and outed myself."

• • •

We had Sunday to ponder the details. I managed to convince Watson to examine the paint on his coat, by calling, "Watson! Crick-Watson DNA model!" But we couldn't make heads or tails of it. We tried every hardware store in town, trying to pinpoint specific colors and analyze chemical composition. It turned out to be some sort of airbrush body paint. This gave Watson an excuse to phone our lady client, informing her of our new discovery. I tried calling, "Matchmaker, matchmaker, make me a match...*honk, honk*!" but I couldn't make him understand that this paint matched the color that I'd seen on the clown.

We were smartly dressed for school Monday, ready to attend the faculty meeting. Watson was dressed in a suit, but sported a red bow tie; he had told me that it was to make him appear professional but also kid-friendly. I personally thought that the accessory made him look like a sociopath. I find television to be quite educational in the realms of pop culture and bizarre human nature, and according to the shows, Watson would never have an eye for fashion.

We didn't really intend to put on a kids' show, in spite of our front. Like I may have mentioned before, I hate children, and I was fully prepared to sabotage our act if they actually liked our routine, Horus forbid.

There were twelve of them in all, seated around an oblong table. They were paying attention to my beauty, of course, and although I pretended to eat it up, I observed everything.

Only two people were giving each other furtive glances. A rat-faced woman drummed on the table in a display of impatience. The other person of interest, an overdressed man with a barrel chest, rapped back a quick response. The exchange went into my steel-trap memory.

"What kind is of parrot is he?" someone asked.

"*She* is an African gray. She's gray, and um, she's from Africa," Watson weakly tried to elucidate. "Her name is, um, Cuddles."

Cuddles? I understood why Watson had to change my name if we were undergoing a secret mission, but...Cuddles? I grumbled, "Surely you're joking, Mr. Feynman."

They all exploded into laughter at that. Watson tensed. "Come on, Sherlock," he pleaded nervously. "Let's sing them a song. You remember your part, don't you? 'Where is thumbkin, where is thumbkin...'"

I was still sore that he told them my name was Cuddles, and decided I would substitute my response with a different line. "I'm Rick James, bitch!" I replied on cue. To show my appreciation for my colleague's excellent stage persona, I lifted my tail and voided my bowels on his shoulder. Much to my delight, I could see his face reddening. Because he was in front of a committee of schoolteachers in a professional setting, protocol prevented him from rebuking me with his usual quip: "No shit, Sherlock!"

We were politely thanked for our time, and assured that we would be contacted should the need arise. Meaning, of course, that we mercifully didn't get the gig. But by the time we left the room I had a good profile on everyone and every tiny exchange.

• • •

We met Miss Rodowsky at her classroom after school. We birds are not known for our keen olfactory senses, but the charming old building smelled clean to me. Colorful artwork made by students and teachers alike festooned the halls at every turn, and much of it was themed on the values of kindness and cooperation. Perched on Watson's shoulder as he walked up to the second floor, I could see how teachers like our client took such pride in shaping the minds of the next generation.

She was just finishing up some one-on-one tutoring with a young man, a rather uncommon sort. He was far too large to be in elementary school, and the way he turned and looked at me led me to believe that there was something different about this child. "Thank you both for coming," she addressed us warmly. "I'm just wrapping it up with Jerome here. He's trying to adjust to the Spanish teacher who comes once a week."

"Wrong words, wrong words!" the kid protested.

"Yes, I know, Jerome, they are wrong words for English class, but this is a whole new language," she replied with infinite patience. The boy turned to see me and suddenly froze, keeping his eyes on me. I bobbed up and down once, and he laughed. Miss Rodowsky beamed. "Animals certainly have a way of reaching autistic people."

Of course we do, I thought. So Jerome was autistic. I could relate to this kid quite well. No one really knew what was going on in his head, just like no one really knew what's going on in mine. This was quite possibly the only child I actually liked.

"Well, Jerome is smiling for once, so at least something good came out of this day," Miss Rodowsky sighed. She crumpled up a piece of scratch paper and threw it in the trash.

"Q, L, Y, T, R!" he exclaimed.

She cleared some papers and made a space for Watson to sit down, accidentally knocking a can full of pencils off of her desk.

"S, S, A, M, T!"

"I don't know why he does that," sighed Miss Rodowsky. "He sometimes just randomly spouts off letters."

No, it's in response to sound, I thought. *He hears something in the crumpling of paper and the falling of pencils. There's some sort of pattern that the rest of us aren't paying attention to.* I wondered if it was Morse code. From my formative years living with the old telegrapher, I had learned to recognize it, but I had never been taught it—and why would I have been? Scientists tend to only bother with teaching language skills to primates. Anyway, it was time to put this theory to the test. I climbed down Watson's arm, wandered across the desk, and pecked the hard surface once.

"A!" he sang. *Aha.*

I then tried something I'd heard about on VH1. I pecked out the rhythm to the intro of a Rush song.

"Y, Y, Z!"

"Ah, so he knows his classic rock!" Watson exclaimed brightly.

No, you twit, he knows Morse code, I tried to project into my half-witted assistant's mind. The clever Canadians that constituted the band Rush had written the oddly timed tritone into the introduction of their famous instrumental to sound out *Y-Y-Z*, the code for the Toronto Pearson International Airport. Like I said, television is most educational these days, so long as it isn't geared for children.

I knew one more basic code. I rapped out S-O-S, which the young man identified right away.

"Wait a minute…that's S-O-S…this kid knows Morse code!" exclaimed Watson. "Sherlock, you really do know your codes!"

Actually, Morse code is technically a cipher—a code replaces every word, and a cipher replaces every letter. But I wouldn't expect a featherless dolt to remember that.

"Sherlock, did you take note of those teachers drumming on the tables? It was annoying at the time, but now I think they were actually communicating with each other," pontificated my slow-witted accomplice at long last.

I'd have told him that from the get-go if only I'd had the words. Relieved that even humans could eventually catch on, I opened my beak and clicked out exactly what I'd heard being hammered out at the meeting.

"B-A-X…T-E-R…B-U-N-N-Y!" Jerome sang. And then the response: "C-O-N-T-A-C-T…S-L-O!"

Miss Rodowsky's jaw went slack. "Baxter Bunny? Like the cartoon? What in the…" Her incredulity rendered her speechless. "What does this have to do with the Core testing company?"

We three sat in silence for a moment, but Jerome was on a roll. Happy to be able to have some common ground on which to communicate, he sang:

"Who's a symbol of this cult that's made for you and I?
B-A-X, T-E-R, B-U-N-N-Y."

Miss Rodowsky made the sobering connection. "'Made for you and I?' See, they can't even get their grammar right! Let's have a closer look at this publisher that everyone is trying to push down my throat." She rifled through her desk and came up with a Rabbit's Foot Textbooks catalog. Printed on the bottom left corner in tiny letters was *Baxter Enterprises*. "This is no coincidence of names. If there's any business that has to do with children, they cash in on it. They manufacture everything from toys to video games. They even have their own cartoon series. Why wouldn't they also have a subsidiary that publishes textbooks?"

Watson's brow creased. "If there is a big publishing company with big money behind it, that means that they could be in cahoots with testing companies all over the country, not just SLO. There has to be some sort of liaison."

"Remember the binary message?" Miss Rodowsky said. "*Books arrive Monday.* Someone went ahead and ordered new textbooks for me behind my back! I know everyone seems to want this new series in the school, but why is everyone so motivated?"

They perused the catalog until they found a tiny ad: *Get Rabbit's Foot Books in your school, receive commission!* And it got even more devious. According to the policy, whoever recruited more sellers got an even bigger slice of the pie, like a pyramid scheme. Arranging an alliance with the testing companies provided the best financial bonuses of all.

"Whoever is behind this, we have to catch them as they pick up the books," Watson said, suddenly looking alert. "Would they have some sort of meeting place? Sherlock, who were the people sending messages?"

I gave Watson a look. No one had formally introduced me to these people, which would have given me a way to associate sounds and faces. How could I explain that it was the rat-faced woman and the one that looked as if someone had stuck a ramrod up his…well, anyway, I had no way to describe them.

Miss Rodowsky sighed. "Let's just go. There is one warehouse where all of our supplies are delivered. Let's take your vehicle. If there are other teachers involved, they'll recognize mine in a heartbeat."

• • •

The three of us cramped in Watson's car, sitting in the parking lot of J. R.'s Educational Supplies, was not my idea of a good time. I wanted my warm house, I wanted the TV, and I wanted a snack. "Sunflower seed!" I squawked.

Watson groaned. "Sherlock, I keep trying to tell you that you can't have too many! Veterinarian's orders! Doctor Milazzo told us that one sunflower seed to a parrot is like a candy bar to a human. And even if I wasn't concerned about your health, seeds make you act like you're on steroids!"

I growled.

He sighed. "Okay, okay, we'll have a sunflower seed when we finish this mess! Help me nail these culprits, and I'll even give you two, okay?" It would have to do.

I didn't know what we were supposed to be looking for, but a brand-new SUV rolled up into the parking lot. Miss Rodowsky made a startled noise in her throat as the familiar-looking driver entered the warehouse. It was the rat-faced woman I'd seen beating out the rhythms at the faculty meeting.

We followed her into the warehouse, where she received several crates of books. We overheard her saying, "Yes, I'm Roxanne Cramer, here to pick up a shipment. The invoice is made out to Zoë Rodowsky, but I'm authorized to collect them."

"Well, isn't that kind of you," said Miss Rodowsky, stepping out of the shadows.

The other teacher stood slack-jawed for a second. I watched her beady eyes flick toward the exit, so I decided to play my final trump card. I launched myself off of Watson's shoulder and dive-bombed Miss Cramer. She shrieked, but I backed her into a corner, flying back and forth while she shielded her face. I snarled, "Go ahead, make my day!"

She swung her purse at me. It missed, but a small plastic bottle flew out. It hit the concrete floor and broke open, spilling white goo. Airbrush paint.

The purse flew out of her grip and hit the ground. The rat-faced woman gaped as another bottle went rolling out. "You don't understand!" she spluttered. "I need that t-textbook commission! If teachers were getting p-proper pay, I wouldn't have to m-moonlight as a s-s-stupid clown!"

"Cry me a river, Roxanne," said Miss Rodowsky. "I get the same wages as you, and you don't see me in big floppy shoes, do you?"

"It was the only j-job I could do on the side."

"Roxanne. You don't have to put on the red nose," said Miss Rodowsky sternly.

Miss Cramer was desperate. "Lester Ventress was in on it too! He was tapping out the codes with me in the meeting today!" she bawled. "The guys at Baxter had made us a sweet deal—a commission for every textbook sold. It was a win-win situation! The system was popular with the children, and popular with the parents as well, since aptitude scores are going up—"

"Even if the information is false?" interjected Miss Rodowsky. "Roxanne, not only are you manipulating the school system for profit, you have also engaged in larceny, vandalism, and arson. There is also a dead man in the picture, so manslaughter is on your hands, if not murder! How convenient of you to set a fire—perhaps on your way home from a gig—while you were disguised as a clown. Who's going to recognize you from afar? Did you know in advance how flammable airbrush paint is? I looked it up, and it is considered a HAZMAT."

"I will have you know that I was very careful when I set that fire," she began.

"Then you can explain all of that to your attorney," intoned a new voice. The police seemed to have caught the tail end of the conversation, including the fortuitous confession. In the wake of Miss Rodowsky cutting down Miss Rat-Face to size, I had forgotten that Watson was able to make himself useful by notifying the gendarmes. "You have the right to remain silent." I was fascinated by the proceedings. It was just like *Law and Order* without the catchy music.

"Roxanne?" our client queried in a softer voice after they had clapped the handcuffs on our motley miscreant. "I just wanna know one thing: how did so many of you guys know binary and Morse code?"

The other woman shrugged. "We all watch the History Channel, I guess."

Miss Rodowsky heaved a huge sigh as they led away Miss Cramer. No doubt she was feeling all sorts of emotions, but she never lost her cool. She bade us both goodbye, promising to swing by on the morrow. She had to go home and process all of the revelations, and I couldn't blame her.

Watson was most definitely relieved. "At least we didn't have to deal with another body. Right, Sherlock? Sherlock?"

He was wrong. If he didn't have my Horus-damned sunflower seed, there would definitely be a body, or at least lots of blood.

• • •

"Well, it turns out that nine teachers were in on this thing," said Watson, twirling his spoon in his teacup. "You did more than stick up for these children; you blew the whistle on quite a bit of corruption!"

Miss Rodowsky was still morose. Shabby beyond recognition, the homeless man had finally been identified as the former music teacher at the school. Once the budget cuts forced him to lose his job, he had apparently fallen into hard times, but his last endeavor had been an attempt to save the books. And he had been her friend.

She buried her face in her hands. "Not only am I seriously bummed out about the fate of this guy, but now I have to spend the summer testifying in court. I was hoping to just read and hang out with my Dobies."

"Dobies? As in Dobermans?" queried Watson with a sudden brightness. "I love Dobies! I would have gotten one a long time ago except that…" He checked himself with a wary eye on me. "I couldn't *possibly* want for a finer pet than my Sherlock over there." He flashed me an ingratiating smile. I weaved my head back and forth, since I couldn't roll my eyes.

There was definitely a spark of chemistry between my roommate and our client. She invited him to her house so that he could get his doggie fix, and his eyes lit up. I was about to rain on his parade, as I often enjoyed doing, but then I stayed my claw. *Why not?* I thought. I liked the human woman, and she might get Watson out of my nest. Then I could watch that upcoming show about the Voynich Manuscripts in peace.

As they left for Miss Rodowsky's house, I still couldn't resist calling out a parting shot, "Bowm-chicka-WAH-waaaahh." Then I let myself become engrossed in the TV, ready to see if my theories about the Voynich were correct. I was certain that I would have it figured out by morning, although I knew it would take these humans forever to give me verbal cues.

The commercial for Cheez-Its certainly looked enticing. Perhaps I did want a cracker after all.

ABOUT THE AUTHORS

JIM AVELLI's first novel, *A Spider's Vow,* was recently released and he's hard at work on the follow-up.

KEITH R. A. DECANDIDO is the author of a truly absurd amount of stuff. Recent and upcoming work includes *A Furnace Sealed,* first in a new urban fantasy series about a nice Jewish boy from the Bronx who hunts monsters; the Marvel *Tales of Asgard* trilogy of prose novels starring Thor, Sif, and the Warriors Three; the *Stargate SG-1* novel *Kali's Wrath; Mermaid Precinct,* the latest in his fantasy/police procedure series; the *Heroes Reborn* novella *Save the Cheerleader, Destroy the World;* the *Super City Police Department* novellas *Avenging Amethyst, Undercover Blues,* and *Secret Identities;* short fiction in *Aliens: Bug Hunt, Altered States of the Union, A Baker's Dozen of Magic,* BuzzyMag.com, *Joe Ledger: Unstoppable, Limbus Inc.* Book 3, *Nights of the Living Dead, The Side of Good/The Side of Evil, V-Wars: Night Terrors, The X-Files: Trust No One,* etc.; and twice-weekly rewatches of classic TV shows in the *Star Trek* and *Stargate* franchises, as well as the 1966 *Batman,* for Tor.com. Keith is also a second-degree black belt in karate, an editor, a musician, and probably some other stuff that he can't remember due to the lack of sleep. Find out less at his web site at **www.DeCandido.net**.

AUSTIN FARMER is a performer in Southern California, and his band's original music can be heard on ABC, Fox, and Nickelodeon. This is his first short story published in an anthology. You can find him online **@mraustinfarmer**.

DAVID GERROLD is a Nebula and Hugo award winning author of over fifty books, several hundred articles and columns, and over a dozen television episodes. TV credits include episodes of *Star Trek, Babylon 5, Twilight Zone, Land Of The Lost, Logan's Run,* and many others. Novels include *When Harlie was One, The Man Who Folded Himself,* the War Against the Chtorr septology, The Star Wolf trilogy, The Dingilliad young adult trilogy, and more. The autobiographical tale of his son's adoption, *The Martian Child,* won the Hugo and Nebula awards for Best Novelette of the Year and was the basis for the 2007 movie starring John Cusack, Amanda Peet, and Joan Cusack. His web page is **www.gerrold.com**.

New York Times-bestselling author **JONATHAN MABERRY's** latest series, Rot and Ruin, has just been optioned for film, and other works of his are heading for the big screen as well. He's a multiple Bram Stoker Award-winner and has written for Marvel comics. He's been named one of today's top ten horror writers. His website is **www.jonathanmaberry.com**.

GAIL Z. MARTIN is best known for her Chronicles of the Necromancer (Solaris Books) and Ascendant Kingdoms (Orbit Books) epic fantasy series, and her Deadly Curiosities urban fantasy series (Solaris Books). Her short stories have been in over 30 US/ UK anthologies. Her web page is **www.GailZMartin.com**.

HEIDI MCLAUGHLIN is a *New York Times* and *USA Today* bestselling author. Originally from Portland, Oregon and raised in the Pacific Northwest, she now lives in picturesque Vermont. Her works include: The Beaumont Series, The Archers and The Boys of Summer.

JODY LYNN NYE has published more than 40 novels and 150 short stories and may be best known for the books she has written in Robert Asprin's Myth Adventures series as well as her own Mythology 101 series. Her latest books are *Myth-Fits* (Ace Books),

Wishing on a Star (Phoenix Pick) and *Rhythm of the Imperium*, third in her Lord Thomas Kinago humorous space opera series (Baen Books) Her web page is **www.jodylynnnye.com**.

BETH W. PATTERSON's most recent novel is *Mongrels and Misfits*. Her short stories have appeared in the anthologies *Rise of the Goddess*, *Poets in Hell*, and *Tales of Fortannis: A Bard Day's Knight*.

MARTIN ROSE writes a range of fiction from the fantastic to the macabre. His early stories found homes in *Necrotic Tissue* and *Murky Depths,* and numerous anthologies such as *Urban Green Man, Handsome Devil, Ominous Realities,* and *Dread. Bring Me Flesh, I'll Bring Hell* is a noir, dark novel of a zombie private investigator, recognized as one of "Notable Novels of 2014" in *Best Horror of the Year, Vol. 7.* Upcoming work slated to appear in *Vastarien: A Literary Journal* and *Heroic Fantasy Quarterly.* He resides in the pine barrens of New Jersey, but believes the Jersey Devil was burned out long ago in the region's numerous wildfires. More details available at **www.martinrose.org**.

HILDY SILVERMAN is the publisher of *Space and Time*, a fifty-year-old magazine of fantasy, horror, and science fiction. She is also the author of several works of short fiction, including "The Vampire Escalator of the Passaic Promenade" (2010, *New Blood*, Thomas, ed.), "The Darren" (2009, *Witch Way to the Mall?*, Friesner, ed.), "Sappy Meals" (2010, *Fangs for the Mammaries*, Friesner, ed.), "Black Market Magic" (2012, *Apocalypse 13*, Raetz, ed.), "The Bionic Mermaid Returns" (2014, *With Great Power*, French, ed.), and "Tweets of the Damned" (2015, *Sha'Daa Facets*, McKeown, ed). In 2013 she was a finalist for the WSFA Small Press Award for her story "The Six Million Dollar Mermaid" (*Mermaids 13*, French, ed.).

Baen Books published **RYK SPOOR's** first novel, the urban fantasy *Digital Knight*, as well as collaborations with Eric Flint on *Diamonds are Forever* and the hard SF Boundary series. In 2010, he released *Grand Central Arena*, his bestselling solo salute to the Golden Age of space opera. Two years later the first volume in his Balanced Sword epic fantasy trilogy, *Phoenix Rising*, was released.

MIKE STRAUSS is a part-time freelance writer with credits on Yahoo News and from Sword & Sorcery Studios. He has had four stories published in the *Tales of Fortannis* anthologies.

MICHAEL A. VENTRELLA's third novel, *Bloodsuckers: A Vampire Runs for President*, was released in 2014. He edits the *Tales of Fortannis* short story collections, and has had his own stories printed in many anthologies, including Janet Morris's *Dreamers in Hell*, *Rum and Runestones*, *Twisted Tails*, and *The Ministry of Peculiar Occurrences Archives*. His website is **www.MichaelAVentrella.com**.